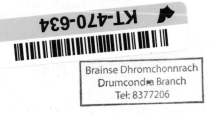
JEFF LINDSAY is the award-winning author of the *New York Times* bestselling *Dexter* novels, upon which the international hit TV show *Dexter* is based. He has also written two dozen plays and, among many other things, he has worked as an actor, comic, voice-over artist, screenwriter, columnist, singer, musician, bouncer, DJ, teacher, waiter, chop-saw operator in a foundry, TV and radio host, gardener, sailing instructor, and girls' soccer coach. Jeff is married to writer-filmmaker Hilary Hemingway. They have three daughters.

JUST WATCH ME

JEFF LINDSAY

ORION

First published in Great Britain in 2019 by Orion Fiction,
an imprint of The Orion Publishing Group Ltd.,
Carmelite House, 50 Victoria Embankment
London EC4Y 0DZ

An Hachette UK Company

1 3 5 7 9 10 8 6 4 2

A CIP catalogue record for this book is
available from the British Library.

ISBN (Hardback) 978 1 409 18661 8
ISBN (Trade Paperback) 978 1 409 18662 5
ISBN (eBook) 978 1 409 18664 9

Printed and bound in Great Britain by Clays Ltd, Elcograf, S.p.A

MIX
Paper from
responsible sources
FSC® C104740
FSC
www.fsc.org

www.orionbooks.co.uk

This is for Gus. He showed the way and waited while I found it.

And for Hilary, without whom there is nothing worth finding.

CHAPTER

1

It was supposed to be almost spring. It didn't feel like it. Not if you were standing outdoors on the brand-new Nesselrode Plaza. A hard and bitter wind with a cold edge to it blew across the wide-open space of the plaza. Nobody was surprised. This was Chicago, the Windy City. It was tough to be shocked when it lived up to its name.

But this wind was *cold*. The plaza itself was only half a block from the lake, so the wind was straight from Canada, and it'd had plenty of time to lose warmth and gather strength as it blew down from the Arctic Circle and across Lake Michigan.

Most people would have put their heads down and hurried across the large open space to find some shelter from the wind. The small crowd gathered here in the arctic morning air didn't have that option. So they clustered together around the podium that stood in the center of the plaza, in the shadow of a huge statue. It was brand-new, too, so new it was still draped with a cover, pending the dramatic unveiling. And the people who stood waiting, stamping their feet and trying to hunch away from the wind, devoutly wished it would be unveiled quickly so they could go someplace warm.

But of course, few of them were here by choice. They were mostly reporters and civic leaders, here because they had to be. The new Nesselrode Plaza was supposed to be important, the keystone to revitalizing this area of the lakefront. A US congresswoman was in attendance, a handsome woman in her fifties. Next to her stood a gray-haired African-American man, a state senator, and an elderly man so bundled up against the cold you could barely tell his species, let alone that he was a prominent federal judge. There was even a tall, rugged-looking man, with a neat beard that didn't hide the large scar running down his cheek, in the full dress uniform of a Coast Guard admiral.

And of course Arthur Nesselrode himself was here, the billionaire who had donated the statue and given the plaza its name. That meant the mayor had to be here, too. And the mayor had to give a speech that fit the occasion, made Arthur Nesselrode feel truly important and therefore happy to write more big checks in the future—and that meant a *long* speech.

Circling the perimeter of the small and shivering crowd were a couple of armed guards, hired because this was an expensive statue, made by a famous modern artist. There had been rumors that a cartel drug lord wanted the statue, rumors the mayor took seriously.

The guards did not. "Nobody's gonna steal this fucker," Denny Kirkaldi said to his partner, Bill Greer. He pointed at the base of the statue. "Lookit—twelve bolts, thick as my wrist, holding it down, and the fucking thing has to weigh ten tons."

"Twelve and a half," Greer said. Kirkaldi looked at him with surprise, and Greer shrugged. "It was in the paper."

"Well, so twelve and a *half* tons. *Tons*, right? So who's gonna steal something that weighs twelve and a half tons? That's fucking stupid!"

Greer shook his head. "We get paid, even if it's stupid."

"We should get paid extra for stupid," Kirkaldi said, "when it's this fucking cold."

Greer just shrugged. "It's not that cold," he said.

But it was cold, and the wet wind off the lake made it feel even colder. As the mayor's speech went on—and on—it seemed even colder to the people who had to stand and listen to the praise being heaped on Arthur Nesselrode. Those who knew Nesselrode, or knew about him, were well aware that there was not very much praiseworthy about him. He had made his billions as owner and CEO of Nesselrode Pharmaceuticals. His company owned patents on a number of important drugs—the most significant being Zanagen, the most effective of the new gene-based treatments for a number of difficult, and formerly fatal, cancers.

Zanagen was truly a miracle drug, and the mayor mentioned it prominently in his speech. But as a politician, he very wisely didn't mention that Arthur Nesselrode had set the price for his wonderful remedy at half a million dollars per dose. No amount of criticism in the press, pleas from doctors, or even censure from the US Congress could shake him from this grotesquely inflated price.

Nesselrode did not become a billionaire by acts of kindness and charity. Anyone who'd had the misfortune of crossing him would readily testify that he was not a nice man. Some even suggested he was a sociopath, and therefore immune from any feelings of guilt or shame. But Nesselrode was aware that public opinion could affect stock prices. And so he was here today to bolster his image by donating a huge $50 million steel statue to the city of Chicago and paying millions more to build this plaza that carried his name.

The money was insignificant to Nesselrode. He could give away this much every day for a month and still have a few billion left over. And like most men with this kind of wealth, Arthur Nesselrode felt himself insulated against the normal slings and arrows of life. But wealth was not sufficient to insulate him from the temperature. He

3

was cold, and he didn't like it. But the mayor was praising him, after all. It takes a better man than Arthur Nesselrode to cut that short.

"Jesus, lookit that," Kirkaldi said, pointing out over the lake, where an enormous helicopter was circling. "Thing is huge!"

Greer glanced up. "Chinook," he said. His partner stared at him. "I serviced them in the Corps," Greer explained. "They can lift seventeen tons. Plus crew."

"Well, I hope the fucker stays away, we got enough wind," Kirkaldi said, and the two resumed their circuit of the statue.

And the mayor went on with his speech. He was well over ten minutes now and didn't seem to be slowing down. Arthur Nesselrode glanced at his watch for the seventh time. Even hearing how wonderful he was had started to get tedious. He had been told the ceremony would be brief—a quick speech, and then the mayor would hand him an electronic box with a toggle switch. Nesselrode would then say a few words himself and flip the switch, which would cause the veil to slip off the statue, and then the fountain would start up at the base, and they could all go back to work. Nesselrode wanted to be back at work. He was working on a hostile takeover of a French company that had had some promising results with a new synthetic insulin.

And damn it, it was really *cold*. Nesselrode wasn't dressed for it, and he didn't like it. He was not accustomed to being inconvenienced, even by the weather. And so, as the mayor passed the fifteen-minute mark in his speech of praise that even the billionaire himself knew was a load of crap, he acted.

When the mayor paused to take a breath, Nesselrode stepped forward. With the confidence only billionaires can feel, he placed an arm on the mayor's shoulder and pushed him to one side. He grabbed the microphone and, with a large and incredibly false smile, said, "Thank you, Mr. Mayor, you're much too kind. And on behalf of Nesselrode Pharmaceuticals, the true House of Miracles, I would just like to say, to you and to the people of Chicago, it is a great honor and privilege to be able to give you this wonderful work of art. And so," he said, lifting the large electronic box resting on the podium, "I hereby dedicate . . . Nesselrode Plaza!" He raised the box high over his head and flipped the toggle switch.

Several impressive things happened at the same time.

There was a brilliant flash of blue light from the electronic box, accompanied by a sharp and crackling *BANG!*, and Arthur Nesselrode pitched over and lay motionless behind the podium, smoke rising from his blackened hands. This was followed immediately by twelve sharp and rapid explosions, one after another, from around the base of the statue. And while the crowd was still stunned and blinking, the Coast Guard admiral stepped forward and began shouting orders.

"Clear a space here! Give him some room!" he said as he knelt beside Arthur Nesselrode.

The mayor knelt beside him as well. "Jesus, what happened?" he said.

"Electric shock. Came from that box," the admiral said as he felt for a pulse. "This man needs immediate medical attention!" He pulled a radio from his pocket and spoke urgently into it. Then he turned his attention back to Nesselrode and began to give him CPR. "All right, that's my chopper offshore," he told the mayor. "We'll airlift him to the hospital."

"Uh," the mayor said. "Don't you think we could—"

"Screw it!" the admiral snapped, pressing hard on Nesselrode's chest. "I need you to time me here! Start the count!"

And the mayor, who had seen CPR performed on TV, looked at his watch and began counting out loud.

"What the hell happened?" Kirkaldi demanded. "What were those explosions?"

Greer shook his head. "Around the base of the statue," he said.

The two of them hurried over, and Greer knelt to examine one spot still smoking from the series of blasts. "It's sheared the bolt," he said. "All the bolts!"

"Shit," Kirkaldi said. "This thing could fall over, crush somebody!" He frowned at his partner. "Why would somebody—"

Greer stood up. "Terrorists," he said. "We better tell the mayor."

Kirkaldi nodded. "You tell him, I'll move the crowd back."

On the podium, the Coast Guard admiral continued CPR compressions on Nesselrode's chest while the mayor counted for him. "I've got a pulse," the admiral said. He glanced up. "And here's my chopper." He stood up and waved at the helicopter.

With a huge swirl of wind, the Chinook descended toward the platform, lowering a medevac basket. "Clear away!" the admiral yelled. "Mr. Mayor, you need to get all these folks out of the way."

The mayor nodded and began to urge the crowd away, off the platform. He was the last person down, and as he stepped onto the top stair, he turned just in time to see Nesselrode, in the medevac basket, rising up into the air—

—and a second thick steel cable with a large metal hook on the end unspooling downward, to the admiral's waiting hand. Frowning, the mayor paused on the top stair. What the hell . . . ?

His puzzlement grew as the admiral grabbed this second cable, stepped to the front of the platform, and swung out toward the statue. But the mayor's confusion turned to alarm as the admiral, perched on the statue, whipped the cable around it several times, stuck the hook into the wrapped cable, and then climbed upward, hand over hand, and disappeared into the side door of the helicopter.

"Jesus Christ," the mayor said. He couldn't think of anything else. He just stood mute as the powerful Chinook climbed upward, taking the statue with it. One of the security guards appeared beside him, lifting his pistol to fire at the chopper. The mayor slapped his hand down. "Mr. Nesselrode is in there!" he said, and the guard kept his pistol lowered.

The two stood side by side and watched as the helicopter flew away, far out over the lake, the brand-new $50 million statue dangling beneath it.

And with Arthur Nesselrode, billionaire big-pharma CEO, inside.

Arthur Nesselrode came slowly back to consciousness with no idea where he was or what was happening. His entire body ached—but especially his chest. It felt like he'd been beaten. Beneath him he felt a hard and cold surface, and it was thrumming with vibrations from some kind of powerful machine.

It took several minutes of concentration and hard work, but he finally managed to open his eyes. Hovering above him was a face he didn't know. He frowned, tried to focus. The man was wearing a uniform—the admiral who had been standing on the platform behind the mayor? But that made no sense—

"You're in a helicopter," the admiral said. He reached behind him and slid open the chopper's door. Immediately, the freezing wind whipped in at them. "See?"

It was terribly uncomfortable, but it revived Nesselrode a little bit. He blinked and licked his lips. "Medevac . . . ?" he managed to say. His voice was an unfamiliar rasp.

The admiral smiled. It was not a reassuring smile. "Not quite," he said.

Nesselrode shook his head. It hurt. "Then . . . why?"

"Insurance," the admiral said. "To keep them from shooting at me."

Nesselrode closed his eyes again. Nothing was making sense. Unless—

He opened his eyes again. "Tell me again how much you charge for one dose of Zanagen?" the admiral said.

"That's . . . ," Nesselrode croaked. He frowned. "You—you're not . . ."

"You guessed it!" the man said. "I'm not really an admiral!"

Nesselrode tried to sit up and discovered that his hands and feet were duct-taped. With that, the last piece clicked into place. Of course; he was being kidnapped. "I can pay," he rasped. The man in the admiral's uniform didn't answer. "I . . . have money. Lots of it," Nesselrode said.

"Enough to buy anything you want?"

"Yes," Nesselrode said.

"Wow," the admiral said. He grabbed Nesselrode roughly and sat him up in the chopper's doorway. Lake Michigan gleamed far below. "Could you buy a big fancy yacht?"

"Yes," Nesselrode said.

"Well," the admiral said, "now would be a really good time." And he pushed Arthur Nesselrode out the door, leaning out and watching until he saw a tiny splash far below in the freezing water of Lake Michigan.

"Bastard," the admiral said. Then he closed the door.

I watched my buyer's guys secure the statue onto the bed of a huge semi rig. They looked like what they were—thugs. But they did it right, so I just stood and waited.

When they were done, the older of the two guys took out a cell phone, made a call, nodded, and came over to me. "He sent it," the guy said. "Wire transfer. Just now."

I took out my own phone, checked my bank account. It showed that the deposit really had been made. All of it, which is never a sure thing. I mean, if somebody is as rich as this guy was, they have to have big holes in their morals. Look at me.

"Paid *in full*," the thug said. He looked offended. "He *said* so!"

"Of course it is," I said. He turned to go. "Just a second," I said. I got my little black electronic control box and flipped a switch.

"What's that?" he asked, frowning at me.

"The bomb," I said. "I just disarmed it."

He shook his head. "What bomb?"

"The one inside the statue," I said, giving him a really big and cheery smile.

He goggled at me. "There's a bomb in the statue?" he said, kind of stupid.

"Trust—but verify," I said. "Have a nice day!" Before he could tell me what he thought about that, I was into my waiting car and away, $50 million richer.

And no happier. In fact, I was feeling dirty, mean, edgy, and antsy. Fifty million reasons to feel good, and I didn't. I mean, the money was nice. And the whole thing had come off without a hitch, just like I had planned it. No reason to do anything but smile and sing happy songs as I drove away. But I just kept looking in the rearview mirror and hissing. Why?

Because. It had all been too easy, and I hate that.

I don't know why that is. It just is. If it's too easy, I always feel like it's got to be a trap, or I made some stupid mistake, or—hell, I don't know. I just don't like things to be too easy. And in spite of the cold, this had been a stroll through the fucking park on a summer day. It was done, and I had the money to prove it, and now all my nerves were standing up and vibrating like somebody was whacking at them with a dull machete. Mom had an expression for this feeling. She'd say, "Somebody's walking on my grave." And right now, I had the Boston Marathon stomping all over mine.

Usually I get over that feeling pretty quick. This time, it stayed with me. I drove for half an hour, thinking about why that was.

Nothing came to me. I put on the radio, spun the dial, and found Talking Heads, "Once in a Lifetime." I like that song a lot. That made me feel even meaner, like somebody was bribing me to cheer up.

I pulled off at a transfer point I'd set up. It was a deserted spot on a country road, well hidden by a screen of trees. That's why I'd picked the place, because it was totally isolated. I'd left another car there, along with a change of costume. I peeled off the false scar on my face, and then my admiral's costume. I dropped it all into the back seat of the car I'd arrived in. Beard, hat, shoes with four-inch lifts. It all went in. From my bag in the trunk of the other car I pulled out a jar of thermite. I took it to the first car and poured the whole thing onto my costume.

I changed into a charcoal-gray suit and brown oxfords. Hand-tailored shirt, silk tie, gold cuff links, and a Movado Museum watch on my wrist. I tossed a little box on top of the thermite, got into the new car, and pulled back onto the road. I was half a mile away when I heard a muffled *WHOOMP* behind me. In the rearview mirror I watched a cheery glow climb up above the trees, and for a few minutes I was at least satisfied, if not really happy. The fire was the real end to the job. It wiped away the last link to the admiral, and to the guy who gave the statue to the thugs. It's one way I stay successful. On every job, I make sure nobody—*nobody*—knows what I look like.

Starting with the identities I wear to work. So, thermite and the first rental car exploding, all that. There would be no trace left by the time I hit I-94. Not a scrap that anybody could connect to the guy who stole the statue. More important, not even a microscopic trace of my DNA. I didn't have to check. I'd done this enough times. That identity was totally destroyed, nothing but ashes—and goddamn it, that had been easy, too. And now I was right back into feeling mean and antsy.

I drove back toward Chicago. I found a radio station playing really *old* oldies. Lovin' Spoonful, Paul Revere, even the Nightcrawlers. Really good background music. It helped me think. By the time I got

to Windsor Long-Term Care Nursing Home, I'd figured out why I felt
shitty. The thing was, *everything* had been too easy lately. Everything
I tried worked perfectly, the first time. I was just too damn good. Does
that sound conceited? It's not. It's the plain damn truth. I am the best
there is—maybe the best there ever was—and I hadn't missed since I
was sixteen and tried to steal a cop car.

The last couple of years, almost everything I did had gone like
clockwork. No matter how stupid-hard something looked, it never
was. It wasn't that I wasn't giving myself any serious challenges. I was
pulling off stuff that looked impossible—like stealing a twelve-
and-a-half-ton statue—and making it look routine. But I just wasn't
finding anything that tested me, and there's always a tremendous danger that comes from that: a danger of getting stale, smug, so that
sooner or later I really would make a mistake. In my line of work, mistakes have very big consequences. Like, life in prison is actually the
best one. So the answer was obvious, even if it looked kind of stupid.

I needed to find something I couldn't do.

Find a heist that was beyond impossible, something ridiculous, unthinkable, stupid, totally out of the question. And then I needed to do it.

Sure, absolutely, why not. I parked the car a few rows back from the
nursing home's front door and sat there for a minute thinking about
that. And then I thought, what the fuck, that was a stupid idea anyway.
I put it out of my mind and went into Windsor Long-Term Care.

It took me a little less than an hour to make the arrangements to
have Mom moved. The nurses were all sad to see her go. After all, most
of their patients sit and complain all day, shit in their pants, and wander off. Mom always behaved beautifully, the perfect patient. She was
no trouble at all. Mom had been in a coma for years, what they call a
persistent vegetative state. No wonder the nurses loved her.

I did, too. For different reasons. I gave her a kiss on the forehead
and told her that. Maybe she could hear me. Probably not.

When Mom was loaded into the ambulance and on her way, I drove on to the airport, O'Hare. Seeing Mom hadn't made me feel any better. I used to think she could get better if I just found the right doctor and threw enough money at him. I don't believe that anymore. But I still throw a lot of money at keeping Mom alive. And at keeping her near me, wherever I have a job.

I turned in my rental car and took their shuttle to the terminal. I breezed through security, no problem, and to the gate for my flight out. I fly commercial right after a job. I mean, even before this particular payday I could afford a private jet. But that attracts the kind of attention I like to avoid until things settle down a bit.

So I drank a cup of coffee until it was time to board. I settled into my seat, pulled the in-flight magazine out of the pocket in front of me, and opened it at random. I glanced at a full-page picture. Then I looked harder.

Time stopped. I just kept looking.

The article was nothing. Just a simple, dumb-ass puff piece, like all the stuff in those mags. Stuff to do in far-off cities, other stuff to take your mind off the fact that you're rocketing through the sky at four hundred miles per hour, and if one little piece of the plane stops working, you're going to drop like a rock.

But this article was titled "Coming to America!" I didn't even need to read it. All I had to see was the picture, and I knew. This was it.

I had found something impossible.

I read the article, and I was sure. It absolutely could not be done, not ever, and I had to do it. I studied the picture some more. I'd never seen anything like it. It was so beautiful it made my teeth hurt. I had to see it for real. And then I was going to steal it.

When the plane landed in New York, I bought a seat on the next flight to Tehran. And I was smiling as I boarded.

Denny Kirkaldi was nervous. He'd done his job and hadn't done anything wrong. He'd protected the crowd instead of the statue, sure— but who could figure somebody would just *take* the fucking thing like that? And those were important people, too. He knew he'd done the right thing. But the FBI guy had a way of just looking at you that made you feel guilty even if you weren't. It made you want to tell him stuff, whatever he wanted. So Kirkaldi tried. "Like I said," he told the Fed, "I was moving the crowd back. I never even saw the guy 'til he went up the rope into the chopper."

"Cable," Greer said. "He went up a steel cable."

"Whatever. Thing is, I didn't see him. So . . ." He trailed off. The FBI guy was looking away, over at the hole in the ground where the statue had been.

"The uniform was authentic," Greer said. "Coast Guard admiral."

The Fed went down on one knee beside the hole to look at a sheared bolt, but he still didn't say anything. That made Kirkaldi even more nervous. "Lookit, Mr.— Uh, hey, what do we call you, anyways?"

The Fed stood up and looked at them. "Special Agent Frank Delgado," he said.

"Yeah, well, lookit, Mr. Delgado. Special Agent, whatever," Kirkaldi said. "The guy's in Rio or something by now. You're never gonna catch him now."

Special Agent Delgado looked at Kirkaldi without a word, holding his gaze a little too long. Then he turned away and looked out over the lake.

"I already know who he is," Delgado said. He turned back around to face the two guards, and there was something new in his eyes. "His name is Riley Wolfe."

CHAPTER

2

I admit I was surprised. Iran is not at all like what you hear on the news. But there it is—it turns out it's not a mean, scary, hostile place where they're all lying in ambush ready to gut every *ferenghi* infidel who comes in reach. In fact, a lot of the people are friendly and ready to help you find things. Just stay away from the Revolutionary Guards. These are the guys who must have started all the stories about hostile natives. They really don't like you, and they're not shy about letting you know it.

Everybody else? They're proud of their history and happy to show it off to you. And holy shit, do they have history. Not stuff they teach you in school, either—at least, not any school I went to. For starters, Iran, which used to be called Persia, was once the biggest empire the world has ever seen. It was ruled by the Great King, and he was no dummy. Every place he conquered, he set up a governor—a satrap. He'd choose some local guy so his new subjects wouldn't get all up in their feelings. And he let the conquered people keep their own religion and customs—just as long as they paid tribute and loyalty to the Great King. Smart—and it made the Persian Empire a pretty good place to live, considering what things were like back then. It also brought in a lot of tribute.

Important historical note? "Tribute" means "treasure." Like silver, gold, and jewels. And it poured into the empire for hundreds of years.

But the empire died, and the new Persia was Iran, which was an Islamic Republic. That meant they were guided by their interpretation of Islam. So they got rid of most of the corrupt, pre-Muslim trappings of the old Persian Empire—except for one really important item:

The Crown Jewels of the Persian Empire.

Remember all that tribute the Great King raked in? Like I said, a lot of it was jewels. And I don't mean cute little diamond chips like you save up for to give your girlfriend. Because the Great King made people really nervous back then. If you pissed him off, he could come down on you with the best fighters in the world, of which he had over a hundred thousand.

This was a time when "soldier" usually meant a farmer who owned a sword. And an "army" was maybe three or four thousand of these guys.

But the Great King's soldiers were full-time killers, trained from birth. So picture this: You flip the finger to the Great King, skip your tribute. And all of a sudden you and a few of your buddies are standing in a line and holding pitchforks, while ten thousand armored Persians on thoroughbred horses ride down at you shooting arrows. And those guys could all put an arrow through a wedding ring while they were riding full speed.

So most of the conquered people stayed serious about the whole tribute business. They even competed to see who could send the Great King the coolest stuff. And when they sent him jewels, they sent him *JEWELS*. Huge gems, rich settings, completely unique things like the world had never seen before and hasn't seen since. It added up to a pretty nice collection, and a lot of it is still there in Tehran, on display at the Central Bank.

I landed in Tehran, checked in to my hotel, and went. I paid my 200,000 rials to get in, which makes me sound like a high roller—like, for that price, I should get to take a few diamonds home with me. But 200,000 rials is only around six bucks, so I paid it without flinching and went inside to take a look.

Ask any Iranian. They'll tell you the crown jewels are the finest, rarest, richest, most dazzling collection in the world. They're right. I have seen the best, all over the world, and I have snatched a lot of it, and I am very hard to impress. But this stuff? The Crown Jewels of Iran?

I was knocked stupid.

I mean, jaw on the floor. Forget to breathe. Just stare—the whole thing. I only saw some of it, the tiny fraction of stuff on display. There's a whole huge vault filled with more—so much it looks like those old cartoons of Scrooge McDuck's vault, piled high with riches you can't even imagine. But just the stuff I saw . . . I mean, you just stare and think it can't possibly be real. There's just so damn much bright, glittering stuff—gold and jewels everywhere, stuck onto swords and hairbrushes and mirrors and chairs—it's got to be fake!

It isn't. It's all real. Nothing else even comes close, not anywhere in the world.

And how much is all that worth? Forget it. You can't even begin to put a price tag on the whole collection. But I can tell you it's so valuable, it's used to back Iran's currency, the rial.

And here's another clue. Forget about the whole collection for a second and think about this: One single piece is said to be worth more than $15 *billion*. That's right. "Billion" with a *b*. Just that *one piece*.

The Daryayeh-E-Noor. The Ocean of Light.

It's the largest pink diamond ever, so big you think it can't be real. And really, you can't even call it a diamond. That's like saying Einstein was kind of clever. The Daryayeh-E-Noor is so huge and so freaking *beautiful* that you just plain can't compare it to anything else. But when you see it, you start to think $15 billion may be a bargain price.

And it is real, and I was looking at it. If I was stunned by the other stuff in the collection, I was lights-out when I saw this gorgeous monster. Couldn't move. Couldn't do anything but look at it, imagine holding it, feeling the cool pink facets of that gigantic beautiful gem on my hands, my face . . . I'd seen the picture on the airplane, and that had been enough to bring me all this way. It didn't come close to the shock of seeing it for real—it's like the difference between looking at a nude picture and hopping into the sack with a real-life *Playboy* model. It took me away, outside of the world, off to a place where there was no clock, no walls, and no other people, nothing at all but me and the Ocean of Light, and I swam in it until it was closing time and the guards came and led me out. I walked away still feeling it, still dizzy from standing so close. And I went back to my hotel with one thought stuck in my head.

The Daryayeh-E-Noor.

I had to have it. And that was impossible.

The upside? That was just what I'd been looking for. And I had found it. I had my challenge. I'd found something that would not be too easy, no matter what I tried. It was as close to impossible as it gets. That didn't matter. I was going to take it.

How?

Well, it was the biggest pink diamond in the world, but it was still jewelry. If you have larceny in your heart—and some of us just can't help it—you know that jewels are light, easy to conceal and carry, and they pack a really high value into a small package, the perfect target for anybody with roaming fingers. Even the Daryayeh-E-Noor would be easy to carry away.

But this is a mean world, and nobody trusts anybody. So sad but true, and the Iranian government had thought of that. If you have anything close to a three-digit IQ, you'll take one look around you and know none of the crown jewels were going anywhere. Because sitting there in the Central Bank, in the heart of the Islamic Republic, in the middle of eighty million people, including a whole lot of the Revolutionary Guards, who are really well armed and truly don't like you, the jewels are safer than they would be in a radioactive pit of cobras rigged with claymore mines and surrounded by SEAL snipers. You might get in, but you would never, ever get out of Iran with any of the jewels. At least not alive, which I consider an important part of any plan.

So it's not even a challenge. It's hopeless. The crown jewels were in Tehran, safe, and they weren't going anywhere.

Until now.

Remember the headline of that article from the in-flight magazine? "Coming to America"? Know what that meant?

The Iranian crown jewels are coming to America.

Why? Politics. It was all spelled out in the article I read on the plane. The jewels are coming to America because a few cool heads on both sides were trying to move Iran and the USA a little closer together. So the two nations had decided to "foster a better understanding of each other's unique cultural heritage in order to promote a spirit of tolerance and mutual respect." For some reason, they figured that the best way to do that was by swapping national treasures.

And so the US will send to Tehran an original draft of the Declaration of Independence, the text of the Gettysburg Address—in Lincoln's very own handwriting—and the US flag from the Battle of Baltimore, the one that inspired F. S. Key to write "The Star-Spangled Banner."

The choice for Iran was a whole lot easier. They're sending a selection from the crown jewels, including the incomparable Daryayeh-E-Noor.

That's right. The Ocean of Light is coming to America.

After a great deal of debate, it was decided that the imperial collection would be displayed at the Eberhardt Museum, a small private institution in Manhattan. It was established at the turn of the twentieth century to house the art collection of nineteenth-century American robber baron Ludwig Eberhardt. And it's still privately owned and controlled by Eberhardt's descendants.

Weird choice? Not really. Because old Ludwig was a truly heartless, greedy bastard, and he collected a huge fortune. That means the museum has a mind-blowingly huge endowment. And because it's private they can spend that money any way they want without worrying about government budget restrictions. Which means state-of-the-art electronic security, stuff nobody has ever seen before, regardless of expense. Since it is a smaller venue, human security can be a lot tighter, too.

And it will be. Aside from the cutting-edge electronic measures, the jewels will be guarded night and day by a detachment of elite armed security guards from Black Hat Security. Every one of them is a retired SEAL, Green Beret, Force Recon—all former members of America's elite Special Forces. And in case they fall asleep on the job, the Islamic Republic of Iran is sending a full platoon of the Revolutionary Guard.

All of these security measures are totally serious and impressive. More than enough to persuade any sane thief that stealing the jewels is a really bad idea, unless your idea of a good time is getting shot.

But America is the land of opportunity, and you can't display the world's richest collection of jewelry in Manhattan without somebody trying to steal it.

And Somebody, most definitely, is going to try.

More than try—Somebody will think of a way to get past all the lasers and sensors and infrared beams and who knows what else. And that Somebody will figure out how to get past the former SEALs and Rangers and Force Recon guys from Black Hat, and past the bearded, itchy-fingered wackos in the Revolutionary Guard. And that Somebody will get his own itchy fingers on one or two of the Iranian crown jewels, put them in his pocket, and get clean away with the greatest score anybody has ever made in the whole fucking history of heists.

Think that's crazy? Suicidal? Impossible? It is. Think it can't be done?

Watch me.

CHAPTER

3

Manhattan has visitors all year long, even in a July as hot as this one was turning out to be. People come from all over the world to visit this great city. Tourists flood the streets, clog the restaurants, jam the subways and buses. For the most part, the natives shrug it off. It takes a lot more than a plague of tourists to shake a New Yorker. They are hardened to the sight of flocks of strangers gawking up at the tall buildings, and mostly they don't mind. They've come to think of the tourists as strolling ATMs.

The man who got out of the cab at Park Avenue and 62nd Street that Tuesday in July was clearly a tourist, and he would not attract any second looks—not in Manhattan, not on a brutally hot day like this. He was average height, average build, and had light brown hair of medium length. The clothes he wore were just what any summer tourist was wearing: lightweight cargo shorts, a bright Hawaiian shirt, and blue Nikes with white crew socks. He wore large sunglasses, of course, and a blue baseball cap that read "NYC" on the front, and he had a small nylon backpack over his shoulder. He paid the cabbie, carefully counting out a 10 percent tip, and then he turned and sauntered easily up the sidewalk toward 63rd Street.

After crossing 63rd, he pulled a camera out of his pack and slung it around his neck—the first noteworthy thing about him, since cameras have become a relic of the past, almost totally replaced by cell phones. But this camera had a top-notch telephoto lens, and it soon became clear why this man preferred it over a cell phone. As he paused and took careful photos of the older and more interesting buildings along his way, concentrating on the decorative strips around windows and doors, it was obvious that he was an architecture buff. Perfectly natural—only a camera can capture detail the way this man wanted it.

At 64th Street, he paused a bit longer and took quite a few shots of the unusual old building there. That was easy to understand, since this was a very rare building indeed. It had been designed by Beauford Harris Whittington, one of Stanford White's lesser protégés, and although it had many of the features made famous by White—columns, an imposing facade, frenetic gingerbread around the roof's edge—it lacked the flair of the buildings White had designed personally, like the Metropolitan Club. Instead, it was solid, a little imposing, with a look somewhere between a bank and a fortress. And that is exactly what the nineteenth-century robber baron had in mind when he commissioned it to house his growing collection of artwork. He demanded something that was not a mere building, but a fortress, a vault, a structure that would tell people there were treasures inside, but they were *his*, and they would stay that way, safe, secure, inviolate.

His treasures were still there, still safe, and the robber baron's descendants had carefully grown the art collection until it was one of the finest private collections anywhere. And the building that still kept them safe had become mildly famous, among a certain circle. So if the man with the camera took a lot of pictures, from many different angles, it was perfectly understandable. After all, what fan of nineteenth-century American architecture wouldn't want to study the Eberhardt Museum?

After walking all around the museum, taking pictures from every angle, the photographer moved on. He walked up to 66th Street, and before he crossed Park Avenue, he paused for one last long look at the Eberhardt, a look of distant calculation on his face. Then the light changed, and the man moved on, across Park and then across town.

Most people who visited the Eberhardt Museum did not care about its architecture, of course. They actually went inside, for the paintings. The collection of Baroque and Renaissance masters was well-known, and for those interested in art of that period, the Eberhardt was a must-see. Six days a week, the museum attracted a crowd of art students and tourists. There was a modest admission fee—which would go up significantly when the jewels arrived—as well as a small café and, of course, a gift shop. There were benches, the galleries were long and cool, and the café had a pleasant shaded atrium. All these features added together made the museum an agreeable stop on a hot day, for the culturally inclined. Although the Eberhardt was far from being the most popular museum in Manhattan, most days saw a steady flow of visitors trickling through to admire the paintings, statues, and other artifacts on display.

This Wednesday afternoon was no exception. The long gallery given over to Baroque masters had its usual sprinkle of art lovers. A young woman and a man of about the same age—obviously students by their clothing—huddled together on a marble bench in front of a Vermeer. The woman was sketching while her companion whispered urgently in her ear about the blue tones in the painting. A small group of Japanese tourists marched through, clustered around a tour guide with an upraised flag. An elderly couple held hands and gazed long-ingly at a small but exquisite Caravaggio. Other visitors moved past them in ones and twos, and no one paid any special attention to the rather fat man in a seersucker suit with an Atlanta Braves cap perched atop his round and sweating face. The fat man came slowly down the long room and paused, wheezing, by a large metal door bearing a sign that read, "EMERGENCY EXIT ONLY—ALARM WILL SOUND."

No one noticed, either, that he had paused and wheezed at every door and window inside the museum, or that the Braves logo on his cap had a very small pinhole hidden carefully in the middle of the bright red tomahawk logo—a pinhole that close examination might show contained a tiny dot that seemed to reflect light. But the pinhole was very small, and no one had any reason to stare or come closer. The fat man took his time, consulting a laminated map of the museum—only $14.95 in the gift shop—and looking carefully at several of the paintings before moving on to wheeze at the next window. After that, he stopped to lean on a marble pillar, next to one of the museum's uni-formed security guards. The guard looked up, took in the man's size and his red and sweaty face.

"Are you all right, sir?" the guard asked the fat man.

"Oh, yes, yes, I'm gone be jest fine," the man answered in a thick South Georgia accent. "I jest carryin' around too much weight these days," he said with a smile, patting his great wobbly belly. "'Specially in this heat! Got to catch my breath."

"Well, you take your time," the guard told him.

"Thank you kindly, sir." After a minute the fat man's breathing leveled off to a more normal pace. "Lovely collection you all have here," he said at last. "Wonderful. But I guess it don't hold a candle to those Persian jewels y'all are getting in." He cocked his head. "You seen 'em yet?"

The guard snorted. "No, and I'm not going to see 'em, neither—unless I pay my twenty-five bucks like everybody else. Which I won't do—not to get into the place I work at for fifteen years."

"Pay your— Why, they surely won't send all you guards home with a treasure like this on display?"

"Yes, they will," the guard said, obviously disgusted. "Because we aren't good enough for the job. They're bringing in a whole new crew from Black Hat."

"Black Hat—you mean they're *outlaws* or somethin'?"

The guard shook his head. "Naw. They're professional soldiers—you know, mercenaries."

"Mercenaries!" the fat man exclaimed. "Well, I never heard tell of such a thing!"

"Right? And me with six years in the Army, ten years a New York cop, and I ain't good enough for the job."

"Well, bless your heart," the fat man said. "Don't seem right."

"Ah," the guard said. "Those Black Hat guys? Bunch of trigger-happy assholes—but they sure as hell know what they're doing."

"Do they now?"

"Hell yes. They're all ex–Special Forces guys. They get recruited right out the Rangers or SEALs, you know. Best-trained, best-equipped private army in the world. And if that ain't enough—" The guard lowered his voice as if he were imparting confidential information. "There's going to be a bunch of hotshot Iranian soldiers, from The Revolutionary Guard."

"Why, I heard of those old boys!" the fat man said. "They supposed to be meaner than a bucket of copperheads."

"Damn straight," the guard said. "Anybody tries to pull something funny, they're just itching to shoot 'em."

"Well, well," the fat man said. "I guess those jewels are gonna be pretty safe."

"You can bet your life on it," the guard said. "Anybody tries anything, they're gonna end up dead."

"Well, sir, I sure do wish I was going to be in town to come see those jewels when they get here. Yes, sir, that's gone be somethin' to see all right. Oh," he said, holding up the laminated map. "Now where would I find that Leonardo da Vinci sketch y'all are so proud of?"

"Next gallery over," the guard said, pointing to the right. "Take it easy, buddy."

"Yes, thank you, I will," the fat man said, and he wandered off slowly to find the Leonardo sketch—

Except that as soon as he was around the corner, he turned *left* and went straight out the front door, climbed into a cab, and was gone.

The next night, right after the night security staff came on duty, Freddy Lagerfeldt took his first trip around the outside perimeter. Freddy had been out of the Army for two years, and he loved this job. He even liked working the night shift since it paid fifty cents an hour more, and that wasn't bad, times being what they were. New York at night didn't scare him at all. He'd grown up in Queens—and after two tours of Afghanistan, the East Side of Manhattan at night was absolutely soothing.

Freddy took his time, checking the doors, shining his flashlight into all the small dark spots, working his way around the building until he came to the back. An alley there led to the loading dock, and a large dumpster was pushed back to the wall opposite. Normally, Freddy would just shine the light, have a good look, and move on. The dumpster was filled with all the garbage from the café, among other fragrant items, and in this heat the smell tended to be overwhelming.

But tonight, when Freddy shone his light down the alley, he saw something that hadn't been there before: a battered shopping cart piled high with tightly wrapped bundles. Freddy was pretty sure it didn't belong to the museum, and so it shouldn't be there. It looked an awful lot like a homeless guy's cart. Freddy had nothing against the homeless, but they could cause trouble sometimes, and it was his job to keep that from happening. He held his light high and stepped carefully down the alley for a closer look. As he approached the cart, he saw a figure wedged in between the shopping cart and the dumpster. He stopped and shone his light on it. "Hey there!" he called.

The figure moved, squirming as if trying to wriggle its way into the wall to hide, and mumbled something Freddy couldn't make out. "What's that? Hey, are you all right?" He took a cautious step closer, shining his flashlight on the figure's face. It was a man, scrawny, ragged, and incredibly filthy. He had a large and bushy black beard covering most of his face, and the rest of his features were hidden by a dark and greasy film of smudged filth. "Hey, buddy," the guard said.

"Veteran. I'm a veteran," the figure said. "Let me be, let me be, I'm a veteran, please, I need a place to sleep, just let me be."

"Huh," Freddy said, coming to a stop. After his own time in Afghanistan, he knew that a surprising number of his old Army buddies ended up like this, too torn up by memories to do anything but huddle in the dark and fight the demons of PTSD. "All right, buddy, take it easy," Freddy said. "Nobody's going to bother you tonight."

"Veteran. I'm a veteran," the man mumbled, and scrunched back down again.

"So am I, buddy. You rest easy here for tonight, okay?" The figure just mumbled. Freddy moved a little closer and crouched down. "I did two tours in the sandbox, pal," Freddy said. "I know what you're going through. I'll make sure nobody bothers you tonight. But just tonight, okay? In the morning you got to move on."

"I'll go, I'll move, I have to, I—I can't stay, not anywhere, because, you gotta know, it gets so loud and I—please, okay, I'm a veteran—"

"Yeah, I got that," Freddy said. He stood up. "You just take it easy. You'll be safe here tonight." He looked down at the filthy, scrunched-down figure, and then, thinking it could have been him instead of this guy, he added, "Don't worry 'bout nothin'. You just get some sleep." And he turned away and out of the alley.

When he was gone, the filthy figure got to his feet, watched the mouth of the alley for a moment, and then ran straight up the side of the building to the roof.

For many years there have been rumors, even urban folk tales, about hidden Things under the streets in Manhattan. There are stories of unknown and unexplored tunnel networks, vast caverns, elaborate Victorian train stations that were somehow forgotten—or deliberately hidden, if your tastes bend toward sinister conspiracies. With these stories go tales of mysterious tribes of pale subterranean humans who never see the light of day. There are tales, too, of tribes of creatures that are not quite human—the Mole People, who have been spoken of in frightened whispers since the 1800s.

And who knows? Some of these stories may well be true. But there is no doubt at all that if the Mole People or any other strange population is really there under the streets of New York, they live in the long stretches of abandoned tunnels that branch off from the main subway arteries that service the city.

Andres Maldonado had heard these stories. He could hardly avoid them—he'd been working for the MTA for twenty-three years now, and the last fifteen he'd been driving the Lexington Avenue local, which was a route that had plenty of history all its own. People said some crazy stuff about this route, like about the old City Hall station, which was closed but still there. He hadn't seen anything in that area himself, but who could say these people were wrong?

Andres knew there were several other spots along the route that looked like hastily blocked side tunnels. He asked about them, and he heard more stories—about the Mole People, the Homeless Army, the Lizard People, and some that were even less believable. He'd never seen any signs that these tales might be true, but who knew? He was old enough to understand that there's plenty of weird shit in the world that nobody really knows about. His uncle back in Puerto Rico had seen *chupacabras*, many times, but nobody wanted to believe him. Andres believed; it was his uncle, after all. But he was smart enough to know that, for the most part, nobody wants to admit things like that are real.

So as he slowed for the 59th Street station, he was not terribly surprised to see a figure up ahead in a dark jumpsuit and a helmet with a light on the front caught in the glare of the train's headlight. Andres swore and felt the sweat pop out on his face. There was nothing he could do; he was too close to stop now. He was going to hit this *pendejo*.

The guy looked up—it was definitely just a guy, so Andres could tell that at least it wasn't one of the Lizard People. For half a second the guy stood there, frozen. Then he scrambled frantically up and into one of those blocked tunnels, pulling a duffel bag after him.

The train roared past the spot just as the guy vanished into the hole, and Andres blew out a breath and shook his head. What the hell; that had been way too close. And what was that *hijo de puta* doing there anyway? Probably just some goofy Millennial asshole trying to explore and write a book about Underground New York. No—not a book, a website. That's what they did nowadays, websites. And he'd sell T-shirts or something, too.

Whatever; he hadn't hit the dumbfuck *pendejo*, so it was none of his business. Andres put it out of his head and brought the train into the station.

As he did, the guy in the jumpsuit was catching his breath just inside the opening he'd made. He'd planned on making it a little bigger, but the oncoming train had forced him to crawl through before he cleared the passage. It had been sealed for a lot of years, and unsealing it had been tougher than he'd expected. He took a deep breath and listened as the train rattled past. That had been way closer than it should have been. But one of the crossbeams blocking the hole had been replaced with steel rebar and anchored in concrete. He hadn't planned on that, and it had taken him much too long to remove it.

It didn't matter. Close was still a miss, and he had a job to do. He worked his way toward Park Avenue, along a tunnel that had not been used in living memory. Rubble had fallen from the walls, and even from the ceiling. There were still train tracks underfoot, but they were rusted, broken in many places. So he picked his way along carefully, until the tunnel ended abruptly at what had once been a stop for a long-gone train route. Here he paused, shining his light across the old platform. There was a marble arch on the back wall, but whatever doorway it had framed was gone, bricked up and then plastered over. He moved his light around the vaulted ceiling, which was decorated with a surprising amount of nineteenth-century detail work, and a mural of the Rape of Europa, badly faded and peeling but still visible. The man smiled and took out a map. He examined it carefully, checking it against a GPS on his wrist. Then he nodded and refolded the map.

Next he opened his duffel bag and took out an orange device, about the size and shape of a rifle case. At one end of it was a hand grip, with some kind of electronics mounted on it. He flicked it on and stepped onto the platform and over to the far wall, the one with the sealed arch, and began moving slowly along the wall to his right, watching the dials while holding the other end of the gadget up to the wall.

For the next hour the man went back and forth, covering every inch of the wall with the orange device. Whatever he was looking for, he didn't find it. He put the orange thing back in his bag and took out another piece of equipment, a black box with twin antennae on top and a meter of some kind on its face. He spent another half hour with this, along the same wall, but when he was done, he was still unsatisfied. He shook his head and mumbled, "Solid fucking steel." He stared at the wall for a while, but that didn't seem to help. So he put the box away, took out a bottle of water, and sat on the ground.

For a long time he just sat, sipping his water, sometimes looking over at the wall and then at the ceiling. Finally, he gave this up, too. "Shit," he said softly. Then he stood, dusted off his hands, and went back down the tunnel toward the platform for the Lexington local, bag over his shoulder.

Angela Dunham was a busy woman. Ordinarily, as assistant curator at the Eberhardt Museum, she did not need to work at the frantic pace she was at now. It was true that her boss, Benjy Dryden, the curator, was a cousin of the Eberhardts, and he was not a man who believed in the virtues of hard work—at least, not for himself. He did expect it from his assistant, and that kept Angela occupied.

Normally, that was not a huge burden. Angela loved the work, and it seldom demanded more of her than she could give in an eight-hour day. But now, with these bloody crown jewels coming in, she was in constant tumultuous motion, arranging extra insurance, overseeing the installation of all the new security—which meant dealing with the men from Tiburon Security, and they were a bit frightening, in her opinion. Curator Benjy kept himself remote from all of it. Angela even had to supervise the design elements for the exhibit—it just never ended. There were so many details that required her attention, and it seemed to her like she never got two seconds to sit down and drink her coffee anymore.

Angela had acquired a taste for coffee—practically an addiction, she admitted to herself. Of course, that was partly because it was new to her; she'd grown up with tea, drank PG Tips all the way through her master's at University of Birmingham, back home in the UK's Midlands. But when she'd come to America to take this job ten years before, she'd grown fond of coffee instead. Among other things, it made her feel a bit more like she belonged here. She'd come to relish the ritual of pouring a cup, sitting and sipping for a few minutes while she mentally organized her day. But the last few weeks had been so hectic she scarcely had time to pee, let alone sit and sip.

So when her assistant, Meg, told her that a Mr. Beck was here to talk to her about electronic security, she did not see the visit as an annoying interruption, as she usually would have. Instead, she welcomed the chance to sit at her desk, just breathe and talk for a few relatively calm minutes—and, of course, have a wee small spot of coffee. "Send him in," she said, and poured herself a cup from the thermos on her desk.

She'd had only one sip when Mr. Beck came in. He was a stocky man in a gray suit, probably in his fifties, with a bristly gray mustache, gray hair in an old-fashioned brush cut, glasses with big black frames, and a bow tie. "Ms. Dunham," he said, holding out his hand with a business card in it. "I'm Howard Beck, from Cerberus Security Systems."

He spoke with a middle-aged rasp in his voice, but he seemed nice enough. Angela took the card and inclined her head toward the folding chair across from hers. "Sit down, Mr. Beck. Would you like some coffee?"

"No, thank you. That's very kind, but no. Doctor's orders." He smiled apologetically.

"Well, I hope you'll forgive me if I have a bit myself?"

"Oh, of course, absolutely—I still love the smell, but I'm not allowed to indulge." He shook his head. "Arrhythmia, they tell me. My heart."

"I'm so sorry," Angela said. "Still, it could be worse, I suppose?"

"Oh, yes, much worse, I don't have any complaints," he said. He allowed her another sip, and then broke the silence by saying, "Ms. Dunham, I know you're a very busy woman—"

"You have no idea," she murmured.

"—so I'll cut right to the chase. I know the Eberhardt has always had top-notch security—but the Iranian crown jewels are going to paint a great big bull's-eye on your museum. And if anyone is taking aim at it, they are going to be better than anybody you can imagine."

"Yes, I'm quite certain you're right."

"They'll know everything there is to know about how to get around any kind of alarm or sensor you can possibly have—they've seen 'em all and beat 'em all before, many times. So if you really want to keep those crown jewels safe, you're going to need a few things that these light-fingered gentlemen have never heard of. And that's where Cerberus Systems comes in. Confidentially, Ms. Dunham, I can help you do a system upgrade that is so far beyond state of the art that some of our components are not even on the market yet."

"Really? That's very interesting, but—"

"In fact, I can promise you that with a new Cerberus System in place, you will be getting a few new developments that have never been installed anywhere—and that means the bad guys don't know how to beat 'em." He nodded, once, with confident satisfaction.

"Mr. Beck—I'm sorry, but we have already hired a firm to upgrade our security system."

"Yes, ma'am, but with all due respect—they can't have the kind of cutting-edge technology Cerberus can offer."

"Yes, but really, Mr. Beck—"

"Most of these other people don't think about somebody tunneling in underneath, to your basement—Cerberus has you covered there."

"We've been promised full electronics in the basement, actually. And I'm afraid—"

"Now before you say no, hear me out on this one thing: the roof."

Angela waited, but he said nothing, merely nodding with a serious expression on his face. "I can assure you, we do have a roof," she said at last into the awkward silence.

"Yes, ma'am, I know you do. But is it equipped with laser sensors that can detect any movement or shift in pressure from anything that weighs more than fifty pounds?"

"As a matter of fact, the firm we hired has informed me that they will install something in that line, yes." She gave him a very British superior smile. "As well as an armed human presence, of course. On the roof and at all other possible access points."

"Oh," Mr. Beck said. He looked a bit deflated, Angela thought. "If you don't think I'm being too pushy, could I ask you the name of that firm? Because—"

"Tiburon Security," Angela said. There was a gentle knock on her door—three soft raps; it was her assistant, Meg. "Come," she called.

Meg stuck her head in, a worried look pasted onto her pale, round face. "It's the swatches," she said. "For the drapery?"

"I'll be right there," Angela said. She looked at her coffee cup and sighed: It was empty. "Mr. Beck—I'm afraid I really can't give you any more time."

"Yes, ma'am, I understand, and I thank you for the time you have given me." He stood up. "Tiburon is very good, but if there's any sort of problem . . . ?"

In spite of herself, Angela smiled. "I'll be sure to call. Thank you, Mr. Beck."

"Thank *you*, Ms. Dunham," he said. He nodded his head in something that was almost a bow, and then went quickly out. And with a last regretful look at her thermos, Angela followed him out a moment later.

Chief Petty Officer (ret.) Walter Bledsoe sat behind his desk in the front office of Tiburon Security. It was a plain-looking office, although a veteran of the Navy might have recognized the way it was organized as highly reminiscent of a Naval Office, Operations, Special Warfare Command. That's how Bledsoe set it up. It was what he was used to. And it was his post. He was an organizer, a facilitator. He was not one of the pointy-headed guys who worked with the high-tech stuff. They were all veterans of the Teams, but the geeks kept to their workroom in the back, and he sat out here and faced the world.

And because everybody in the Teams is expected to pull his weight and perform multiple tasks, Bledsoe was also Tiburon's receptionist. Most days he didn't mind. The people who came in here were generally flag-rank assholes, but in twenty years in the Navy Bledsoe had made a career out of handling desk jockeys and pogues just like them, guys who thought their shit was pure gold. He ran into even more of the dickless shitbags now that he was a civilian, but the same techniques worked on them, and Bledsoe was an absolute artist at putting them in their place, civilian or flag rank, without anything that could be called outright insubordination.

A small electronic tone sounded, and Bledsoe looked up from his paperwork. The high-def monitor on his desk showed a man approaching the front door—average height, wiry build, dark and shaggy hair, wearing pressed khakis and a white shirt neatly tucked in. He also sported a pair of large glasses with bright cranberry-colored frames. "That's just fucking *darling*," Bledsoe muttered. He watched as the guy looked again at a slip of paper in his hand, comparing it to the number on the door. "Well, come on, Tinker Bell. Push the fucking button, fucknuts," Bledsoe muttered.

As if he'd heard, the man reached up and punched the small black button beside the door. Bledsoe moved the mouse over his computer monitor and clicked to open the door. A moment later, the stranger stood before him. "How can I help you . . . sir?" Bledsoe said, deliberately being a bit snarky.

"Uh, I'm looking for a—I mean, I was hoping you might have a job opening?"

"A *job*? *Here*?" Bledsoe said. He gave the man a slow and insulting once-over before shaking his head and adding, "You sure you got the right place? We don't do much ballet here."

"No, I—I mean, Tiburon, right? And, uh, yeah. Yeah, that's— You know, I heard about what you guys do, you're cutting-edge and so forth, and that's—oh!" He pulled an envelope out of his pocket and placed it in front of Bledsoe. "Uh, my résumé? It's— I have a master's? From Stanford? Electronic engineering? I specialize in surveillance and security? And, uh—I got a job at one of those start-ups, you know, Silicon Valley? But, uh—" He gave a one-syllable laugh. "They went belly-up, like, before they even paid me? So, uh . . ." He trickled to a halt and blushed as he saw that Bledsoe's face had taken on a look of pitying disbelief.

"Listen, buddy," Bledsoe said after letting the guy sweat for a minute. "I don't know what you heard, but we only hire guys from the Teams."

"The teams? You mean—I was on the tennis team in high school . . ."

He stumbled to a stop again as Bledsoe shook his head and said, "No, sport. Not tennis. SEAL Teams. We only hire guys we know from the SEAL Teams."

"But—but I have a *master's*—I know I could help—"

"Not gonna happen," Bledsoe said firmly. "Not never, not nohow." He cocked a dubious eyebrow. "Unless you wanna enlist and try for a spot on the Teams first?"

The poor guy just opened and closed his mouth like a goddamn fish. He was obviously suffering, but what the hell did he expect? Bledsoe let him stand there and sweat and swallow convulsively for a moment, and then he finally said, "Seriously, buddy. No fucking chance. Okay?" Bledsoe clicked his mouse, and the door swung open, startling the stranger into a small jump. "Have a nice day," Bledsoe said, and the guy swallowed one more time, looked around, and then bolted out the door like he was being chased by Apaches. "Fucknuts," Bledsoe said. "Dumb-ass cock-breath fucknuts." He flipped the résumé into the trash.

CHAPTER
4

My desk was littered with shit. It usually isn't. Unless I'm working, putting together some totally new plan. Which I was—or anyway, I was trying. And the crap storm on my desk told the story: photographs, charts, brochures, maps, papers stacked just high enough to hide the empty food wrappers—it was a mess that would have made Mom faint dead away. But she wasn't going to see it. Nobody was except me. I couldn't take a chance that somebody might notice it wasn't what it looked like, which was a pointless shit heap of random papers with no connection. A closer look would show that each piece of this particular shit heap had some connection to the Eberhardt Museum. There were detailed photographs of every window and door, inside and out; close-ups of sections of the roof—especially the area around the skylight; floor plans of every inch of the museum, and even seismic maps of the area under it, along with an ancient map of the subway system. I had busted my ass to collect all this, turned myself into a sweaty fat redneck, spent the night by the dumpster in rags. I tried everything, covered every inch of the place you could possibly think of, and even a lot that you would never imagine—that's kind of my trademark—and guess what?

None of it was worth a rusty rat's ass.

There was just No Fucking Way In. Not even for me. Riley Wolfe. The genius of gems. The king of kleptomania. The greatest thief who ever lived. I was stuck on the outside of what could be the greatest heist in history—but only if I could get inside the museum.

And I couldn't. No way.

"Shit," I said. "Shit, shit, *shit* . . ." It didn't help, no matter how many times I said it. No brilliant plan came to me. Not even a stupid one. I was on the outside looking in. And once the jewels arrived, it would get a whole lot worse. I wouldn't even be able to get close enough to look in the door.

I picked up a sheet of paper and snarled at it. My checklist. The starting point for my most amazing and impossible job ever. I scanned it, waiting for some overlooked weak spot to leap out at me. Roof access—nope. Basement access—not possible. Alarm system—brand-new unknown tech, so forget it. Infiltrate tech company—uh-uh, not happening with those 12-gauge assholes. Doors, windows, walls, floor, nothing. Every single possible entry point on the list was crossed out. And no matter how many times I stared at the paper, nothing new magically appeared.

I balled it up and let it fall. It was worthless. I was worthless. I couldn't come up with a single thing they hadn't covered. Why? Because I couldn't break out of brain-dead, ordinary, garden-variety thief thinking. Everything I thought of was something any two-bit wannabe would try. *Oh, I know—go through the skylight!* Sure. And land in front of a couple of trigger-happy assholes with automatic weapons. "Standard," I mumbled. "Total normal-ass bullshit. *Think*, damn it."

But the thoughts were not coming. I'd made my rep by coming up with things nobody else ever could—and by *doing* them. And before I did them, just to be extra safe and thorough, I always went through all the ordinary tricks, the dumb-ass things any clown could do—the kind of stuff the cops actually hoped you would try because they'd seen it before and they were ready for it. I checked it all out anyway, always. And usually, that would help me see some totally new and beautiful plan to get what I needed.

This time? Nothing. I hadn't expected anything, and I didn't find it. But what I did find was enough to scare away anybody else. I'd thought the security at the Central Bank in Tehran was stiff. This was a lot worse. What they were doing to the Eberhardt was practically *Star Trek*, like two hundred years ahead of everything else.

So I tried harder. And because nobody else would think of it, I did research on Ludwig Eberhardt, the dynasty's founder, the old asshole who built the place. I did enough research to write a fucking thesis. I learned things about him I would bet nobody else in the world knew. And I even got one quick moment of hope when I learned about the private train track the old bastard had built so he could ride his luxury Pullman car from his home all the way in to his museum.

I almost got squashed by a subway train, but I found the tunnel old Ludwig's track was in. And it was just another dead end. Just like all the other dead ends that were piled up on my desk. All of them garbage, useless. Unworkable, even fatal. And I was out of ideas.

I thought I needed to find something impossible. It was starting to look like I'd done it for real.

"Shit," I said one more time. It still didn't help. "There has to be a way. Goddamn it, there's always a way."

I glanced around the room without really seeing it. It was small and cramped, but it was all I needed right now. There was a bed, a dorm-sized refrigerator, a hot plate—and behind a tattered old shower curtain, there was a sink and a toilet. The room was in an old building south of Williamsburg, and it smelled like a public toilet. But what the hell, I've had worse. I can get used to anything, and nobody else was coming in here. I had paid a stupid amount of cash for three months' rent and a guarantee that I'd be left alone, to "finish my novel."

The room hadn't been much before I got there. It was worse now. A lot worse. It looked like someplace where the worst frat on campus had competed with an indie band for craziest party. It was a close contest, and garbage won. It wasn't my usual habitat. Mom made sure I grew up so that I am generally pretty neat. It just makes everything easier if you can find what you need. But when I'm working out a plan, I'm somebody else. I don't even notice what's around me.

Which was a good thing: I had turned this room into a total dumpster fire. There were heaps of dirty dishes, old pizza boxes, cans and bottles and wrappers, all of it just flung wherever, into every inch of the room—except my desk and one other area. In a corner near the door was a clothes rack, the kind you might find backstage in a theater. Hanging from it were pieces of the people I'd become to check out the Eberhardt—a seersucker suit that was about eight sizes too big for me, a wrinkled mass of filthy rags with a bushy beard perched on the hanger, coveralls, and a few more ordinary articles of clothing. Beside the rack was a table holding more carefully arranged items: a pair of glasses with cranberry frames, a couple of wigs, and so on—all carefully preserved, just in case I needed them again before this job was over.

But it was starting to look like this job was over before it started.

"Shit," I said one more time. And because I hate to repeat myself, I added, "Fuck a shit-piss." I said it a little too loud, but the garbage soaked up the noise. And anyway, it didn't help. My gray cells weren't churning out anything. It just wasn't happening, and it had to. It abso-fucking-lutely HAD to. To the very depth of my soul, if I have one—and I kind of doubt it?—I totally believe that no matter what the goal,

41

there is always a way to achieve it. It's not that I'm any kind of California brown-rice, new age optimist. I've had a hard life so far, often violent, starting in my childhood. The kinds of thing I've lived through would knock rosy optimism out of the Dalai Lama. So I've got no delusions, illusions, or confusions about what life really is. It's a fucking mess, a flying shit storm with a sharp knife. Life mostly sucks, and then you die. But I also believe—no, I absolutely fucking *know*—that whatever rotten shit pit life dumps you into, there is always a way out. Always. That's the only real piece of faith I've got: There Is Always a Way.

But this? The Eberhardt Museum? If there was a way in, I hadn't found it. Usually, that would be like using spurs on a thoroughbred. It would whip me up and make me think of something new, something no one could hope to anticipate. That's what kept me going. That's who I was: Riley Wolfe, the guy who never quit and always won. Riley Wolfe, who took every obstacle as a challenge to greatness. Riley Wolfe, the greatest thief who had ever lived. I always found a way— *always*—to get what I was after.

Until now.

I couldn't grab it if I couldn't get inside to where it was kept. And this time, there was no way in at all. Nothing.

"Nothing *yet*," I muttered. "There's always a way . . . *Has* to be . . ." I tried like hell to believe it was there. And I would find it. I *had* to find it. What was at stake was more than the incredibly rich payday. This was who I am, goddamn it. If I couldn't do this, I wouldn't be *me* anymore. Because it was totally fucking impossible, and that meant I had to do it, whatever They might say.

Who's They? The ones who told me I couldn't, whatever it was. They've been telling me that my whole life, since I was a kid. And as I got older and the things They said I couldn't do got more complicated, I kept doing them. There was always some fat-ass, born-into-money jerkwad standing in my way and telling me to give up and crawl back to Loserville with the other poor boys. And it didn't matter. I found a way. I did it. Always, ever since I was so young and stupid that I let their fat-faced sneers push me into all the dangerous, crazy bullshit stunts they said I couldn't do. Always, since the very first time, I found a way and came back to wipe the stupid smirk off their fat faces.

But this time . . . ?

I blew out a frustrated breath and closed my eyes. Nothing came to me. No wonderful, unexpected key that would unlock the doors of the Eberhardt. All I could see were lethal obstacles and unbreachable walls, and me on the outside again with no way in. And I *hated* that, being outside. It made my skin pucker, made me feel small and stupid and dirty, like I was trapped in a box with the walls closing in and the air hissing out so I had nothing to breathe, no way to move, nothing to do but curl up and wait for it to squeeze me out of life. Trapped inside the small and ragged kid I had been, surrounded by bigger, cleaner, better-dressed kids sneering and pushing me and telling me I wasn't even shit to scrape off their shoes, and I would never be anything else but nothing.

Go on, rag boy. Run away, back to your double-wide.

That still ate at me like it had just happened. I put my head down. My stomach was feeling sour and had started to churn, because it looked like they were right and there was nothing I could do about it, like I was back at the beginning again. Just a kid without a clue . . .

"It's like this, son," my father said. We were sitting in the grass of the front yard. A mild wind blew gently across us, cooling the sweat we'd worked up from playing catch. "People are sheep."

I looked at him. I mean, I kind of knew what he was saying, but . . . "Everybody, Dad?"

He smiled. "Weeeeellll . . . there's a few sheepdogs—just to keep the sheep in line, you know. But most people . . . Yeah. Just sheep."

"Are—are you a sheep, Dad?"

My father turned and looked at me with a lazy smile. "No, son. I am definitely not a sheep." He ruffled my hair. "I'm not a sheepdog, either."

I frowned, trying to make sense of it. "Why do people just, you know, stay sheep?"

"It's safe," my father said. "It can be dangerous to leave the flock." Dad looked off into the distance. "Very dangerous," he said softly.

"Are . . . Are you in, um . . . danger?" I asked.

Still looking away, my father nodded. "Almost certainly," he said.

I felt a lump grow in my throat. The next day was my birthday—ten years old!—and I didn't want anything dangerous to happen, not to Dad, not to me . . . not before the party. "Then why?" I asked. "Why do you have to, you know, be in danger?"

Dad looked at me, very serious now. "It's the price you pay, son. You want the truly good things, you have to put your neck on the chopping block now and then. But it's a whole lot better than being a sheep." Dad put a hand on my shoulder, squeezed. "You try not to be a sheep, too . . ."

I didn't really know what Dad meant—not then. But I said, "I'll try" anyway. And then all of a sudden Dad was gone and he never said how not to be a sheep. Mom didn't know, either, and things got bad. And before I knew what was happening, I was in the middle of a circle of boys and they were pushing me around and laughing at me, and I just had to let them because they were bigger and there was a lot of them and what could I really do? And they pushed harder and talked tougher and I got more and more scared and I started praying that somebody might come help me, but there was nobody who would, nobody who could, there was only me against them, all of them together and me all alone, the whole flock of them getting louder and—

And then, just like that, I knew what Dad had meant.

And I looked around at the circle of faces all scrunched into fake mean expressions—and all I saw was sheep.

They weren't really tough, dangerous guys. They were boys, scared boys, and they were pushing me around and jeering at me because they thought they could. Because there was a whole bunch of them and only one of me. Because, damn it, they were just sheep, and that's what sheep did. They picked on the one they thought was weaker, different, until they felt better about being sheep.

Right then and there, just like that, I knew I wasn't one of them, would never be one of them, and I didn't have to try anymore. And I didn't want to try because I didn't want to be one of them anymore.

So I knocked away the hand on my chest. And I smiled. I could tell right away that worried them, scared them a little even—because that meant I was not a sheep.

Right then and there, everything changed.

Riley Wolfe was born.

"All right," I said. "I'll do it. But it's gonna cost you."

The biggest, loudest, sheep-est one stepped closer. "You'll DO it, rag boy? You'll climb all the way into the old quarry?" He shoved—

And this time, I shoved back. The big sheep stepped back, stunned. "I said I would, and I will. And I'll bring back the taillight from the Studebaker at the bottom. For proof," I said. I shoved the big one again. "But it. Will. COST you."

The big kid looked uncertain. "You can't climb into the old quarry," he said. "All the kids who tried it died."

And that was true, or at least it was the local legend. The old quarry was the place that every parent warned their kids to stay away from. It was a death trap—a hundred feet straight down, the walls made of soft and crumbly stone. And at the bottom, nothing but a pool of fouled water. Somebody had pushed a car into it years ago, a 1958 Studebaker

Lark. The tail end of the car stuck up tantalizingly, a target for the best rock throwers.

"Nobody can climb down there. It's too dangerous," one of the other sheep said. The others nodded.

"Then you can't lose your money, can you? So let's see it."

"There's no way," they said.

"There's always a way," I said for the first time. And as I said it, I realized that it was true; it HAD to be true. It was the whole explanation for how not to be a sheep. Sure, it could be dangerous. Dad had said so, and he was right. Climbing into the quarry was going to be risky as hell. But it could be done. There Was a Way. Always. It was a basic law of life for anybody who could grab it and believe it. And I did, and it filled me up with its truth, lifted me far above the bleating sheep and the crappy double-wide and all the hungry dreams I'd been squashing because there was no way they could ever happen. But now I knew better. There was a way. There had to be. "There is always a way," I said again.

And there was. There was a way down into that old death trap of a quarry, and I found it. And the sheep paid. Almost a hundred dollars altogether, a huge amount of money back then. I still remembered the look on Mom's face when I gave it to her, the slow smile spreading over her face as she counted it out. "Oh, my," she'd said. "We're going to be living the life of Riley."

She liked to tease about that. "Living the life of Riley." I didn't know what that meant then, but I liked the name. And I kept it.

And I kept that flash of insight, that there's always a way. All these years in between that first time I put my life on the line and now. And all to get a stupid fucking taillight from a 1958 Studebaker Lark. It felt great taking the money from them, better than just having money, because they were fat, stupid *sheep* who had things I didn't, and it almost felt like I was doing a good deed to take stuff away from people like that. But as nice as it was to get the money, I think I liked just doing it even more. Just to see the look on their face when I showed them that yeah, I fucking well *could*.

That feeling stayed with me. It even grew. It always felt better to take it away from the rich sheep. They always thought they deserved to have what everybody else couldn't because they had money. So that turned into what I wanted most—not just the stuff; the stuff taken from the rich sheep. And no matter how well they protected it, I always found it, and I took what I was after.

But this time . . . Where was the way? What was left to try? What was I missing? What was the one thing nobody would ever even think about—nobody but Riley Wolfe?

Go ahead, rag boy. Run away—

Back to the double-wide . . .

I still heard those voices in my head, getting bigger and louder, sneering, daring me, telling me I would fail—and I knew I would, because I wasn't shit, I was just rag boy, trailer trash, and I always would be . . .

I picked up the brochure from the museum and scanned it again: ". . . founded in 1889 . . . unique example of Stanford White's influence . . . still owned and managed by Eberhardt's descendants, who take an active role . . . recognized worldwide as one of the finest . . ."

"Shit," I said one last time. I'd read the thing a hundred times. The words hadn't changed, and they still didn't tell me anything I wanted to know. I crumpled the brochure in disgust. The fucking Eberhardts and their fucking family museum. "Rich fucking assholes." Exactly the sort of privileged shitbag, scumbag sheep I hated the most. Not merely rich, they were rich from *inheriting* money—they'd done nothing at all to deserve it. I could just about feel their smug superiority from here. Their kind were my favorite target, and that made this deadlock even more frustrating. A perfect target, a legendary score—and I couldn't get to the starting line.

I wadded up the brochure and flung it away. It fell on an impressively big stack of other crumpled papers. I'd tried everything I could think of, every possible angle, and I had nothing but a heap of crumpled paper and a headache. I told myself I was very damn good at what I did, absolutely the best, and if I couldn't see a way in—well, maybe there just wasn't one this time. It didn't make me feel any better. It just made it hurt in a way that went much deeper than the disappointment of missing a great score.

I blew out a long, frustrated breath and leaned back in my chair, running a hand through the bristle of dark blond hair on top of my head, cut short so the wigs would fit. So far they had, and the disguises had been near perfect, and they hadn't gotten me anywhere. The Eberhardts were just too good, too thorough. I had never before seen anything like this. They'd sealed up that museum so tight that the only possible way to get in was to buy a ticket.

I took another deep breath and tried to focus. The frustration wasn't helping. It was taking over my brain. I needed to push away all the bullshit, uncoil the knots building up inside. Relax and get to a creative place. So I reached for the Bose headphones around my neck. I slipped them up onto my ears and picked up my mp3 player. It was stupid expensive, definitely not just an iPod. It had on it all the hundreds of hours of music I needed, music from all time and all the world. I don't give a shit about genres in music. Since I learned the music I liked mostly by myself, I never learned to care if it was rap, rock, or even bebop. I just care if it's *good*. There was a mood or a moment for just about anything, even Balinese monkey chant. So my player was pricey, but it was the best, and that was what mattered. Money was for spending, and I never gave it a second thought. Besides, I'd made plenty, and getting more was easy. I thumbed up the volume and hit PLAY.

At once, the music flooded into me—Miles Davis, *In a Silent Way*.

Perfect soundtrack for letting your mind float away from problems and off to a peaceful place where the solution to the Eberhardt Museum would finally happen. I just needed to relax, let it come to me. I closed my eyes and let my mind glide. Forget the museum, forget the guards, let it all go and just drift . . .

The gentle breeze blew, and Dad squeezed my shoulder. "Try not to be a sheep, son."

"I'll try," I said, even though I didn't know what that meant. And then Mom was calling from the porch of the big Victorian house and we were walking across the wide lawn together and going in for supper, going in to that big wonderful old house, MY house—except that when I got there, Dad was gone and the house had turned into a battered old double-wide trailer and Mom was crying and there was nothing in the fridge so there was no supper after all and no money and Mom was crying, so I knew I had to do something and I did it but I didn't mean to and then he was falling, falling, spinning and endlessly falling away, and I could only stand there and watch him falling, spinning and falling, and now it's me falling, turning slowly and falling, and I can't—

I woke up with a jerk. I tried to shake off the fumes of that black-cloud feeling, but it was no good. The asshole Eberhardts and their inherited billions and electronic systems had me beat. And as for a human door in, forget it. You didn't bribe or blackmail Black Hat or Tiburon or, God help us, the Revolutionary Guard. And even the museum senior staff was mostly the fat-ass Eberhardt family anyway. A whole fucking family of entitled asshole sheep who did nothing except sit on their fat pimply butts and count their inherited money and keep out anybody who wasn't one of them, so getting past them was just as impossible, unless—

It hit me like something heavy falling on my head—but it felt *good*. Really, truly, amazingly fucking *GREAT*!

"There's a way," I said out loud. "Goddamn it, there IS A WAY!"

I jumped out of my chair and kicked through the heap of crumpled papers until I found the brochure from the museum. I threw it on the desk and smoothed it out, and this time I read through it slowly and carefully.

When I was done, I just sat there and smirked for a minute. It was there. It was really and truly right fucking *there*. And it was so obvious—and at the same time so totally un-fucking-thinkable!—that only Riley fucking Wolfe would ever see it, let alone try it.

It was there. I had my way.

I switched the music over to something with a feeling of celebrating—David Bowie, *Ziggy Stardust*. And as the opening guitar chords crashed into my headphones, I leaned back and closed my eyes again—but this time, I was working. And as I began parsing the details, I was still smiling. "There is *always* a way," I told the rich-bitch asshole fucking Eberhardts. "Always." And I pushed away the last of the black cloud and its double-wide memories and began to plan.

CHAPTER

5

Two days later, I was still feeling the high when I went to see Monique. I was going to make this happen. And Monique was a big part of the setup. And of the finish, when we got there. *If* we got there, I thought. But I pushed that away, too. Having an answer made me feel too good to doubt it. It also felt good to have a reason to see Monique.

Like always, I paused just outside and peeked in Monique's window. Creepy, I know, but I can't help it. I mean, I am not a Peeping Tom except with Monique. That's partly because she used to paint naked, which is something truly worth seeing. And except for one night of celebration—which she says will never happen again—I don't get to see it.

That is tragic because, like I said, Monique is worth seeing. She's twenty-eight, with one of those slim bodies that doesn't look like much when it's covered up—especially covered up with the paint-spattered coveralls she always wears. But as I found out that one wonderful night, when the coveralls come off, Monique's body is a true play-ground. The curves are subtle, but they are elegant and they beg your hands to wander. Her coffee skin feels like somebody took satin and improved it. Her lips are full and sensuous and taste like some kind of wild berry. And when she gets wound up—

Anyway, that's a night I will never forget. And I swear, I will find a way to repeat it.

When I looked in now, she was in front of her easel—dressed, un-fortunately. Her hair was pulled up and back, she had a paintbrush between her teeth, and she was frowning at an Impressionist painting I recognized on her easel. A blown-up section of the original was on a computer monitor to her left. She glanced at it, then went back to frowning at the easel. I was pretty sure the frowning wouldn't last long. She'd figure it out—Monique always figures out these things. That's why she's so damn good at what she does.

Monique is an art forger. A really good one.

Maybe the best in the world.

I had checked out her background. You have to know about the people you work with—I mean, if you want to stay out of the slam. So I checked. And I'm pretty sure Monique didn't start out with the thought of working the dark side of the street with wicked people like me. She came from a respectable Pittsburgh family, mother a pediatri-cian and father a well-known professor of moral philosophy at Pitt. Monique had gone to Harvard on the fast track for an advanced degree in art history, her passion. But after taking a few studio classes, she discovered that she had a real talent for painting. And beyond that, she had an absolute genius for imitating other painters.

On a bet, egged on by her boyfriend, Ron, Monique had made a near-perfect copy of one of the paintings in Harvard's museum, the Fogg: She chose Renoir's *Chez la Modiste*. And because she was a little bit vain and had a very quirky sense of humor, she'd signed it with her name, but disguised to look like Renoir's.

Monique's plan was to sneak her copy into the Fogg Museum and put it side by side with Renoir's—just a joke, a lark, a fun way to say, "Look what I can do!" And she'd done exactly that, leaning her copy against the wall under the original and successfully slipping away without detection.

Or so she thought. But someone else had come along right afterward and taken the original, hanging Monique's copy in its place.

It took the Fogg a week to discover the forgery. It only took the detectives three days to find Monique's name in the signature and then find her. They had not been amused. Neither had the Fogg Museum or the university—and neither had the judge. I always suspected the judge, a true Boston Southie, saw a black girl trying to pull a fast one. And her boyfriend, Ron? He was really helpful—to the police. He told them that yeah, Monique did the forgery and snuck it into the Fogg Museum, and he didn't know what she did with the original. Ain't love grand?

So the evidence was all against her. It was more than enough. Monique was expelled, sentenced to jail, and shamed. Even her parents, who paid for a good lawyer, washed their hands of her. Turns out they were kind of social climbers, even her dad. So much for moral philosophy.

Six months into serving her sentence, Monique was released. Ron, her talkative boyfriend, had been nabbed trying to sell *Chez la Modiste*, the real one, to an undercover agent of the FBI. "I argued down to second-degree accessory and forgery," the lawyer told Monique. "So it's time served—but you've still got the felony on your record. Best I could do."

Her parents, surprisingly, were waiting for her. They gave her a check for $10,000 to "get settled"—and told her not to call them anymore.

In spite of all that bullshit hitting her right in the face, Monique was grateful. Because she had learned three very important life lessons from the experience: Never trust anybody, screw them before they screw you, and love sucks. And when she had that figured, she was ready to play on Team Riley.

Like all great players, she found her own way over to the dark side. She took the money from Mom and Dad, moved to New York, and used the cash to set up a studio. And then she went into business doing the one thing she was good at and could still do with a felony on her record.

She did that the smart way, too. She nosed around until she heard rumors of a gallery owner who was supposedly selling copies and charging for the real item—without telling the customers, of course. Monique thumbed through the dealer's catalog, made two brilliant copies as a calling card—and her career was launched. She'd even branched out into sculpture and objets d'art because there seemed to be nobody else covering that corner of the market. She turned out to be just as good at that as she was with painting. Her copy of Dudu the Scribe, a Sumerian votive figure, was breathtaking. So between the objets and the paintings, she'd made damn good money and built a reputation. Even better, I found her, which was good for both of us, especially financially. I'd put a lot of money into her pocket.

The relationship had grown. Turns out, Monique had a flare for costumes, too. She started helping me design my disguises, making sure they were clothes that were right for who I was supposed to be. And accessories? Let's face it, that's not a Guy Thing. I would never have gotten that right. Monique did. She was a genius at figuring that stuff out—watches, ties, briefcases, and especially shoes. I relied on her now for all that—and maybe I relied on her too much? You might say I have trust issues—but the truth is, trust is something I can't afford. You trust somebody in this game—*anybody*—and sooner or later they're the ones who drop the dime on you.

So I don't actually *trust* Monique—but it's awful damn close. And anyway, it's in her own best interest to keep me working. Because, like I said, she helps me, and I help to make her rich. She could even afford to take a job for the love of it now and then.

Like now, the thing on her easel. The idea of Monique working on this painting was so sad, it finally got me moving. Knowing it did not say anything good about my character, I stepped in and snuck up behind her, as close as I could get without touching. Hard not to touch—she smelled like patchouli oil mixed with cinnamon, and the curve of her bare neck was right there, inches away. And if I stood there any longer, I was going to bite it.

"You have to use a finer brush." I spoke softly but almost in her ear, and Monique jumped a foot into the air. Very satisfying.

"Jesus *fuck*, Riley!" she said, turning on me with a raised brush, like she was going to stab me. "How the fuck did you get in here?"

I shrugged. "The window was open."

"Of course it's fucking open! Why shouldn't the fucking window be open?! We're on the twenty-fifth fucking floor!"

"A really pleasant climb, too," I said. It was. No real challenges, so I could relax. Let my mind go.

"Jesus fuck," Monique said again. "You and your fucking par-kay."

"It's par-*kour*," I told her. Not for the first time.

"Whatever," she snapped. "Just cut it out. Why do you have to pull that shit on me anyhow?"

"Weeeellll," I said with a shrug and a very small smile, "I like to surprise you."

"So next time, surprise me and knock on the fucking door like everybody else, all right? I don't paint naked anymore—thanks to you."

"Tragic," I said. "Your work loses that other dimension."

"I wish you'd disappear into another dimension," she said. "You're going to give me a heart attack someday you go on like this." She blew out a long breath, deliberately calming herself. "Well, shit. All right, so what is it this time? I'm kind of busy."

I raised an eyebrow at that. "Busy, Monique? Really?" I tipped my head to the canvas. "With Mary Cassatt? I mean . . ."

"Fuck you twice, Riley," she said. "You don't know shit."

"Sorry," I said. But in fact, I DO know shit. A lot of it. For one thing, I know Cassatt was strictly second rank, and not worthy of Monique's time.

"Anyway, I like her," Monique said, still sounding defensive. "She was from Pittsburgh, same as me." She glared at me, daring me to say that being from Pittsburgh never made anybody a great painter. And honestly, it was on the tip of my tongue, but I'm no fool. I bit down and didn't say it.

"And what the hell, Riley, she's a hell of a lot better than she gets credit for," Monique said. "But because she's a woman, nobody gives a shit about— I mean, look at the detail, the color!" she yelled at me, pointing to the monitor. "Every fucking bit as good as Degas!"

"Maybe," I said. "But nobody else thinks so, and there's no real money in doing a Cassatt."

"Tough shit! I *like* doing it!" she said. "And it's for a respectable decorator who pays up front!"

"Respectable? Really?" I said, and I couldn't keep a little bit of smirk out of my voice. "A respectable interior decorator?"

"That's right! Is there something wrong with that?"

I shrugged. "Not that I can think of," I said. "Although I didn't know you could be respectable and still sell them fakes."

"My fakes are worth what they pay," she said.

"And the rich assholes deserve it. I totally agree, you know that,

Monique. And your work is fantastic, usually better than the original," I said. Maybe laying it on a little thick, but it was true. "It's just that as good as you are and as hard as you work, I just think you should be making more money."

"I make plenty of money."

I snorted. "With a Cassatt? Come on, Monique, Cassatt doesn't bring top dollar."

"Well, goddamn it, she *should*! Just because she was a woman—!"

"Probably," I said. But I knew I had her here. "You know you're not going to change the market. And like I said, the chump change money is a waste of your talent."

Monique rolled her eyes. "Meaning you have something that isn't a waste of my incredible, one-of-a-kind talent? And a Riley Wolfe Project always comes first?"

I looked at her for a moment. I couldn't be sure if she was being sarcastic. I mean, the part about me—definitely. But I couldn't tell if she really did appreciate how good she was. And she really was the best, in my opinion. That was one big reason why I'd brought her something that was going to be the biggest challenge I'd ever faced. I had to have the best if I was going to pull this off. And another reason was that I liked her. I don't like a lot of people. It's counterproductive. I mean, if Monique sucked at what she did and I used her because I liked her, I'd be in the slammer very damn quickly. It's always your "friends." I mean, who else knows enough to kick you into the shit? Nobody wants to admit it, but it's true: It doesn't pay to have friends, because you have to trust them, and that never works out.

"Well?" Monique said. "What do you need that only a great artist like me can provide?"

I smiled. I was pretty sure I had her on the hook. "This." I dropped a photograph on her computer table. "And this." A second photo.

Monique glanced at the pictures and looked at me, shaking her head. "Rauschenberg and Jasper Johns. I can do those in a week each—and I can name four guys in the metro area that could do these for you. Cheaper, too."

I smiled bigger, my shark smile, and I could see it made Monique very uneasy. "I could name *seven*, almost as good as you," I said.

"Fuck you, Riley."

"I said '*almost*,' Monique," I said. "You know I don't do almost."

Monique looked back at me. She could see I was serious now, and for some weird reason that made her smile. "I know that," she said, in a softer voice, and the tone of it made my blood start to bubble. "That's one reason I put up with you."

She wasn't doing anything but looking at me and smiling, but I felt like pawing the ground and snorting. "What are the other reasons?"

"Money's good," she said. "And you never miss."

I swallowed. My throat was so tight it hurt. "Anything else?"

"Sure." Her smile got bigger and a little bit wicked. "One of these days, you *will* miss," she said. "I kind of want to see that."

That hit me. I mean, what the hell? She wanted to see me go down in flames? "What the fuck, Monique," I said. "Why?"

She shrugged, but she was still smiling. "Perfectly natural," she said. "Everybody wants to watch a cocky bastard get skunked."

"'Cocky bastard.' Thanks, that's nice."

"It's accurate," she said. "Just because you always find a way to pull it off—I mean, you act like that's a given." She just looked at me for a minute. I wasn't sure if I wanted to slap her or kiss her. Maybe both. Then she shrugged. "Anyway," she said, "mostly I really do want you to keep winning. Except," she said, raising a perfect, paint-spattered hand, "for the Bet."

Now I had to smile. "Sooner or later, I'll win that, too," I said.

"You won't," she said. "You can't." She flicked at the two pictures with her finger. Then she frowned and cocked her head at me. "This contemporary stuff isn't your usual turf, Riley. What's up?"

For just a minute, my mind zoomed off Monique and onto the prize. "Something big. *Huge*," I said. "Jesus, Monique, when I pull this off—goddamn it, everything changes forever! This is—"

"A Jasper Johns copy is going to change everything forever? That's not possible, Riley."

"But it is," I said. The excitement poured through me as I talked, and some of it must have splashed onto her because she bit her lip and her eyes got big. "These paintings are just the beginning, just seeding the ground. But what they are going to lead me to, Monique—what these two drab contemporary pieces are going to help me do—Jesus Christ, it's going to be the most awesome—!"

"Ouch!" Monique barked. I looked down. Without knowing it, I'd grabbed her by the wrists, and I guess I was squeezing. I dropped her hands.

"It's huge, Monique. It's abso-fucking-lutely huge."

She rubbed her wrists and looked again at the photos. She shrugged: simple stuff. "When do you need 'em?"

I gave her a tight grin. "Soon. Probably . . . three weeks?"

"'Probably'?"

I shook my head. "Timetable isn't really set in stone. But—" I suddenly remembered the important part. "Oh! Here . . ." I fumbled in my pocket and pulled out two small pieces of this morning's *New York Times*. Each piece was no more than a strip with a partial headline and today's date. I held them up. "Very important," I said, passing the two strips of newspaper to Monique.

"Riley, what the hell . . . ?" she said, glancing at the papers and then back to me, to see if I was joking. I wasn't. "All right, I give up. What am I supposed to do with these?"

"This is the best part," I told her. "You glue one strip onto each canvas—the lower left corner, left as you face the canvas, very important. Crucial. And then . . . you overpaint it, hide it. But not *too* well. You know, so it can't be seen, but if you look for it—boom! There it is!"

Monique shook her head. "What the fuck, Riley, you mean you *want* people to know these are fakes?"

Showing all my teeth in a savage grin I really felt, I nodded. "That, my darling, is the entire fucking point."

Monique kept her eyes fixed on mine, but I didn't say anything more. She knew me well enough to know I wouldn't, either. So she sighed, shook her head, and said, "All right, sure, why not. I'll make two perfect fakes and make sure people *know* they're fakes. But someday, maybe you'll tell me why?"

I just smiled. "Maybe," I said. Then I clapped my hands together and got serious again. "So!" I said. "Can you do it?"

"Hmp," Monique said. I could tell she was still just a little pissed I wouldn't tell her. "You said three weeks?"

"To be safe," I said. "Like I said, it's hard to be really sure. You know how these things go."

"No, I don't know, Riley, because I've got no idea what 'these things' are this time."

I just shrugged. We both knew I wasn't going to tell her. "Can you do it?"

She looked at me a little longer. Then she picked up the photos. "Well," she said thoughtfully, "a couple of days to finish the Mary Cassatt, then a week each for these two . . . I mean, if nothing goes wrong?" she started.

"What could go wrong?" I said. "Two people who are the greatest on earth at what they do—what the *hell* could go wrong, Monique?"

"I don't know," she said. "Global warming might drive up the price of paint." But she couldn't help one more try at opening me up. "But damn it, Riley—this is routine stuff. I mean—it's really going to shake the whole fucking world?"

I smiled. I was feeling the excitement again. "Let's just say these paintings are going to open a door?"

Monique shook her head wearily. She knew there was no point in asking for any more detail. "All right, fine, we'll open your goddamn door," she said. "Three weeks, usual rates. And then what? If your door actually opens?"

I couldn't help it. Like I said, I was really *feeling* it. And I wanted Monique to feel it with me. I crept closer, just a half step, but she didn't back away. I locked eyes with her, and my voice dropped to an intense purr just above a whisper. "Then, Monique," I said, and I saw the hair go up on her neck and arms. "Then you will make me something amazing, something absolutely spectacular, and I will use it to perform the most astonishing disappearing act the world has ever seen."

Monique shivered. Her eyes never left mine, and for just a second she leaned forward, toward me. But as I swayed forward to meet her, something snapped awake inside, and Monique shook herself and stepped back. She took a breath and put on a face that told me she wasn't getting sucked in by animal magnetism and melodrama. "And what's the payoff, after all these ifs?"

I felt the shark smile spread onto my face again. "Eight figures," I told her.

"Not bad," she said.

"That's just *your* end, Monique," I said.

For a moment Monique forgot to breathe. She stared at me like she wanted to see some sign that I was kidding. And of course, I wasn't. She saw that. "Jesus Christ, Riley," she said after a long pause. "What could possibly—"

I held up a hand. "It's all hypothetical," I said. "For now."

"Jesus Christ," she said again. She knew there was no point in asking for any more information. So she thought about it for a minute. I could see the wheels turning, and she started chewing on her lip as she figured it. She looked incredibly hot when she did that, and I wanted to help her. But I didn't. I let her work it through—eight figures. That meant . . . ten million dollars? Twenty? Which meant *my* end would be—

"For Christ's sake," she finally burst out. "What in the name of God could be worth *hundreds* of millions of dollars?"

I just shook my head.

"You do mean *dollars*?" she asked, one eyebrow raised.

"Dollars," I said happily. "In cash, untraceable. More dollars than you have ever seen before or will ever see again."

Monique took a slightly shaky breath.

"Well?" I said. "Are you in?"

"Hell yes," she said in a husky voice just one step away from sex.

That hit me like a two-by-four. I leaned close to her, and once more she unconsciously leaned toward me, too. That much money can do that to anybody. Closer still and her breathing got a little ragged. And then my breath brushed across her face, and for just a moment I was sure that—but no, goddamn it! At the very last instant Monique turned her head to one side and my lips landed on her cheek. I held my lips there a second too long, thinking maybe—but no. Not going to happen. I sighed and stepped back. "All righty then," I said. I eyeballed her one more time and then turned and walked toward the window. "I'll see you in three weeks," I said.

"Riley, use the fucking door!" Monique called, but it was too late. I was already out the window and away into the night. But just before I got out of range, I heard her say to herself, "*Eight figures! Jesus Christ, Riley!*"

CHAPTER

6

The night air was cool. But after the heat I'd just gone through with Monique, it wasn't cool enough. I needed a cold shower. An ice bath. Something about her got me going like nobody else. But Riley's First Law: The job comes first.

So save those thoughts for later. Out the window and away. This time I went up, climbing easily to the roof. There was a nice raised lip around the roof, and I stood on it for a moment, breathing in the night. There was electricity running through me, and I felt twenty feet tall and invincible. It was not just seeing Monique, although that was a lift of its own. Maybe even more this time, as if the sight of her was a first small reward for a plan that was riskier than anything I'd ever tried. In a weird way, seeing her, having her in on it with me, made me sure it was going to work. Shit, it almost *had* to work—and it would be my greatest achievement ever when it did.

So I just stood there for a few minutes, watching the lights of the city and feeling pure delight. Say what you want about anyplace else.

New York is the greatest city in the world. The air is different here. Just breathing it makes you think you can do great things. And goddamn it, I was going to.

I took one more big hit of New York air. And then I gave in to the pure joy and electricity, ran to the far edge of the roof—and launched myself into space. For a moment I was flying, feeling the air rush past. Then the adjoining roof came up at me. I tucked, rolled, and let the momentum lift me up, onto my feet, and off the edge to the next roof.

For ten minutes I raced across the rooftops, up walls, leaping out into the night air time after time and running full speed along the narrow rooftop ledges and then down the side of buildings and out into space again. It looked and felt like I was Spider-Man. I mean, I'm not. I'm just really good at parkour. It's a way to move across a city like you really are Spider-Man, but without using webs. The French came up with it. Funny how many cool but very odd things come out of France. I was over there, and I saw it, and I knew I had to learn it. I saw right away that it would be incredibly useful as a tool of my trade. What I didn't see until I got good was just how much fucking *fun* it is. It makes me feel like I own the night and everything in it. And it keeps me in top shape, which is also a good idea in my profession.

So I let it rip, really blew out the carbon. When I finally came down to the street, in a dark alley, the elation that had sent me into my parkour jag had settled down to a quiet burble. I walked toward the subway, still thinking about Monique. Not professionally; I wasn't worried about the two paintings. I knew she'd do a near-perfect job. She always did. No, I was thinking about that night two years ago. Couldn't get it out of my head.

I had just pulled off a very big score—not as big as this one would be, but way more than average. With Monique's help, it came off perfectly. We got drunk to celebrate, one thing led to another, and somehow we ended up in bed.

Sex is almost always a good idea. It's fun, therapeutic, good exercise. But that night it was something else. We did the same stuff everybody does, but somehow it took us to a brand-new place. And yeah, I do mean "us." She was feeling it that way, too—I know it. And naturally, I thought it would be a terrific idea to keep it going, turn it into a semiregular thing.

Monique did not agree. She said it was a mistake, a onetime thing that shouldn't have happened, and it wasn't going to happen again. I tried to make her see how dumb that was. After all, we both liked it a lot, more than with other people, right? And I was really persuasive, too. The best I could do was talk her into the Bet.

I smiled when I thought of that. "There's always a way," I said. The Bet was my way back into Monique's bed.

I went into a bodega a few blocks from my train station. I needed to buy a razor. But when I opened the door, I heard angry voices yelling. Two voices, one raspy and with a Hispanic accent, the other higher-pitched, much younger.

Over by the cash register a man with a large mustache and a larger belly held a boy by the hair and hollered at him. The kid looked to be about ten, scrawny, and he was trying desperately to get away without losing his hair and yelling back at the same time. Scattered on the floor at their feet were a bag of chips, two Little Debbie pastries, a bottle of Gatorade, and a handful of Slim Jims.

I knew right away what was going down. The kid got caught shoplifting. And from what the store owner was yelling, it wasn't the first time, but it would damn well be the last.

I couldn't figure why, but all of a sudden I felt the Darkness slipping in. It's what happens when somebody is in my way, or when they're some kind of threat to me. It's like Riley fades into the background and whatever it is that lives in that dark cloud takes care of the dirty work. And there was just no fucking way in the world it should happen now.

65

I mean, because some fat guy was yelling at a kid? Why did that matter to me?

I froze there in the doorway and looked harder. The bodega guy was yelling, and the kid was trying to squirm away, and it was nothing to do with me. They could kill each other and it wouldn't matter. I could find some other place to buy a razor.

But still, the scene had a familiar look, like something I should remember. It stumped me for a second. Then I got it. *That's me a few years ago.* The painful memories came back, from the time when I was learning about life the hard way, by making stupid mistakes. And yeah, I'd been caught shoplifting, more than once—but never for the same mistake twice.

I pushed away the Darkness and just watched the struggle a few seconds more, remembering. And I knew I should avoid the hassle, find a different bodega. But the kid yelled again, in pain this time, and the owner said something about the police. Something kicked over inside me. And before I knew what I was doing, I was crossing the floor and putting a hand on the bodega owner's arm.

He looked up at me, angry. "Hey, the kid's just hungry," I said. "We all been hungry, right?"

"That's twenty-five dollar of hungry this time," the guy said, really pissed off. "And he been in here before, who knows how many times?"

I reached into my pocket and took out my roll. I peeled off a fifty and placed it on the counter, raising an eyebrow at the owner. The man scowled. "I tole you, he been here before!" he said. "An' he come again!"

"No, he won't," I said. I put another fifty down on top of the first one. "I guarantee it."

The owner looked at the money, licked his lips. "I gotta call the cops," he said, but all of a sudden he wasn't as angry.

I could see those two big bills working on him. It made me smile. "No, you don't gotta call the cops," I said. I put one more fifty on top of the first two. And then, to make sure the bodega owner knew that was it, I put my roll back in my pocket. "Kids shouldn't go hungry," I said.

The owner's eyes were glued on the money now. "I catch him here again, that's it," he said.

"He won't be back," I assured him. "Okay?"

The owner looked at the kid, then at the money. Then he made the three bills vanish. "Get him outta here," he said.

Cash. The sovereign remedy for everything.

I took the kid by the arm and led him toward the door. The boy thrashed in my grip. He was stronger than he looked, or maybe just desperate. His jerking and yanking threw me off balance, and I bumped into a couple of shelves on the way out. But I finally got him through the door and onto the sidewalk. I didn't let go. I frog-marched the kid down to the corner and turned right. The side street wasn't as busy, so I stopped. I pushed the kid against a wall and faced him squarely, looking him over. The boy was scrawny, undernourished, probably a few years older than my first guess. Maybe twelve? Probably Central American. Salvadoran or something. "What's your name, kid?"

"Monsy," the kid said sullenly.

"Where's your mom?"

Monsy shrugged. "Probably fucking some dude so she can shoot up again," he said.

"Father?"

"Who the fuck knows," Monsy said.

I just nodded. It was about what I expected. Just the way I grew up, stealing because if I didn't, I'd go hungry. I mean, Mom never whored, but for the kid it was about the same. I looked at him. Monsy met my eye for the first time. "Listen, mister, I don't care how many dollars you pull out, I ain't gonna do that stuff."

Yeah, same deal. It was exactly what I would have assumed at that age. The street teaches hard lessons. Some stuff never changes. I shook my head and smiled. "I'm not a chicken hawk, kid," I told him.

"Yeah, sure, a hundred fifty bucks cuz you a nice guy."

"Money is easy," I said.

The kid actually managed a sneer. "Yeah, sure it is," he said. But his eyes went wide when I reached under my jacket and pulled out a bag of chips and a handful of Slim Jims. "How the fuck—oh!" Monsy said with a sudden look of comprehension. "When you bumped the shelf?"

"Watch and learn," I said. "And don't go back to that bodega."

"I'm not stupid," Monsy said.

"Then stop acting like you are," I said. I reached into my jacket and flipped him one last thing, a Little Debbie cupcake. He caught it, and I turned to go. "Later, Monsy."

I could feel his eyes on me as I walked away. I didn't care. And I didn't mind the hundred fifty bucks at all; it's just money. Besides, it felt good to do a good deed like that. And anyway, I'd slipped a razor into my pocket at the same time, without paying. Riley's Second Law: Free is always better.

CHAPTER
7

Special Agent Frank Delgado was an unusual man. Not because of his appearance; that was completely unremarkable. He stood five foot ten, had a stocky frame and dark hair. You would pass him in the streets of any US city without a second glance. Delgado's abnormality came in other, less visible areas.

He said no more than he had to, kept his thoughts to himself, and maintained a stone face that showed almost nothing, no matter what the circumstances.

And as a special agent of the FBI, he lacked many traits that are virtually part of the uniform. His hair was just a little too long, his suit was never quite pressed, he did not communicate well with other agents working with him, he seemed to lack automatic respect for superiors—suffice it to say that he would not have lasted two weeks if J. Edgar Hoover still ran the Bureau.

But Frank Delgado got results. No one argued with that. If he set out to nail a criminal, that criminal was as good as nailed. Over a seventeen-year career with the Bureau, Delgado had a success record that was the envy of his peers.

There was, of course, one glaring exception. Three times he had failed in his pursuit of a wanted criminal. Three times—the same criminal. And the same result: Special Agent Delgado could not make the collar. In Delgado's most recent run-in, just a few months ago in Chicago, he had missed his man by a matter of only hours. But he had still missed.

Aside from that, his record was remarkably good, and Frank had earned some true respect. With that went a certain amount of tolerance for his somewhat unorthodox behavior.

And so it was perfectly normal for Special Agent Frank Delgado to walk into his supervisor's office without knocking. On top of his reputation, Delgado had enough seniority to get away with it. In fact, he had been offered his boss's job himself and turned it down. He said he didn't like paperwork. The man who now held the job, Special Agent in Charge J. B. Macklin, was well aware that Delgado had been the AD's first choice for this position. It didn't bother him anymore. At least, not too much.

But Macklin was a little irritated that Delgado just came in and sat down in the chair facing him across his desk without saying a word. So he finished reading the report he'd been working on, signed it, and pushed it into his out-basket before he sat back and gave Delgado his attention. Delgado didn't speak, though. He just sat and looked back. "What's up, Frank?" Macklin said at last.

"Riley Wolfe," Delgado said.

"No," Macklin said automatically. This was not the first time Delgado had asked to take off after Riley Wolfe. The master thief was, in his opinion, an unhealthy obsession for Delgado. Especially after the near miss in Chicago. Delgado said nothing and showed no disappointment, but Macklin was sure it rankled, and he suspected it was one reason Delgado had turned down the supervisory job—he wanted to stay in the field until he caught Wolfe.

Delgado's face showed nothing, but he shook his head. "I need to," he said.

"Why, Frank?" Macklin said. "Or, more to the point, why now?"

"I know where he is now," Delgado said.

Macklin blinked. "Where?" he said.

"New York," Delgado said straight-faced.

Macklin waited, but there was no more. "You got something more specific?"

Delgado gave one short shake of his head. "No," he said.

Macklin stared at him. "Just that? He's in New York? As in New York City. You know he's there, with nine million other people."

"That's right."

"For God's sake, Frank—seriously? You don't even know what he looks like. And you think you can find him? In New York?"

"Yes."

Macklin studied the semi-maverick agent. Delgado was known for saying little and showing less, and that was tolerated to a point. But if he wanted to take off solo on something that would probably turn into another wild-goose chase, Macklin, as his supervisor, needed a few details.

And of course, Delgado offered none. "Did you have a tip, Frank?" he asked at last. "Somebody saw him in Times Square? Or on a Greyhound headed to Port Authority? He posted on Facebook? Anything like that?"

"No," Delgado said.

Macklin sighed. "Okay, I'll bite. How do you know he's in New York?"

"He has to be," Delgado said.

"Sure, that works. He has to be there. And you can find him, pick him out of the nine million other people in New York," Macklin said, letting a little sarcasm color his voice. "Because you are part basset hound and part Sherlock Holmes?"

Delgado ignored the mockery. "I can find him," he said, "because I know what he's after."

"You know what he's after," Macklin said, disbelief clear in his tone.

"Yes."

Macklin sighed. "Okay. What?"

"The Crown Jewels of Iran," Delgado said. "At the Eberhardt Museum."

"Jesus Christ," Macklin blurted, shocked in spite of himself. If anything at all happened to threaten the crown jewels while they were in the US, the international complications would be enormous, and mostly disastrous. And if Riley Wolfe was after them, it certainly rated sending someone to stop him. "And you know this *how*?"

"I know Riley Wolfe," Delgado said.

Macklin again waited for more, and again there was none. He spread his hands in disbelief. "That's it? You think he's going to try because you *know* him?"

"Yes," Delgado said.

Macklin looked at Delgado; then he sighed again and leaned back in his chair, lacing his hands behind his head. "Frank," he said. "Even if you're right—and I don't believe you are, not without some kind of proof—but if you are right . . . why do you think you can catch him *this* time?"

Delgado sighed, the most emotion Macklin had ever seen from him. "I failed before because I didn't know him well enough," he said.

"You just told me you know him."

Delgado shook his head once. "Not well enough," he said. "Or I would have caught him."

"And you plan to, what—to somehow get to know him better?"

"Yes."

"But you already know him well enough to know he's going after the crown jewels," Macklin said, tapping his pen on the desk a little too rapidly.

Delgado nodded. "That's easy," he said. "I know *what* he will do—but to catch him, I need to know *why*."

"Other than a few billion dollars?" Macklin asked dryly.

Delgado just nodded again. "Something happened to him. Something *turned* him this way. I find out what, I find a weakness."

Macklin leaned onto his desk and rubbed the bridge of his nose, mostly to give himself a moment to think. It was clear to him that Delgado had gone a little buggy on the subject of Riley Wolfe. In fact, this was starting to sound borderline crazy. But a certain amount of tact was required here, with a special agent of Delgado's talent and seniority, and Macklin could be very diplomatic when he needed to be. "Frank," he said, after what he hoped looked like a reflective pause, "you've read the profilers' report on Wolfe, right?"

Delgado shrugged. "It's mostly wrong," he said.

Macklin stopped himself from saying something he shouldn't and took a deep breath instead. He let it out and said, "All right, fine, the finest profilers in the world are wrong and you're right. But Frank—the crown jewels? Do you know how tight the security's going to be at the Eberhardt?"

"Yes," Delgado said.

"They're bringing in some security technology straight from the DOD labs," he said. "And they've hired Black Hat to stand guard around the clock. Those bastards are good, and they're ruthless."

"I know," Delgado said.

"On top of all that, the Iranian government is taking their own measures, INCLUDING," he said, wagging a finger at Delgado, "a full platoon of the Revolutionary Guard. And those bastards make our bastards look like tame kittens."

"All right."

"The Eberhardt will be under constant surveillance by every electronic and human means known to man, and some means that, in my opinion, have to be back-engineered alien technology," Macklin said. "And you think Riley Wolfe is going to get around all that?"

"I know he's going to try," Delgado said.

"Goddamn it, Frank," Macklin snapped, rocking forward in his chair. "It's impossible!"

Delgado just nodded, twice this time. "That's exactly why he has to try," he said.

Macklin felt his control slipping. The way Delgado just sat there, stone-faced and so goddamn sure of himself—it would make Mother Teresa lose her cool. But he took a deep breath and leaned back again. "On the very small chance that you're right—Riley Wolfe is going to get around unbeatable military-grade electronics, get past a bunch of trigger-happy hired killers, and somehow get out again with the jewels—what exactly do you plan to do to stop him?"

"I don't know," Delgado said.

"Well, that's fucking perfect," Macklin growled.

Before Macklin could say any more, Delgado opened a file folder and slid it onto the desk. "Look," he said. "First arrest, sixteen years old."

"All right, so?"

"There's no record of a Riley Wolfe previous to this arrest," Delgado said, and when Macklin just frowned, Delgado very patiently added, "'Riley Wolfe' is not his real name."

Still frowning, Macklin pushed the folder away, leaned back, and crossed his arms. "Why does that matter?"

Delgado's eyebrows twitched, as if he'd stopped himself from showing irritation. "It's the key to his entire personality," Delgado said. "Why did his birth name force him to change, and why change it to 'Riley Wolfe'? What do those two names mean to him?" He frowned and spread his hands, a huge display of emotion for him. "If I know his real name, I know his real story," he said simply. "If I know his real story, I know why he has to be Riley Wolfe and do impossible things."

Macklin shook his head. It was the longest speech he'd ever heard from Delgado—but it wasn't enough. "And you want to do what— track down Wolfe's real name? So you can catch him before he steals the crown jewels?"

"Yes," Delgado said. And then he just looked blankly at Macklin.

Macklin looked back, chewing his lip. What Delgado was saying was not, after all, completely nuts. But it also wasn't an efficient use of a senior agent's time. Being completely honest with himself, Macklin admitted that he could not think of a way to make this look good in his report to the AD, and that was maybe more important than it should be. Macklin wanted to be AD himself someday. And Delgado truly had nothing to back up his premise—that Wolfe was going to try for this impossible target, and that finding his backstory was the way to stop him.

"Help me out here, Frank. Give me something tangible. Anything at all—even an anonymous tip?" Macklin said, raising an eyebrow. Another agent might have taken this as a hint and perhaps made up something to justify the mission. Delgado stayed mute. "And you really think you can stop him by finding his real name," Macklin said.

"That's the only way," Delgado said, with absolutely no uncertainty on his face.

Macklin just shook his head. "Even without one tiny clue, tip, or hint—even when it goes against what our profilers have said—you want to take off on some goddamn odyssey to find the real Riley Wolfe. Because you're dead certain that's the way to catch him."

Delgado moved his head up and down about half an inch. "There's not the slightest doubt."

"No," Macklin said. "Without any kind of evidence to back it up? No. I can't justify the man-hours, or the expense."

Delgado still showed no expression. He simply looked back at Macklin for an uncomfortably long time. Then he nodded and stood up. "I understand," he said.

"Good, thank you, Frank," Macklin said, surprised and relieved.

"I have six weeks' accumulated vacation time," Delgado said. "I'm taking it, starting tomorrow." And he turned to go.

"What? Wait! Goddamn it, Frank!" Macklin said. But his office door was already closed, and Delgado was gone.

Macklin shook his head, sighed deeply. "Goddamn it," he said again. Then he pulled the next folder from his in-tray and went back to work.

Dawn the next morning was gray, and a fine drizzle fell over suburban Virginia. Frank Delgado didn't really notice. He was up well before the sun, and by the time the first soggy gray gleams of light showed in the sky, he'd showered, shaved, and had his breakfast. And then he made one small gesture to his heritage and drank a second cup of Cuban coffee before he headed out the door.

He walked briskly down the front walk and threw his luggage into the back seat of his personal vehicle, an eight-year-old Yukon. There wasn't much, just a small suitcase, a laptop, and a briefcase. He closed the door and climbed into the front behind the wheel. On the seat beside him he placed the file folder. It was a copy, but still technically a breach of regulations since he was on private time. It was exactly the kind of rule he tended to break routinely, and he wasn't worried about the consequences. If he was successful, anything up to shooting the

AD would be forgiven. Especially since Riley had apparently killed that billionaire Big Pharma guy in Chicago, and big money always makes big waves.

He flipped open the folder and studied the top page again. That arrest for B&E, the first official record of Riley Wolfe's existence, had taken place in Syracuse, New York. Delgado knew the town slightly. He didn't like it much. But that was his starting point. And he had a feeling he wouldn't be in Syracuse very long. His instincts told him that Riley Wolfe had gone to Syracuse for a specific prize, and his trail would very quickly lead out of town to a more relevant locale, maybe even Riley's hometown.

He could have made a phone call to the Syracuse cops, or sent an email. But Delgado was after more than bare facts. He wanted to put his nose down on the ground Riley had walked on. He wanted to get a true scent of this elusive criminal. He needed to poke around in the places that had formed Riley Wolfe. That meant going to those places, finding people who knew him, talking to them face-to-face. That was the only way to get an accurate picture of Riley and what made him tick.

So he would go to Syracuse, even though he didn't like it. Finding the key to unlock this master criminal's psychology was what mattered. Delgado would go anywhere to do that. And he had six weeks to get it done.

Special Agent Frank Delgado nodded. He knew what he was good at, and patiently tracking down a lead was part of it. Six weeks was enough time. He flipped the folder closed and started his car. Then he headed out the driveway and down the road to find Riley Wolfe.

CHAPTER

8

Michael Hobson was one of the top corporate attorneys in New York City. He had a practice that demanded a minimum of twelve hours a day. On top of that, like most rich and important men, Michael was also on a lot of corporate boards. So there were meetings, conferences, briefs to read—it all kept him very busy indeed. So busy that he seldom seemed to have time for distractions of any kind, which included, in his mind, his wife. So he was understandably peeved when his secretary buzzed him to say that a Mr. Fitzer, from the SEC, was here to see him. Michael spent a full three seconds looking out the large glass window that made up the entire back wall of his fifty-second-floor, mahogany-paneled office, and wondering if he should tell the man to make an appointment and come back later.

Three seconds was all it took. A man like Michael Hobson didn't need a problem with the SEC. Besides, their officials were professional, smart, and competent and wouldn't waste his time. So he said, "Send him in," to his secretary and then swiveled his chair to face the door.

The man who came in a moment later was the very picture of a young and hungry attorney. He was average height, fit-looking, with medium-length brown hair and a hearing aid in his left ear. He wore rimless glasses and a fashionable stubble of beard, and his suit was good without being ostentatious. He walked in briskly and offered Michael his hand. "Mr. Hobson? I'm Bill Fitzer, from the SEC Division of Enforcement."

His grip was strong but not overbearing, and Michael motioned him to a chair. "I didn't realize you were from Enforcement, Bill," he said.

"That's right," Fitzer said with a polite smile. "I'm afraid crime is something of a ruling passion."

"A private practice would pay a lot better," Hobson said, probing just a little. "And it would certainly give you more than enough exposure to crime."

"I'm sure you're right," Fitzer said. "In fact, that's what I want to talk to you about."

Hobson was instantly on guard. "Really," he said. "Is there some kind of problem with . . . one of my clients?"

Fitzer smiled, a brief professional expression that meant nothing. "I'm sure it's nothing, Mr. Hobson. Probably an excess of caution. But if I might have a few moments of your time, I would like to ask a few questions about Elmore Fitch."

"Elmore Fitch is not actually my client."

"Perhaps not," Fitzer said. "But it's mostly for background? And I believe you've had some dealings with Mr. Fitch in the past two years?"

"Who hasn't?" Michael said wryly. "Elmore is all over the landscape. It's impossible to avoid him if you want to get anything done in this town."

Fitzer nodded and reached into his glove leather attaché case. "So we have heard," he said. He took out a small but very sophisticated digital recorder and placed it on the desk, closer to Michael.

Michael raised an eyebrow. "Really? You're recording this?"

Fitzer nodded. "It guarantees accuracy, and it lets me concentrate on the questions. Do you object to a recording, Mr. Hobson? I can assure you it will not be used against you in any way, nor will its contents be shared with anyone outside our organization."

Michael hesitated. He found the idea of a recording irritating, but he couldn't say why. And since it made sense, he really couldn't object. "A recording is fine," he said. Then he glanced pointedly at the wall clock to his right. "Let's get this done, Bill."

"Very good," Fitzer said. He leaned over and pushed the RECORD button, giving his name, Michael's name, and the date, before pushing the recorder closer to Michael. "I'd like to start with a few questions about Mr. Elmore Fitch's corporate structure—I believe you are on the board of one of his companies?"

"Two, actually," Michael said.

Fitzer nodded and said, "Please state the names of those companies and how long you have been a director—oh, damn it!" He clutched at his hearing aid and yanked it out of his ear. Michael could hear a loud, high-pitched tone coming from the thing. Fitzer fumbled with it for a moment and then muttered, "Damn it," and dropped it into a pocket.

"Problem?" Michael asked. Fitzer didn't respond. Michael smiled, raised his voice, and said again, loudly, "Is there a problem?"

Fitzer looked up. "The battery is dead. I'm sorry, it should have lasted another day, but . . ." He shrugged. "I'm practically deaf without it. An IED in Afghanistan." He pointed to the recorder. "I'll have to rely on that thing. And possibly ask you to repeat once or twice?" He raised an eyebrow. Michael spread his hands in a what-can-you-do gesture, and Fitzer nodded. "Sorry for the inconvenience," he said. "Let's continue?"

Fitzer jumped right back into it, asking for names and dates and details as he led Michael through a series of increasingly complicated questions about Elmore Fitch and his corporate maneuvers, prodding Michael into giving longer and more detailed answers. Fitzer was an efficient interrogator, but he tended to be blunt, even confrontational, and with his hearing problem he would ask Michael to repeat his answers—more than the "once or twice" he'd promised. And as the questions got more aggressive and the request to repeat his answers got more frequent, Michael found himself getting closer and closer to losing his temper. When Fitzer asked about one of Elmore's most distasteful forced mergers, Michael was on the very edge of anger.

"As an attorney, what did you advise Mr. Fitch to do about this merger?" Fitzer asked.

"I told him to get out of the deal," Michael answered through clenched teeth.

"To do what?" Fitzer asked, his head cocked to the side.

"To get. Out. Of the. Deal," Michael said, nearly snarling.

Fitzer shook his head. "Sorry?"

"Get out!" Michael shouted. "I told him, 'Get! Out!'"

"Ah. Uh-huh," Fitzer said, and then he looked down at his notebook and moved on to the next line of questioning. He kept pushing, prodding, coming at his subject from every possible angle so that, among other things, Michael could not possibly guess what he was really after. That had to be deliberate obfuscation, and although Michael admired the technique, as an attorney himself he couldn't help trying to guess what Fitzer was fishing for.

But after twenty minutes of questions, Michael still hadn't figured it out, and he was very happy to see Fitzer go.

When the door finally closed behind the SEC investigator, Michael took a deep breath to calm himself. Then he glanced up at the wall clock and said, "Shit." He had less than ninety minutes before he had to leave for the airport to get his flight to Zurich. So he put Fitzer and the SEC out of his mind, picked up a file, and went back to work.

SEC investigators don't use parkour. So I had to go all the way back to Williamsburg by train. The whole way, I had to stand there holding the strap like I was just any old asshole in a suit. I let jerkoffs push me and step on my feet, because that's what somebody wearing this suit would do. And in a funny way, I didn't really mind. Because the last preliminary piece was done, and I was ready for the Main Event. Or anyway, I was ready to get ready for it. So when I got back to my crappy rented room, I went right to it.

The Sierra Club types like to say, leave nothing behind except footprints. That wasn't good enough for me. Footprints are loaded with DNA. So if I left one behind, I was dead and fucked. So Riley's Fourth Law states: Leave nothing behind. Clean up like your life depends on it, because it does.

I don't mind. I've been cleaning up since I was a kid. Before she fell apart, Mom was always a real fanatic about keeping everything clean. She swept, she mopped, she scrubbed—and she taught me to do all that, too. I did it, and I got good at it. Not because I really cared but because *Mom* cared. I scrubbed the floors because it mattered to her.

Mom wasn't in my crappy little room in Williamsburg. And she would never see it. She'd probably never see anything again. I was still on my knees scrubbing anyway. I hit every single inch of that floor with a good stiff brush and the strongest cleaner I could get. Just like I'd already done to the walls, the door, everything in the room. I finished up by the door so I could go out and dump the bucket in the alley.

Then I put it, the brush, all my cleaning supplies into the dumpster and went back up to my room.

I stood in the doorway for a minute, looking around the room. Except for one folding chair, the furniture was already gone. The costume rack was in storage over in Jersey City. All that was left was one suit. It was draped over a folding chair. The chair was pulled up beside the door so I could push it in front of a long mirror hung on the back of the door. I had cleaned it, but it didn't help a lot. It came with the room, and it was just as worn as the rest of the place. There was a small suitcase and a black leather Polo briefcase on the floor beside the chair.

I scanned carefully for anything I'd missed. Nothing. The place was clean. So clean even Mom would've been impressed. Every surface that might hold a fingerprint or a small smear of DNA had been scrubbed with carbolic acid and then industrial-strength cleaner. When I was done, there'd be no sign that I had ever been here. Except that the ratty little room would be cleaner than it had ever been before.

When I was sure I hadn't skipped anything, I stepped in, locked the door, and moved on to the next step. The last step. Because everything else was done. All the pieces were in play. It was all ready to go, the whole brilliant scheme, except for one thing:

Me.

I stripped, put my clothes in a garbage bag, and washed as completely as I could in the rusty little sink. I dried off and shaved in the cracked plastic mirror hanging above the sink on a nail. Then I scrubbed the sink and put the soap, towel, razor, everything into the same garbage bag and moved over to the big mirror.

I sat in the chair to put on the suit and the black wingtips that went with it. But first I reached into the briefcase and pushed PLAY on my mp3 player. Tupac, "All Eyez on Me." Then I opened the little suitcase, turned to the mirror, and went to work on Me.

Every professional has rituals that go with going to work. I know;

I've done a lot of different jobs, at least for a while. You know, as a cover for doing my real job. A pro does the same meaningless things each time, things that really don't make sense or have anything to do with their job. They probably wouldn't admit it, but they do it for luck. Because they can't believe the job will come off if they don't. So they do a few small superstitious things because they did it last time, and the time before. I do, too.

The cleaning isn't part of it. That's just being careful. If I leave any clue behind, no matter how tiny, I'm leaving a way for somebody to get lucky and figure out who I am. It's after I've cleaned up that the rituals start.

The music is first. The same playlist every time. If the prep takes longer, the playlist repeats.

When I've got the music going, I move to step two: the mirror. For a few minutes I just look at my face and listen to Tupac. When I have a perfect picture of who I am, I start to become somebody else.

I'd already changed who I was a half dozen times setting this up. This time was for real. This time, it would have to be better, and it would have to last for a while. There was no way to know how long, so I had to make someone who would last. I had the tools. I'd done the research on this New Me, and I'd done the creative part, too. Filling in the blanks, like where I was from, my parents' names, my high school, all that shit. And I'd gotten all the documents to prove it—driver's license, passport, Social Security card, all of it. You might be surprised to learn how easy it is to get all that stuff. And if you're willing to pay, you get documents so good that nobody could possibly know that's not really you.

I'd done all that. Now it was time for the final step.

I can do makeup, prosthetics, all that. I've studied with the very best people I could find. There's no point in learning from somebody who isn't the best. And I didn't mind paying top dollar for top talent.

So I'm good at that kind of thing. But this time wasn't about makeup. I was changing *Me*. Who Me actually *is*.

The costume was first. As the music changed to Iron Maiden, "Hallowed Be Thy Name," I started to get dressed. "Riley" would not normally wear a suit. This new person did, and putting it on forced me to leave Riley behind and let the new identity take over and guide my speech and movements.

Any good actor will tell you that what you wear tells your audience a lot about who you are. It also tells *you*. With Monique's help, I'd picked what I thought was the perfect suit. It was expensive, but not crazy-rich expensive. It was the best New Me could afford. I put it on slowly, watching how it hung on me. I moved my arms, my legs, my torso, and watched what happened when I did. I started to feel how somebody who wore this suit would move. It was different.

Survivor's "Eye of the Tiger" began to play. I moved in time to that for a few minutes, watching myself in the crappy mirror. When I got how I moved now, I draped the jacket over the back of the chair and picked up my tie. It was a great expression of who I was now; flamboyant but beautiful silk, hand-painted in imitation of a Gustav Klimt. I knotted it in a loose Windsor that showed a casual nonchalance mixed with superb taste. When it was tied, I reached up with my thumb and forefinger and pushed it slightly crooked. Not a lot; just enough so most women would want to reach over and straighten it.

As I finished the tie, "Freddie Freeloader," Miles Davis, started up. I sat in the chair and started on my hands.

Everybody's hands tell a story. Even the way you clip the nails is different depending on where you come from, what you do, what you think of yourself. Are they clean or dirty? Chewed or manicured? Square cut or round? I trimmed my nails neat but short. From my makeup kit I got a small bottle of blue stain. I worked it into the heel of each hand. Then I scrubbed at it until it was just barely visible. It looked like what a draftsman's hands might show after hours of leaning on a drawing or plan as he worked.

From the top tray of the little suitcase I pulled a signet ring. Nothing outrageous, a class ring from a pretty good prep school. Again—Monique's suggestion. Her brother went there. I don't think I would have thought of a class ring or known about this school. It's not my world. It is hers, or it was before she moved into mine. I put the ring on the pinky of my left hand as Yo-Yo Ma came on, playing the Prelude to Bach Cello Suite #2 in D Minor.

I finished my hands in just another minute and stood up. I looked in the mirror for the first two suites. I studied New Me. One tiny flaw, no matter how small it seemed, and the entire job could be torpedoed. So I looked hard. Everything seemed perfect—but *seemed* was not enough. It had to *be* perfect. Two more minutes of hard inspection. If there was any kind of flaw in my appearance, I couldn't see it. And if I couldn't, the odds were very good that no one else would, either. People see what you tell them to see. I was sure they'd see what I wanted them to this time.

Okay. Time for the last ritual.

I sat in the chair, opened the briefcase, and took out two photographs. They looked like they had been printed by a computer, and they had been. They were securely stored on several flash drives and on a cloud account so I could always access them. I closed my eyes for a few seconds, took a couple of slow, deep breaths. Then I opened my eyes and looked down at the first picture. It showed a young boy, nine or ten years old, and a man in his thirties. They were playing catch in a well-kept yard. Behind them, down a hill, you could see green, rolling countryside.

Off to one side, just visible in the photo, was a large house. Victorian architecture, two stories, with a couple of cupolas and a front porch, with a strip of gingerbread trim running above it. A 1992 Cadillac Eldorado sat in the driveway.

The music changed to Barbra Streisand singing "Happy Days Are Here Again." I shuffled up the second picture. It showed a woman of around forty. Her face was careworn, and her hair was a bit wild, but she was smiling. I sat and looked at the picture until I could hear her voice again. "We are living the life," she would say. And I would smile back and say, "We sure are."

The music switched one last time: Alice Cooper, "Vengeance Is Mine." I felt my breathing slow, and I kept all my focus on the picture.

The song ended. The sudden silence was a little bit of a shock, like waking up too quickly. I took a deep breath and stood up. One final scrub of the area, getting any tiny traces I might have left. Then I looked in the mirror one last time. You maybe couldn't name anything specific, but the face was subtly different. The way I held my head, the movement of my eyes, all changed.

Riley Wolfe was gone.

I smiled. It was a good smile: worldly, amused, guardedly friendly, and not at all like Riley Wolfe. "Baa," I said. I looked at the smiling reflection for a moment. Then I switched off the smile, spun away from the mirror, and headed out the door.

Showtime.

CHAPTER
9

The ballroom of the midtown hotel was crowded, packed with Manhattan's wealthiest, most socially exclusive set. They wore fabulous clothing and immorally expensive jewelry, displayed glittering wit, and walked around smug with the knowledge that they could painlessly write huge checks to whatever the noble cause was this evening. It was why they were here, of course: to write checks. Most of them could not have said what the noble cause was tonight—in fact, it was a foundation for fostering war orphans—but they came anyway. That was partly because they believed they should write those checks, some from desire to do good and some because their accountants suggested it. They also came because everyone else in this dazzling stratum of society would be there, and they knew from experience that the surest way to get yourself talked about was to be absent from an event when the other check-writers gathered. Because in spite of their wealth—or perhaps because of it—very few of them would overlook a chance to snipe from behind. The shots could be lethal—and, occasionally, even true.

From the outside, though, it was a world of glamour and privilege. Any ordinary person looking into the room would have been struck dumb with longing to be included in such a magnificent company, and at the same time crushed by the knowledge that it could never be, for these people were clearly the top of the food chain, the glitterati, the richest and most accomplished people in the greatest city in the world.

While most normal human beings would have been thrilled to be in such company, would have traded ten years of their life to belong, to be welcomed into this group, on this bright and wonderful evening, Katrina Eberhardt Hobson was not normal, and she was definitely not thrilled. She felt no elation at having a well-earned hereditary place among these fabulous people. In fact, she had reached a point where she hoped they would all spontaneously combust so she could go home and take off the expensive heels that were pinching her feet and change into equally expensive slippers. She would gladly have traded ten years of her life to be almost anywhere else. Because Katrina was bored. Hugely, monstrously, totally, and completely bored. So bored that her head was pounding, and her hands ached from being clenched; so bored her mouth hurt from constant fake smiles, her teeth ached from grinding, and her throat hurt from stifling screams of frustrated, soul-crushing tedium she had endured for over two hours now.

She'd had four glasses of a truly appalling pinot grigio, and that hadn't helped the headache, and she'd even spent twenty terrible minutes listening to Samantha Perkins, who was the most god-awful gossip in New York and always knew the salacious details of every sordid affair, and the only result was that Katrina was a tiny bit drunk, increasingly homicidal, and now aware that the graybeard CEO of a major bank was having an affair with a much younger foreign investor—a *male* investor. Katrina longed with all her soul to run from the ballroom, flee for her sanity, her very life—but she could not. Her husband, Michael, was on the board of directors of this foundation, and because he was in Zurich on business, it was Katrina's duty to attend and represent him.

It was not the first time. Michael was often away on business. And when he was home, she rarely saw him, either. Of course, he was a busy man, and an important one. But when Katrina had married him, she'd been led to expect a little more, and she couldn't help but feel a kind of sour disappointment with her marriage every now and then. And she did resent covering for him like this, just a little bit. But she had been raised in an old-money family who taught her that social responsibility was part of the deal. On top of all that, Michael did so much charity work, and nearly all of it for kids, so she couldn't really justify feeling any resentment at all toward him. For the most part, she kept the fake smile in place and carried on.

"Noblesse oblige," she whispered to herself. Just a reminder that she had to keep up appearances, no matter how desperately she wanted to throw her painful shoes at somebody and run from the room.

She thought about getting another glass of wine, decided it was a bad idea, and twitched her painful false smile back into place. Soon it would be time for the dreadful meal—a warm and limp salad, choice of unthinkable fish or inedible beef or vegan, whatever that would turn out to be. And then a series of soul-crushingly earnest speeches crafted to make the checks a little bigger. Katrina knew the whole program by heart. She had grown up wealthy and married even more money, and in her lifetime, she had attended hundreds of events just like this one—thousands of them—and they never varied, except for a few dull details. Tonight was no different.

—except for one small thing. Tonight there was actually a brief moment of interest in the program, one little thing that kept her in the ballroom when her entire being was screaming to be back in her big old house: the silent auction. Oh, there had certainly been silent auctions before. Most of the charity events had them, and Katrina had quite often bid on something, just because that, too, was part of her job. But tonight . . . Tonight some lunatic had donated an item that made Katrina quiver, and even drool with lust. Tonight, some incredibly lucky soul would bid on, and win, a perfectly *gorgeous* Hans Hofmann painting.

And Katrina was going to be that lucky soul even if she had to murder everyone else in the room.

The painting was a fantastic splash of primary colors, a swirl of rigid shapes and ragged edges, titled *Ad Astra*, and Katrina wanted it on her wall at home more than she wanted to breathe. So she would stand here with her fake smile and her aching head and her throbbing feet. She would endure Samantha's dreadful leering stories and the nauseating dinner and the painful speeches. And as her just reward for suffering through all this terrible inhuman suffering, she would damn well go home with *Ad Astra*.

Finally, after four more conversations she couldn't remember two minutes later, with people who were even less memorable, she heard a large silver bell ring three times, the PA crackled, and the announcement she'd been waiting for came.

"Ladies and gentlemen, the silent auction is now open for bids." There was a bit more, a reminder to be generous and so on, but Katrina didn't hear it. She was already moving at full speed across the room to the table that held the clipboard with the bid sheet for *Ad Astra*. Behind the table, the painting was displayed on an easel. An armed security guard stood to one side—this painting was not the only valuable item on display.

In spite of her haste, Katrina was third in line, and she waited impatiently as the first two bidders dithered, nibbled at the pencil, looked at their bank balances on their smartphones, and finally, with horrid, deliberate sloth, slowly wrote down their bids. When they had finally finished, Katrina lunged for the clipboard and quickly read the first two bids—both insultingly low for such a treasure, in her opinion, both well under seven figures. Katrina smiled. If this was an example of what the other bids would be, the Hans Hofmann was as good as hers. She reached for the pencil where it lay on the table, frowning as she considered her bidding strategy. Huge bid now to frighten away the competition? Or something small and then come back later, at the last minute, to enter the final winning bid?

But before she could decide, a soft and confidently amused voice murmured from just behind her, almost in her ear, "It's a fake, you know."

Katrina jumped. She'd been concentrating so completely that she hadn't heard or sensed anyone moving that close. Holding the clipboard like a shield, she spun around.

A man stood there with a cheerful, almost mocking smile. A good-looking man, in an understated way. He had a gleaming shaved head and a neat beard, and he wore a suit that Katrina was quite sure came from a Savile Row tailor. On an impulse she didn't understand, she reached out and touched the lapel of his suit. "Richard James?" she blurted.

The man lifted an eyebrow in surprise, then said, "Ah. The suit? I thought you meant me. No, actually, it's from Henry Poole, just a few doors down Savile Row."

Katrina frowned. "You don't have an accent."

The man laughed, a very pleasant sound, Katrina thought. "It's a relief to hear that. I've been told for the last few years that I *did* have an accent—a bloody Yank accent. I'm just back from a stint in London."

Katrina found herself liking this man, and as she realized that, she remembered what had started their conversation. "Why do you say this painting is a fake? It certainly looks like a Hans Hofmann to me—an absolutely *gorgeous* Hans Hofmann."

He nodded. "You have a good eye—but it's a very *good* fake," he said.

"I don't believe you—I don't *want* to believe you!"

"That's always a dangerous posture when you're considering a purchase like this," he said.

"And how on earth would you know whether it's a fake, Mr. Expert?" Katrina demanded.

"Actually, that's part of my job," he said, with a display of very good, very white teeth. "Or it was. I worked for Sotheby's—in London? Because I'm a Yank, I was their expert on modern American." He shrugged. "To be honest, I would have preferred German Expressionist, but—"

"All right, fine, you really are Mr. Expert," Katrina said, abruptly feeling cranky. The thought that someone would take away her Hofmann was truly annoying. "So what makes my painting a fake?"

He took her arm and led her to a spot as close to the painting as they could get, with just the clipboard table between them and the easel. He had a strong grip, but warm and gentle, too, and again Katrina caught herself thinking that she liked this man—and perhaps in a somewhat dangerous way. *It's the wine,* she told herself. *Four glasses— that's all it is.* But the feeling stayed with her.

"Look," he said, leaning toward the brightly colored canvas. He waved a hand in an up-and-down direction. "Vertically, the composition, it's really good, very Hofmann. The shapes and colors, all very authentic. But look over here, this patch above the bottom right. See it?"

Katrina frowned at the painting. "The pink rectangle? What about it? What's wrong with it? You don't like pink?"

Again he showed his teeth—and again Katrina felt a small thump of excitement in her chest. "I don't mind it at all. Neither did Hofmann. But *this* pink—"

"It's *too* pink?" she asked, favoring him with a small smile.

He returned it. "The pink itself is wrong," he said. "It's called Passion Pink, it's made by DelMar, and it was first put on the market in 1984."

"Shit," Katrina said. "Hofmann died in 'sixty-something. 'Sixty-eight?"

"'Sixty-six, very good," he said, and Katrina found herself liking his approval, too. But very much *not* liking the idea that she would not go home with a Hans Hofmann.

"Shit, shit, shit," she said. She looked longingly at the painting. "You're really sure?"

"Absolutely," he said. "It costs me money to be wrong, and I'm not rich."

She glanced at him; the Savile Row suit, the fact that he was here tonight, had made her assume he belonged. If he was some kind of climber or gold digger, she would shake him off quickly and go back to being bored. She raised an eyebrow. "Really? Then what are you doing here?"

His smile was different this time, softer. "I can easily afford a ticket and a small donation. I'm not *that* poor. And for me, orphans are . . ." He shrugged, looking rather vulnerable. Then he abruptly straightened up and spoke briskly. "And anyway, if I can save a lady from getting ripped off by a fraud, it's worth it. And that painting *is* a fraud."

"Shit, shit, shit, SHIT," Katrina said, staring at the treacherous canvas. "I really want that painting."

"Even though it isn't a real Hofmann?" he said mockingly.

"Almost, yeah," she admitted, and he laughed. After a moment, she did, too. She straightened up and threw down the pencil. "Well, now what?"

"I could buy you a drink," he said. "To make up for spoiling your evening."

Katrina bit her lip and hesitated. Like all who live in enormous wealth, she was eternally on her guard. People were almost always friendly because they wanted something—money for a cause, or a personal project, or a foolproof investment. This man didn't really *seem* like he was after anything—or at least, she corrected herself wryly, not after money. But he had already admitted that he didn't have real money, which meant she was right to be wary. And another glass of wine, on top of the four she'd had, was not a good idea, either. On the other hand, he'd shown no sign that he knew who she was—and she really had a good feeling about this man and didn't want to let go of him, not just yet. "Well . . . ," she said. "Oh! I'm sorry, I'm Katrina Hobson." She held out her hand and he took it. She watched him carefully for any sign that her name meant anything to him but saw nothing.

"Randall Miller," he said. He reached into his pocket and came out with a business card. He handed it to Katrina, and she looked at it with real curiosity. It read:

RANDALL MILLER
Dealer in Contemporary Art
Interior Design Consultant

"Design consultant! Well, that's funny," she said. "I'm doing a massive redecoration on my house—that's what I wanted the Hofmann for."

"Oh, I didn't— Aw, crap," he said. "I really didn't know—I mean, now it looks like—I wasn't dunning you for business, honest," he said, and he looked flustered, which Katrina thought was cute and kind of endearing.

"I know," she said, patting his arm and wondering if it was true. "But it's a funny coincidence. Anyway, I have someone under contract for the work."

"Oh, good," he said, looking a little relieved. "Who are you using?"

"Irene Caldwell?" Katrina said. "She came highly recommended."

"Yes, she's very good," Randall said. "And anyway, as much as I'd be happy to help you, I am completely booked right now. I have this massive project that really—" He shook his head. "Ah, listen to me.

Talking shop when there's a thirsty lady right in front of me." He offered her his arm in a way that was gallant and still mocked the very idea of gallantry. "Your Grace—how about that drink?"

"I'd like that," she said. "But I've had a couple already, so please, stop me if I start a strip tease or something?"

He laughed. "I'm not sure I can promise that," he said. "But I'll try."

She took his arm, and he led her over to one of the three bars in the ballroom. He sat her at the closest table while he went to get the drinks. In just a minute, he returned with her pinot grigio and what looked like a martini for himself. "Well," he said, sitting next to her and raising his glass. "Cheers. Chin-chin. *Sláinte. Salud.*"

She raised her glass in return. "*Prosit!*" she said with a smile.

"That's right, I left that one out," Randall said. "So, uh, to get the awkward questions out of the way right away"—he nodded at her wedding ring—"you're married, right? Or is it—forgive me, but are you, um, a widow?"

Katrina took another sip of wine to cover her thoughts while she tried to think of how to answer. She felt very relieved that the man obviously didn't know who she was. But she had no idea how to answer the question without seeming . . . what? Wanton? Open to something beyond flirtation? It would have been lovely simply to tell the truth, that Michael was away on business—but did that sound like an invitation? He was clearly attracted to her, and she didn't want him to get the impression that it was mutual— *But it is*, she thought, and fought to push the thought away. *Screw it, the truth*, she thought.

"Michael is in Zurich on business," she said, and couldn't stop herself from adding, "He's away on business a lot."

"That's a shame," Randall said. "You must miss him."

Katrina bit her lip and took another sip to keep herself from blurting out more truth. She put down her glass and gave him a small smile. "And how about you? Is there a Mrs. Miller?"

Randall shook his head. "Nope. Never found the right one. It's just possible that my standards are too high," he said ruefully. "Like with art? I just can't be satisfied with 99 percent of the crap they pass off as art nowadays."

"I know just what you mean!" Katrina said, relieved to be past the awkward stuff. She told him of a show last month—in a reputable SoHo gallery, too!—that had been an appalling waste of time and space. He responded with something similar he'd seen in London, and they relaxed into a safe zone, just two art lovers enjoying a drink, and each other's company.

Afterward, Katrina couldn't remember much about what they'd said, just that it was light, inconsequential, amusing stuff. On top of being truly knowledgeable, he had a way of making you like him, trust him, a quality that was a combination of charm and believability. And Randall was very funny, in a dry kind of way Katrina thought he might have picked up in England. He made her laugh, which was something she hadn't been doing a lot of—certainly her husband seldom even brought a smile to her face nowadays.

When dinner was announced, Randall took her to the head table and thanked her for a lovely evening. His seat was far away in the back of the room, and she watched him go with real regret. And later on, when the interminable damn dinner and endless speeches were finally over, she looked for him as she left the ballroom. But of course, he'd been seated in the back—the "cheap seats," as he'd called them. So he must have left much more quickly than Katrina could manage since she also had to stop and say a few words to all the important people she met on her way out. There was certainly no reason why he would wait for her, a married woman. They'd had a pleasant half hour of talk, and that was the end of it. Katrina went home, to her massive modern palace, and went to bed alone.

But she could not get Randall Miller out of her mind.

CHAPTER
10

The two paintings were easy, just as Monique had known they would be. The Rauschenberg was a simple matter of matching the images and the colors of the paint-over. The Jasper Johns was a simpler design, since he didn't usually deal with images as complex as Rauschenberg, and it went much quicker. She was finished with both paintings in only two weeks, which gave her a little free time. She thought about taking a quick trip to the Islands, maybe Antigua, or working on something of her own, or even just hanging around her apartment, watching TV and eating too much.

Nothing really appealed to her. Leisure was not something she appreciated; Monique hated having nothing meaningful to do, no task she could focus on. It made her restless, cranky, even a little mean.

For two days she fretted, paced, ran meaningless errands around the city, and let the self-loathing of not working build up until she felt like screaming and kicking small animals.

And thinking about Riley and the mysterious job he had for her just made it worse. And of course the ridiculous things he said about the size of the score, which made her even madder. Ten figures? *TEN?!* For the love of God, was he serious? And that was just *her* cut? It was flat-out impossible. Where would that much money come from? And how could he hope to get his hands on it? And what on earth would she do with that much money anyway?

Early on in working with Riley, she had discovered they had something important in common: Neither of them was truly driven by money. Oh, it was lovely stuff, and wonderful to have too much of it, and neither one of them was an ascetic of any kind. But it was not what motivated either one of them. For both of them, it was the challenge, the feeling of stepping all the way out there on the thinnest branch of the tree and plucking the ripest apple, the one nobody else could get.

So Monique knew that with a payoff this big, the risk had to be equally big. Whatever Riley had in mind, it would be dangerous, impossible, ridiculous, something no one else would even consider conceivable. That went for her part in it, too. Not that she would be risking her life, probably. But certainly there would be a large element of risk. Which was just fine with her. And after all, there was the money . . .

But for the love of God, what would she do with that much cash? And then she thought, with an uncharacteristic giggle, she didn't have a thing to wear while spending it! It was such an absurd thought—but she enjoyed it. And she realized it had helped her decide what to do with a few free days and just before she went completely off her rocker, too. *Why not?* she thought. *I deserve something wonderful.*

Before she could even figure out what she had meant by that, or what justified it, Monique had booked a suite at the Mandarin Oriental spa for two full days. She checked in with little more than a bathrobe and slippers and spent an hour looking through the menu of services offered by the spa. And then she made appointments for every single one. She spent the two days running through everything the spa offered: Oriental Essence massage, Calm Mind Retreat, Thai Yoga massage. Then onto Clearing Factor, aromatherapy, and Restorative Detox Wrap. She went to bed after the first day feeling as if her body was made of overcooked spaghetti.

The second day she dove into the beauty treatments: Áyurvedic Facial, HydraFacial, and all the more traditional options. She left the next morning feeling like a completely different person—and half convinced she looked like one, too. And she dove directly into part two of her program. She went on a tour of Manhattan's high-end boutiques, indulging in an absolute orgy of shopping and spending some rather large chunks of what she still secretly thought of as her Ill-Gotten Gains. She bought an entirely new wardrobe and took it back to her studio, where she laid it out, sorted it, and gloated over it. Some of it she would probably never wear—but she *could*, she told herself, and that was what mattered.

She was still admiring her new glove leather boots when the door's buzzer sounded. Frowning, puzzled at who might be calling on her now, she looked through the peephole. Although she had never seen that particular face before, she had seen several others wearing the same jacket. And she knew the owner of that jacket changed his appearance the way other people change shirts. It was Riley Wolfe.

She rolled her eyes and opened the door.

I thought I might surprise Monique—either because of the way I looked or because I was using the door this time instead of the window. No such luck.

The door swung open, and Monique stood there with the same half-pissed-off expression she always wore. I liked to think she put it on so I wouldn't know she liked me.

"You're three days early," she said, tapping her right foot.

I just looked at her for a few seconds, and I had to smile. "You knew it was me," I said. "Even though I used the door."

Monique snorted. "Don't get too excited. It's that stupid jacket," she said. She had to say my Yankees jacket was stupid. She was a Pittsburgh Pirates fan, of course. She stepped to one side. "Come on in."

"I knew you wouldn't need three whole weeks for those two paintings," I said as she closed the door behind me. "I bet you finished two days ago and you're bored out of your skull."

"I finished *five* days ago," Monique said. "And if I was bored, what do you think *you* could do about it?"

"Oh, I can think of something," I said.

"Well, think of something else."

"All right," I said. "Almost as good—the paintings?"

She just shook her head. "Come take a look."

She led me over to a corner of the studio where two easels stood side by side. She'd thrown a bedsheet across the top that hid whatever was on them. I was itching to whip off the sheet and look, but I knew better. Monique has a dramatic streak. She likes to do things with a little flair. You know—showmanship. Or is it show-*woman*-ship?

Anyway, I waited while Monique flipped a switch on the wall. A handful of track lights came on, and the easels were flooded with light. And only then did she whip off the sheet. "Ta-da," she said with quiet pride.

I had been sure the pictures would be perfect, and one quick glance said they were—from a distance. I mean, I expect perfection from Monique, but I never take anything for granted. I had to be absolutely sure. I took a magnifying glass from a pocket and moved up to the first canvas, the Rauschenberg.

Monique and I have done this before. She knows how I work. So as I began, she got comfortable in a nearby chair and started flipping through an Italian art magazine, *Espoarte*. She didn't really speak

Italian, but as an art-history buff she could usually get the gist of what she read. Besides, *Espoarte* was mostly about the gorgeous pictures any-way. So I stopped thinking about her and dove into the Rauschenberg.

I am not a huge fan of modern painting. Too much of it is like jerk-ing off; it's fun for the guy doing it and doesn't mean a whole lot to anybody else. But I kind of like Rauschenberg. I don't know why. One thing is, it has texture. You can look at photos of Rauschenberg's work without really getting a true sense of it, and that kind of keeps you from appreciating what he's done. You need to see the real thing—because the *feeling* of it is a big part. You want to run the palms of your hands across the canvas.

Monique knew that—hell, she knew it a whole lot better than I did. And as I got up close and personal with her copy, I had to admit she'd copped it beautifully. The way she'd laid on the paint was pure Rau-schenberg, and the bumpy, gritty surface of the canvas was just right. I wanted to rub my cheek on it.

I didn't. I just looked, and I took my time. I went over every inch of that canvas, looking for any small mistake. I mean, I was pretty sure there wouldn't be any, but everybody has to sneeze or burp or some-thing, and that's all it takes. What's the thing they say about the glitches in the *Odyssey*? "Homer nodded," right? So if Monique had nodded, I needed to find out now. After twenty minutes, I had to admit that if she had, she'd done it somewhere else. The canvas was flawless.

I looked at the bottom left corner last, the spot where I'd told her to put the *Times* clipping. At first pass, I couldn't see it. I got closer, used the magnifying glass—and there it was. Once I had seen it, it stuck out like a sore thumb. Before that, it was invisible. Monique had pulled off that trick of making something undetectable until you see it, and then you can't *un*-see it. I don't have any idea how the trick works, but I've seen it enough times to know it does. I had to smile, looking at it. Then I straightened up and moved to the second painting.

I'm not as fond of Jasper Johns. He's a little too simple and neat for me. I can't feel any heartbeat in his stuff. I guess it's just me, because plenty of people pay big bucks for his paintings. So it didn't matter if I didn't like the painting. I just had to make sure it could pass for the real thing. I went over it just as carefully as I had the Rauschenberg. It was a lot simpler in terms of composition and color and content, but once again Monique nailed the trick with the *Times* clipping.

When I was done, I took a few steps back and looked them both over again. And if I took more time staring at the Rauschenberg, who can blame me? I was pretty sure they would both pass almost anybody's inspection. Shit, I was positive. And even knowing that the *Times* clippings were there, I couldn't see them from three steps away. Monique had totally killed it. The paintings were perfect.

"Fucking *beautiful*," I said. I mean, I didn't want Monique to get all full of herself, but I couldn't help it.

I heard a rustling behind me and turned. Monique had closed her magazine, leaving one finger to hold her place. "What did you say?" she said, kind of polite and distant.

I took two big steps over to her, grabbed her shoulders, and hugged her. She didn't really return it, but I didn't care. She'd made me the cheese for my rat trap—two perfect hunks of cheddar. "I said, *fucking beautiful*," I told her. "Totally excellent! Monique, you hit it out of the park!"

She shrugged, but I could tell she was pleased. "What did you expect?" she said. That made me want to kiss her, but when I moved in for it, she held up the magazine between us.

I was so excited, I didn't really care. I stood up straight and reached into my pocket.

A tiny smile tugged at the corners of Monique's mouth. "Really, Riley," she said. "You act like you didn't think I could do this."

I pulled a piece of paper out of my pocket and handed it to her.

"Bullshit!" I said. "I knew you'd do it. In fact, I was so sure, I already wired the money for these two to your account. The Hong Kong one?" Hong Kong was the new Cayman Islands—a really good place to stick money when you didn't want anybody to know about it. They didn't ask questions, just stuck your cash in an anonymous numbered account.

Monique nodded and glanced at the paper. She did a small double take. She looked up at me with a raised eyebrow. "A tip? Really, Riley?"

"Fuck, yeah," I said. I realized I was kind of bouncing on my toes—but what the hell. I was jazzed about her work, seeing her two paintings done so perfectly. It made the whole impossible thing I was trying to pull off more real—and made me feel it working. Like my plan was some kind of machine, and we'd just started it and could hear the engine purring for the first time. "You earned that and more," I said.

Monique watched me bouncing for a few seconds. Then she shook her head and stuffed the receipt into her pocket. "And now what?"

I gave her a big, toothy leer. "We could celebrate," I said.

"Or not," she said. "I meant, what's next? With your super-duper top-secret I'm-a-genius ten-digit amazing plan?"

"Weeeeelllll," I said. "I mean, celebrate was the first choice—"

"Nope, not gonna happen," Monique said, a little too quickly. "I mean the *work*, Riley. You said there was something big after these two paintings."

I couldn't help it; her saying that gave me a picture in my head of the next step, and that made me serious. Because it was a real buzzkill. Ugly, dangerous, and totally necessary. It was the Riley Wrinkle, the one thing nobody else would ever dream up. Because it was stupid, wicked, lethal, and impossible. Which made it irresistible to me once I thought of it. "Yeah, it is big," I told Monique. "E-fucking-*normous*."

"And you're not going to tell me what it is?"

I stared hard at Monique. It was Riley's Third Law: Nobody gets told anything until they need to know it. But I couldn't help thinking that just maybe, if I told her—well, shit. I'd seen a whole lot less loosen up a woman's defenses and turn *absolutely not* into *oh, hell, why not*. More than that, she was as close to a partner as I had ever had. Like I said, I almost trusted her.

But this was probably the biggest, most complicated plan I'd ever come up with. And no matter what anybody tells you, rules are *not* meant to be broken. Not when they're Riley's Laws of Survival.

So I just shook my head. "Nope, not gonna happen," I said. I didn't realize I was mocking her until after I said it. Monique did; she looked a little pissed.

"Are you *ever* going to tell me?" she said. Very cranky, too.

"Yeah, sure I will," I said. "When it's time."

"'When it's time,'" she said, and now she was mocking me. "Well, fuck, that's just fine. And what the fuck does that mean?"

"When I know it's working," I said. I tipped my head at the paintings. "When these two masterpieces do their job."

"Which involves somebody discovering that they're forgeries," Monique said.

"Several somebodies," I said. "And the more, the better."

"Which means they will probably get thrown in an evidence locker by a couple of ham-handed cops, where they will gather dust and get all banged up and torn and eventually thrown away."

I shrugged. I hadn't thought of it that way. But she was right, and it really was too bad. They were wonderful paintings. I would've hung them both up in my living room, even if I had to build a bigger living room. But that's the way it goes. "Yeah, probably," I said. "I mean, if everything falls just right . . . ?"

Monique got out of her chair and looked at the two paintings, like she was feeling a little bit of maternal affection for them. "I worked my ass off painting them."

I leaned around and glanced at her butt. "Nope, still there," I said.

Monique sighed. "You have a truly twisted mind, Riley."

"Thank you, that's very sweet," I said. "I just hope it's twisted enough." I looked at the paintings, too, and I was feeling it again. The kind of excitement that whips through your veins and lifts you up to a new place. This was going to work. I bounced again. "This is it, Monique. This is the big one."

She didn't say anything. I looked over at her. She was staring at me, her head tipped to one side. "Maybe it is," she said softly. "I've never seen you like this before."

"I've never *been* like this," I said. "Goddamn it, if this works—"

"'If'?" she said. "You've never said 'if' before, either. Only 'when.'"

I took a big, deep breath and thought about what had to happen. About how many different pieces had to fall just exactly right . . . "If," I said at last. "This is a very big *if.*"

Monique stared at me, looking amazed. "What the fuck . . . ?" she said. "Riley Wolfe uncertain?" I just shrugged. But Monique licked her lips and took a half step closer. "Tell me," she said in a kind of husky whisper. That and licking her lips had me ready to howl at the moon.

"Monique," I said. My mouth was really dry and that was all I could manage.

"Tell me what it is," Monique said. She moved a tiny bit closer. "What's the target, what's your plan—tell me, Riley . . ."

I almost told her. I mean, she had me hypnotized. I don't know if she knew what she was doing to me, but she was sure as shit doing it. Almost . . . "No," I got out. My voice sounded like I'd been gargling sand. "I can't."

She licked her lips again and stood there watching me for another few seconds. And just when I couldn't take any more without grabbing her and flinging her down, with me on top—

Monique shrugged and stepped away from me. "All right," she said. "I guess I can wait."

She turned away. I swallowed, which was harder than it was supposed to be. I wanted to say something to make her turn back and face me again. But I didn't. I had to work tonight—and there was Riley's First Law in the way: The job comes first.

"You can keep that sheet," she said. She nudged with her toe the sheet she'd used to veil the paintings. "To wrap up my beautiful babies."

I tore my eyes off her back and shook myself. "Thanks," I said. I zipped up my jacket and took a deep breath. I let it out, wrapped the paintings in the sheet, and left. I really did have to work tonight, and it was not going to be easy.

CHAPTER
11

Actually, the first part *was* easy. The alarm system was an old friend. I'd dealt with a dozen just like it. Two dozen. It was ancient technology. Even being careful, watching for some improvement I wasn't expecting, it took me only a couple of minutes.

It was almost sad. I mean, it's amazing that people who have plenty of money and plenty of reason to lock up carefully—these are the people who scrimp on security. Maybe they had great insurance. For their sake, I hoped so.

It was a simple, no-sweat climb up to the roof, too. The only part that was even close to hard was that I had to do it twice. The paintings were too big and awkward to carry them both up at the same time. Aside from that, simple.

And then the alarm. There were two sensors touching each other at each door and window, and if they came apart—if the door or window was opened—it set off the alarm. Primitive. Only a little better than balancing a tin can full of rocks on the doorframe. I could've gotten through the sensors blindfolded.

I didn't. In fact, I took it nice and slow, watching for something unexpected. I had learned the hard way that when everything is sliding along slick as owl shit on a river rock, something bad is probably coming along to make up for it. Riley's Fifth Law: If you think it's easy, you're missing something. Superstitious, maybe, but I feel like you always end up paying for "easy."

So I kept both eyes open. I went all the way around the roof a couple of times, looking for anything I might have missed—cameras, sensors, a neighbor watching from a window. I scanned all the nearby buildings, too, and the street below. Nothing; it really was as uncomplicated as it looked. Unusual, but not impossible. I shrugged off the antsy feeling and went to work.

I took my time. The skylight was set into a metal frame. That makes people think, *Wow, metal, it's secure.* Except—guess what? It isn't secure at all. Because the frame holding the glass pane is held by ten screws. And the genius who installed this thing left the screw heads exposed. All I needed was my battery-powered reversible drill and a small Phillips-head bit. Five minutes, even taking it slow, carefully undoing each screw and laying it on a piece of tape so it wouldn't roll away and get lost. Slow and steady and simple. None of the screw heads was even stripped.

Then I was just as careful lifting off the cover to the skylight. I set it carefully to one side and then took out my coil of nylon cord. I tied off the roof end of the rope on a big sturdy stanchion. Then I dropped the loose end through the place where the skylight had been and slid down with the first picture under my arm.

It only took a couple of minutes to shimmy back up and bring down the second canvas. And then I went to the inside vault. The alarm and lock on the vault were about on par with the outside alarm system. I disabled the alarm with a piece of tinfoil. The lock on the vault was an old tumbler type and much harder. I put my stethoscope on it, and it took almost thirty whole seconds to open it. I put Monique's pictures inside, took out the two they replaced, and reversed the whole process. Lock the vault, climb back to the roof, reseat the skylight, and rearm the alarm.

I wrapped the two pictures carefully, then slid to the ground in the alley beside the building. I'd parked a van there. It read "NIGHT WATCHMAN SECURITY SYSTEMS" on the sides. I slipped the pictures inside, padded them carefully, and climbed into the driver's seat. And then away into the night, happy it had all gone right. I took it as a good sign. If the whole thing went this well—

I know. A really big if. But so far, a piece of cake. A really good start, and that was something. I mean, I knew it wouldn't last. In a way, I didn't want it to. I wanted a challenge and the feeling that I was doing something impossible. Because I was. But so far, it was pretty standard stuff. It would stay standard for one more day, nothing really out of the ordinary.

But after tomorrow? I just might find myself wishing for something this simple again.

The life of a top-end decorator is hard. It's a fight for many long years to reach the top, and when you make it—*if* you make it—it's a much harder fight to stay there. But Irene Caldwell was a fighter, and a good decorator, and she'd made it to the top of the list in the tristate area by outworking the competition, offering the best at a fair price. Her knowledge of the latest designers, furniture, and modern art was second to none, and she always found a way to please her clients while still nudging them toward wonderfully good taste. She had worked her ass off to get where she was—

But there were times when she wondered if it was worth it.

Like this morning: Her train had been delayed, and then it came to a dead stop between stations, where it sat for thirty-eight minutes while the rush hour crowd, already jammed in elbow to elbow, stood helplessly in growing pools of their own sweat. And of course there was absolutely no cell phone service in this particular spot, so Irene could not even call her morning appointments to tell them she was delayed. When the train finally got moving again, she was already an hour behind schedule, and that made her furious. Irene was a bit of a control freak, which was probably part of the personality that made her so good at what she did, and to be stuck like that, completely help-less, was intolerable. In addition, she demanded punctuality from herself and detested tardiness in others, and here she was an hour late before she had even really started her day.

Irene practically ran when the train finally disgorged its load of fuming passengers. Once on the sidewalk, she had at least managed to call and let her first appointment know she would be late, but apologizing just made her angrier, and by the time she got to her SoHo studio, she was ready to peel the skin off anybody who crossed her path. She clicked off her studio's alarm, tapping her foot impatiently. It always took a few seconds for the whole system to turn off—it was a very good alarm system, necessary since Irene quite often kept some very pricey artwork in her vault—which had a separate alarm of its own, of course.

The light on her alarm clicker finally blinked green, and Irene unlocked her front door and hurried into the vault. She had to pass her work area, where the large wall clock told her she was now an hour and three minutes late. "Damn, damn, damn," she said. She shut down the vault's alarm and hurriedly grabbed the painting she was going to deliver this morning, a wonderful Jasper Johns. She'd gotten it for a decent price and made a nice little profit when she passed it on to her client. She felt absolutely no guilt about that; her client was Elmore Fitch, a crusty, bad-tempered billionaire who gave lavishly to White Nationalist causes. He had basically chosen the picture because the artist was white and famous, and because the colors matched his couch. Irene found a small satisfaction in a little extra pinch when the client was such a Philistine. *Ars longa, assholes brevis,* she told herself.

Irene took the painting out to her worktable and laid it down carefully, looking at it with love. Gorgeous. As always, Irene was thrilled just to be in the presence of such a great work. My God, this was a superb picture—but did the colors seem a little brighter and fresher this morning? She frowned briefly, running her eyes up and down the canvas. Nothing had changed—it was probably just a trick of the lighting. Sometimes the morning light, coming through the skylight, made everything seem brighter. And paintings did not refresh themselves sitting in a vault overnight. Irene just looked for a moment longer, letting the painting set her off into a small, idyllic daydream. Someday, she would have a Jasper Johns of her own. And maybe a Rauschenberg, like the one in her vault that she would deliver tomorrow. Someday—

Her wall clock ticked loudly, snapping Irene out of her brief reverie. An hour and *five* minutes late now. "Goddamn it," she said. She wrapped the painting carefully and then hurried out the door to make the delivery.

Fall was finally here, and it was one of those days that makes you want to stay in Manhattan and live forever. The sun was shining, the air was so crisp and clean you could take a deep breath and not cough— even in Times Square. And although it wasn't so cool I needed a coat, you could tell that kind of cool was coming and pretty soon I'd need a whole lot more than an old Yankees jacket. But for now, it was perfect. The kind of day when even hard-ass New Yorkers smile a little as they walk through the streets.

And they were walking. Everybody walks in New York, but on a day like this one they actually seemed to like doing it. Weather like this yelled at the locals that you better get your ass outside and enjoy it while you can, because winter is coming and it will be a bitch this year.

I walked for a while, too. And I took it kind of slow. Hell, I'm not immune to feeling good now and then, even when I'm working. Which I was. I wasn't forgetting that or neglecting something connected to this job. Like I said, Riley's First Law: The job comes first. But it wasn't going to affect anything at all if I took two extra minutes and chilled in the fall's first great day. And as soon as I got my fill of strolling along with my hands in my pockets and started to feel guilty, I ducked into an alley like Spider-Man changing into his costume. I didn't change. But I did zip up to the rooftops.

I moved a lot faster up on top. That made up for the two or three minutes I'd wasted in the street. "Lollygagging," Mom would've called it. She came out with these ancient Southernisms like that sometimes. I never did figure out most of them. Like, if you gag on a lolly, that slows you down?

Whatever, I didn't lollygag on the rooftops. I raced across the city—uptown, down to street level to cross Fifth Avenue, then up again and crosstown to West End and down at 66th Street. I loved traveling by parkour on a day like this one. Every time I launched into space, it felt like I would live forever.

When I finally came down at 66th, I was smiling. It was a short walk to my goal, one of the last working phone booths in Manhattan. I love these old things. Don't get me wrong, I'm not anti-tech. I use cutting-edge techno toys every day, and the edgier, the better. But I still think it's a true shame that phone booths are dying out. Especially for somebody who every now and then needs to make a call that doesn't leave any kind of cell signal, no ID, nothing at all to track you. Sure, somebody could figure out where the call was coming from. But by the time they could do anything about it I'd be long gone.

That was exactly what I had in mind this morning. So the old phone booth at West End and 66th was perfect.

I slid into the booth, no problem—can you believe nobody was using it? Not even to piss in? I dropped a quarter into the slot and dialed a number I'd memorized this morning. After three rings, a woman's voice came on. She sounded like a cross between a robot and a high-priced hooker, a pretty good trick, if you think about it.

"Grey Wolf Securities, Elmore Fitch's office," she said. "How can I help you?"

"Yes, hello," I said in a British Oxonian accent I'd used before. And I have to say, it was pretty good. "I'm calling from Sotheby's? I have an extremely important message for Mr. Fitch."

"I'm sorry, Mr. Fitch is in a conference," the woman said, and her reply sounded so automatic it might have been recorded.

"Well, of course he's in a conference," I said, trying to sound amused and patronizing. I mean, there's more to doing Brit than just the sound. You've got to cop the attitude. "If he wasn't in a conference, I'm sure we'd all be terribly worried. So be a dear girl and simply convey a message, won't you? As I said, it's rather urgent."

"Yes, sir, and what was your name, please?"

"Tell Mr. Fitch that the Jasper Johns painting he purchased recently is a forgery," I said, very happy, like all Brits are when something goes wrong. I mean, for somebody else. "If he'll carefully examine the lower left-hand corner of the canvas, he'll see proof of this. He will have to look rather closely, but I assure you, the proof is there. Lower left, yes? Can you do that like a good girl? Brilliant."

114

"And your name, sir?" the woman repeated.

"Now please make sure he gets the message immediately, or even sooner, all righty? Brilliant. Ta," I said, and hung up the phone. I was sure I'd been just superior and annoying enough. That, combined with the Oxonian accent, and the poor woman would have to assume I was the kind of asshole who can only live at the high levels. I had to be important and official, and she'd deliver the message. "Brilliant," I said to myself, and I snorted. I mean, why do they always say that? Stupid habit. Fucking Brits.

And then I dropped the whole lighthearted Limey thing and walked back down West End. The phone call and the parkour were fun, but that part was over now.

From here on, things got serious.

CHAPTER 12

Frank Delgado got to Syracuse bright and early his second day. He'd last been there about twelve years ago. Not much had changed. It was still Syracuse. The leaves already had changed colors and fallen to the ground, brown. And he still didn't like Syracuse much.

The police station was in the same place, and Delgado parked, went in, and presented his credentials. No problem. And the cops found the file easily enough. Of course, there was a little routine foot-dragging first. Delgado had expected it. He'd been in the field his whole career with the Bureau, and he knew very well that no local cop worth his badge was going to jump up and run through some hoops just because a Fed asked him to. But Delgado was patient, and eventually, when the locals had proved they didn't give a shit about any Fibby, they turned him over to a Sergeant Valducci, a fireplug of a man in his fifties, broad across the shoulders, with arms like Popeye. Valducci was bald on top, with a short white fringe and massive black eyebrows.

"We love to cooperate with the Bureau, Special Agent Delgado," he said, and his gigantic black eyebrows moved as he spoke. "Let's hike on down to Records."

Delgado nodded and followed the sergeant.

"Well, shit," Valducci said when he'd pulled the file. "This is sealed—court order, the perp is a minor."

"*Was* a minor," Delgado said. "It was twenty years ago."

"Uh-huh," Valducci said. "But it's still sealed. That might mean he went straight, never arrested again . . . ?" He raised his giant eyebrows inquiringly.

Delgado said nothing.

"Oh. Like that, huh?" Valducci said. The sergeant frowned and brushed some dust off the folder. "I can get this unsealed, but it'll take some time. Couple weeks minimum, and more likely months." He shrugged and looked at Delgado. "Unless you can pull some Bureau strings?"

Delgado looked back and studied Valducci's face. One important reason he needed to see inside this folder was that the copy of the arrest report from the FBI files had no accompanying photograph. This might have been omitted originally to protect a juvenile. It might also have been removed later, for more sinister reasons. Either way, Delgado was still not entirely sure what Riley Wolfe looked like. So if Valducci was stalling, continuing the old Cops vs. Feds game, Delgado wanted to find a way around it and open the folder.

But the dark eyes under the massive eyebrows looked back at him with nothing but patience. Delgado nodded. The sergeant wasn't being a jerk. A file sealed by a court has to be unsealed by a court. Just as Valducci said, that could take weeks or months, and Delgado could end up using his entire leave just to get to his starting point. Unless—

"Is there anything written on the outside?" he asked.

The sergeant glanced down, turned the folder over, nodded. "It says, 'Remanded to custody of Jefferson County Probation Department,

Juvenile Services.'" He glanced up again. "Jefferson County, that's Watertown. North of here?"

"I know where it is," Delgado said.

"So what it means, they knew him up there, they came down and got him." He slapped a hand against the file folder and waggled his eyebrows one more time. "You don't need this thing. Jefferson County'll have what you really need."

Delgado nodded. "Thank you," he said. And he was gone before Sergeant Valducci could put the folder away.

The drive north to Watertown took a little over an hour. Delgado took Interstate 81 all the way, and the traffic eased up after Liverpool, a few miles outside of Syracuse. He drove at a steady eighty miles an hour, until he reached Watertown. He left 81 on the Arsenal Street exit. That took him straight through town—a town that had grown much larger and busier since the last time he'd been to Watertown, on a security case at Fort Drum. And Watertown had grown because Fort Drum had gotten bigger and more important. There were a lot more census-conscious franchises like Arby's and Taco Bell, which wouldn't open a location unless the population hit a certain density. But it wasn't just size; the flavor of the town had changed, too. There were even a couple of sushi restaurants, which would have been unthinkable in the decaying, blue-collar Watertown Delgado had known before.

There were so many new shops and strip malls and cafés that Delgado wasn't quite sure where he was. But the county probation department office was right on Arsenal, so there was no chance of getting lost. Twenty minutes after leaving the interstate, Delgado was standing in front of a desk and showing his credentials to a trim, middle-aged African-American woman who wore a lavender blouse and an expression that said she'd seen everything, and it mostly just made her weary. The sign on her desk read, "MAVIS WOLCOTT—Director Juvenile Services." She frowned at his badge for a few moments, then flicked her glance up to his face.

"All right," she said. "How can I help the FBI, Special Agent Delgado?"

There was a steel folding chair against the wall. Delgado moved it closer to the desk and sat. "I'm collecting background on someone who was in your system twenty years ago," he said.

Ms. Wolcott's lips twitched. It was probably intended to be a smile, but it didn't make it that far. "A little before my time," she said.

Delgado nodded. "I'd like to see his file," he said.

"Does he have a name?"

"Riley Wolfe," he said.

Delgado was watching closely for any sign of recognition, but there was none. "What's your interest in Mr. Wolfe?" Ms. Wolcott asked.

"He's a dangerous criminal," Delgado said.

Since she did not know Frank Delgado, Ms. Wolcott waited for details. He offered none. Finally she raised her eyebrows and said, "Well, I don't see why not. I guess." She picked up the phone on her desk and, after a moment, said, "Trish? I'm sending somebody down to see you. No, an FBI agent. Delgado. What? He can tell you that himself." She hung up and said, "Trish Wolcinski, in Records." And as he stood to leave she said, "Fair warning, Special Agent Delgado? Trish loves to chat."

Delgado just nodded. "Thank you for your help," he said.

Ms. Wolcott's warning had not been an exaggeration. Before Delgado even had both feet into the records room, Trish was already talking.

"You must be the FBI guy, right? Yeah, of course, I mean, who else would you be? Not that many people come here—I mean, duh, records, right? Who really cares enough to want to get all dusty? But I gotta say, you don't really, really *look* like an FBI guy. I mean, no offense or anything, but you know. You look more like a drug cop, right? What is that, DEA? I mean, those guys are more—not that I'm, you know, it's just—see, I'm from Detroit, you know, I just came here cuz my hubby was at Drum? Tenth Division? And he deployed and I thought, what the hell, it's not such a bad place. I mean, it gets colder than you can believe in the winter—that's, you know, that's why they put Fort Drum here, okay? Because the winter is—"

"I need to see a file," Delgado said, much louder than he'd intended. It didn't seem to bother Trish.

"Sure, of course, why else would you be here? But I gotta say, most of our files are on computer now? Which is totally NOT a lot easier and more convenient like they said it would be—"

"It's from twenty years ago," Delgado said.

"Okay, sure, no problem. And it's a local juvenile who was in our system at the time, right? I mean, Mavis didn't say, but I just figured that—"

"He used the name Riley Wolfe," Delgado said. "I don't think that's his birth name."

"Uh-huh, uh-huh, they do that sometimes, I mean, I guess it's a good idea and all, if you're breaking the law, and so they get away with—"

"The relevant date is here," Delgado said. He passed her his copy of the arrest report from Syracuse.

"Right, there it is, okay. Yeah, that's not gonna be on computer, that'll be an actual old-fashioned paper file, which means it's gonna be right over here—you know, they were going to put all the old paper files onto computer a few years ago? But they suddenly, I mean the government, I guess, I don't know which one, local or, you know, Washington? Anyway, it was probably some jerk in Congress saving money, but like suddenly we didn't have a budget, so—"

Trish whirled away toward the back of the room, talking full speed and running a finger along the front of the file cabinets as she chanted the dates, interspersing that information with haphazard comments about computers, filing, winter, her husband—there was so much, all of it random noise, that Delgado tuned her out and didn't notice what she said again until the flow of talk stopped abruptly.

"Huh," she said suddenly. She looked up at him and frowned. "It should be right here, but . . ."

Delgado crossed the room to the open file drawer, where Trish held a finger on an olive green hanging file. "Right here," she said definitely. "You can tell, this is where it would be, matching the date and the—"

"You're sure?" Delgado asked.

"Oh, absolutely positive, not the tiniest bit of doubt, it oughta go right here, and you can see, there's even this empty hanging file where it went? Which means it was here, and now it isn't, and that has to mean—"

But Delgado didn't hear what it had to mean. He was out the door before Trish could finish her sentence. He already knew what it meant.

Riley Wolfe had been here first.

Of course, he thought. *Naturally he'd cover his tracks.* There was no way to know how long ago—it might have been twenty years ago or yesterday. Getting in and out of this room would be child's play for someone with Riley's skills. He might have come during the day in one of his disguises. Just as easily, he could have gotten past the security at night. It didn't matter how he'd done it; it was done, and there wasn't much doubt who had done it.

And although Delgado was a little disappointed, he already knew his next move by the time he got to his car. Watertown was still small, and twenty years ago it had been smaller. That made finding some things a lot easier. A few moments with his phone and Google, and he had the address.

Delgado drove south for about a mile before he came to Watertown High School. It was the only high school in Watertown, except for a Catholic school, and Delgado chose to go with the odds and try the public school first.

His badge got him into the principal's office very quickly, where a worried woman in a pantsuit sat behind a desk that read, "JANE CRONK, Principal." She stood up as he entered and offered her hand. "If this is about one of our students, I'm going to have to see a whole lot of paperwork from a judge," she said by way of welcome.

Delgado shook her hand, then sat down. "A former student," he said. "From twenty years ago." He hesitated, not used to volunteering anything, then added, "I'm collecting background information."

Ms. Cronk stood a moment longer, watching him. Then she said, "Hmp," and sat back down. "I guess that's a little different." She leaned back in her chair. "All right," she said. "What can you tell me, Mr.— Do I call you 'Agent'? We don't get many federal agents in here, and I'm not sure of protocol."

"Special Agent Frank Delgado," he said. "Frank is fine."

She gave him a brief, businesslike smile. "All right, Frank. What can you tell me about this former student?"

"Not much," he said. "I was hoping you might have a teacher on staff who was here back then."

"Twenty years ago? I think we have three," she said. She ticked them off on the fingers of her left hand. "Mr. Deutsch, the industrial arts teacher, has been here twenty-seven years. Ms. Caprino, I think it's about the same, maybe twenty-eight. She teaches English? And Mr. Berdichevsky has been here for a whopping thirty-four years." She raised an eyebrow.

"The shop teacher first, please," Delgado said. He thought for a moment. English sounded like a class Riley Wolfe would skip whenever he could. "What subject is Berdichevsky?"

"Algebra," Ms. Cronk said. "And he does the chess club."

Delgado nodded. "I'll talk to him next."

Ms. Cronk tilted her head to one side. "No interest in the English teacher?" she asked.

"If needed," Delgado said.

"All right." She pointed to her left. "Conference room down the hall there. You can use that." She turned to lead the way. "I'll tell Abbie to bring them in one at a time." She paused in the doorway, hesitated, then turned around to face him. "Would you like some coffee?" she said, a little uncertainly.

"Yes. Thank you," Delgado said. Ms. Cronk nodded and spun away.

The coffee was pretty bad. Delgado didn't care. He sat at the conference table and sipped as Cronk's assistant, Abbie, brought in the first teacher, Mr. Deutsch. He was a burly guy with a buzz cut and a large tattoo on his forearm. Delgado glanced at it, just long enough to recognize the eagle, globe, and anchor of the US Marines. Deutsch sat across from Delgado practically at attention as Delgado questioned him. He answered carefully after thinking over each question for several seconds. But all Delgado learned was that Deutsch had served two hitches in the Corps, mostly embassy duty. He'd never heard of anybody named Riley Wolfe and didn't really remember any students from twenty years ago, except one kid who'd cut off a finger in the band saw.

Mr. Berdichevsky was no better. Riley had always shown remarkable planning skills, and Delgado had thought that because of that, there was a chance he'd been a chess player. But Berdichevsky had no helpful answers. Perhaps his memory was going; he showed more signs of advanced age than Deutsch had, and the broken veins around his nose indicated a heavy drinker. In any case, he was no help.

From a habit of thoroughness more than from any real hope, Delgado sent for the third teacher, the English teacher, Ms. Caprino. She came in with quiet grace and confidence, a pleasant-looking woman around fifty, with unnaturally red hair. She sat down, smiled at him, and crossed her hands on the table in front of her.

"Thank you for speaking with me, Ms. Caprino," Delgado said.

She inclined her head. "Abbie said you were asking about a former student? One of *my* students?"

"I don't know," Delgado said. "I don't even know his real name."

Caprino cocked her head. "Really. Do you know his *un*-real name?"

Delgado almost smiled. He liked this woman. "He calls himself Riley Wolfe," he said.

To his astonishment, Ms. Caprino threw back her head and laughed, a long, loud, raucous laugh that practically shook the furniture. Delgado watched her laugh, liking her even more. The laughter was so genuine, so infectious, that he could feel the corners of his own mouth twitching.

"Oh, dear," Ms. Caprino said at last. She wiped a tear from the corner of her eye. "Oh, my." She chuckled briefly, then controlled herself again. "I always knew that boy would make something special of himself."

"He has done that," Delgado said.

"Oh, my. And I assume this is not a background check for a high-profile government job?"

"No, it isn't," Delgado said. "You knew him, then?"

"Yes, I knew him," she said, still smiling. "And I liked him, Mr. Delgado. I recognize that he was not always . . . but that boy was smart, and he absolutely loved to read." She looked down, her smile turning fond as she remembered. "He was always asking me to recommend new books for him—some very advanced titles, too." Caprino looked up and met Delgado's eyes. "There aren't very many high school students who read *Swann's Way*, you know."

"I can't imagine why not," Delgado said. "Can you tell me his birth name, Ms. Caprino?"

She shook her head and smiled ruefully. "As far as I knew—as far as any of us here knew—Riley Wolfe *was* his birth name. Now, he was new to the area. But all the official paperwork said 'Riley Wolfe.' And seriously, a fifteen-year-old kid—why would he change his name? And *how*? I mean, all the records he'd have to fake just to enroll in school—transcripts, birth certificate, Social Security, you know. A fifteen-year-old boy?" She smiled. "Of course, as I said, he really was quite precocious."

Delgado leaned forward slightly. "You say he was new to the area?"

"Yes, of course, nobody had ever seen him before. And he didn't really go out of his way to make friends."

"Do you know where he lived before he moved here?"

"No, I don't think I ever saw the transcript, and he didn't say. But the paperwork had to have been in order—there was never any question of it—and he really was a very good student."

Delgado nodded. He wasn't terribly surprised by what Ms. Caprino called Riley's precociousness. The Riley Wolfe he had come to know would have had no problem, either morally or practically, with forging papers. But it did make him wonder if young Riley had really been quite that good—or if he had had adult help. "Did he ever say anything about his home life?" he asked.

Ms. Caprino shook her head. "Not a lot. He mentioned his mother, and I think he cared for her a great deal."

"Most boys care about their mothers."

Ms. Caprino's head shake got more vigorous. "Not like this," she said. "He was absolutely devoted to her. The way he talked about her . . . And that was why, just before his senior year—he came to see me? To say good-bye—because he was scheduled to be in my Advanced Placement class?"

Delgado frowned. "Something happened to his mother?"

"She had a stroke," Ms. Caprino said. "She couldn't work anymore, even at Friendly's." The teacher shook her head. "Riley came to see me, to tell me he had to drop out to take care of her." She smiled sadly. "And to ask for a final reading list."

"Did you see him again?"

She shook her head, and the sadness on her face grew. "No. Never saw him nor heard from him again. I heard they moved away shortly afterward." Before Delgado could ask, she added, "And no, I have no idea where they went. As far as I know, nobody here in Watertown heard." She sighed. "I would've liked to . . ." Ms. Caprino looked down at her hands, then abruptly shook her head and sat up straight. "Anyway," she said. "I believe he was very close to his mother. Even before the stroke."

"It was just Riley and his mother? No father or siblings?"

"Not that I ever heard about."

"Do you know where he lived?"

Caprino made a face. "No," she said. "But I know he was sensitive about it for some reason. And . . ." She grimaced and looked away, and Delgado was quite sure there was something she wasn't sure she wanted to tell him. So he just waited. It was a technique that had served him well many times. He sat with no expression, his hands folded in front of him, motionless, looking like he'd been carved from wood.

Ms. Caprino looked back at him, smiled tentatively. Delgado's expression did not change. She looked away again, sighed, and finally looked back. "All right," she said. She spread her hands ruefully. "There was . . . an incident." Caprino sighed again, heavily this time. "It seemed so out of character. He was such a good student and . . ." She shook her head. "I didn't see it, but— All I know is, in homeroom one morning, another boy said something to him, just a remark about Riley and his big house on the hill." She sighed. "Riley absolutely flew at that boy. He had to have stitches, and Riley was suspended for two weeks. It could have been— I put in a good word for him, or he might have been expelled. I believe the homeroom teacher did, too, which helped, I think."

"Another teacher?" Delgado asked. "Do you remember who it was?"

Caprino shook her head. "It's been an awfully long time. And my memory isn't what it was. But it was the music teacher—a Mr. Fraser? Fisher? Foster?" She smiled sadly. "I really can't remember, I'm sorry. He retired, oh, perhaps twelve years ago?"

"Is he still living?" Delgado asked. "In the area?"

"I have no idea," Caprino said. "I barely knew the man. He was— I would not say 'odd' except that this is Watertown?" She smiled. "In any case, he kept to himself for the most part."

"Did Riley have a girlfriend that you know of?" he asked her.

She pursed her lips. "I saw him with girls, but never the same one for very long." She sighed, shook her head. "Riley was a lonely boy, I know that. And I'm pretty sure he didn't actually *like* the bad eggs he hung around with—" She shrugged. "In any case, it's not something I would have asked him about."

"You mentioned 'bad eggs'?" Delgado asked. "His friends?"

"'Friends'—well, I don't know if that's the right word here. There were a couple of boys he hung out with, but . . . ," she said. She made a face, and again, Delgado almost smiled. Even after twenty years, she looked disapproving. "They were not really good students—'not good' meaning socially as well as academically. But Riley was— Do you remember high school at all, Mr. Delgado?"

"Call me Frank," he said. "I remember."

She smiled again, a little warmer. "All right, Frank. I'm Eileen."

He returned the smile briefly, then prompted, "High school?"

"Yes. Well, if you remember, you know that everybody has to have a clique, a group to hang out with. Like birds need a flock. If you're a complete loner, the other birds will peck you to death—in a flock or in high school." She raised one eyebrow at him.

"I remember," he said again.

"So Riley hung with the bad kids because he could," she said. "Protective coloration, I think. I mean, I can't really believe he actually liked any of them. Aside from being pure trouble, they were— I have to be careful what I say. Um—the other boys were very *limited*." She lifted an eyebrow, and Delgado nodded, understanding. "Certainly none of these 'friends' read *Swann's Way*. Or anything else, most likely. Their only real talent was for trouble. But Riley?" She looked at him with an expression every cop sees a thousand time, the look that pleads for understanding. "He was so bright, and so . . . He wasn't a bad kid, Frank—not really—and the books he read, I mean, he absolutely *devoured* everything in the library. It was just—" She sighed. "I guess it's the old story of a good kid hanging with a bad crowd. Those other boys were . . . primitive."

"Can you remember any names?"

"Well, I know two of them—they're still here, in Watertown." She gave a quick snort of wry amusement. "It's still hard to get away from Watertown, except into the Army or prison. And these two—" She shook her head. "I will just say that I don't think they went into the Army." She sighed. "Anyway, Jimmy Finn works at the Kwik Lube on Washington Street. They work on my car? And Rodney Jankowski . . . Hm . . . I saw him at the county fair two years ago, we didn't really have a lot to say, but Jimmy Finn might know how to find him. If not—he should be in the phone book. Oh! I mean, you can Google him. Phone book." She laughed briefly. "I'm afraid I'm dating myself."

Delgado actually smiled at last, a rare thing for him, but he liked this woman. "I remember phone books," he said. He stood up. "Thank you, Ms. Caprino. You've been very helpful."

She stood up, too. "Oh, my, you almost sound like you mean that," she said.

"Actually," Delgado said, "I do."

Abbie, the principal's assistant, informed Delgado that she'd been a student here and of course she remembered the music teacher's name. "Lester Foley," she said. "He was kind of, I don't know. A little . . . different? But he really loved music, and he made us listen to all kinds of stuff."

And at Delgado's prompting, Abbie dug into a cabinet and even found a file. "Oh," she said, glancing into the folder. "Oh well." She took out the folded page of a newspaper. "There's this lady, Mrs. Ashton? She comes in twice a week, like a volunteer?" Delgado nodded that he understood what "volunteer" meant, and Abbie went on. "Well, she's been putting things into the files. Like updates? About all our old teachers and, you know, if somebody gets in the paper?" She fluttered the newspaper. "And so here, this is Mr. Foley's, um, obituary? So . . ." She shook the paper apologetically.

"All right," Delgado said. It was a disappointment, but not a major one. "One more thing," he said. "If a new student came here from out of the area, would he be required to submit a transcript from his previous school?"

"Oh, yes," Abbie said. "Absolutely. Even if he was homeschooled, there are standardized test results and so on, so the principal can determine if the new student is actually up to grade level."

"How long are those records kept?"

She pursed her lips. "I couldn't say exactly? But the student you were asking about—from twenty years ago? I'm pretty sure they don't keep them *that* long."

Delgado was pretty sure, too. But he was never willing to leave something at "pretty sure." "Could you check, please?"

"Of course," Abbie said. "Wait here? It'll just take a minute."

Delgado waited. The wall clock ticked loudly, and he felt the first stirrings of hunger. A gaggle of students went by in the hall. The clock ticked again, and then Abbie came back. "Like I thought," she said, smiling like it was a triumph to be right. "Those records went missing years ago."

"Thank you for your help," Delgado said. He wasn't surprised.

Delgado got into his car and took out his notebook. And then, for a few moments he just sat, thinking over what the English teacher had told him. There were threads, possibilities . . .

Delgado was a careful, step-by-step thinker, which was one of the reasons for his success. He never tried to jump from *A* to *L* without filling in all the letters in between. So he did not try to form any tentative conclusions. Instead, he flipped open the notebook and wrote "MOTHER" in block letters. Ms. Caprino had said she thought Riley cared about his mother. Well, most boys did. And they'd been close even before the mother's stroke. Had she taken an active role in his identity change? More than that—was Riley's mother his criminal mentor? That might mean she had a criminal record somewhere—something to check when he found their original name. Next to where he'd written, "MOTHER," he wrote in, "Record?"

In any case, Mother had clearly gone along with the identity change. To think that she was either ignorant or disapproving of it was ridiculous. She would have had to have a driver's license and so on in the name of Mrs. Wolfe. If she was not a criminal herself, why would she help out with forging documents?

Delgado thought about it for several minutes, unconsciously chewing on his pen. When he found her legal name, he could check for a criminal history. But if there was none . . . Why would a straight mother help her son commit some serious crimes?

That was easy. To protect him, of course. From what? Something even more serious. There was no way to know what, any more than he could guess what had caused mother and son to move to this frigid, remote town and change their names. But the more he thought of it, the more Delgado thought it was probably the same traumatic event. That made sense, more than thinking it had been two life-changing calamities in a row.

So what had been that traumatic event? It was vitally important to find out—it had been the cause of a relatively normal young boy changing into a devoted criminal. The first step in the career of Riley Wolfe. But there was no way to know what had happened—not yet. At the moment he didn't even know *where*.

Delgado chewed the pen some more until he tasted ink and, with a start, realized what he had done. He pulled a fresh pen from his briefcase. This time, he merely tapped it against his blued teeth as he went back to his train of thought.

All right: Putting the cause aside for a moment . . . the boy and the mother are close. The mother has a serious stroke. The boy drops out of school to take care of her. And soon after they move away.

Delgado realized his teeth hurt and then understood why. He frowned and put down his pen. The mother would need full-time care. She would *still* need it, if she was still alive. It might make sense to track her down. And then wait for Riley to visit her, which he would— IF she was still alive and IF they were still close. And, the biggest IF of all, IF he could find out what name she was using.

131

But that could be anything. And so far, he had no leads to finding it. He shook it off and went back to his notes.

The next item he thought was important was the "big house on hill." Delgado wrote that down, then underlined it. After all, Riley had pummeled a boy for mocking it. He didn't think that house was here in Watertown. This part of upstate New York did not have a lot of hills, and even fewer with big houses on them. Aside from that, he was already known as Riley Wolfe when he got to high school here. That would have been a near-impossible trick if he'd lived here all along under another name and then suddenly changed it.

Delgado tapped the page with his pen. He did not have enough information to guess where Riley had come from before Watertown, so there was no real point in beating his brains out about it. But he underlined "big house on hill" again, before dropping down two more lines and writing "books." He had no idea where that bit might lead, but if it had been a big part of Riley's youth, it might prove important.

Delgado thought a few more minutes, going over all the English teacher had said. When nothing else jumped out at him as important, he looked over what he'd written. It was a good start.

Delgado closed the notebook, started his car, and drove east.

Jimmy Finn had a car up on the rack and was taking off the tires with a pneumatic wrench. But when Delgado showed his badge, the young woman behind the counter practically sprinted into the service bay to fetch him. There was a window between the office and the work area. Delgado saw the woman waving her hands excitedly and Jimmy looking over at him, obviously worried. For a moment it looked like he might bolt. But he took a deep breath, put down his wrench, and followed the young woman back into the office. He came directly to Delgado and then jerked to a stop. The young woman bumped into him from behind, then took a half step back and watched anxiously. Finn stood there, clenching and unclenching his hands, until Delgado took pity on him.

"Mr. Finn? If you don't mind, I'd like to ask you a couple of questions," he said, trying to sound mild.

"I, I—about what?" Finn said, looking like he might hyperventilate. "I mean—because my parole officer said—"

"You're not in any kind of trouble, as far as I know," Delgado said. He tilted his head toward a doorway that led to a waiting room. "Can we talk in there? It'll only take a few minutes."

"But then why—I mean, if it isn't me, then, you know. What?"

"Let's go sit, maybe have some coffee?" Delgado said.

The young woman spoke up anxiously. "I made it fresh just like an hour ago," she blurted out.

"I'm sure it's fine," Delgado told her, pointedly adding, "I don't want to keep you from your job."

She gulped but didn't move. The phone began to ring.

"Mr. Finn?"

Finn looked at the doorway, then at the woman standing so close behind him. Then he turned back to Delgado and blew out a loud breath. "Yeah, okay," he said. "Go on, Ellie," he told the woman, and she scurried back behind the counter and picked up the phone.

Delgado followed Finn into the waiting area. There was a coffee-maker, a stack of magazines, and a wall-mounted TV blasting a midday show, five women all talking at once. Delgado reached up and turned it off. He poured himself a cup of coffee and raised an eyebrow at Finn. "Want a cup?"

"Yeah, no, no, I don't," Finn said. "Look, I'm not gonna rat anybody out or— I mean, I don't even know anything worth shit anymore—"

Delgado nodded and gestured to a chair. "Have a seat," he told Finn. He waited until Finn sat, then took a nearby chair. He sipped his coffee. It was terrible, worse than what they'd given him at the high school, but it was hot.

"So, so, so what's this about?" Finn stammered. "I mean, it's been a long-ass time since I—since, since—" He slammed his mouth shut and gulped, looking guilty. "So, what?" he said.

Delgado took another sip, watching Finn sweat. "Riley Wolfe," he said at last.

"Jesus *fuck*," Finn said, barely above a whisper.

"He's a friend of yours?"

"Oh, jeez, I mean—I ain't heard from Riley in like—I mean, this was high school, and he left when it—I mean, really, that was the last time I—years ago, okay?" He gulped and took a deep, ragged breath. "What, uh . . . what'd he do?"

"That's the last you heard from him? In high school?"

Finn nodded vigorously. "Junior year. He left that summer, after junior year, because his mom, and I never, uh—I mean that's a long time ago, right? And, uh . . ." He trickled to a stop and gulped again.

Delgado watched Finn. He was extremely nervous. Anyone might be nervous talking to an FBI agent, but Finn seemed panicky far beyond that. Part of it was certainly guilt, probably because of some past criminal act. But Delgado was getting a whisper of a message from his instinct, and he trusted it. "Mr. Finn," he said matter-of-factly, without raising his voice. "Did you know it's a felony to lie to the FBI?"

Finn had been pale before. Now he turned green. "I, I, I din't know that," he said in a gravelly whisper. He pushed a lock of dank hair off his forehead. "I, I got a kid now," he said. "I can't, I can't go back to—"

Delgado nodded and waited.

"Look," Finn said at last. It took him two tries, and he had to clear his throat before he could speak. "Shit," he said softly. He hung his head. "It was like maybe ten years ago?" he said in a pleading tone of his voice. Sweat rolled off his face. "And it was just, I din't—" He stopped, looked up, and licked his lips. "I seen him," he said hoarsely. "I seen Riley."

"You saw him here? In Watertown?"

"Shit, yeah. I sure as shit never got away from Water-fuckin'-town, except for—and now, I got to report to my parole officer, so—yeah, it was here. Riley was here." He nodded and wiped sweat from his face with his sleeve.

"Where did you see him?"

"Salmon Run Mall. He was comin' out of Dick's, you know, Sporting Goods? And his hair was different—I mean, different color and all, too? Blond. But I knew it was him, and I go, 'Riley! Yo, buddy!' And he's all like, he didn't hear me, and he goes back into Dick's, and I thought, what the fuck, and I followed him." He gave a snort that might have been laughter and wiped his forehead again. Then he looked up at Delgado and said, "Okay if I smoke?" Delgado nodded, and Jimmy took out a crumpled light-blue pack of generic cigarettes. He lit one with a kitchen match, inhaled deeply, blew out a cloud of smoke. "Yeah. Anyways, I'm like two steps into Dick's, and I feel, like, it has to be a pistol. Stuck in my ribs, right here?" Finn lifted an arm and pointed to a spot on a level with his heart. "And this voice says, I don't know, something like, 'Don't say nothin' just keep smilin' and come with me.' And I can't exactly see? But it's gotta be Riley, right? And so what the fuck, I do what he says."

Finn took another puff. "He takes me to the food court, it's like right there close, and he sits me at a table and leans in close to my ear and says, 'Call me Andrew,' and he pokes me with the gun again and sits down beside me." Finn nodded. "It's him, like I figured it had to be. It's Riley. And he's all smilin' and shit, goin', 'Hey, Jimmy, wassup?'" He shook his head and laughed, and opened his mouth to say something but instead slammed it shut and looked around nervously.

Delgado waited. Finn stared down at the floor and puffed his cigarette. Finally, Delgado said, "Did he tell you why he was in Watertown?"

Finn blew smoke out his nose and nodded without looking up. "He said he was just cleanin' up some old shit. I din't ask what. I mean, you don't, not with somebody like him."

Delgado was reasonably sure that the shit Riley was cleaning up was removing all the files about himself from the school and from Juvenile. He was also sure Finn was telling the truth about not pressing Riley for details. That was in the rules that went with the life, and he knew them as well as Finn. So he just sat and waited a bit longer. Finn finished his cigarette and ground it out on the floor with his foot. "That was the last time you saw Riley Wolfe?"

Finn nodded vigorously. "Swear to God."

"Did you hear from him? Phone, letter, email, anything at all?"

Finn shook his head, just as enthusiastically. "No. Never. Not once, not nothin', on my kid's life. That was it, we just sat at the food court for like half an hour, and that was it, honest to God." He gulped, wiped his forehead again, and took a deep, shaky breath.

Delgado watched Finn sweat without sympathy. When he was sure Finn was done, he nodded. "Do you have any pictures of Riley?" Delgado asked.

"Pictures? No, uh-uh. He's not even in the yearbook. It was like a thing with him, ever since he—" Finn stumbled to a stop and gulped again. "Lookit, this was a long time ago, okay? But, uh—I mean, we were kids. Poor kids."

"Why didn't Riley want his picture taken?"

Finn sighed. "It started ninth grade. There was Riley and three of us. And after we, uh . . . He wouldn't let anybody take a picture after we started, uh . . . We *boosted* stuff."

"Who were the other two?"

"Rodney Jankowski," Finn said. "And Tommy Steuben."

"Do you know where they are now?"

"Sure," Finn said. "Tommy's dead. He got drunk and ran his car into a tree three years ago. Rodney, he's back in the slammer. Midstate."

Delgado nodded. "What kinds of stuff did you steal?"

Finn flinched a little at the word "steal." But he nodded and went on. "Riley got a brand-new Walkman. It was a real big deal to him, he always had it on him. Fuckin' loved music, all the time. And you know. Clothes, cool shoes, and like *Hustler*?" He shrugged. "Stuff kids would take. You know."

"Did Riley have any other friends?" Delgado asked. "Maybe a girlfriend?"

Finn gave a snort of amusement. "Oh, man, *a* girlfriend? Not Riley. He totally was a player. I mean, he had a line of bullshit like you never— Shit, Riley could talk a nun out of her panties."

"Never somebody special?"

"Naw, not Riley," Finn said. "Strictly flavor of the week. And *every* week, right? I never got how— I mean, there was just something about Riley. What, charm? I guess so. He could turn it on and the chicks were just crazy, did whatever he wanted."

"Any other friends?" Delgado prompted. "Or just the three of you?"

"Just us," Finn said. "I mean, we was pretty tight, but . . . I dunno. It was always like, I mean, we knew Riley was like, you know. We did what he wanted?"

"Do you know where he went when he moved away from Watertown?"

Finn shook his head energetically. "No. Naw. Uh-uh. It was weird, like—one day they was just gone. Never a word, nothing."

"Did he ever say where he lived before Watertown?" Delgado asked.

Finn shrugged. "Naw, he didn't say shit about that—and after he beat the shit out of Cal Simpkins in homeroom, we didn't ask, neither."

Finn frowned. "I dunno, though. Once or twice he said stuff, like—I mean, he'd say, like, 'Y'all coming?' Like a hillbilly or something." He snorted. "His mother was worse. She was like *Gone with the Wind*, you know?"

"You met Riley's mother?"

Finn shrugged. "Couple times, you know. I'd stop by their place to pick him up. Once or twice we stopped at the Friendly's when she was working, waiting tables, and we'd stop to, you know. So Riley could talk to her, maybe give her a few bucks or somethin'." He shrugged again.

"Do you know what her name was?" Delgado asked. "His mother's first name?"

"Uh, lessee, yeah, you know—I mean, she had a name tag on her waitress uniform? So . . . Shirley? Somethin' like—no, wait, Sheila. Yeah, that's it."

"Sheila?"

"Absolutely."

Delgado nodded. "So Riley was close to his mother?"

Finn snorted. "Sick close. Like she was the girlfriend that gave the best head in—" He jerked to a stop, looked at Delgado, and actually blushed. "I mean, you know," he finished lamely. "They were real tight."

Delgado nodded encouragingly. "He was closer to her than most guys are to their mothers," he said.

Relieved, Finn nodded vigorously. "Yeah, that's it, you know. It seemed funny, a guy that hung up on his mother, that's all." He smiled and shook his head. "But hey, believe me, nobody ragged him about it. I mean, all the girls he got? Nobody would even *think* about he was gay or anything."

"And the mother had a strong Southern accent," he said. "Any guess what part of the South?"

"Naw, who can tell?" Finn said. "But you know, totally Southern. No doubt."

Delgado nodded. He knew very well that most people couldn't tell a South Georgian from an Appalachian accent. For now he was satisfied to know that Riley was from somewhere in the South. It wasn't much, but more than he'd had. He had one more question, something Finn should know. "You said you stopped by his place. Where did Riley live?" Delgado asked.

"What—you mean, uh—like, *here*? When he—in high school?"

"Yes," Delgado said.

Finn shook his head sadly. "Beat-to-shit old trailer, maybe a mile down Evans Road—it's out by the airport? Practically at the end of the runway." He snorted. "Piece-of-shit dump. All they could afford."

"Is it still there?"

Finn snorted. "If it hasn't fell over," he said. "Thing was close to rusting out back then."

Delgado studied Finn a moment longer. Then he nodded and stood up. "Thank you for your time," he said.

Delgado found Evans Road easily enough. It was a left turn off Route 12F, just before the airport. There were very few houses; it was mostly scraggly trees, brush, and a couple of fields. He didn't see any trailers, but he drove slowly down the road to the end, where it dumped out onto Route 180. He doubled back along Evans Road, going even slower. Finn had said "at the end of the runway," so Delgado drove past a tiny old graveyard to a spot where he could see the airport through the trees. There was a rutted, half-overgrown dirt road, or driveway, and he turned down it. It led him toward the airport through trees that grew increasingly close to the rutted dirt road, and finally to a place where an old maple had fallen, blocking the way.

Delgado parked his car and got out. The tree blocking his way had clearly been there quite a while; it was already half rotted through. Even so, there was no way he could get his car past. He took a flashlight and a pair of work gloves from his car, carefully picked his way over the tree, and followed the old road on foot.

Another fifty yards and the road broke out into what had once been a clearing. It was mostly overgrown now—but at the far end, Delgado could see the wreckage of a double-wide trailer.

He pushed across the clearing through the encroaching scrub. Halfway through it, he hit a patch of thorns, some kind of bush. Delgado had no idea what it was, but the thorns tore his pants in two places, and his skin in three. He pulled on the work gloves and disentangled himself.

Moving more carefully now, Delgado worked around the thorns and closer to the trailer, and finally he was standing at the front steps. They were rotted through, of course. So was the trailer itself. It sagged in the middle as if some huge creature had been sitting on it. The front was intact, except for the windows, but the door hung on one hinge at a crazy angle.

Delgado walked slowly around the wrecked trailer. At one end, the encroaching brush was not quite as thick, and he crouched to look underneath. Shards of linoleum hung down where the floor had fallen through. There was a litter of rags, unidentifiable plastic items, and what looked to be half an old wooden chair. He stood up and completed his tour around the trailer.

At the far end, he paused again. The outer wall here had rotted through, and there was a large hole. Delgado worked over to it carefully, watching for any more of the vicious thorn bushes. He peered through the hole and inside the old trailer. The interior was dim, and he flipped on his flashlight and shone it around inside. There wasn't much to see. The inside was as ruined as the outside. As far as he could tell, there was no furniture or anything else left in there. And with gaping holes in the floor in several places, it would be almost suicidal to try to get in and look.

Delgado stepped away from the trailer and worked around to the front again. He leaned in the front door and flicked the flashlight's beam around. Nothing but ruined emptiness.

Delgado took a couple of steps back. For several minutes he stood there, not really looking at the trailer anymore. Birds chirped absent-mindedly. A very small wind stirred the leaves around him. He didn't notice. He just stood and thought. Then he turned and looked around the clearing. There was nothing to see but plant life. Delgado chewed his bottom lip for a moment and then nodded. He walked back to the spot at the end where he could see underneath and carefully pushed up close. Getting down on one knee, he stuck his head under and looked up. Above him, the floor was still mostly intact. It seemed an acceptable risk, and he crawled cautiously under the trailer.

At the first pile of rubbish he paused and sorted through it carefully. He found a piece of porcelain, half of a coffee cup. It was the kind of cheap souvenir mug you could buy at most tourist stops, and he examined it carefully. Very faintly, he could make out faded red letters: "RU," and under that, "F." Ruby Falls? It could be, if Riley really was from somewhere in the South. But it could just as easily say "RUGBY FOOTBALL." Or "rubber fangs," "ruined feet," or a thousand other things. He put down the shard and crawled forward to the next heap of trash.

He sifted through the junk again, but the items he could identify were no better: The filthy, matted sleeve of a sweatshirt. Two broken plastic plates. A twisted metal fork. Rags, bottles, and rusted cans. Plenty of nothing.

But Delgado was a patient man, and he worked his way to the bottom of the pile. And finally, his patience was rewarded. Just underneath a mound of decomposing something mixed with shards of glass, a corner of something familiar stuck out, and Delgado felt his heart flutter. He carefully brushed away all the gunk on top and took the corner between gloved thumb and forefinger. It came free, and Delgado smiled.

A license plate.

It was old and battered and grimy, but it was intact. Since it had been on the bottom of the heap, the letters and numbers had not faded away completely. Delgado was amazed to note that his hands were trembling slightly as he tilted it to catch the light.

Green letters across the top spelled out "Georgia." A faded peach made the O, and in the upper right corner a green sticker read "96"—the year this plate had been valid.

Even better, at the bottom was the word "PICKENS." That would be the county of issue.

Delgado closed his eyes. For a moment he just breathed, listening to his heart race and then begin to slow down. He crouched there in a garbage heap under a moldering trailer, clutching a grubby old license plate and feeling something close to bliss. And then he opened his eyes, crawled back out from under the trailer, and walked down the road to his car.

He was still smiling as he drove away.

CHAPTER
13

Three weeks after the benefit dinner, Katrina was still thinking about Randall Miller. Not obsessively, not constantly, not even frequently. But every so often, he would cross her mind, just the image of his warm smile and lovely white teeth and the feel of his strong but gentle grip on her arm. Katrina was hardly a giddy young girl, and she told herself she was being stupid to spend any thought at all on somebody she would probably never see again.

But the thought was there in her mind as she waited for her decorator, Irene Caldwell, to arrive for the day's work. And that wait proved to be much longer than it should have been. Irene was scheduled to arrive at ten—but at 11:30 there was still no sign of her. She wasn't answering her phone, either. That was very unlike Irene, a responsible and hardworking woman who was always punctual. At first irritated, Katrina began to grow alarmed at the thought that something might have happened to Irene—and the redecoration not even half done! She was just considering what she could do to find out when her phone rang. Glancing at the screen, she saw with some surprise that it was Tyler Gladstone, her attorney.

"Hello, Tyler, what a surprise," she greeted him.

"And a slightly unpleasant surprise at that, I'm afraid," he said. "Do I remember correctly that you are currently employing Irene Caldwell?"

Katrina's stomach lurched. So something bad *had* happened. "Yes, I am," she said. "What happened? Is she all right?"

"As far as her health goes, she's fine," Tyler said.

"Tyler, please don't be mysterious. What on earth has happened to Irene?"

"At the moment, she's in police custody," he said.

"Police?! Good God," Katrina said.

"Yes, but she'll probably be turned over to the FBI in a few hours," he said. He chuckled. "I'm sorry, that's not exactly reassuring, is it?"

"But that's—that's preposterous, I can't believe it," Katrina said. "What could Irene possibly do that— Jesus Christ, Tyler, the FBI?! What did she do?"

"Actually, that's how I found out," he said. "The police called me because they want to talk to you."

"Me? Talk to *me*?! Tyler, for the love of God, what do I pay you for? Can't you take care of it?!"

"I'm afraid not. Apparently, a couple of the high-priced authentic masterpieces Ms. Caldwell has been selling are forgeries," he said. "The police would like to know if there are any more, and they know she's sold a few pictures to you."

"Holy shit," Katrina said, sinking into a chair.

"Since the call came from Elmore Fitch, the authorities take it quite seriously, and they would like to know what you might have to say on the subject."

"Holy shit," she said again.

"They may want a slightly more comprehensive statement, Katrina," Tyler said dryly.

Katrina didn't hear him. She was looking at the wall directly across from where she sat. Her brand-new Rauschenberg dominated the wall, delivered just days ago by Irene Caldwell. It represented a considerable investment—and if it was fake? She was badly shaken, not merely by the thought of the money but by the very idea. Fakes—from Irene Caldwell?

"How did he know?" she blurted out.

There was a short pause before Tyler said, "I'm sorry . . . ?"

"GodDAMN it, Tyler! Elmore Fitch couldn't tell a Van Dyck from a Vermeer! How did he know his painting was fake?"

"Oh, yes," Tyler said. "Apparently, he got an anonymous tip? He was told these particular fakes have a newspaper clipping hidden in the lower left corner. With a recent date?"

Katrina lurched to her feet, still clutching the phone convulsively, and stumbled over to her gorgeous new Rauschenberg. She was dimly aware that Tyler was talking, but she didn't hear a word of it. She bent down and stared at the lower left-hand corner of the painting. It took a moment, but she found it: a small strip from the *New York Times*.

With a date from just a few weeks ago.

Her Rauschenberg was a fake.

Just before she screamed, she realized Tyler was speaking again, and she forced herself to focus.

". . . told them you would speak to them at my office, and they agreed, but they would like it to be today. Apparently Mr. Fitch is twisting a few political arms? So can you drop by this afternoon? Say, three o'clock?"

Katrina looked at the painting again and felt a sudden shiver of anger. "Bitch," she hissed. If Irene Caldwell had cheated her, it was *totally* worth a trip into town to make sure she paid for it.

And then louder, to Tyler, she added, "Three o'clock. I'll be there."

Katrina went to the interview still angry, and glad of an opportunity to strike back at Irene for what she regarded as a true crime—forging great art. But two minutes into it, she realized that the two sour-faced cops had no idea what a Rauschenberg was. "Wasn't he that comic? On *Saturday Night Live* couple years back?" one of them said, straight-faced.

The other cop was looking at a rumpled piece of paper. "Jasper Johns. That mean anything to you?" he asked.

"Not personally," she said. "He's a great artist, though."

"Uh-huh," the cop said dubiously.

"You know Elmore Fitch?" the other one asked.

"Oh God," Katrina said, and she could not repress a shudder. "I've met him."

"Yeah, we have, too," the cop said, and his buddy shook his head.

"Is he implicated in some way?" Katrina asked.

"We thought maybe you could tell us," he said.

"My client has told you she barely knows Mr. Fitch," Tyler said.

"Yeah? I'm sorry. I didn't get that," the cop said.

"Can you tell us about the paintings Irene Caldwell sold you?" his partner said.

"Were they insured?" the first cop asked.

Katrina described the painting, but the cops kept interrupting, steering her into one narrow area. All they really seemed to care about was how much she'd paid, how much the painting was really worth, why she let Irene Caldwell rip her off, and if her insurance would cover the loss. This last area began to expand, until Katrina understood that the cops wanted to implicate her in the scheme somehow. When she realized that, Katrina looked at Tyler, whose frown had been growing over the last few minutes.

"This is going nowhere," she told him, and he nodded.

"That's all, gentlemen," Tyler told the cops.

The older one frowned. "We may have more questions later," he said.

"I doubt it," Tyler said crisply. "I'm fairly confident the FBI will take over—probably by this evening. But if not—please get in touch with me, and I'll arrange something again." He stood up. "And now if you'll excuse us?"

The cops looked at each other, but they got up, and after a significant glance or two, they left.

"I'm sorry about that, Katrina," Tyler said when the cops were gone. "If I'd known they would try to implicate you—"

"It's ridiculous!" Katrina fumed. "Goddamn it, I'm the *victim* here! And to try to connect me to that loathsome Elmore Fitch—"

"Yes," he said. "But you're both rich, and they're cops."

"Jesus Christ," Katrina said. "I hope that woman rots in jail 'til she dies."

"Probably not that long," Tyler said. "But she'll do some time."

It was small consolation for Katrina. She was still furious when she got home. She had trusted Irene, and she had loved that painting—and goddamn it, it was *fake*? She felt offended, abused, even violated. She was so angry that it wasn't until she sat down in her half-finished living room that she realized that on top of everything else, she needed to find a new decorator.

"Oh, shit," she said. "Shit, shit, *shit*." That seemed like the capping insult to the whole situation, that she would have to call around and get recommendations from friends, and each one of them would want all the details about how on earth oh-so-art-savvy Katrina had been tricked out of a few million bucks. And then it was 50-50 whether whoever her friends recommended would be any good at all—and the way things were going, she'd probably end up with a few more art forgeries anyway. They were popping up all over the place lately! She really didn't want to put herself through that. But how could she avoid it? Apparently, as much as she thought she knew about modern art, she could not spot a fake. So what she really needed was a decent decorator she could trust who knew modern art and *could* spot a fake.

With that thought, of course, Katrina also thought of somebody who fit the bill. And the fact that just thinking of him sent a little flutter rippling through her stomach had nothing to do with anything. She grabbed her purse and rummaged for the business card, pulling it out and setting it on the couch beside her while she dialed.

It rang four times, and then a crisp male voice said, "Randall Miller."

"Hello, Randall," Katrina said. "This is Katrina Hobson. From the awful banquet?"

"Of course! How are you today?"

Katrina thought he sounded glad to hear from her, which was nice. "A little pissed off right now, I'm afraid," she said.

"There's a lot of that going around right now," he said. "Damn it, no! Excuse me a second . . ."

Katrina heard Randall's phone clunk down onto a hard surface, and then his voice in the background berating someone—she couldn't quite make out why. A few moments later, he came back on the line.

"I'm sorry," he said. "It's this shipment of Mexican tile. And the workers are trying to—" He blew out a long breath. "Never mind, that's my problem. How are you—oh, I already said that, didn't I?"

Katrina laughed in spite of herself. "You did. But I think I can forgive you," she said. "Especially if you'll tell me you can come finish my redecoration."

"What? But what about, ah—was it Irene Caldwell?"

"That's right," Katrina said, and some of the anger came back to her. "Irene is going to be busy making license plates for a while."

"Making license— You mean she's been arrested? Good Lord, for what?"

Katrina filled him in, as much as she knew, and Randall seemed deeply shocked. "My God," he said. "Irene Caldwell, an art forger?"

"Apparently so," Katrina said. "Please, Randall, please tell me you can help me out with this. My whole house is upside down, there's nowhere to sit, and I—I could really use your help. Please?"

He hesitated before answering, and Katrina realized the palms of her hands were sweating. "I . . . would love to," Randall said at last. "But this project I'm working on now is— Damn it, the other phone line is ringing. Could you hold for just a minute?"

"Of course," Katrina said. She waited, chewing on her lower lip, wiping her hands on the couch, listening to the rapid thump of her heartbeat, and wondering why this redecoration suddenly meant so much to her, and only admitting to herself that it might not be all about the redo seconds before Randall came back on the line.

"Katrina?" Randall said. "I am truly sorry, but I have to go over to Jersey City—there's some kind of problem with the paint, it doesn't match the swatches, and I have to go out and threaten the dealer with bodily harm."

"I'm sorry," she said. And then, biting her lip as she plowed straight into the kind of self-centered focus she despised in others, she said, "But is it— Please, Randall, can you finish my house?"

There was a brief silence on the other end, and then she heard him blow out a long breath. "I don't see how, not for several months. I'm sorry, Katrina—I really do wish I could help."

"Oh," she said, feeling a huge weight of disappointment that was out of proportion with merely losing a decorator. "I'm sorry, too, Randall." She heard herself sigh, and then, forcing cheerfulness she didn't feel, she said, "I really hope your project goes well, Randall. And kick that paint dealer right in the swatches."

Randall laughed. "Thanks, I will. I'm sorry, too, Katrina."

After they'd both hung up, Katrina sat, chewing on her lip and thinking nothing more constructive than *damn. Damn, damn, damn . . .* Where would she find somebody now? Somebody she could trust, with taste that agreed with hers? There was no one, not on such short notice. *Damn . . .*

Katrina got up and circled around the room, glaring angrily at the draped furniture and empty walls, and repeating her litany of *damn* as she wandered through the other rooms of the huge house. Most of them were worse than the living room, stripped of furniture, walls spattered with primer. *Damn!*

She had just switched back to *shit* when her phone rang. "What!" she snapped angrily.

"Oh, dear, did I catch you at a bad time?" After a moment of disorientation, she recognized the voice—it was Randall. But calling back so soon?

"Randall! I thought you were off to Jersey City."

He gave a two-syllable laugh. "I was," he said, and Katrina thought he sounded rather happy all of a sudden. "But tell me—do you believe in kismet?"

"I'm not even sure what it means," she said.

"It means that I just hung up on the person who hired me for this massive project. And apparently their business just went belly-up, and although they said I can keep the Mexican tile, they can no longer pay me."

"Oh, that's wonderful!" Katrina said.

"Well, I'm not sure they'd agree with you," Randall said. "But what the heck, I do. I really like the tile."

Katrina laughed. "You know that's not what I meant. Can you do the job for me?"

"Text me your address," he said. "I'll be there in the morning."

CHAPTER
14

The clock beside the bed said it was 3:18. It was a cheap hotel room clock, so it didn't say "A.M.," but it was: 3:18 in the morning. I had been lying there with my hands behind my head for four and a half hours. I hadn't slept. I couldn't. I just lay there and went over everything in my head. And every five or six minutes, the memories would come back at me.

It happens sometimes. I am definitely not nervous, sensitive, high-strung—none of that shit. I mean, try disarming a high-tech alarm if your hands are shaking from nerves. That's not me. And I don't get all into feeling worried, like, *Oh no, what if something goes wrong?* That's just not me, either. But sometimes the past comes back at me. Right before I get into something, right when I really need a good night's sleep, I can't do it. I remember instead. Maybe that's worse than nervous.

This was one of those times.

I was all the way back in time to the old quarry again. Just couldn't put it out of my head. And I wasn't remembering the good part, the way I'd felt when I climbed all the way back up with that taillight in my hand, and I stood there looking down at where I had been and felt like some kind of god instead of a ragged-ass kid. No, I couldn't get that. When the memories hit me, I never got the good ones.

Instead, I get this part. The one that changed everything. The first time I got the Darkness. And it comes back at me completely clear and fresh, like it had happened this morning.

Bobby Reed was a brickhead. The only way he managed to pass sixth grade was by copying from other kids. He could always get away with that because he was the biggest kid in the class. And his family was a big deal in town. They had money, and Bobby's dad was a judge. So he got away with being stupid. And a lot of other stuff. Like being a bully.

We were standing at the old quarry again, the one everybody's parents told them to stay away from. I guess that's why we went there. It was the same one that I had climbed into, grabbing the taillight and climbing out again. And Bobby was pushing at me. Maybe because being here, looking down into the quarry, and seeing one missing taillight on the old Studebaker—maybe that reminded Bobby that I had done something he could never do. Maybe that made him feel small and worthless. Like he really was.

I don't know. Whatever the reason, he was in my face and on my case. Bobby had pushed at me from day one. He always found something to pick on. Today it was my mother. "I bet she never married your daddy," he said. The other boys, the ones who hung with him because they were afraid of him, all snickered. "I bet she don't even know who your daddy was."

"Be fair, Bobby, coulda been a lot of guys," his brother Clayton said. And all the other boys laughed.

"Isn't that so?" Bobby said, poking me in the chest. "Don't know your daddy, do you?" Poke, poke poke.

Before my climb, before I knew I wasn't a sheep like them, I would've taken it. Maybe made some joke, tried to change the subject. But the new me poked back.

"And maybe you don't know *your* daddy, either, Bobby," I said, poking at him, the same spot he poked me. "'Cause you sure don't look like that old guy your mama's with." Poke. "Truth is, Bobby, you look a lot like Mr. Swanson, the mailman."

Bobby turned bright red. "You take that back," he said.

"Why would I take it back? It's true!" I said. "You got the same nose!"

Bobby turned even redder. I liked that I'd gotten to him. So I kept going. "Don't get mad, Bobby, maybe you can be a mailman when you grow up. Just like your real daddy."

Bobby didn't say anything. He probably couldn't think of anything. Instead, he swung at me. It would've taken my head off if it had connected. But I expected it. I ducked under. As the force of his punch took Bobby around, I stuck my leg out and thumped him with my shoulder.

All I meant to do was bump him. Maybe knock him down. I guess I figured that if he went down, I could get away before he got up.

That didn't happen.

The bump worked perfectly. And Bobby tripped over my leg just right. But he didn't fall to the ground. Because we were standing on the lip of the old quarry. So Bobby went over the edge.

I was right there, right on the edge when he went. I saw the look on his face when he realized what was happening to him. And I stood there watching as he fell. I couldn't do anything but stand there. And I didn't try. Not because I knew it was useless. More like I wasn't really involved, like it was happening to somebody else and I wasn't really there. Like I was inside a dark cloud watching something on TV. That was it, the first time the Darkness came. And from inside it I watched. Bobby fell, his body turning slowly in a circle, spinning in the air, and falling. Falling. Seemed like forever, like he was never going to stop falling. But it wasn't forever. I kind of wish it could be, because I can see he's about to hit the rocks. And just before he does, it's like our eyes meet—I mean, it's impossible. He's too far away, and moving too fast, and there's just no fucking way. But it feels like that anyway, like our eyes meet, and his expression says, "It's your fault."

And then he hits the rocks.

They say that people remember what they see better than what they hear. Maybe that's true. But I will never be able to forget the sound of Bobby Reed hitting the rocks at the bottom of the old quarry. Like somebody dropped a bowling ball into a huge pot of pudding. Kind of a heavy *SPLAT*. It echoes off the walls, comes up at me in waves, and that sound will stay in my head forever. *SPLAT*. And there's no way in the world you can think he's okay. Not after that sound. Bobby is dead.

I don't really feel bad about it. First, because I was inside that dark cloud for the first time, so it felt like it really wasn't me it was happening to. And anyway, it wasn't really my fault. Bobby pretty much did it to himself. And he was a truly stupid kid, a bully, and thought he was king shit because his family had money. The world was better off without him, like it is without all the overprivileged assholes I've run into since. Him dying like that didn't bother me. But the sound when he hit? That's stuck in my head and it's never going away.

SPLAT.

A nd now it's 3:32 and I'm still awake.

And just like every other time that memory comes back at me, I sit up in bed in a room I don't recognize. I'm in a midtown hotel, being somebody I have to be. Because I am on another job. A truly epic lift this time. Maybe the best and the greatest ever, and I should be excited about doing it. I should be high on adrenaline, giddy with the thought that Riley Wolfe is about to do something nobody else in the world could hope to do. And I am going to do it in the Riley Wolfe way, a way nobody else could ever even imagine. Doing it, even thinking about it, has been filling me with excitement for the last few weeks, and it should be filling me now.

It's not.

All I can think about is that goddamn sound.

SPLAT.

I get out of bed and walk into the bathroom. I see my face in the mirror—except, of course, it's not my face. I stare at it. For a minute I can't remember my real face. It doesn't help that I'm wearing some-body else's right now. Especially somebody who doesn't even really exist. So I stare into the mirror. I try to see *Me* in there somewhere. I can't see it. I can't remember it. I'm somebody else, and for a long min-ute it feels to me like I was always somebody else and I don't know who *Me* is and maybe I never really existed at all except as a whole series of Somebody Else's Faces.

It's that stupid fucking memory.

It knocks me on the head every time.

I pull my eyes away from the mirror, splash water on my face—on *his* face. Because it still isn't *Me*.

I straighten up from the sink and look in the mirror again. But this time I pull away and leave the bathroom. Dangerous things, mirrors. You have to watch out for them. If you're not careful, you can get stuck in there. They hypnotize you, pull you in, take you away to a place where nothing is real, especially you. It's hard to pull out again.

But I manage. I sit on the edge of the bed and think for a while. The clock said it was 3:35. In a few hours, things would start happening and I needed to be alert, ready for anything. But I was pretty sure I still couldn't go to sleep.

I looked out the window. New York wasn't asleep, either. It never sleeps. Just like the song says. Isn't it nice when something lives up to its reputation?

I thought about going out, maybe heading across town on an aimless parkour jag. That usually cleared my head, washed out whatever ailed me. But this time? It felt too much like running from something.

So I sat on the edge of the bed. Just sat.

After a while I stretched out with my hands behind my head. I lay there and thought about what I had to do in the morning. I lay like that for a long time, just thinking about doing it, telling myself I'd be fine, I could do it, nothing to worry about. I kept telling myself all that, over and over, until I saw morning light out the window.

Then I got up and went out to do it.

CHAPTER

15

P lease don't be impressed," Katrina told Randall as she led him up
the rose-lined path and into the house. "Really, it's just a house."

"No, a house is someplace where people *live*," Randall said,
looking up at the glass-and-metal facade.

"Well, for goodness' sake," she said. "I mean, I live here."

"Mm, no," he said. "This is a castle. A place like this, I think you
have to *dwell*."

Katrina opened her mouth to protest that really, she wasn't a
princess—but just in time, she caught the expression on his face. It
was the look of a man trying very hard to look serious while delivering
the punch line to a joke he wasn't sure his audience would get. "In that
case," she said somewhat primly, playing along, "I shall have to demand that you enter on your knees."

"Ouch," Randall said. "Very well, Your Grace."

And as if they were wired to the same switch, they snorted with
amusement in unison.

That was when Katrina knew they would get along very well. And over the next few hours nothing changed her mind about that. She took Randall through the whole cavernous house, and he took it all in, making notes on a small tablet, which he also used to take photos. And all along the way, they made small jokes together, discovering that they shared a slightly off-kilter, very whimsical sense of humor.

Katrina found that Randall was everything she had hoped when she first met him. Although he was thoroughly professional and very knowledgeable, he was also warm, human—and yes, damn it, he was *charming*. In the few hours they spent walking through the house and making preliminary plans, Katrina realized she had smiled more than she had in the previous six months.

And at the end of the day, Katrina watched him walk away down the path, thinking, *I really like this guy.* But a small nagging voice in the back of her head told her it had noticed the way she watched Randall climb into his car, her gaze lingering on his butt, and the little voice whispered, *Just be careful you don't like him a little too much.*

Throughout the next few weeks, the feeling grew. Katrina told herself it was just a friendship, two souls who had a lot in common and liked each other. But when Michael came home on one of his rare visits between business trips, she couldn't help comparing him with Randall. Her husband did not do well by comparison. Randall was so much more . . . well, *nice*. Pleasant. Fun to be with, charming, funny, attentive. And if she was honest with herself, he was a great deal more attractive, too.

Not that she would ever actually *do* anything about that. Even though she thought he might be having the same kind of feelings about her. She wasn't an adolescent. She was full-grown and totally married, and as her grandfather had often said, she had made her bed and could bloody well lie down in it.

But every now and then, she would look at Randall and feel that small warm feeling in the pit of her stomach that seemed like something more than friendship. And even though she pushed it away, it always seemed to come back.

Nothing will ever happen with him, she told herself. *It's wrong, it's adultery, and it just won't happen.*

But that didn't stop her from thinking about it.

Michael Hobson was the problem.

The obstacle. The stumbling block, the hurdle, the hitch, the hindrance. The bastard was in the way.

Was "bastard" just my opinion? Because he was in my way?

Maybe. Everybody else said Michael Hobson was a good man. He gave a lot of money to charities—especially kid's charities. Make-A-Wish, Children's Defense Fund, March of Dimes, St. Jude's Children's Hospital—they all had Michael on speed dial. It didn't stop there; he gave his time, too. He worked with the courts as an advocate for children in trouble with the law. He always said kids were important, that helping them was just something he had to do.

But Michael's epic goodness didn't stop there, with helping kids. He was way too Good for that. Just to round things out, he did a lot of pro bono work for the Innocence Project, too. So anybody who looked at his record would totally have to say he did everything a truly good man could do, and a lot more. A freaking saint. And all that free work meant lost billing hours, too. At the rate Michael charged, that was a lot of money lost.

Not that money is important, right? I mean, not when you're doing something you love, helping kids. And anyway, Michael could afford it. Because as one of the top corporate attorneys in New York City, he made at least eight digits every year. And there was more—a lot more. In one of his early cases he'd defended the head of a big hedge fund.

The guy was a true scumbag, and he got caught fair and square. But Michael Hobson went in against big odds and a federal prosecutor who wanted to run for governor, and somehow Michael won the case. Scumbag or not, the CEO was grateful enough to let Michael in on some very lucrative deals. Over the years that had grown, like only a shady hedge fund can grow, to a total that might make a Saudi prince blink.

So in spite of the pro bono charity work, Michael still had plenty of money, and he wasn't bashful about spending it. There's an old saying that Beverly Hills showed what God would do if he had money. Michael could have shown God a few tricks. He built an enormous modern house on the shore in Connecticut, on thirty acres of wooded land that sloped down to the water and looked straight across at Long Island. Lots of glass and steel and angles, and twenty-four thousand square feet of space inside. A rose-lined walkway led down to the water, where just to one side, so it wouldn't interfere with the view, a beautiful fifty-foot Marquis sport yacht bobbed at the dock.

There was a barn and paddock for the horses, a large attached garage with room for eight cars, and a huge infinity pool, complete with a hot tub and a cabana that was bigger and better furnished than most middle-class houses.

Inside, the main house was totally smart-wired to a computer so you could make it do anything just by calling out the password and a command. It would even bake you a quiche and then wash your dishes, as long as you stuck them in the dishwasher. So Michael didn't really need a domestic staff hanging around and getting all up in his privacy. Michael liked privacy. You might say he needed it.

And the house had a high-tech, temperature-controlled wine cellar, a gigantic kitchen that any gourmet chef would envy, and a full gym. There was also a room you could call a "home theater" only because it was in a home. Aside from that, it was more luxurious and better equipped than any movie mogul's screening room. It held both the most modern electronic equipment and a row of old-fashioned projectors, since there was a large library of classic 16- and 35-millimeter movies in an adjacent temperature-controlled vault.

Like I said. Totally awesome house. Furnished by an incredibly rich person who didn't mind spending it. And Michael had shown true good taste by installing a wife in the house who was a genuine trophy, the real deal. She wasn't a bimbo with implants who'd been a stripper until she got chosen runner-up in the 2015 Miss Mango pageant. Instead, Michael had married the daughter of one of America's great old-money families. Michael's wife was a woman of good breeding, exquisite taste—and an enormous trust fund of her own.

So when you looked him over, Michael Hobson was a guy who had it all. You couldn't even hate him for it because he gave so much back, to kids and so on. He really looked like some kind of modern urban legend, and he really seemed to be what everybody said he was—a truly good man. The kind of guy who made having money look Good. A living saint.

I killed him anyway.

Some guys like to kill. I'm not one of them. I mean, if it has to happen, if you have to go or the job flops, okay, I'm sorry, better luck next life. But I don't really like it. And I know it should bother me. It doesn't. Right before, it's like I stop being me. The Darkness comes over me, like mental armor. I go into it, and it's not me doing stuff. It's like I'm watching a movie in a small dark theater. Not that it's ever fun. I usually try to find some other way first.

I didn't try too hard this time. Not with Michael Hobson. There wasn't any other way. More important than that, the miserable shit deserved to die. And I didn't mind making that happen.

He made it pretty easy. Not just because he had it coming. But it was the middle of the night, and he had just flown in from Abu

Dhabi—some kind of conference. And when he came home, he didn't go upstairs to see his wife. No "Hi, honey, I'm home," not for Michael Hobson. He went right to his soundproofed office, like he always did. And then he sat down and went to work.

He had to be tired. So tired he sat with his back to the door and counted on the security system. I would have to say that's almost always a mistake. It sure was for Michael. He turned on the system and thought that was the end of it.

For him, it was.

He was sitting at his desk, staring at his computer screen. He was concentrating hard, and he was dead tired, and he wouldn't have heard me if I'd come in with a brass band. Like I said, a little too easy, and that always makes me nervous. So I stopped for a few seconds, right in the doorway, and I looked around.

The security system was a good one. I mean, it wasn't so good I couldn't hack it. I did. It was high-tech but pretty standard equipment— surprising how much useless crap they sell to people who could afford something better. Anyway, there were no surprises, and I was sure I'd disabled all the sensors, cameras, the whole system. But I took time to look around the office anyway, just to be sure.

Michael had done one hell of a job on his man cave. It was a beautiful room, decorated in a very definite taste—classical masculine leather and dark wood—and absolutely no care about what it cost. Two walls were set with floor-to-ceiling mahogany bookshelves full of law books and other reference volumes. One wall was all glass and looked down a sloping wooded lawn to Long Island Sound. On the wall opposite the window, there was a painting I knew right away. It was one of Edouard-Henri Avril's erotic pictures. Some of them can bring a pretty good price. This one showed an older man with a much younger one. It looked like the original. But I didn't see any sign of overlooked security measures or anything else that might give me trouble. I eased the door shut behind me and took a breath. And then—

The Darkness came. I stepped into it.

I watched my feet move quietly across the room. I got closer . . . And Michael Hobson just kept staring at his computer screen like his life depended on it. It didn't. But it sure helped me end it.

He had no idea I was there. He yawned and stretched once, and I froze. But then he went right back to his computer screen. I saw myself slip across the floor to a spot behind him, and he still didn't notice a thing. But he sure as hell noticed it when my gloved hand clamped over his mouth. He noticed even more when I jammed the razor-sharp blade into his neck. In fact, he noticed that for a full fifteen seconds, as the blade went in and out several more times.

That wasn't really necessary. My first stab had been perfect. It slid in just right and severed his spinal cord. The stabs after that were just for show. Michael tried to struggle, wriggle away from the pain and the gloved hand. He tried—but for some reason his limbs didn't listen to him. Maybe the cut spinal cord.

So he just sat there, trying to move, trying to moan, not making any progress with either one. He just sat until his sight went dim and his body started to relax. And then Michael Hobson stopped struggling and just let go, sliding down the long dark slope into nothing at all.

I was sure he was dead. That first stab had been placed perfectly. But I waited anyway. Not for any creepy ghoulish reason. I've watched the terrible and beautiful trip down the Dark Hall into death before. I don't get off on it. But I watched and waited a full minute anyway, just to be sure. And after a minute, I was. Michael Hobson was dead.

And just like that, the Darkness blew away. I blinked. I looked at the dead body, but it didn't matter. It was just an empty suit, and I had real work to do.

I had a picture to paint. *Still Life with Dead Asshat*. And I had to get every brushstroke just exactly right. I started with the lifeless body. When I let it go, Michael's head flopped forward and thumped onto the computer's keyboard. I took one step back, looked him over. Something was a little off; it looked like I had dropped him. I mean, I had—but I didn't want it to look like that. I readjusted one arm so it looked like he had raised the arm to defend himself and then dropped it when he died. Much better picture. Next, I took a small Ziploc bag from my jacket pocket. Inside was a short piece of what looked like ordinary Scotch tape. It wasn't. It was a specialty item, well-known to forensics geeks, designed to lift fingerprints. I took the tape out of the bag carefully. Then laid it onto the handle of the blade sticking out of Michael Hobson's back. Gently, steadily, I rubbed the back of the tape. Then, just as carefully, I peeled up the tape and took a look.

A clear set of fingerprints in a light brown powder now stood out on the handle of the blade. Right where they should be. I put the tape back in the bag and the bag back in my pocket.

From a different pocket, I took out a second plastic bag. I opened it and took out a few thin fibers, too small and light to be wire—hairs. Human hairs, belonging to somebody very specific. I put one beside the knife's handle, one on the floor beside the desk, and a couple more on the dead guy's hand and shirtfront.

I stepped back again and looked; so far, it was perfect. Now for the kill shot.

I pulled out a file drawer from the left side of the desk. Taped to the back of the drawer was a flash drive. I held it up and looked to be sure. Yup. This was the Money. In block letters, the flash drive was labeled "TRUE MENTOR." This was something Michael hid, in a place where nobody would find it but where he could get at it quick and easy when he wanted a peek. Which he did a lot. This was the *real* Michael Hobson.

"Bastard," I said softly. Just holding it in my hand made me want to kill him all over again. But there was still work to do. So before I could puke and ruin the picture, I pushed the flash drive into a USB port on Michael's computer. Using the keyboard was a little awkward. I had to work around the lifeless head lying there. But I managed. In a few seconds, images came up on the screen. I didn't want to look, but I had to be sure.

They were the right pictures, all right. "Fucking bastard," I whispered again. Couldn't help it. And anyway, Michael Hobson wasn't going to hear me. I turned away from the pictures. If I looked any longer, I really would puke. I didn't want to see them, even by accident. But Michael Hobson did. Or he had.

Almost done. I stepped back and looked the scene over. It was close to perfect—but "close" is never enough. It needed one more dramatic touch. My eyes fell on Michael's briefcase. Yup, that was it. I knocked it onto the floor and scattered a few pages from inside it onto the carpet. Now the scene told it all: dramatic struggle ending in tragic death. The body sprawled across the desk, obviously murdered. A very small drip of blood had made a stain on the carpet—a true fucking tragedy, because it was beautiful Persian, probably seventeenth-century and therefore worth a great deal of money. Unfortunately the bloodstain would lower the price. A shame, but unavoidable—and worth it in any case.

One last thing: From the desk beside the dead asshole, I picked up his cell phone. I took out a small electronic box I'd bought from a guy in Atlanta. A truly handy tool—everybody should have one. I plugged it into the phone and waited. In just a few seconds the phone's security code ticked into place. I unplugged the little device and started typing a quick text message. I read it through twice to be sure it sounded right.

Then I hit SEND, replaced the phone, and stepped back to look over my work.

It looked right. More than that, it made me smile. I couldn't help it.

Like I said, I don't love killing, and I don't get off on dead bodies. No, it was the picture that made me smile. Why not? I bet Leonardo smiled when he looked at the finished *Mona Lisa*.

My picture, in its own way, was just as good. I'd stabbed Michael with his own letter opener. Like most of his stuff, it was a rare and valuable antique. Turkish, sixteenth-century. The blade was filigreed silver, which was lovely to see, and razor sharp. But the real joy of the piece was the handle. It was ivory, and it was carved to look like a large penis.

And now, stuck into Michael's back with my last hearty stab, that handle stuck straight up in the air. It looked exactly like Michael's spine had somehow sprouted an erection.

I kept the smile for a minute. It wasn't just funny by itself. Considering what was on that thumb drive, it was very close to poetic justice. The miserable shit got just what he deserved.

I looked around a last time, checking for any small item out of place, anything that might contradict the story I wanted to tell, anything I might have dropped. There was nothing, not even a scuff mark from my feet.

Good. The scene was perfect. It said exactly what I wanted it to say. I turned away and left as quietly as I'd entered, pausing in the hall just long enough to turn the security system back on.

CHAPTER
16

Katrina woke slowly, from a sleep deeper and more deadening than she could ever remember having before. Light showed around the edges of the heavy drapes; it was morning. Katrina closed her eyes again, just for a moment. Her brain felt like it was wrapped in cotton, and her whole body was in a state of the most delicious numbness. She thought she could just lie there with her eyes closed forever. She felt good all over—and of course, that made her feel guilty. She was *committing adultery.* The phrase echoed down at her from her childhood, part of her family's strict moral tradition, and a very strong and deeply rooted voice told Katrina that adultery was bad. And so it really shouldn't feel good.

But it did; it really, really did. It made her feel young again—young and, astonishingly, *innocent.* That made no sense at all to Katrina, but she couldn't argue with it. She felt rejuvenated—emotionally, spiritually, and, of course, physically. Not just because the sex was great—and it was—but something more, something that would have filled her with elation even with mediocre sex. It had to be the relationship itself. It seemed *right* somehow, as if this man was the one she should have been with all along, and not stuck in the cold and empty marriage with her husband, Michael.

Michael, who never had time for her; Michael, who was always away on business; Michael, who had made love to her perhaps four times in the last six months—each time hurriedly and distantly, as if he were dutifully performing some chore.

No, this was very, very different. This was fun, fulfilling, and if it was adultery, well, so be it. Because it was also the best anybody had made her feel in a long time. She stretched slowly, reveling in the sensation of feeling good all over, inside and out.

Beside her, Randall mumbled something in his sleep and then she felt him twitch, take a deep breath, and turn over, and in a few seconds his breathing steadied into the deep and regular pattern of someone still deep asleep. Katrina couldn't help herself; she opened her eyes and rolled over onto one elbow to look at him. The sight of him made her smile. The affair was still new, still delightfully fresh—and, well, *wrong*. And she still got a little thrill out of seeing him stretched out beside her, his lean, hard body relaxed in slumber, his beard tousled from their lovemaking, and his lovely sensitive face looking so much younger and more innocent as he slept.

Katrina sat up. She remembered most of the previous evening. It had seemed like they couldn't keep their hands off each other, and they'd stopped fighting off the urgent need and gone to bed early— very early. But she'd had a little more to drink than usual. A lot more, actually; two cocktails at dinner, and then most of the bottle of wine they'd brought upstairs with them—an excellent Château Margaux— because Randall only sipped at his and kept saying it was a shame to waste it as he refilled her glass. The bottle and the glasses were gone now, and she smiled again. It was so very like him to get out of bed and tidy things up. She was absolutely certain that when she went downstairs she would find the two wineglasses washed and put away, and the bottle tucked neatly into the recycle bin. That was Randall: neat, thoughtful, and absolutely delightful.

But he'd left the half-empty dish of cocoa-powdered almonds on the bedside table. He'd been very funny about the almonds, insisting she try them. She thought they were a very odd choice, especially with red wine. But he told her that she had supplied the wine, so it was only fair that she let him provide the accompanying snack, and in any case he said chocolate went extremely well with red wine, and he'd practically forced her hand into the bowl. And he'd been right, oddly enough. Chocolate *did* go with red wine, even the Margaux.

Katrina shook her head, marveling at how quickly this new relationship had become important. Because suddenly it seemed like one of the most significant things in her life, and that was impossible, foolish, dangerous—because she was committing adultery.

With her decorator, for God's sake. A man she hardly knew. Granted, he was a very good-looking man, and his taste was exquisite. And she *felt* like she knew him—they laughed at the same things, and often. And he was so good at what he did; somehow, he managed to locate some absolutely amazing pieces, and at reasonable prices. But not even the gorgeous new furniture and artwork could possibly explain or excuse sleeping with the man. She was *married*, and she'd never before even thought of cheating on Michael. She was well aware that many in her social circle had affairs—perhaps even most of them. But she did not, nor did anyone in her family. It was just unthinkable for an Eberhardt, part of the Victorian code of behavior instilled in all Eberhardts as they grew up. But here she was, sunk into the quicksand of infidelity and, worse, absolutely *loving* it. And although the details of how it had started were a little fuzzy, she was quite sure Randall Miller had not forced himself on her.

Since the night she met him, Katrina had found Randall attractive. Physically he was lean and very fit, and his shaved head and neat beard gave him a dashing look. But more than that, he had a sense of humor that matched her own perfectly. He made her laugh, and that is far more important to a woman than any bulging biceps. Lord knows Michael didn't give her many laughs—or anything else, except an open checkbook. And since Katrina had inherited a great deal of money of her own, that was one thing she did not need from her husband. What she needed was a little attention, some affection, a few smiles—and yes, damn it! A little bit of sex now and then! Katrina was a young and healthy woman, with normal healthy appetites, and Michael was not feeding them.

And Randall was.

Katrina didn't really remember how it had started. Michael was away on business, of course. Katrina and Randall had been sitting together on the old couch in the main living room, comparing pictures of designer furniture for the room. She had her heart set on Perry, which Randall thought was too stodgy. He was pushing a three-piece Vetrina sofa. They'd been sitting there arguing happily, heads together over the photos, and then suddenly . . .

It was Randall who pushed away from her. "Katrina," he'd said, his voice shaking. "We can't—this is wrong. It's, it's— You're married."

"Married in name only," she said bitterly. And then she had to stifle a giggle because she couldn't believe she had really said that. What hackneyed old movie had that line come from? "I'm sorry," she said. "I know it's wrong, Randall. I just . . ." She shrugged. "I've been married to Michael for five years, and—I mean, he's never home. Even when he is, it's . . . What. Maybe once a year we have sex." She felt herself blushing, but she went on anyway. "I need more than that, Randall."

"I won't be your sex toy, Katrina," he said

"I didn't mean that, Randall, really," she said. She took his hand. "I really like you, you know that. We have fun together, we like the same things, we laugh at the same things. And if there's sex, too—is that so bad?"

Randall sighed and turned away from her, looking deeply troubled. "I just—I mean, the way it looks is so"—he shook his head—"'gold-digging designer preys on heiress,' you know?" He looked up, and there was a little anger in his eyes. "I don't want to be anybody's pet, Katrina."

"I don't want a pet, Randall," she said, taking his hand. "I want a friend."

"A friend with benefits?" he said.

She saw a smile twitching at the corners of his mouth and felt an answering one growing on her own lips. "Why not?" she said.

"It's just—I mean, it's still just wrong," he said. "You're *married*." He looked down, then up at her again. "And you know, there is the money thing, which is a very big—I mean, it's just impossible to ignore."

"How about if I promise not to give you any money?" she said.

His lips twitched again. "Wow," he said. "You would do that for me?" And he looked at her, a long, straight-faced look, and then suddenly they were both laughing, and somehow that led to more kissing, and then—

And then here she was, a month later, lying in bed with him, naked, and feeling absolutely wonderful about the whole thing. Randall was everything she hadn't known she wanted and more—a fantastic lover, sure, but so sweet and thoughtful, too, in so many ways, like with washing the wineglasses. Of course, he remained very prickly about the money issue. He refused to allow her to spend anything on him, not even for little things. And to her surprise, she kind of wanted to buy him things. Nothing ostentatious or ridiculous. Just impulse buys, like a ring, or a nice Italian sports coat. Just something to say she cared.

But Randall refused everything. He said it was insulting and silly to spend it on him. She told him that was the point, but he was very stubborn about it. He really didn't understand that her kind of money was *supposed* to be spent on silly, impulsive things—and she wanted to spend it on him. And seriously, she could buy him a Ferrari in every primary color, and it wouldn't put a noticeable dent in her bank account.

Still, if that was Randall's only fault, it was one she could live with. Other than that, he was as close to perfect as a man could be. He didn't even snore. Not very much, anyway.

Katrina stretched once more, enjoying the glow, and the movement must have been enough to wake Randall. "What time is it?" he croaked in a voice that was still more than half asleep.

"I don't know," she said, flopping over to rest her head on his chest. "You threw away my old clock—"

"It was *hideous*," Randall muttered.

"And you made me turn off my phone so we wouldn't be disturbed."

"I *hate* phones," he grumbled. "And you need to pick a *decent* clock for this room."

"I don't like digital," she said, running a hand over his chest. "And I like that Waterford."

"Nineteenth-century crap," he said. "Won't go at all with the rest of the room."

Katrina chortled, a low throaty laugh she hadn't heard from herself in years. "Now you sound like such a designer."

Randall grunted. "I am," he said. Without getting up or dislodging her, he reached over to the bedside table and fumbled for her phone. A moment later he handed it to her. "Here," he said. "Clock. Phone. GPS, weather station, music player, web surfer—"

"And a whole lot more. So why do you hate them?"

"I need foibles," he said. "A real artist has to have foibles."

This time Katrina giggled. "You make 'foible' sound like a sex act." And putting on her deepest voice, she leered at him and said, "Come here, little girl, I'm going to foible you."

"To you everything is a sex act. So what time is it?"

Katrina turned on her phone, and in a moment her wallpaper blinked into life—a Hans Hofmann painting, in memory of the one she didn't get. The time was plastered across the picture in big white numerals. "It's 7:17," she said.

"A.M. or P.M.?" Randall asked. He put a hand on her back and rubbed gently. "I guess I should go soon."

"Well, I don't see—oh, shit!" Katrina stared at her phone in horror as it began to ding and display calls and texts she had missed while it was turned off. And the second one—"Oh my fucking God," she moaned. She lurched upright in bed.

"What is it?" Randall asked anxiously.

"Oh God. Oh God," she repeated numbly, and handed the phone to Randall.

The first message on the screen read, "*Michael. Missed call. 3:49.*" But the second . . . "Holy shit," Randall said, handing the phone back.

Katrina took the phone and, hoping she'd made some kind of weird mistake, looked at the screen again. And there was the text message, exactly the same as the first time she'd read it.

Hey Kat—home around 5. C U 4 brkfst—Michael

And just to give her terror one more little boost, the clock ticked over: It was now 7:19. "Randall, he could come in here any second! Ohmygod, he's home already!"

For half a second, Randall stared at her without moving, his mouth hanging open. And then he leapt out of bed and lunged for his clothing, and a moment later Katrina did the same. He was completely dressed in an amazingly short time, while Katrina was still fumbling with her blouse. Of course, women's clothing tends to be more complicated, but even so, Randall was quick as he pulled on his shoes and jumped to his feet. "I better go," he said. "I can only—" He hesitated and gave her a strange look—part pleading, part scared. "Katrina," he said. "What if he . . . hurts you?"

"I'll fucking kill him!" she said.

"But he could—I mean, maybe I should stay and—"

"Go," she said, tugging the blouse over her head. "I'll take care of Michael, if he dares to— Go, Randall. I'll call you later. If there is a later." Her head popped out the top of the blouse in time to see him nod, spin away, and hurry out the door.

She heard his rapid footsteps on the stairs as she pulled on her socks. One of them snagged on her toenail, and she yanked, ripping both the nail and the sock, and she flung it away, snarling. In spite of her brave words about "taking care of" her husband, she was close to panic. She didn't fear any physical violence, not from Michael. But all her guilt about adultery came at her, nearly overwhelming her. What would her family say? Her older brother, Erik, had very old-fashioned ideas about marriage and the family name. She tried to calm down, reminding herself that Michael usually went right into his home office when he got home. The office was soundproofed, and with the door closed her husband wouldn't know if a bomb went off in the hall. *So relax, Katrina,* she told herself. *So far, so good . . .*

And then—

Voices.

One of them Michael's.

"Oh God, oh no . . ." Katrina froze, straining to hear what was being said. Randall spoke, hesitatingly, and Michael answered. By the overtones in their voices she could tell they were in the large high-ceilinged hallway near Michael's home office, but she could not make out the words. Randall spoke again, defensive now, and then Michael cut in, yelling, "Get out! Out! Get out!" A moment later the front door slammed. The alarm system beeped to announce that it had been turned back on and armed—that had to be Michael, locking up. Only Katrina and her husband knew the code.

And then, silence.

Katrina sat, unmoving, until she tasted blood. She'd bitten through her lower lip. She unclenched her jaw and sat there, waiting, half expecting Michael to come thundering into the room to confront her. And what would she say? Yes, she was guilty. She had slept with Randall—and *liked* it! It was incomparably better than anything Michael had ever done, and she would do it again!

Katrina bit her lip again, felt more pain. That was probably not the smartest thing to say. She needed to keep her cool, whatever Michael might say. But that was much harder than it sounded, mostly because she had no idea what he would say. She was not even sure he really loved her, not from the way he'd behaved ever since they got married. So he might not even show anger. Would he be cold and distant? But he was *always* cold and distant! That's why she had wanted—had *needed*—what Randall gave her. So not coldness, not anger—then what?

The longer she waited, the more her uncertainty grew, until it occurred to her that *this* was Michael's response. He would ignore her. Wait for her to make the first move, make her come crawling to him, trembling and ashamed. It was an extra piece of humiliation, to force her to come to him, humbly and penitently, and beg him for forgiveness.

Well, forget it! She would do no such thing. She was perfectly content just to sit here and do nothing. Let Michael stew in whatever emotions he might be feeling, if any; she was fine where she was. Katrina crossed her arms and remained seated on the edge of the bed, thinking, *Fuck you, Michael. Come and get me!*

But he didn't come. The longer she waited, the more her defiance faded. And finally Katrina couldn't sit still any longer. She lurched to her feet—and then paused. What was she thinking of doing? She took a ragged breath, clenched and unclenched her fists, and stood indecisively. Maybe she should just slip out to the garage, take a car, drive into Manhattan, and wait . . . but wait for what? Whatever was going to come of this, wasn't it better to get it over with right away? If Michael wanted a divorce, fine, he could bloody well have one. She could walk away from this marriage and never look back. She didn't need him, or his money, or this enormous house. She was a complete person, and she had plenty of her own resources—emotional as well as financial. And as for Michael—what could he really do? Call her names?

Katrina took a deep breath, put some of the old Eberhardt steel in her spine, and marched out the door and down the stairs.

The hall was empty when she reached the first floor. In fact, the whole house felt empty. Had Michael stormed off, maybe to the apartment he kept in the city?

Katrina felt a small spark of hope, which she immediately pushed away as shameful. She wasn't afraid, and she was going to face him now and have it done. Just to be certain, she stuck her head around the corner and looked down the hall, toward the front door. Michael's coat was there on the rack—so he was still here, in the house. And that almost certainly meant he was in his office, his normal habit when he came home.

Anger sparked. So he would act like he always did? That's how much it mattered to him that he'd found a strange man alone in the house with his wife—at seven in the morning?

It was infuriating. Katrina stomped toward the office, ready to give Michael a full broadside blast of anger and contempt.

The office door was closed. Katrina turned the knob and found it unlocked. She pushed it open and peered in.

It was a beautiful office. Michael had excellent taste, although somewhat old-school and definitely male. It was one of the things that had originally made him seem attractive to Katrina; he surrounded himself with beautiful objects, the kind of antique furnishings that reminded her of her grandfather. And even though the rest of the house was ultramodern, with lots of steel, glass, and angles, Michael's home office reflected his true taste. It was all classical masculine leather and dark wood with absolutely no regard for expense.

In the center of the room, beside a beautiful seventeenth-century Persian rug, sat Michael's desk, a massive rolltop of old dark wood. A computer monitor and keyboard were perched incongruously on the desktop, and there was Michael, slumped over, apparently asleep.

Katrina was momentarily stunned—how could he fall asleep like that? She'd heard him yelling at Randall; he had to know. Did he really care so little?

Her anger flickered high again. She stepped into the room, now completely determined to put him on the defensive. "Damn it, Michael!" she said—and stopped as her brain registered what she was seeing. ". . . Michael . . . ?" she said. It was almost a whisper, but that didn't matter.

Katrina was fairly certain Michael wouldn't hear her, no matter how loud she called him.

CHAPTER

17

The police arrived fairly quickly. In Katrina's neighborhood, they usually did. Cops are ultimate realists, and they know how the world works. Slow response and sloppy service tend to piss off rich guys. Piss off a rich guy, you're looking for a job. And Katrina and Michael Hobson were very, very rich. So even though most cops would not really go out of their way to give rich people a better kind of law enforcement, it was a good idea to let the rich folks think they did. Katrina's 9-1-1 call got a very quick response.

First on the scene was a patrol unit, two uniformed officers with over thirty years on the job between them. They arrived, took one quick look at Michael's body to verify that he was dead, and then went to work. There is a well-established routine for a homicide, and both officers knew it well. Hoffner, the senior of the two, led Katrina gently away to the kitchen. There he politely asked her for a cup of coffee. Over the years he'd found that giving somebody a definite task settled them down, and coffee created a chummy atmosphere that made a witness more likely to talk freely. He had also found that the smell of coffee usually covered any unpleasant odors from a homicide. And there are odors, almost every time. So if you wanted your witness to calm down a bit and answer questions rationally, it helps if they're not thinking, *Oh my God—that stink is Herbert's intestines!*

So Hoffner asked for coffee, and Katrina bustled about making a pot. He asked a couple of simple questions as Katrina worked, noting down her answers as well as his own observations: Witness's hair was tousled, clothing a bit mussed—probably just out of bed. Witness appeared greatly agitated but not hysterical, and so on.

Hoffner's partner, Officer Beard, was junior by seven years, and so he got the dirty end of the stick, doing the grunt work. He immediately secured the area around the crime scene—Michael's office—and then began a careful perimeter search. By the time he finished that and returned to the house, the detectives had arrived.

Officer Beard led the two detectives to Michael's office, informed them that the victim's wife had discovered the body approximately twenty minutes ago, and that no one had been in the office since their arrival on the scene. Then he took up station beside the office door and the two detectives, pulling on latex gloves, went into the room.

They paused just inside and surveyed the room. "Nice office," the younger one, Detective Melnick, observed. His gray-haired partner, Sanders, just nodded and went to one knee just inside the door, looking at the scuff marks on the floor. Melnick took two steps in toward the body, and so he saw it first and jerked to a halt. For a long moment, he was absolutely speechless. Then, when he tried to think of something to say, nothing came. Melnick wanted to be a captain someday, and he was enrolled at the community college to better himself with that in mind. He wanted to say something really cogent, something that reflected the B-plus he got in his psychology course, but what finally came out was "Holy shit."

Sanders looked up at Melnick with one raised eyebrow. "You gonna hurl?" he asked with mild scorn. "First dead guy?"

Melnick shook his head. "Lookit," he said, nodding toward the victim. "You're not gonna believe this."

Sanders sighed heavily and got slowly to his feet. He looked at the corpse, expecting to see nothing out of the ordinary. But what he saw was a surprise, even to him.

After a first quick glance he had seen only the handle of a knife protruding from the victim's back. But this was not an ordinary knife. The handle was beautifully carved, from ivory, it looked like. And the loving and skillful hand that carved it had fashioned it into a perfect likeness of a penis, now sticking straight up in the air. The sight of it was enough to make even Sanders grunt with surprise, which annoyed him. He covered it by saying merely, "Uh-huh. How 'bout that."

"The handle," Melnick said. "The handle of the knife?"

Sanders nodded. "Yup. Looks like a dick," he said, straight-faced.

Melnick, in spite of his lofty ambition, tried for a true cop zinger. "Kinda small one, don't you think?"

Sanders didn't even look at him. "You're the dick expert," he said.

Defeated, Melnick moved around his partner and bent over the body where the blade stuck up. "It's ivory. Isn't that illegal now?"

"You want to write him up?" Sanders asked. He nudged in beside his partner. "Multiple stab wounds," he said.

Melnick frowned. "Doesn't look like he struggled much."

"Mmp. One of the first stabs musta been the lucky one," Sanders said. "Cut the spinal nerve."

"But the killer kept stabbing anyways," Melnick said thoughtfully. "So . . ." He glanced at Sanders. "Not a professional job. Killer was upset? That works with the multiple wounds, too."

Sanders nodded at his partner. "Yeah, that makes sense. So, upset about what?" He knelt beside the opened briefcase. "Be nice to know if anything was missing from the case."

"Yeah, but . . . ," Melnick said. He tried to shape the scene with his hands. "Briefcase looks like it fell, maybe during a struggle? Except the guy's already at the computer, working. Right? So the killer comes in, stabs him, takes out whatever . . . and THEN drops the briefcase? I mean—if he wanted something from the briefcase and the guy's dead, he just takes it, probably takes the whole case, and then puts it back so nobody notices something's missing. But it's on the floor, like busted open? And they didn't fight for it 'cause the wounds are all in the back, and . . . it doesn't add up." He looked inquiringly at his partner. "Set dressing? Make it look like a robbery gone bad?"

Sanders said nothing. He'd already reached the same conclusion. He glanced up at the desktop. "Hey, the screen saver is on," he said.

Melnick reached for the mouse. "Let's see what he was working on when he got stabbed," he said. He twitched the mouse, and the computer screen came to life. "Oh Jesus fucking Christ," he said.

Sanders leaned in and looked at the screen. For a moment he was speechless again. "Shit," he said at last. He looked around the room slowly, then back at the screen, then at the knife. "I think I wanna talk to the wife," he said.

Katrina had seen enough cop shows on TV to know that it was never good news when the detectives asked you to "come down to the station and answer a few questions." It usually meant they thought you were guilty. But of course, she was *not* guilty, so really, what was there to worry about? There wasn't really any point in calling Tyler, her lawyer. This was just a formality, probably taking no more than an hour. And in all honesty, Katrina's kind of wealth—enormous and inherited—has an insulating effect. Even if you are a very good person, a vast fortune makes you tend to believe, consciously or not, that you are protected against being arrested or otherwise inconvenienced.

So Katrina was a little bit alarmed to receive the invitation to answer a few questions, but not really worried. And the two detectives were so polite, asking if she was comfortable several times as she rode to the station in the back seat of a patrol car. She told them she was, thank you. But Katrina was not comfortable. Not at all. Not because the car's seat was lumpy. Her discomfort came from her thoughts. First, because her husband was dead from a violent murder. Of course, that would make anybody uncomfortable. Even if they didn't really like their husband.

But far worse was wondering if somehow Randall was the killer. He certainly had a motive—and she had heard Michael yelling at Randall! Right before the front door slammed. He could easily have killed Michael and then hurried out.

But then the alarm had gone back on—*after* Randall left! Only Michael knew the code, so he had to have been the one who turned it back on. Randall couldn't possibly have done it—and so he couldn't possibly have killed Michael. But that meant the killer was already in the house—except how and when did the killer *leave* the house? After the place was swarming with cops?

Katrina could not make sense of it. And the two detectives with their constant fake concern for her comfort didn't help. And it didn't stop. They were even polite when they took her fingerprints—"Would you be willing?" and it was "just a formality." Katrina agreed, thinking it would help prove her innocence when none of her prints were found in Michael's office.

The politeness continued when they took her to an interrogation room. They even gave her a cup of coffee. True, it was really terrible coffee. But it was not at all the kind of rough treatment she'd seen on

TV shows, and for that, at least, she was grateful, and she sipped from a Styrofoam cup as they all sat at the table.

"Mrs. Hobson," the older detective said in a kind of sympathetic way—although he did emphasize the name a little, as if to remind her that she was married—*had* been married—to a person who had just been murdered. "I'm Detective Sanders. This is Detective Melnick." They both nodded courteously. "It must have been a terrible shock for you."

"Awful," Melnick agreed.

"And I'm sure you're not a violent person, not normally."

"But seeing something like that?" Melnick said, shaking his head sorrowfully.

"It might have turned anybody violent," Sanders agreed.

"Even Mother Teresa," Melnick said. Sanders glanced at him, eyebrow raised. Melnick shrugged. "She was a nun?"

"I'm pretty sure even the DA would understand," Sanders said, turning back to Katrina. "It's called 'extenuating circumstances.'"

"It means you had a reasonable motive for what you did," Melnick said. "They take that into account."

"Of course, it *is* still murder, isn't it?" Sanders said.

"It is, no question," Melnick said. "Murder." And the two of them looked at her solemnly, just looked, and let the silence grow.

Katrina looked back. Her mouth had gone dry, and she felt like all the air had gone out of the room. "What . . . what are you . . . ?" she stammered. She knew perfectly well that they were accusing her of killing Michael, but it seemed like such a stupid idea that she couldn't think of any response that made sense.

"I guess you never had a clue about Mr. Hobson," Sanders said. "Until just a few hours ago."

"And when you found out like that? Had to be a terrible shock," Melnick said.

"So you snapped," Sanders agreed. "Understandable—I mean, your own husband."

"A pedophile," Melnick said, shaking his head. "Terrible."

Katrina felt her jaw drop, and for a moment she couldn't breathe. "He was— Michael didn't . . . What . . . ?" she managed at last.

"You see?" Sanders said to his partner. "She didn't know."

"No wonder she was so angry," Melnick said. Then he turned back to Katrina. "But you must have noticed something? Some little quirk of behavior that made you suspicious? Not even once?" They both looked at her expectantly, but she could only shake her head numbly.

"So you didn't know he was a board member of True Mentor, did you?" Sanders asked.

"Of True—of, of, what?"

"True Mentor," Sanders said. "It's an organization that believes having sex with young boys helps them grow up right."

"They're pedophiles," Melnick explained. "Even worse, they're self-righteous pedophiles."

Katrina could only stare. What they were telling her was utterly impossible. It was as if they had told her Michael was actually a large cactus trying to pass as human.

"You're right," Melnick said. "She really didn't know."

"Well, that explains it," Sanders said, nodding pleasantly. "You had no idea what your husband was. So when you find out he's in an organization that seduces young boys—"

"SNAP!" Melnick said.

"So you picked up the knife—" Sanders said.

"I think it's a letter opener," Melnick said.

Sanders looked at him. "Pretty sharp for a letter opener."

"Very sharp," Melnick said. "One good stab would have done it."

"But you stabbed him seven times," Sanders said, looking mildly at Katrina.

"Which usually indicates great anger, or shock, or both," Melnick chimed in.

"In this case? Definitely both," Sanders said.

"Honestly?" Melnick said. "A lot of people would thank you for killing a pedophile."

"Of course, we can't do that," Sanders said sorrowfully.

"Not officially," Melnick said, winking at her.

"But we do understand—and I think the DA will understand—why you killed him."

At last, Katrina found her tongue. "I didn't," she said. "I just—no. No. No. I, I— This is some kind of— It's a terrible mistake!"

"Yes, murder is always a mistake," Sanders said.

"Even a pedophile," Melnick added.

"For Christ's sake!" Katrina snapped. "I didn't kill Michael! And I had no idea that he was—I mean, if he even was! Which is crazy!"

The two detectives just looked at her with identical bland expressions.

"Well, good God," Katrina said. "You can't really believe I— Michael was much bigger than me, and stronger, and I couldn't even— and I never go into his office anyway, so how could I—"

"That's a really nice security system you have at your house," Sanders said abruptly.

"State of the art," Melnick added.

"My—what?" Katrina replied, confused by the sudden change of subject.

"Security system," Sanders said. "Alarm, motion detectors—"

"And cameras," Melnick added happily. "There must be fifteen, twenty cameras."

"And they all record," Sanders said.

"Unless somebody turns 'em off," Melnick said.

Sanders nodded. "Which they can't do unless they know the pass codes."

"How many people know those codes, Mrs. Hobson?" Melnick asked politely.

Katrina just blinked.

"The codes," Sanders said.

"You know. To turn the whole thing on and off?" Melnick said.

"He means the security system," Sanders said.

Melnick nodded. "And the cameras, too."

"Who knew those codes?" Sanders repeated.

"I, I guess—just Michael and, uh . . ." Katrina swallowed hard. "Just me now, I guess."

"No housekeeper, cook, nothing like that?" Sanders said, raising an eyebrow.

"Maybe a butler—or a majordomo?" Melnick smiled and turned to his partner. "Really rich people go for that one. Majordomo. Very *regal*," he said.

"Did you have a majordomo, Mrs. Hobson?" Sanders asked blandly. "A *regal* majordomo who knew the pass code?"

Katrina could only shake her head numbly.

"Well then, see, that's the thing, Mrs. Hobson," Sanders said, leaning forward and lowering his voice confidentially. "The two cops that got there first say the alarm was on—you turned it off to let them in. Is that right?"

Again, Katrina nodded, trying to fight down the sick feeling that was growing in the pit of her stomach.

"And the cameras," Melnick said. "Somehow they got turned off for a few minutes—while your husband was getting killed."

"So you see the problem," Sanders said. He leaned back and shook his head. "The alarm is *on*. Nobody can get in. Only two people in the house, and one of 'em ends up dead." He spread his hands.

"Which is really only a charming puzzle if you're Agatha Christie," Melnick said. "Which we are not."

"I think Agatha Christie is even dead," his partner added.

"That's right, she is."

"So you see what we have to think here, Mrs. Hobson?" Sanders asked, again politely—but this time that bland and even tone seemed harsher than a snarl of rage.

"With the whole alarm thing, you know," Melnick said mildly.

And then they both just looked at her.

Katrina fought for air. The inside of her mouth felt like sandpaper and she couldn't swallow. And her brain seemed frozen. She fought for something to say—anything. There had to be a few simple words, some elementary phrase, that would make them see how ridiculous this was—how totally *impossible*—to think she had killed Michael. But she couldn't think of anything, and her head was throbbing, and the room seemed to be getting dim and wobbly. And the two detectives just looked at her with matching expressions of mild and patient curiosity. And just when she thought her head would explode, the room's door popped open.

A woman in uniform stuck her head in. "Detective Sanders?" she said. She held up a file folder. "They said you should see this ASAP. Uh, forensics?"

Sanders nodded and got up. As he stepped over to take the folder, Katrina felt a small trickle of relief. She'd seen *CSI* enough times to know what forensics was. And the ASAP part—it was obvious that they'd found some kind of evidence that implicated the real killer. So now they would have to let her go. She was innocent, for God's sake— and they had to know the kind of political pressure her family could bring; it could make things very unpleasant for the detectives. She took a deep breath and waited while the room steadied a bit and reminded herself not to be too harsh on them—after all, they'd made an awful mistake, but they were just doing their jobs, and really, they'd been very polite to her.

Sanders was showing the contents of the folder to his partner. The two of them looked at her, and Sanders smiled. *Here it comes,* Katrina thought. *Now they apologize and let me go. And I will be gracious.*

It didn't quite go that way.

The two detectives settled back into their chairs and exchanged a glance. "Where were we?" Sanders asked innocently.

"Mrs. Hobson was about to explain that she didn't kill her husband," Melnick said with the same fake blandness.

"That's right, she didn't do it," Sanders said, looking at Katrina.

"No, I didn't!" Katrina said. "And I have no idea who did do it—but whoever it was, they're getting away while you waste time playing games with me!"

"This isn't a game, Mrs. Hobson," Melnick said.

"Nope, we don't play games," Sanders said.

"Then let me go—and find the real killer!" Katrina snapped.

Sanders shook his head. "See, that's the problem," he said reasonably. "We think we *found* the real killer."

"We think it's you," Melnick said.

"That's just plain stupid!" Katrina said.

Sanders nodded. "Sure, why not. After all, we're just stupid cops. But here's the thing, Mrs. Hobson." He held up the folder in his hand. "This is the preliminary lab report," Sanders said. "They found some fingerprints on the knife."

"Very good prints, too," Melnick said. "Very clear."

"Your fingerprints," Sanders added.

"On the knife," Melnick said.

"You know—the *murder* weapon?" Sanders added. And they both looked at her expectantly.

The room began to wobble again. "That's not . . . I didn't—"

"The prints show up so nicely because whoever made the prints—"

"Your prints," Melnick added happily.

"—they had cocoa powder on their fingers," Sanders said.

"Cocoa powder that's an exact match for the cocoa powder we found in the dish beside your bed," Melnick said.

"Your bed where forensics says that last night you had sex with somebody. They also say your husband did *not* have sex in the last twenty-four hours," Sanders said.

"Who was he, Mrs. Hobson?" Melnick asked, and he was definitely emphasizing the "*Mrs.*" "And what time did he leave your house?"

Sanders nodded at her. "We kind of need to talk to him, too."

"Just so it all kind of fits together," Melnick said.

"Motive, means, and opportunity," Sanders said. "Plus the prints and the DNA evidence."

"This is really the kind of case that makes the DA love us," Melnick said. "She doesn't like to work too hard?"

"She won't have to work very hard at all with this. Open-and-shut case," Sanders said.

"Open-and-shut," Melnick agreed, and they nodded at each other.

"So it might be a good thing to let it all out now, Mrs. Hobson."

"Confession is good for the soul," Melnick said.

"It's also good for reducing your sentence," Sanders said. "You may want to think about that."

And the two of them just looked at her, with matching expressions of mild and patient amusement.

Once again Katrina was unable to breathe. She just stared back at them as they swam in and out of focus and the room seemed to tilt to one side. When at last she could get a little air into her lungs, Katrina closed her eyes for a moment and tried to steady herself. When she opened them again, nothing had changed. She was still in an interrogation room, and the two detectives were still looking at her with mild interest. She took one more breath. "I want my lawyer," she said.

CHAPTER

18

Sergeant Fraleigh had seen pretty much everything in his years as a cop—a lot of things over a lot of years. Nowadays, only seventeen months before mandatory retirement, most of what he saw just made him tired. Especially when his sciatica was kicking up, which it definitely was right now. And his acid reflux. Between the two, his patience had dissolved, and he was in no mood for bullshit. Of course, since he had the desk today, he was bound to get some. But when it finally came, he wasn't happy about it.

Still, he'd kind of known something was coming. So he didn't actually roll his eyes at the young man standing in front of him at the precinct desk. And thanks to his long years of practicing that special cop technique for suppressing his emotions, he did not say any of the filthy, blistering things that he wanted to say. But he did, most definitely, put on an expression that left no doubt to those thoughts, and he also let out a long-suffering sigh. "Say that again . . . sir?"

The young man swallowed visibly and shifted his weight. But he also jutted his chin and repeated what he'd just said. "I want to confess," he said. And then he just stood there.

"You want to confess," Sergeant Fraleigh said wearily. "And you couldn't find a priest, so you came to me?"

"No, I— It's murder," the guy stammered. "I killed Michael Hobson."

Fraleigh was well aware that there had been a murder, and the vic's name was Hobson. A rich guy. It was already getting a ton of coverage on the news. And every time that happened, the wackos came out of the woodwork to confess. Real killers *never* strolled in and confessed. The guys who did were after attention, and they were always out of whack in some sad way. Maybe they didn't get breastfed, or they never learned proper self-esteem in middle school. Whatever; one or two nutjobs always wandered in and confessed after a splashy murder.

This guy wore a nice suit, looked clean and respectable—he didn't look like a wacko, but who did nowadays? They were all raised to feel special, entitled, and nobody gave a shit about responsibility or anything else, and eventually, it seemed to the sergeant that they all flipped out, one way or another.

"You killed Michael Hobson," he said, in a voice that was flat—but would still peel paint at ten paces. "You're sure it was him?"

The young guy flinched, but he stood his ground. "Positive," he said.

Sergeant Fraleigh closed his eyes for a moment. He did not actually pray. He wasn't a religious man. But he did ask for strength, if anybody was listening. Of course, nobody was listening. When he opened his eyes, he didn't feel any stronger, and nothing had changed. The guy was still standing there, fidgeting. And even then, no sudden strength came flooding into the good sergeant's veins.

Sergeant Fraleigh knew very well Hobson's wife had killed him. The evidence was strong, and the detectives were sure it was her. So this guy was definitely a mental case. "All right, citizen," he said, folding his hands in front of him. "And *why* did you kill Michael Hobson?"

"I—I was sleeping with his wife," the guy said. "He—he came home early, and, uh . . . so I killed him."

That got Sergeant Fraleigh's attention. He knew the detectives were looking for some guy who had been in bed with the widow when it happened. Fraleigh looked the guy over a little more carefully—could this be wifey's sex toy? He wasn't bad-looking. And the suit was a really good one. That usually meant a little money—which didn't guarantee the guy was sane. But it was possible. This could be the guy—maybe. In any case, the detectives would want to talk to him. If he was telling the truth, they had their man. If he was a wacko, it was their problem. Either way, Sergeant Fraleigh would be done with him.

Fraleigh half turned to his left, keeping his eye on the young guy, and said, "Bender?"

Bender, a chubby young African-American cop, came right over "Sergeant?"

Fraleigh nodded at the young guy. "Take this guy down to holding."

"Sure thing. Uh—you want me to cuff him?"

Fraleigh shook his head. "No. We're not booking him yet. But frisk him—and keep an eye on him 'til the detectives get there, okay?"

Bender nodded. "You got it, Sergeant." He took the young guy by an elbow and steered him toward the hall. "Please come with me, sir," he said, and led the young guy away.

Fraleigh watched them go until he was distracted by a loud rumbling sound—his stomach. He glanced up at the wall clock. It was almost time for lunch—Chinese or Mexican? His stomach rumbled again, and he felt his acid reflux flare. That settled it. *Chinese,* he thought, rubbing his gut regretfully. *Definitely Chinese—and no Szechuan.*

R andall sat quietly in a small room, at a table that had more scars than a pincushion. The room had a full-size mirror along the back wall, he noted with wry amusement. Presumably he was supposed to think it was there in case he wanted to touch up his hair before the interview. Surely every living person in America had seen enough TV and movies to know that it was one-way glass so the detectives could watch him undetected. But there was nothing else to do while he waited, so he looked at his reflection in the mirror and tried to imagine who might be on the other side watching him. And if they were merely watching him, why? To see if the long wait would soften him up? For what? He had already confessed to the sergeant out front.

Randall fidgeted nervously, tapping his fingers on the tabletop and rubbing his face. If they really were watching, they'd see how nervous he was. Did that make him look guilty or innocent? He folded his hands on the tabletop and tried to calm down, but that lasted for less than a minute, and he began to fidget again.

He stood up, took a step toward the door, and hesitated, then turned around and stared at the room as he ran a hand over the top of his head. He'd shaved it yesterday, and a very faint stubble had already grown out. He wondered where Katrina was. He was certain she would be treated well, even arrested for murder. But she had to be very upset.

Randall looked over his shoulder at the door. It didn't open. He looked at the big mirror again, rubbed his beard, and then went back to the chair and sat again. He glanced at his watch; he'd been sitting here almost half an hour.

Randall spent a few more minutes fidgeting. Then he stood up again, walked jerkily around the room, pausing at the door, and then sat and fidgeted again, drummed his fingers on the table. He took a deep breath and tried to relax. That didn't work, either.

A few minutes later the door finally opened. A guy with a face like an old catcher's mitt walked in, sipping from a chipped mug in his left hand. The mug was almost as battered-looking as the man holding it. He stood just inside the door and looked Randall over carefully without blinking. "Randall Miller?" he said mildly.

"Yes. That's me," Randall said.

The man nodded and went to the opposite side of the table, sipped some more without looking away from Randall, and then hooked the chair out with one foot and sat in it. He put the cup on the table. "Hello, Randall. I'm Detective Sanders."

"Hello," Randall said.

The detective raised one eyebrow in question. "So you killed Michael Hobson, did you," he said.

"That's right."

He nodded again. "Why?"

"I was having an affair with his wife," Randall said, looking down at the table. "He came home early." He licked his lips, looked up, shrugged. "I didn't mean to kill him, but . . ."

Detective Sanders just kept looking at Randall, watching impassively, not even blinking. It was oddly unsettling because the detective kept a mild, even sympathetic look on his face—but his eyes were reptilian, predatory, and half the time he had that battered old coffee mug up and covering the lower half of his face. "How did it happen?" he said.

Randall cleared his throat. "Like I said, he came home early," he said. "While we were . . ." He looked away, embarrassed, then went on. "I, um, I heard something and went downstairs, and . . ." He shrugged.

"And what?" he said.

"And he came at me, really angry," Randall said. "I mean, it was pretty obvious why I was there so early in the morning, right?"

"Uh-huh. What time exactly?"

"Um, like I said, it was early morning. About 7:15?"

Sanders nodded. "Okay," he said. "So he comes at you—where was that? In the front hall?"

Randall licked his lips and hesitated. "Yyyes," he said at last. "In the hall."

"And how did you get him into his office?" Sanders asked mildly.

"I, uh—" Randall swallowed convulsively. "I said, 'Let's talk.' You know, be reasonable? I—I didn't want Katrina to hear us and worry? And so we went into the office. To talk?"

"Okay," Sanders said. He sipped. "And then?"

"And then, so, uh," Randall said. This was not going smoothly. Something about Detective Sanders and his unmoving old-leather face was truly intimidating, and Randall began to sweat. "So he started to get mad again? And he came at me swinging."

Sanders raised both eyebrows. "And what, you just grabbed up the fire poker and swung back?"

"Yes. Yes, that's right," Randall said. "See, he just kept trying to hit me, and I—I mean, I didn't know what—I mean, I just reached behind me and felt the handle? And he hit me again, and, and I just . . ."

"You hit him with the poker," Sanders finished for him.

"Yes. Yes, that's right." Randall nodded vigorously.

"Okay," Sanders said. "That makes sense. I guess it was an accident. Maybe even self-defense." He sipped again and looked thoughtful. "Except for one thing. How many times did you hit him, Randall?"

"How many . . . ?"

"Yeah, you know. One good swing and he goes down? Two smacks, just to be sure? Or it felt real good and you just kept swinging?" And he looked expectantly and unblinking at Randall.

Randall swallowed loudly. "I—I'm not sure exactly . . . ," he said.

"But more than once?" Sanders said.

"Yes, I—I'm pretty sure it was more than once," Randall said. He didn't actually sound sure of anything.

"Uh-huh. Okay. I guess that makes sense." Sanders slurped loudly from his cup and then set it down on the table—hard. Randall jumped, startled by the sudden loud noise. "Except for one thing," Sanders said—still mildly, in spite of banging down his mug. "However many times you hit Mr. Hobson—with a fire poker—it didn't show." He shook his head slowly. "No bruises, no broken bones, nothing."

"That—that isn't possible," Randall said.

"Sure it is," Sanders said. "Because Mr. Hobson wasn't killed with a fire poker. There's no fire poker in his office. Because there is no fireplace in his office." Sanders smiled, and it was neither a happy nor a reassuring smile. "He was stabbed to death, Randall. With his letter opener."

Randall's mouth moved a few times. It looked like he was trying to say something, probably starting with the letter O, judging from the shape of his lips. But nothing came out.

"So here's what I think," Sanders said. He picked up his coffee cup again, glanced inside, and then set it down again. "I think you really were sleeping with Mrs. Hobson. We'll check your DNA against Mrs. Hobson's sheets and we'll know for sure. But I think it was you. I believe that part. And sometime this morning, you left—hey, was it before or after Mr. Hobson got home?"

Randall just shook his head, numb. After a moment, Sanders shrugged. "We'll find out," he said. "I'm guessing before—unless you know the code for the alarm system?"

Randall shook his head dumbly.

"Yeah. Didn't think so, but we'll see. Anyway. You go back to your own place. And you turn on the TV—and there it is, all over the place. Your girlfriend has gone and killed her husband."

"That's not—Katrina could never—"

"And even worse—she killed him over you!" Sanders said loudly, pointing abruptly at him, and Randall flinched. "So we got guilt, and maybe we got real love?" He raised an eyebrow, but Randall said nothing. "Or maybe you just like getting close to all that money. It's possible. But I guess there's some feeling there, huh?" He shrugged. "So you figure, come on down here and confess, jerk my chain around for a while, and maybe get your lady love out of the slammer. Am I right?"

And he waited for Randall to say something with that same expression of mild patience, just sat there, until Randall finally had to say something or scream. "It's not— There had to be some mistake. Katrina could never . . . never do something like that."

"The evidence is pretty solid," Sanders said. "It sure looks like she did."

". . . Evidence?" Randall said.

"Fingerprints and so on. You know. It looks pretty conclusive, Randall. It really looks like your girlfriend did it." Randall said nothing, and after a moment Sanders went on. "There's maybe one or two small holes? A few things maybe you could tell us?"

CHAPTER
19

Katrina wanted to scream. More accurately, she *still* wanted to scream, had wanted to ever since those two detectives with their Frick and Frack comedy act had accused her of killing Michael.

Even when Tyler Gladstone, her attorney, had finally come down and bailed her out, she was still fighting the desire—no, the *need*—to open her mouth as wide as it would go and let out a pure, loud, air-raid siren of a scream. Of course that wouldn't look good, and she'd battled the urge to give in and let one rip.

But now, as it dawned on her that even Tyler—her very own attorney!—thought she'd done it, she was losing the battle. Oh, he'd been very careful choosing his words, naturally—but she could tell what he meant when he said things like, "It might be difficult to make a jury believe your version of what happened."

"My *version*?! Tyler, goddamn it, what the fuck does that mean?!"

"Katrina, please, calm down," he said soothingly.

"Calm down? You want me to calm the fuck down?! Then fucking DO something!"

"I got you out on bail," he said. "Which was not easy, believe me."

"Well, whoopity-fucking-do! And that's it? You've got no more masterful lawyer tricks up your sleeve?"

"Come on, Katrina, I'm not a criminal attorney," he said. "And for a case like this, with all the evidence against you—"

"Tyler, so help me God," she said. "If you're going to sit there and hint that you think I killed Michael, I really will kill *you*."

He held up both hands, as if to shield himself from her attack. "All I'm saying is, it doesn't look good. The police think they have a strong case, and apparently the district attorney thinks so, too. In fact," he said, lowering his voice, as if he were telling her a great secret, "the DA is going to prosecute this case herself. Which means she thinks it's a slam dunk because she's up for reelection."

"Well, Jesus fucking Christ!" Katrina stormed. "That's fucking great! And so what's your plan, Tyler? To let her win?!"

"My plan," Tyler said, his voice still even and unruffled, "is to bring in an expert." He smiled for the first time, paused for effect, and then said with great relish, "Jacob Brilstein."

"Oh," Katrina said, and for a moment, all the rage drained out of her. Jacob Brilstein was far and away the most brilliant, flamboyant defense attorney in the tristate area. Many times he had taken on an apparently hopeless case and somehow won his client acquittal. "Has he really never lost a case?"

"Oh, I think he may have lost one or two," Tyler said. "He just doesn't get those splashed all over the front page. But damned few losses, Katrina." His smile grew. "Damned few losses."

Katrina perched on the edge of a glove leather sofa. It was a beautiful piece of furniture, and it begged her to lean back and relax into its soothing embrace. But Katrina could not possibly relax. She was still numb with shock and completely bewildered by all that was happening—and the speed at which things were moving. Just yesterday morning her husband had been murdered—and she had been blamed for it and put in *jail*, for God's sake. And now she sat in Jacob Brilstein's midtown office, with a view through his large window of the sun setting over Manhattan. It was a large room that seemed cramped with all the piles of folders and books, and the assortment of bizarre objects strewn around the room: a ball-peen hammer with a red ribbon on the handle, a bowling ball with a chunk missing, five or six toy guns and knives—they had to be mementos of memorable cases. There were also some quiet, reassuring paintings on the wall—the kind Katrina called "motel art"—and a glass coffee table holding a crystal vase with fresh-cut flowers in it. The whole effect was of sitting in an eccentric uncle's odd but comfortable room, an ambience designed to put you at your ease, and that was impossible for Katrina. Murder—jail—interrogation by detectives—! She had been flung savagely into a world she could never have imagined entering, and now she was stuck there! Katrina could no more be at her ease right now than she could fly.

And everybody just assumed that *she* had killed Michael! Which was completely crazy—even if he really was a pedophile like the detectives said. Or maybe *especially* if he was a pedophile! Because if that was true, killing him would have been stupid—she could have divorced him quickly and kept the house, the yacht, whatever she wanted. Pedophiles did not get a good break in divorce court.

But since she knew she didn't kill Michael . . . who did?

The obvious answer was Randall. It seemed unlikely—Katrina felt sure she *knew* Randall. After all, she wasn't stupid; she knew how to judge people, and she couldn't sleep with a man so many times without learning his true character. And Randall was a sweet, mild-tempered, cultured guy—he wouldn't hurt a fly, and she was absolutely sure he couldn't kill another human being.

But she had heard Michael confront him—and she was certain Randall had feelings for her, strong feelings, beyond just the sex. Wasn't it possible that Randall was full of adrenaline from being discovered, and then Michael yelled at him—she had heard that—and Randall just lost it, just for a moment? Wasn't it conceivable that he would give in to a moment of weakness and kill Michael out of love for her?

No. It just wasn't even thinkable. Randall was a lamb, a gentle and sweet man. It was out of the question. He couldn't possibly have killed Michael.

Which left Katrina herself. Or . . . who?

And so she fretted, and sweated, and fidgeted. And Brilstein himself did not help. After a cursory introduction, he had spent over an hour grilling her—worse than the detectives!—asking her very sharp questions, making her go over everything that had happened several times, all the improbable, unbelievable events that had led to this meeting. And now, for the first time, he seemed to relax, and Katrina longed to do the same but could not.

"Well, well," Brilstein said softly as he glanced over the copious notes he'd taken. "Well, well, well . . ." He flipped through a few more pages, nodding, twice adding a quick note, and finally he dropped the legal pad into his lap and looked up at her. "So you may think I'm being jocose if I say, good news and bad news?" Jacob Brilstein said. "But . . . ?" He raised one carefully groomed eyebrow and looked at Katrina with a half smile. "I am actually saying it?"

"I suppose I—I mean, what's the, um, the good news . . . ?"

His smile widened. "Based on what you've told me, it's not nearly as complete a case as they think it is." He lifted one hand and turned it over, back, over.

"That is good," Katrina said.

"Like I said. But the bad news . . . it is very *close* to being complete, and based on what I have already heard from the district attorney's office, the other side thinks it's open-and-shut." He smiled briefly. "They like to say things like that, 'open-and-shut,'" he said with more than a hint of mockery.

"Oh," Katrina said. "So, um . . . and what do *you* think, Mr. Brilstein?"

"Please, call me Jake," the attorney said. "We are going to be spending a lot of time together, so . . . I hope I can call you Katrina as well?"

"Yes, of course," she said.

"Well, Katrina," Brilstein said, "there are one or two holes here— holes I could drive a truck through." He nodded, then frowned. "Don't get me wrong, the district attorney is very good, for somebody who isn't Jewish. Smart. And she will be working her tight little WASP ass off to plug these holes."

"Oh," Katrina said. "Is there a—I mean, um . . ." She trickled to a stop, not really sure what she meant to say.

It didn't faze Brilstein. "Of course there is," he said. "This whole business with the alarm system, for instance, the timeline. You say it was *off* when your husband came home, right?"

"Yes," Katrina said. "Randall had to—I mean, he usually just left quietly, when—um . . ." And oddly, Katrina found herself blushing.

"Naturally," Brilstein said, ignoring her discomfort. "But it was *on* when the cops got there, and nobody knows the code except you and your husband. So the DA is going to hit that hard because there was no one in the house except you and Mr. Hobson." He shook his head. "Which is what they want us to think, right?"

Brilstein stood up abruptly, causing his legal pad to fall to the floor. "But," he said loudly, beginning to pace as though addressing an imaginary jury, "you heard him argue with your boyfriend. And then you heard the boyfriend leave, the alarm came back on—" He spread his arms dramatically. "Yes, of course, that means your husband was still alive when the boyfriend left. BUT"—he lowered his voice—"the DA also wants us to forget," he said, stopping and pointing a dramatic finger, "that before Mr. Hobson turned the alarm on, when it was *off* for several hours—absolutely *anybody* could have come in, any enemy of Mr. Hobson. And once inside, they could easily hide in the office and wait. Isn't that right?" And he spun and looked at her.

Katrina nodded.

"Of course it's right. And in that hours-long period, with the alarm off, that is exactly what happened! An unknown person, with bad intentions toward Mr. Hobson, came into the house, hid themselves, and waited!"

Brilstein paused, and then looked around as if surprised to find he was only in his office. He smiled and sat back in his chair, retrieving the legal pad from the floor. "Once I get the whole True Mentor thing into the record, I can sure as hell make the court believe your husband had enemies." He nodded to himself, glancing down at the legal pad and tapping the pencil again.

And then, just as abruptly, he frowned. "But the boyfriend," he said. He looked up at her, and to Katrina he seemed worried. "Your boyfriend is the wild card here, Katrina. In the first place, just having a boyfriend does not look good—to some of these people, adultery is halfway to murder."

Katrina felt a lump growing in her stomach. She swallowed but said nothing. Until she'd met Randall, she would have agreed.

"Worse than that—apparently, he walked into the police station and confessed that *he* killed your husband."

"Oh my God!" Katrina said. Her heart and stomach seemed to collide, and for a moment she couldn't breathe. She hadn't even thought of it before—but it made a kind of terrible sense. Randall would think he was protecting her, and . . .

"He didn't," Brilstein said.

Katrina blinked at the attorney. ". . . What?" she managed.

"He didn't kill your husband," Brilstein said patiently. "For whatever reason, they're pretty sure of that."

"Of course not—oh, that idiot . . ." Just hearing what he had done made her more certain than ever that he couldn't possibly have killed Michael. She found that she was actually smiling. It was so sweet of Randall—to try to take the blame for her.

"It's not a good thing, Katrina," Brilstein said. "Now that they have him, they're not going to let go of him. They'll want him to testify, and we don't know what he'll say on the stand. And the DA *will* put him on the stand, I'd bet my life on it."

"He won't—I mean, Randall would never—"

"Of course he wouldn't," Brilstein said, and for the first time he sounded irritated—with her. "Until now. You have no idea the kind of pressure they can put on somebody—and if it's a question of testify or take fifteen years in the slammer, you can bet even Vito Corleone would sing like a lark. No, you better get used to the idea that he will testify against you."

The lump in Katrina's stomach lurched upward and then settled back down twice as big as it had been. She would have bet her life on Randall, but when Brilstein explained it like that . . . And after all, how well did she really *know* Randall Miller? She knew he was gentle and cultured—and wouldn't a man like that do anything to avoid the horrors of prison life?

"So there's that. And in addition, we may have something sudden and unexpected thrown at us, and there's no way to stop it or be ready for it." He closed his eyes, sighed deeply, opened them again. "Still, there's hope here." He gave her a reassuring half smile. "I have won cases that were a lot worse, and that's the truth. But this one—" He shrugged. "I won't lie to you. It's an uphill fight."

Katrina: "But that's—I mean, I really am innocent—"

Brilstein waved that away as if it were an annoying plume of smoke. "Of course you are. All my clients are innocent. That has nothing to do with this case, or any case." He looked at her like he was studying her for a moment, then shook his head. "It's like this, Katrina. The court will want to believe you killed your husband." He raised a hand to cut off her automatic objection. "Because you are rich, good-looking, have a lot of money—and on top of that, you're rich." He shrugged. "For some reason, that never gets any sympathy. And it makes reasonable doubt a lot harder."

"I give a lot to charity," Katrina said meekly.

Brilstein laughed. "And we will absolutely keep that off the record."

"What? Why? I thought that would be good!"

"Oh, it's splendid," Brilstein said in a voice rich with irony. "But the moment we tell them, 'My client gave $4 million to charity last year!' every single person on the jury will think, 'More than I make my whole life. And that bitch can afford to throw it away like it's nothing.'"

". . . Oh . . . ," Katrina said.

Brilstein sighed, ran a hand through his thinning hair. "I have a feeling it all hinges on the security system. We can create reasonable doubt by underlining that it was off and some bad actor got in. But if the DA finds a way to counter that, to make the court believe that it was actually turned *on* the whole time—" He took a deep breath. "Well, in that case, we hope for the old Brilstein Luck to kick in."

"Jesus Christ," Katrina blurted. "We're going to depend on *luck*?!"

"Yes," Brilstein said quite seriously. "One of the cops breaks the evidence chain. One of the witnesses says something contradictory. The prosecution asks the wrong question." He waved a hand to indicate an infinite number of possibilities. "A lot of things happen in the course of a trial. Wild cards. You just have to recognize them when they turn up and be ready to take advantage."

"Jesus Christ," Katrina said again. She found it hard to believe that

Brilstein was admitting that her life—her actual, literal *life*—depended on blind chance. If he didn't have the reputation of being the best, she would have fired him on the spot.

"It's not so bad as that," Brilstein said, sensing her despair. "When I say 'luck,' what I really mean is 'instinctive intelligence based on experience.'" He patted the folder and nodded. "There *will* be an opening. And I will see it and jump in. This I promise." And he raised his right hand as if swearing an oath. Then he dropped his hand, paused, and shook his head. "But the boyfriend . . . ," he said.

As if it had been a cue, the phone on Brilstein's desk buzzed, loud and annoying, and Brilstein glared at it. "For the love of— I said no interruptions, and—" He took a breath and picked up the receiver. "This better be good," he said.

Apparently, it was good. Brilstein looked startled, glanced at Katrina, and then snatched up a pencil and legal pad and began jotting down notes. "Uh-huh . . . Okay—and what time was this? . . . Where is he now? . . . Okay, all right, good. Get me the contact information, will you please, Caitlin? Thanks."

Brilstein hung up the phone and looked thoughtfully at his notes. Katrina watched him, feeling only an anxious uncertainty. She was half sure the call had been about her, about her *case*—she would have to get used to thinking of it that way. But there was no way to tell from Brilstein's expression whether it was positive or very bad.

"Well, well," he said at last. "Well, well, well . . ." He put the pad down in his lap, looked up at Katrina, and oddly, he smiled. "In fact," he said, "*very* well."

"What?" Katrina said, and she could hear the quaver in her voice. "What is it?"

Brilstein's smile grew until he was showing an entire mouthful of bright white teeth. "Remember what I said about the old Brilstein Luck?" he said.

Katrina was covered in cold sweat, and her heart was pounding wildly, thumping so loudly she could barely make out what Brilstein was saying. He sat right beside her on the sofa, and she was aware that he was speaking, but the words seemed to be warbled indistinctly in some foreign language. She glanced at him; he was looking at her gravely, and she tried to focus in on what he was saying. ". . . nothing at all, do you understand?"

Katrina clenched her fists until she felt her fingernails dig into the flesh of her palms. "I . . . what?" she said.

"I said—don't say anything at all, Katrina. Nothing, not even hello, not unless I say so, all right?"

Somehow the words got through the fog, and Katrina nodded. "I—yes," she said. "I understand."

"It's crucially important," Brilstein went on. "Vital. We don't know what he's going to say—and, more importantly, who he's saying it for, all right? So just sit tight and hear him out and don't say anything."

Katrina just nodded.

There was a soft knock on the door and a young woman stuck her head in. She smiled at Katrina and then said to Brilstein, "He's here, boss."

Brilstein nodded. "Send him in," he said. He glanced once more at Katrina and held a finger to his lips. She nodded and turned to face the door.

Randall walked in. He seemed slightly unsteady, as if walking on a wobbly floor. He stopped in front of Katrina and Brilstein and looked at her, then at him, then back to her, very uncertainly. His face was pale and sweaty, and there were dark smudges under his eyes. He stood there for a moment looking at Katrina. Then he swallowed and said, "I—I only . . ." He glanced at Brilstein. "I'm sorry, I just— Can I sit down, please?"

Brilstein nodded at a chair, and Randall sank into it gratefully. "Thank you," he said in a raspy voice. He cleared his throat, said, "Thanks," and ran a hand over the top of his head. It came away wet with sweat, and he stared at it for a moment, as if not sure what he was seeing. Then he dropped his hand and swallowed hard. "I just, I don't know where to—I mean how to, uh—" He glanced down at his lap, clenching his hands into fists. Then he looked directly at Katrina. "I just came from the district attorney's office," he said. He looked even more worried. "They, they—she asked me about the alarm? A lot of— I mean, the alarm at your house?"

He waited; Brilstein nodded, and Randall went on. "A lot of questions—and it's like, they think it means something, what I said about the alarm, and, and . . . She said that I was the final proof, a witness that—" He swallowed audibly and looked at his hands again. "She, uh—I mean, the DA? She said that unless I testify—and I mean, if I did, what I said would prove—I mean, to a jury, not—but that any jury would believe that you . . ." He shook his head, his face a mask of bewildered anguish. "But if I *don't* testify . . . Katrina, if I don't testify for the prosecution, I am looking at fifteen years in prison? Uh . . . accessory something?"

"She's exaggerating," Brilstein said. "Probably more like five to seven, with time off."

Randall didn't look reassured; he went right on, as if he hadn't heard. "And she said if I refuse to say anything, it's obstruction of justice, and that's almost as bad, and—and I thought, I can't do that. Fifteen *years*? That's—but I could never . . . I mean, but how could I live with myself if anything I said might, you know—if it could hurt you?"

Randall looked at her pleadingly, and Katrina felt her heart go out to him. But she felt Brilstein's hand clamp down on her arm, and she said nothing. "Go on," Brilstein said.

Randall's glance flicked to him, then back to Katrina. "Katrina,

I—I could never hurt you. But to go to prison for . . ." He swallowed hard again and dropped his eyes. "I—I—I tried to think of what I could do that might—but everything seemed like it was either . . ." He looked up at her and quickly down again. "I couldn't see any way out of— I mean, either you go to prison or I do—or *both* of us—and that was . . ." He took a deep and very shaky breath. "And then I thought, um . . ."

Randall jerked abruptly to his feet, glanced at Katrina, and wobbled over to the window. He stood there for a moment, looking out while he clenched and unclenched his fists spasmodically. "Okay, I know this is . . . I mean, I know we've never talked about our feelings or anything, so it just seemed so—and it hasn't been that long, either, so . . ."

He turned and looked at her, and for the first time he met and held her eyes. "Katrina," he said in a wounded-puppy voice. He walked jerkily back toward her and stood in front of her, swaying slightly. "I could never—really! I can't testify against you—but I can't go to prison, either, and the DA is—I mean, it's like—"

Randall shook his head with a rapid, jerky motion. "I don't know, maybe this is stupid, I'm really sorry, but—I had this idea? It was in some old movie, I can't remember what the—but I Googled it? And it's true! It would mean they couldn't compel me to testify, and I mean I've been thinking about it anyway, just not so soon, but now it's like—"

Once again he swallowed, swayed on his feet—and then abruptly lurched over onto one knee. "Katrina—will you marry me?"

Katrina could only stare. She felt her mouth moving open and closed, like a fish out of water, but no sound came out, and anyway, she wasn't supposed to speak at all unless— She glanced at Brilstein. To her astonishment, he was beaming, a huge smile. And he nodded at her happily.

Katrina looked back at Randall and took a ragged breath. "Yes," she said. "Yes, I will."

CHAPTER
20

Monique could feel herself getting fat and lazy. If not literally, physically fat—no more than maybe a pound or two?—then *mentally* fat. Because she had just been sitting here waiting for Riley, and she hated being idle. She'd never really learned how to do nothing. She couldn't stand to watch TV, and she had no training in how to relax, kick back, mellow out—and no desire to learn. She had been a relentless worker her entire life. If she was not working on *something*, she started to go crazy after just a few days. And it had been far too long since Riley's last visit. She had received a half dozen calls absolutely begging her to take a job—but how could she take on any new projects when Riley might show up at any minute with the job of a lifetime? Whatever it was—

And that was another thing making her buggy. What *was* it?

Ordinarily, it wouldn't have mattered. She'd never asked him for details before—it didn't seem all that important. But this time . . . the way Riley had been acting, not just mysterious but hesitant, as if this time there was some doubt in his mind. Riley Wolfe *never* felt doubt. If he was feeling it this time—why? What did Riley want her to make that could command that much money? Hundreds of millions of dollars—and Monique knew how Riley worked. His payout was usually from the insurance, for much less than full value. That way the settlement was quick and painless for both sides. So if he expected a few hundred million, then whatever he was after would be worth three or four times that much. Which meant . . . a *billion dollars*?! Two billion? There were no more than a handful of objects in the entire world worth that kind of cash. And Monique couldn't think of one of them that was even a remote possibility.

Obviously, Riley could. Riley *had*.

If Monique had had some project to occupy her, it wouldn't have mattered as much. But just sitting here waiting for Riley, it was absolutely impossible to stop wondering, turning over the possibilities in her mind, rejecting them all a dozen times—and still wondering. She tried distracting herself by catching up on the long list of movies she'd been meaning to see. Not a single one of them kept her attention for more than ten minutes. She cleaned her studio until it sparkled, organized her paints and brushes, tried on her new clothes in dozens of combinations—and nothing worked.

After a week of chewing her teeth, Monique had had enough. She went to her sparkling-clean, newly organized work area and began to work on a painting she'd wanted to try since grad school. It wasn't a copy; it was an original work based on an abstract expressionist interpretation of West African symbology. She'd abandoned the idea long ago. It wasn't contemporary, and it wasn't something she could sell. But it was interesting to *her*, so she took out her old notes and began to sketch.

For three days she roughed out designs for the canvas, and for three days she rejected them. But on day four, something began to click. She had been playing with a trio of adinkra symbols. One of them looked a bit like two crossed, curved blades—but also a bit like a ceremonial mask. That gave her an idea, and she began evolving the adinkra until it began to take shape as a powerful abstract form. Looking through her sketches, Monique began to feel a small tickle of excitement. This could be good. She could see it on a large canvas, limned in black to give it more power, and then around it she could take some of the other symbols, evolve them to fit this new pattern, make them into a border for the main shape—

Happily working for herself for the first time in years, Monique began the canvas.

It had been several weeks since the last time I saw Monique. I had been busy, but that was no excuse. I knew her well enough to know how she would take it that I kept her hanging like that. She would be Actively Unhappy—meaning I'd have to be on my guard, or she just might smack me. And Monique *punched*, hard enough to ring your bell.

So I approached her carefully and quietly. She'd left the window open again, which I thought was pretty nice of her. I slid inside, and right away I saw her, working at her easel. It pissed me off a little. I mean, I know I should have found a way to check in with her so she didn't go totally squirrely. But I still couldn't believe she'd take another job when it might interfere with mine. And here she was working on a new project.

And so because I was pissed off, I decided to sneak up on her, which had not been my intention when I came in. I figured it would serve her right if I scared her into messing up the canvas. Probably just another fucking Cassatt or something anyway.

But when I got close enough to see what she was doing, I could tell it wasn't anything like I'd seen her do before. She'd started to put in a big, powerful shape, right in the center of the canvas. It was obviously abstract, but something about it seemed sort of familiar. I moved closer, until I was right behind her, and looked closer. Two big dark lines crossed in the center. They had a kind of West African feeling to them that looked almost familiar—

"An adinkra!" I said as I finally recognized it. Monique jumped about three feet straight up. Very gratifying.

"Jesus *FUCK*, Riley!" she yelled when her feet were back on the floor. "I swear to Christ, I will *kill* you—!"

I know it makes me a bad person to take so much pleasure out of scaring the shit out of somebody—but Monique looked so damn *hot* when she was angry that I had to smile. Just in time I remembered her fists and stepped back. I'm pretty sure I heard her punch whistle as it went through the place where my head had been a second before.

"Hey, hey, take it easy," I said, both hands raised palms up.

"I'll take your fucking head off, scare me like that," she said.

"I wasn't going to," I said. "But then I saw you working on something for somebody else and I thought—"

"For ME, asshole!" she said, and she took another swing that just missed. "I am painting for *me* because *you* left me sitting here chewing my goddamn fingernails and wondering what the fuck was going to happen, or even IF, and who knows when—"

"Jesus, slow down, I'm losing track here," I said. "The painting is an original?"

"It will be," she said, kind of sullen now. "If I ever get to finish it."

"Well, if that's what you want to do." I shrugged. "I guess I can ask Tony Gao to do this job with me."

"You do that and I really will kill you," she said. "Goddamn it, I have been spinning my wheels for fucking weeks! Waiting for you to— Damn it, Riley, I turned down half a dozen jobs, and never a single fucking word from you!"

She was glaring, but she didn't swing again. I thought it might be safe, and I stepped a little closer. "I'm really sorry, Monique," I said, and I meant it. "Things got a little complicated?" I shrugged. "Never mind, all better. We're ready to go."

"Great! Wonderful! We're fucking ready to fucking go!" Monique snarled. "Go on fucking *what*?!"

I felt a wave of excitement whip through me just thinking about it, and I closed my eyes and let myself feel it for a second.

"Riley, holy shit, come on," Monique said. "You're practically scaring me—I've never seen you like this. What the fuck is it?"

I opened my eyes, and I took her hand. A row of gooseflesh ran up her arm. Even gooseflesh looked good on this girl. "Monique," I said. My voice sounded funny to me, like I'd swallowed something wrong. I didn't care—this was going to happen. Everything I had planned, everything I had done to make the plan work—it was all in place, and I could *see* it happening, and it filled me up with a kind of wild joy like I hadn't felt before. And when I had this final piece from Monique . . .

I shivered. She did, too. "Monique," I said again, "we are about to make history. We are going to do something impossible, something so unlikely that there's not a single goddamn person in the world, cop or thief, who could possibly imagine anybody doing it—not even me! Except—" I took a breath, and I could taste it, taste what we were about to do.

"Except *what*, Riley?" Monique said, and her voice had gone soft and husky, too.

"Except . . . we are going to do it," I said. I looked into her eyes, and she looked back, and after a moment her breath went ragged and her knees wobbled. I started to move toward her. But she straightened up and pulled her hands away from mine.

"Do *what*, for Christ's sake?" she said with a frown.

The time had come. I reached into a pocket and pulled out a small packet of photographs. I tossed it onto her worktable. "This," I said.

Still scowling, Monique picked them up, glanced at the top picture—and went very still. Inside and outside of her nothing made a sound; nothing moved. It felt like the entire world thumped to a halt, and Monique just stared at the top picture. "Jesus Christ," she whispered at long last. "Jesus fucking Christ." Since I agreed with that, I didn't say anything.

Monique thumbed through to the second picture, stared at it, then went through all the others, faster and faster. "Fuck," she whispered, "Jesus fucking Christ, oh, fuck," over and over. She came to the last picture and remembered she still needed to breathe. She took in a big lungful of air and then started to shake her head. "No," she said. "Uh-uh, no, can't happen, no way. No, this is just—" And she slammed down the stack of photos. "For fuck's sake, Riley!" she practically screamed. "Are you out of your fucking mind?!"

"Maybe," I said. She had me smiling again. "But I'm gonna do this."

"What you're gonna do is get yourself fucking *killed*!" she yelled. "Every fucking electronic security device in the whole fucking—I mean, things you've never even *heard* of, and—and the *guards*, Riley! They're gonna have armed fucking guards! And the motherfuckers *will be looking* to kill somebody, and you just stroll in and—goddamn it, NO! This is totally fucking impossible!"

"Yup," I said. "And that's why I have to do it."

She stared at me, then shook her head. "You are totally fucking nuts."

"But in a really nice way?" I said.

That pushed her back to being mad again. "Do you even fucking know how much fucking security is around this fucking thing?!" she shouted.

"Yup," I said. "Doesn't matter."

"Doesn't matter," she said. "Doesn't matter. Because Riley fucking

Wolfe is on the job, so it doesn't matter. Because Riley fucking Wolfe is SOOOOO fucking smart it doesn't matter what you do, you can't stop him." At least she wasn't screaming anymore.

"You could say that," I said.

I should have been ready and seen it coming. I wasn't, and I didn't. She smacked me so hard on the side of the head that I saw stars.

"You ignorant, dumb-ass, arrogant, conceited, stuck-up mother-fucking pig!" she said. "I am not going to help you get yourself murdered or—I mean if you're *lucky*, it's just prison forever!"

I didn't say anything. I just waited for the stars to fade so I could see again.

"Goddamn it, Riley, it can't be fucking done," she said.

"I can do it," I said. "I have to . . . if you don't knock my head off first."

"Somebody shoulda knocked your head off years ago," she snarled. "You sure as shit aren't using it."

"Well, shit, Monique," I said, throwing up my hands. "Does that mean you can't do it?"

"It means I'm not stupid enough to try! For God's sake, that thing is—and it's totally impossible! You'll be killed or— No, Riley! Absolutely not!"

I raised one eyebrow at her. "Are you that worried I'll get killed? Wow, so you *do* care about me, don't you?"

"Sure, sure, I care," she snapped. "You're a steady customer, you pay well, you never give me a short count—of course I care!"

I knew she'd say something like that—she almost had to—but it kind of hurt anyway. I mean, it would if I'd believed her. I didn't. I shook my head and took a small, soft step closer. "It's more than that, isn't it?"

Monique hesitated, just a half second. "No," she said, looking away. "I mean, sometimes I think you're—" She bit her lip in that way she had that I found incredibly sexy. "I think you're kind of . . . a friend . . ." She glanced back at me. "Everybody has one asshole friend, right?"

Now it did hurt, and I almost believed it. "That's it?" I said, moving a half step closer. "I'm just the asshole friend?"

Monique bit her lip again. Our eyes locked, and for a minute, neither of us said anything. "Damn it, Riley," Monique said at last. She put a hand on my chest, and just when I was going to return the favor—she pushed me back. Hard. "It's not going to happen again, all right?"

"It is," I said, "when you lose our bet."

"Which I never will!"

"We'll see," I said, and I smiled in a way I hoped looked charming and confident. "But that means you have to do this job for me—or you lose. And besides . . ." I watched her carefully as I put my hands on her shoulders. She kept her eyes on me, and I couldn't read what she was thinking—but she didn't push me back again. I lowered my voice. "You have to picture this, Monique. You've got to *feel* it like I do." I think my voice was shaking a little. Monique still didn't push me away. "Not just the target, but the whole plan, the way this will work—goddamn it, girl! Nothing like this has ever been done before! You are going to be part of the greatest heist in fucking *history*!"

I shook her gently and willed her to feel the excitement like I did.

"And the challenge! You have never even *dreamed* of—oh my God, everything has to be *perfect*, and it's—nobody else would even *think* of trying, Monique! But you and me, together—we can *do* this! I know it!" I took a breath and tried to calm down. It wasn't easy. "I can pull this off, Monique. Absolutely. But only if I have an absolutely perfect copy."

Monique looked back at me. She licked her lips, which almost made me forget what I was talking about, and then she pulled away from me. She picked up the photographs, flipped through them, frowning. She traced a detail with one finger, let out a noisy breath.

"Maybe," she said, talking quietly to herself. "Has to be moissanite—shit, that setting's so busy, so . . ." Suddenly remembering I was there, she jerked her head up. "But Jesus, Riley! How can you possibly even get close enough to—goddamn it, you're going to be killed!"

"Or worse," I said mock-seriously.

Monique shook her head vigorously. "I'm serious!" she said. "This thing is wrapped up tighter than, than—"

"A mosquito's asshole?" I suggested. "A nun's pussy?"

"Fuck you, Riley, I mean it!" she snapped. She waved the pictures at me. "I read about this. They've got dozens of guards, with machine guns, and—you can't possibly— I mean, how, how—what the fuck are you thinking?"

She was very damn serious, so I got serious right back at her.

"I am thinking that I want to do something that nobody else in the whole fucking world could ever, in a million years, think of or do," I said. "And more than that—I am *doing it*." I took a big breath, and the whole thing just blew up and took me over. "It's already *working*, Monique!" I realized I was shouting, but I didn't care. "It is already falling into place! I am more than halfway there, and the rest of it is going to happen, too, I know it! Goddamn it, I can *do* this!"

And I could see that she almost began to believe me, believe I could really do it.

Almost.

Monique shook her head. She looked at the picture again, then back at me. "You're insane," she said. "Totally fucking crazy. There's just no fucking *way*, Riley!"

"There's always a way," I said. "Come on, Monique, yes or no. Can you do it? No—" I held up a hand. "I won't say '*can* you.' I know you can! But, Monique—*will* you do it? Will you be a part of history with me?"

She shook her head and looked down at the photograph. "I can try," she said.

I don't know where it came from, but I heard my Yoda imitation answer her. "'There is no try. There is only do or not do.'"

She shook her head, still looking at the picture.

"Monique, you can do this," I said. "I have every confidence." I paused. "Well, not *every* confidence." Couldn't help it—my favorite joke. I covered it with a small leer. "Of course, if you'd rather say no, then I guess—"

"Fuck you, man. You are *never* going to collect on our bet."

I gave her the first real, big, happy smile I'd worn for days. "I win either way," I said.

"Fuck you."

"Maybe later," I said. "Are you in? Monique?"

She hissed, chewed her lip, shook her head. Then she looked up at me, and before she said it I saw it in her eyes. "I'm in," she said. "But goddamn it, Riley—"

"Absolutely!" I said. I leaned forward and kissed her, too fast for her to stop me. And before she could say anything else, I was out the window and gone in the night.

Monique watched Riley go with an unreadable expression on her face. "Asshole," she said. But she smiled when she said it—until she looked at the photograph again. "Jesus *fuck*, he's totally out of his mind," she said.

She shook her head and reached for her notebook. Monique was a very organized person, especially when it came to work, and she always planned everything meticulously before she began the actual work. She pulled a folding chair over to the small metal worktable, putting her paints on the shelf underneath the tabletop. Still standing, she put the notebook in the space she'd made. Ready to take notes now, she sorted through the small stack of pictures, showing it from every angle. It was possible. In fact, aside from being a bit complicated, very possible. But the sheer fucking *balls* of Riley for even trying—!

She thumbed back to the top picture. "Jesus fuck," she said again, very quietly. For a moment she was overwhelmed. She sank into the chair and flipped slowly through the photos. She thought of materials and techniques, but every one of those thoughts was overwhelmed with the hugeness of attempting something like this. "Shit," she murmured. "Oh, shit."

Monique came back to the first picture again and stared at it for a long time. Then she took a deep breath, nodded once, and began to think it through. *All right,* she thought. *I can do this.* Her hand trembled slightly, but her decision was made. She would do it. She would make a perfect copy of this thing.

She would copy the Daryayeh-E-Noor.

The Ocean of Light.

CHAPTER
21

I t's a little over a thousand miles from Watertown, New York, to Pickens County, Georgia. Instead of driving fifteen hours straight through, Delgado decided to stop for the night in Charlotte, North Carolina. From there it was only about four hours more to Jasper, Georgia, the Pickens County seat. Once there, he'd get the name that went with the license number on the plate he'd found under Riley's trailer in Watertown. And then, wherever that took him in Pickens County, he hoped he'd find somebody with a few memories of Riley Wolfe or his mother, however faded the recollections might be after so many years. What he had learned from the English teacher and from Jimmy Finn in Watertown had been worth the trip. If he could find a similar source in Georgia, it was worth driving fifteen hours more.

So Delgado drove south, the whole length of New York State and on through Pennsylvania, into Virginia. He actually passed within fifty miles of his own house, but he didn't even think about stopping.

He got to Charlotte, North Carolina, a few minutes before 2 A.M.

He found a cheap hotel near the airport, checked in, went to his room, and was asleep in just a few minutes.

Delgado woke up at 7:30. He had the hotel's free breakfast, three cups of their coffee—terribly weak by Cuban standards—and was on the road again by 8:15.

The drive was uneventful. I-77 was minutes away from the hotel, and that took him south to I-85, which ran him through South Carolina and then across the top of Georgia. He pushed a little harder, drove faster, because the anticipation was mounting. But he felt so close—and he was half convinced that the "big house on the hill" was the key to understanding all about Riley Wolfe. When a classmate sneered at it, that had caused an uncharacteristic explosion of savage violence from young Riley. That meant it was vitally important to the boy, which in turn made it a key piece to understanding the man.

So the "big house on the hill" was important, and Pickens County was hill country—the "Marble Capital of the South!" as the county's website said. He just might find the big house there. The thought was so tantalizing that he actually began to whistle, which would have stunned his colleagues at the Bureau.

The county's motor vehicle registration records were kept, naturally enough, at the DMV. The registrations had not been recorded onto computer, the clerk told him, until 2007. She handed Delgado a thick and dusty book that held all the registration information for 1996, the year stamped on the license plate. He took it to a small desk in an unoccupied office and sat.

Delgado reached to open the book and was surprised to see that his hand was trembling slightly. He ignored the tremor and flipped hurriedly through the book to the W section. There were two Wolfes listed—and neither matched the number on the license plate.

Delgado closed the book and frowned. On the one hand, this made things a little more difficult. But on the plus side—he knew that Riley

Wolfe and his mother had gone to Watertown from right here in Pickens County. Since there was no matching record for Wolfe in this book, that meant Riley had been living here under his birth name. He had therefore changed his name between leaving Georgia and registering for school in Watertown. So if he could find a match to the license plate—he would have Riley Wolfe's birth name. But finding a vehicle registration in a printed book—by plate number—is more difficult than finding it by name. It would take much longer since he would have to scan every page until he found a match. If he found it, though—

And still Delgado paused before reopening the book. Some stray thought was nagging at the back of his mind. Something had to have happened here in Pickens County that forced Riley to change his name and move. It seemed highly likely that whatever that was, it had been serious enough to convince his mother of the necessity, too.

What had happened?

If it was that serious, there was a good chance that someone in the area would remember it. That alone would be worth the long drive. So he spent a moment organizing his thoughts on where to look for that someone. Sheriff's office, school, maybe a neighbor if he got very lucky. Newspaper archives? He wasn't even sure there was a newspaper here. He'd have to check. If so, there might even be a reporter who remembered the story, which was a lot better than working through a stack of ancient newspapers. Even if they'd been microfilmed— unlikely for a small town like this one.

Delgado flipped open his notebook and jotted down, "Sheriff, middle school, newspaper?" He would talk to the sheriff first. The newspaper would be a last resort. He didn't like reporters.

Delgado started to close the notebook, and then paused for just a moment to glance at his notes. They seemed pretty skimpy. He had so far learned very few real facts. He was certain Riley's relationship to his mother was important. He had underlined it twice more and circled it. Other than that? Not much. A lot of guesswork, and none of it pointed to a reason for a sudden name change and move. Except, once again, the big house on the hill. He was sure it was real, and something had happened to make Riley's family lose the house. That kind of loss would be huge to a young boy. The house would have stood for everything important: security, status, family, comfort. Had it been here, in Georgia? Had its loss forced the move and name change? Did it become the driving force that made him the master criminal he was?

Delgado had to admit that it was all a fragile construct, but it made sense to him. If he was right, everything led back to that house. He had to admit that it might not even exist except in young Riley's imagination. It could easily have been something a poor boy might dream up, a comforting fantasy. Delgado didn't think so; he thought it was real. But he had never yet solved anything by wanting something to be true, and he knew it was just as likely that the big house was only a make-believe solace for a kid who needed to dream. It could even provide motivation for all Riley had become: *Someday I will have enough money to buy a big house on a hill.*

But if it was real, and if it was here, in Pickens County, Delgado would find it, even if he had to scan every page in the massive DMV book. He closed his notebook, opened the registration record, and began, going from front to back. After forty-five minutes, Delgado had worked up through the *L*'s with no luck. He paused to stretch his neck, sore from bending over the book. And then, for no logical reason, he opened up the book and flipped to the back to look at the entries under Wolfe. And as he ran his finger down the page of *W*'s, he saw the plate number.

Not under Wolfe. Under the name Weimer.

Delgado traced it with his finger tip, as if touching it would make certain it really was the right number. It was. The plate was registered to a Sheila Weimer. Delgado blinked, then flipped open his notebook again. There it was—Jimmy Finn had said Riley's mother's name was Sheila. Not conclusive, but Delgado felt a surge of excitement anyway. The address given was right here in Jasper, on Brittany Court. The street name sounded a bit upscale—could it be the big house on the hill?

He reached for his phone and saw his hand was still shaking from excitement. He paused, took a deep breath, and steadied himself. *I know better,* he told himself. *It isn't over until it's over.* He held out his hand in front of him, and after a moment the shaking stopped.

He picked up his phone and Googled the address. It wasn't very far. Delgado grabbed his notebook and headed out.

Brittany Court was not upscale, and it was not the big house on the hill. There was no hill and no big house, only a cluster of small, one-story duplexes. The units looked old and worn; they'd probably been there in 1996. Still, he had to be sure. And there was a tiny chance that someone who lived here now had been here back then.

Delgado got out of his car and approached the central area, where the mailboxes were. There was a small sign by the mailboxes instructing anyone interested in renting to contact the management company. Delgado wrote down the phone number and, sitting in his car, called it.

Delgado had expected to get a receptionist who would put him on hold, forcing him to listen to terrible music for five or ten minutes before he finally spoke to somebody who could answer his questions. To his surprise, the woman who answered the phone also answered his questions.

"Those units been there for thirty years, but our company bought 'em 'bout eight years ago," she said with a Georgia twang. "So I couldn't anyhow tell you 'bout anybody lived there that long ago. And they always been cheap? So they always had a quick turnover, and I know for a fact ain't nobody been there long enough to remember somebody back then. No, I'm sorry, but the old fella built 'em and owned 'em back then, he died 'bout six months after he sold out to our company. It's like they always say, you stop bein' active and you probably just gonna die. Anyways, that's what old Bill Thomson done. Sold out, retired, and died, one two three."

Delgado thanked her, disconnected, and frowned at his steering wheel. Not the big house on the hill. This little place was already a huge step down from that, if it had really existed. So had Riley and his mother—the Weimers—come to Jasper from somewhere else? Probably; it was unlikely that they would stay in the town where they had just suffered a huge loss in status. But if the big house was only a fantasy, they might have lived here all along.

Delgado shook his head. It was a dead end, at least for now. He would have to move on to his next step, talking to the sheriff. He looked up the address and saw that Jasper had its own police department, separate from the Pickens County sheriff. It wasn't far. Nothing was, in Jasper.

The duty sergeant informed him that he was in luck, and the man to talk to was Clay Bensen. "He was detective here twenty-six years," the sergeant drawled. "Retired 'bout three and a half year ago. But this time a day, you gone fine him over to Molly Bee's." When Delgado looked blank, the sergeant twitched a tiny smile. "That ole diner, edge o' town? 'Bout two mile from here. Dead east." He jerked a thumb in an easterly direction and nodded. "They got meatloaf today, it's worth a try," he said, and went back to a stack of reports on his desk.

Delgado found Molly Bee's easily. It was one of those 1960s space-age diners, with a jagged neon sign towering up, and a big theater-marquee-style sign that read, "MOLLY BEE'S—*Fine Home Cooking!*" He parked and went in.

In the far corner of the diner was a booth with a knot of five men gathered around. No one else was in the diner except a bored-looking woman in an apron resting one haunch on a stool behind the counter.

Delgado walked back to the booth. The man in the far corner of the booth was talking. He looked to be average height, thin and wiry, probably in his sixties. He had a worn-looking face with bright blue eyes and wore a Stetson perched on top of short silver hair. He wore a brown jacket, a Western shirt, and a string tie with a large turquoise clasp. Delgado guessed that would be Bensen. He was the only one of the group old enough. So he stood and waited. The man in the Stetson glanced at him but didn't interrupt his story. When he finished talking, he turned his attention on Delgado. "Detective Bensen?" Delgado said.

"That's right. Something I can help you with, son?" he said. "Or you just admiring my profile?"

"It's not bad," Delgado said. "But I'm hoping you can help me."

"I live to serve others," Bensen said. He cocked his head to one side. "You a cop of some kind, ain't you?"

Delgado fished out his badge and held it up.

"Oh, my, a real-life G-man, everybody bow your heads," Bensen said. Two of his listeners chuckled. "This official business?"

Delgado hesitated for half a second, then decided to trust the old man. "I'm on my own time," he said. "But it's important."

Bensen looked steadily at Delgado and then nodded. "This oughta be good. Pull up a chair, son. Betty? 'Nother coffee here."

Delgado pulled a chair from an adjacent table and wedged himself in at the corner. By the time he got seated, Betty had a cup of coffee down on the table in front of him. "There you go," Bensen said. "It's not real *good* coffee, but at least it's kind of warm." Bensen leaned forward and gazed steadily at Delgado. "Now what can I do for you, son?"

"Two people lived here about twenty-four years ago, a mother and son," Delgado said. "Something made them move. I think it was something bad, maybe criminal. I was hoping you'd remember."

Bensen nodded. "They got a name?"

"Sheila Weimer," Delgado said. "I don't know what name the boy used."

One of the men in the booth muttered, "Oh Lord." Another man jerked to his feet, glared at Delgado, and stalked out of the diner.

Bensen didn't even blink. "Why you want to know about them, son?" he said in a soft voice that held an edge of danger.

Delgado was suddenly in the middle of a ring of hostile faces. He knew he had stepped in something, but he wasn't worried. Instead, he felt a surge of adrenaline. Something *had* happened here. He was right. And Bensen remembered.

"The boy has become a dangerous criminal," he said. He heard someone growl, "Big fuckin' surprise," but Bensen just kept his steady gaze on Delgado, waiting for more. "I want to find him. Arrest him. To do that I need to know more about him. His backstory."

It was very quiet in the diner for what seemed like a long and awkward time. That didn't bother Delgado. If it got him some answers, he would sit here in silence and stare back at Bensen all day.

It didn't last all day. Bensen finally said, "Huh," and leaned back in the booth, and the rest of the men gathered around all took a breath. "Well, I can't say I am surprised," Bensen said. "It was a bad start for that boy, and that don't usually turn out good."

"Can you tell me what happened?" Delgado asked.

Bensen chuckled, one syllable of dry mirth. "'Course I can. But I'm a Southerner, son, and that means I got to lead up to it just right. Put in some background, make a proper story of it." He frowned and steepled his hands on the table in front of him. "I b'lieve it had to be 1996," he said.

"That's right," Delgado said.

Bensen raised one eyebrow. "Is it? That's good to know. Hush up, now, let me tell this."

Delgado couldn't help a small smile. "Sorry," he said.

"It was 1996," Bensen said again. "The world was young, and I could still walk without cryin' from the pain, and I could even get all the way through the night without gettin' up to pee." He looked around the booth, just checking to see his listeners were following. They were. Bensen went on.

"Now there was a woman had come to town just a couple of years before," he said. "Town like this, everybody knows everybody else, but nobody was real sure where this woman come from, nor why she chose to come to Jasper. Sheila Weimer, her name was. And she brought her son with her, young boy maybe eleven, twelve years old. Boy went by the name of J.R. Sheila took a job clerking at Weatherbee's hardware store. J.R. enrolled at the middle school, in the seventh grade."

Bensen paused for a moment before he continued. "That woman kept herself to herself. Kind of held herself back, like she was better 'n what you might think. Couple of the town busybodies, they tried to get her to talk. She'd just give 'em this frosty smile and change the subject. Folks got the idea, and everybody just settled back to normal for a year or so. Nobody much felt like gettin' to know Sheila Weimer after a while." He paused and frowned. "Well," he said, "like I was saying, two or three years go by, the Weimers are part of the scenery, nobody gives 'em a thought. And then . . ."

He was silent again, perhaps gathering his thoughts. Then he pursed his lips, looking directly at Delgado. "You got to understand I spent some time on this. It bothered me. Thing like that—it was real ugly, all around, and I—" He frowned. "Gettin' ahead of myself. Telling it like a Yankee." He shook his head. "Anyway. Mother works in town, boy having some problems at school. Can't seem to fit in, make friends, nothing." He shrugged. "Maybe not his fault. Boy's very first day of school ever, teacher calls the roll. And instead of sayin' 'J.R. Weimer,' she calls out 'Junior Weener.'" He snorted. "Not the kind of thing middle school boys are gonna let go of. Right away, J.R. was 'Tiny Dick' or 'Little Cock.' They rode him hard, and especially a boy named Bobby Reed. He was on J.R. all the time, 'Tiny Dick, Tiny Dick.' He was bigger, not all that bright? But big and strong—plus his family had some money. And that made him one of those boys had what you might call followers—other boys that hung out with him and did what he did. And they all pushed real hard at J.R., and at first it seems like he didn't much push back. So I got to figure it built up inside him . . ."

Bensen was silent for a few moments. Delgado didn't prod him, just waited. "Well," Bensen said at last, "when that boy J.R. finally pushed back, it was one hell of a push. And what most folks believe is, he pushed Bobby Reed into the old quarry." He shook his head. "Me, I'm not 100 percent sure. I think it might maybe have been an accident. Or he did push Bobby but didn't mean for him to fall in like that. The kids that was there that day, they were of two minds about it. At first." He snorted. "'Course, a day or two later, they all swore up and down J.R. pushed Bobby in on purpose 'cause that's what folks wanted to believe.

"Anyways, that's a hundred-some feet down onto nothing but rocks. Coroner says Bobby died right away. Folks really want to believe that because it was near seven hours before anybody got down there to fetch Bobby's body back up." He tilted his head toward the diner's door. "That was his brother Clayton walked out a minute ago?"

Delgado nodded.

"Well," Bensen went on, "by the time I went round to talk to J.R., him and his mother had up and gone. Lock, stock, and minivan." He sighed. "Kid was fourteen years old. I wasn't about to cuff him and toss him in jail. But I sure did want to talk to him 'bout what happened."

Bensen sighed and closed his eyes. He looked like he'd run out of steam and might just decide to take a nap. But when he opened his eyes again, they were full of energy. "I did all the things you'd expect. Put it out on the wire, names and plate number and descriptions. Nothing came back, not ever. After a while I just had to figure they'd changed their names. 'Cause they sure didn't have the means to run for Argentina or someplace like that." His face got even more serious and thoughtful. "And I got to admit that bothered me more. How did a kid and a lady like that manage it? I mean, 'less there was a criminal history I couldn't find. I checked back, and I still couldn't find it, and I had to figure one of 'em just had a natural talent for felony."

Bensen raised one eyebrow. Delgado nodded. The old cop picked up his coffee cup and took a sip. He made a face and put the cup down. "I just can't like cold coffee," he said, pushing the cup away from him. "Guess I talked too long."

"No, sir," Delgado said. "You've been very helpful."

"Sure I have," Bensen said. "Always a big help to let an old man ramble on, isn't it?"

"Do you know where they lived before?" Delgado asked. "Before they came to Jasper?"

Bensen made a wide-eyed face. "Now how 'm I gonna know that? Poor dumb ole country cop like me? Why, shucks, I ain't never heard of no database or nothin'." He snorted. "'Course I know. Like I said, this bothered me. I went over this thing every way I could think. I even checked with your folks at the Bureau, hopin' that maybe just once they wouldn't fall over their own damn feet and land on mine." He made a disgusted face. Delgado kept silent. He was well aware that most local cops don't like the Bureau. Besides, Delgado had the same opinion about most of his fellow agents.

"I wasn't really expecting much, just doing some due diligence?" Bensen said. He waggled his eyebrows. "And what do you know? I got a hit. Nothin' at all on the kid or his mom—but it seems J.R.'s *daddy* had a record. Bunch of financial stuff—check kiting, fraud, you know. And he died just before they arrested him for a Ponzi scheme."

Delgado felt his mouth go dry. This was it—the final piece. And he was certain it would lead to the big house on the hill. "Where?" he said. "Where did that happen?"

Bensen knew he had Delgado hooked and enjoyed it. He let it play out a little longer. "Well, I got a copy of the death certificate. It was dated just a few weeks before Sheila and J.R. showed up here, in Jasper." He smiled, drawing it out. "The old man passed away of a heart attack in the hospital. Not too terrible far from here. In Davidson County, Tennessee." He smiled for the first time, the smile of a man who realized he had just made somebody's day. "That's Nashville, son," he said.

CHAPTER
22

The wedding had been very simple, of course. Katrina wore a basic, off-the-rack Hugo Boss business suit—all she could get on short notice. There were no crowds, no family members, not even any music. It was not at all like Katrina's first wedding, the one to Michael. That had been in St. John the Divine Episcopal, where Eberhardts always got married. The pews had been packed with family members, business associates, paparazzi. This time, it was town hall, and nobody was there except the two of them, Jacob Brilstein, and a clerk. It was so very different that it was hard to think of it as a wedding. Katrina hoped that was a sign that this marriage would be different, too, in spite of being somewhat impromptu.

As the clerk intoned the civil ceremony in a flat voice, Brilstein stood beside them beaming as if it were his own wedding. And somehow, magically, at the proper moment, he pulled a ring from his pocket. Randall put it on Katrina's finger with trembling hands, and a moment later it was over and they came together for the official kiss—which turned into a much longer and more passionate kiss that lasted until the clerk cleared his throat ostentatiously and said in a very loud voice, "Okay, folks, you're married now. Take it home, please."

As a wedding present, Brilstein had booked them a suite at the St. Regis. Katrina managed to hide her disappointment. In the first place, she didn't really care for the St. Regis. More importantly, she found that she was aching with a need to go back to her own house— impossible, of course. It was not her home right now; it was a crime scene, and they would not be allowed in until the police had finished examining every inch of it.

That turned out to be more than a week later, which seemed like a long time, and Katrina was quite sure the police were deliberately slow to punish her for being rich and for apparently dodging a murder conviction. Brilstein had managed to delay the trial for at least six months, and they were both free for now. Unfortunately, the first week of freedom meant freedom at the St. Regis, and Katrina could not be happy. And when they were finally allowed to move back in to her house, it looked like a gang of wild teenagers had savaged the place. The police had been very thorough in examining every inch of every room, and just as negligent in putting it back the way they'd found it. Katrina spent her first three days at home supervising a cleaning crew.

But when the house was finally restored to its former state of half-refurbished glory, Katrina was surprised to find how easily the two of them settled into married life. With Michael, the best Katrina had ever achieved was a kind of disappointed comfort. With Randall, there was routine elation. Every day began and ended happily, together. They fit together like two pieces of the same puzzle, as if they had been together forever.

Slowly, very slowly, something approaching Normal Life returned. But for Katrina, it was a far better Normal than she'd ever had. When she came home from errands, or a meeting of some charity that still wanted her on their board, she had something to come home to—some-*one*. And so even though there was an eventual trial for murder hanging over her head, Katrina was happy.

Randall seemed just as content. Initially, he'd been a bit stuffy about living at her house amid the abundant trappings of ridiculous wealth. Little luxuries that Katrina took for granted seemed to make him very uncomfortable. But he had slowly relaxed into his new life of luxury. He still insisted on doing his work as a designer and art consultant, and he would not take any of Katrina's money. He wouldn't even drive one of the luxury cars that sat in the huge garage unless they were going somewhere together. On the other hand, he soon lost his shyness about using the pool, the sauna, and the home gym.

And surprisingly, wonderfully, the enormous, perfectly furnished kitchen.

Katrina had never really been interested in cooking. She'd taken a course in classic cooking when she first married Michael. But he never came home for dinner, and she quickly lost interest in making coq au vin for one. So for most of her marriage—her *first* marriage—she'd gotten by on eating out, getting takeout, or making a quick egg sandwich.

With Randall in charge of the kitchen, every evening was a different charming surprise. He seemed to delight in amazing her, and she never knew if she was sitting down to a meal of pad thai, pulled pork, or *tournedos du boeuf.* Katrina enjoyed the surprise, and the meals, immensely.

More than that, there was a comforting domesticity to being married to Randall that she'd never experienced with Michael. Katrina got a quiet happiness from the everyday things Randall did: trimming his beard, shaving his head, polishing his shoes, stupid little things that everybody did—but she was watching Randall, her *husband*, do them, and that made all the difference. At last, at long last, marriage had turned into something that met the expectations she'd had for it. It made her feel *complete*.

Marriage—to Randall—made Katrina happy.

Of course, nothing is all flowers and rainbows. Before her arrest for her husband's murder, Katrina had been active in quite a few charities and civic organizations. It was part of the Eberhardt code of noblesse oblige, the absolute obligation to give back. Katrina had always taken that duty seriously, and attending meetings for all the various organizations had given her a busy schedule. And because of her name—and, of course, her checkbook—she had always been greeted warmly, treated with affection and respect.

The first two or three such meetings *after* Michael's death . . . not so much. Nothing was actually said out loud, but a chill was in the air, and Katrina was made very much aware that the other committee members no longer approved of her. Katrina vowed to show them all that she was tougher than they were and their disapproval mattered less to her than a sparrow's fart. And she gritted her teeth, returned frost for frost, and soldiered on.

But there was one date on Katrina's calendar that no amount of spinal steel could prepare her for: the meeting of the Eberhardt Museum's board of directors. Katrina was a board member, of course, as were her two brothers, a handful of cousins, and a couple of what, in bygone days, would have been called family retainers. They had all known Katrina her entire life, and their opinion of her actually mattered to her. She dreaded facing these other board members—and especially her brother Erik Jr.

Erik, the senior sibling, was the head of the family business trust, and a bit of a Calvinist. He took himself and his responsibilities very seriously—a little too seriously, Katrina had always thought—whether those responsibilities were financial, fiduciary, or moral. To Erik, adultery was an unthinkable, unforgiveable affront to God and Man.

Katrina could just imagine what he would have to say about his baby sister being charged with the murder of her husband—and then to re-marry before Michael's body was even cold! And to marry someone so far beneath the Eberhardts, socially and—even more important—financially. He would naturally assume that Randall was a gold digger who had somehow wheedled Katrina into killing Michael to get his hands on her money. And to Erik, gold-digging was even worse than murder.

There would be no sympathy at all from Erik, and Katrina was frightened of what he might say or do. Not that he would become vio-lent, or even verbally vicious. And he couldn't cut her off from her trust fund. But because he had always been in charge, the older brother, she felt afraid of him in a way that she couldn't talk herself out of.

She hoped that her other brother, Tim, would be more understand-ing. He was only three years older than Katrina, and they'd always been close. He was much more tolerant than Erik. He was also gay, which made Erik disapprove of him, too. Erik felt that his younger brother had made a foolish "lifestyle choice," one that brought dis-credit to the Eberhardt name. Protecting the Eberhardt name was one of Erik's major preoccupations—yet another reason he would be furi-ous with Katrina. Tim had no such concern. Even so, Katrina could not bring herself to get in touch with him. What if she was wrong and Tim was cold or hostile? It was better not to know than to risk an un-pleasant knowing.

And so as the day of the museum's board meeting arrived, Katrina was full of dread. But she also had a stubborn streak, and she refused to skip the meeting. She would ride out Erik's disapproval, and maybe Tim's, and let them see that she was not neglecting her duty to the family, whatever they might think of her recent adventures. She even left home early, to make sure she arrived on time, so everyone would see that she was not ducking them, and she had no reason to hide.

Katrina marched into the museum with her spine straight and her head held high, ready for any hostile confrontation at all—and so she was completely unprepared when she was blindsided by a huge, warm hug from her brother Tim the second she walked in.

"Kat!" he said, almost yelling. "Oh. My. God! My sister, the tabloid queen!" He laughed, nearly squeezing the life out of her. "Oh Jesus, I am SOOOOO happy to see you! Are you okay?" And before she could say a word, or even breathe, he lowered his voice confidentially and said, "I *knew* there was something wrong with that Michael of yours. I never trusted him, and I always— But, Kat, seriously, couldn't you just *divorce* him? But you always did take things to extremes."

"Tim, for God's sake," she finally got out, "let me go! I can't breathe!"

Tim stepped back but held on to her shoulders. "God, Kat, I called a hundred times—I was so worried!"

"My phone is *evidence*," Katrina said bitterly. "They won't give it back, and I—" She bit her lip to keep from telling him the truth. He guessed it anyway.

"You didn't call me because you thought I would get all Erik on you, right? For shit's sake—you know me better than that!"

"I do," she said. "I'm sorry, Tim." And then she gave him back a hug. "Next time I'll know better," she said, and they both laughed.

They walked into the boardroom arm in arm, chatting happily. Tim wanted to know all about Randall, and was it just a marriage of convenience or True Love? And then of course all the more personal details—things Katrina wouldn't tell him no matter how much he wheedled.

The happy bubble burst for both of them as they stepped into the boardroom. "I'm so glad you two can laugh," Erik said from his place at the head of the long, polished oak table. "And, Katrina"—he said the name with such distaste it must have hurt his mouth—"I admit I'm surprised you would even show your face."

"Don't be such a prick, Erik," Tim said before Katrina could speak. "Your *sister* has been through a terrible ordeal."

"And whose fault is that?" Erik said coldly.

"You're acting like the Taliban," Tim snapped. "In *this* country we do innocent until proven guilty, remember? Especially with your *sister*!"

"Oh, for God's sake," Katrina finally managed to put in. "Can we stop acting like family and get to business?"

Tim snickered. Erik stared at her but finally nodded once. "Very well," he said, still in frigid tones. "Despite the *distractions*, we certainly have a great deal of *important* business today. The crown jewels arrive in—" He paused, frowned, looked around the room, and then sighed heavily. "Where is Benjamin?"

Katrina looked around the room. Her cousin Benjamin Dryden, known as Benjy by everyone but Erik, was missing. As curator— which meant he was in charge of special events like this one, too—he was expected and even needed at this meeting.

"Anyone, please," Erik said, quite cranky now, "where on earth is Benjamin?"

'd been watching Benjy Dryden for a couple of weeks now. Not 24/7, of course. I couldn't do that and still get everything else done, and there was a lot of "everything else" right now. But I'd kept one eye on him. I knew his habits, his routines—I knew pretty much everything about him. I do my research. I don't like surprises. If I overlook some factoid about a person or situation and it later turns out to be important—that pretty much guarantees a surprise. And it won't be a good one.

So I knew Benjy. I even knew a few things about him I'm pretty sure he wouldn't want anybody else to know. And the bottom line was I had decided that Benjy was just the guy I'd been looking for.

First off, Benjy was family—not my family, of course. No, Benjy was *Eberhardt* family, which was the important thing. Benjy's dad had married Priscilla Barclay, who was Erik Eberhardt Sr.'s sister. So Benjy was a cousin. Not in the direct line, but close enough that he had a big chunk of old Ludwig's money set up in a trust fund. Like way too many people with a trust fund, Benjy coasted and let the money do the work. He had no ambition, no drive, no real interests except looking at paintings and getting high.

And because he was an Eberhardt, he could do that and get by just fine. In fact, his life had been a total picnic so far. He'd been a five-star party boy at Andover. Money and family got him out with a diploma and into Yale, where he cranked it up a notch for his first two years. He took Party Hearty to a near-lethal level. It looked like Benjy was going to be one of those guys who flames out early and ends up dead at forty. But Benjy got lucky.

They say that different people wake up at different times in their lives. I'd have to say from my experience that's only partly true—most people never wake up at all. Anybody who does, there's always some kind of trigger moment that rocks the cradle hard enough to snap their eyes open. They look around and it's like, *Shit—I'm* alive?! And everything is different after that.

But not everybody. Most people spend their lives asleep, not even aware that this is it, a one-way ticket, you don't get another chance. And before you know it, the ride is over and you don't have another quarter. You're gone, and you never really knew you were there.

That was Benjy. Sound asleep, with both feet solidly on that path to permanent unconsciousness. Sometimes literally, because Benjy went through booze and dope at a rate that only a trust fund party boy could sustain. He was a cinch to be voted Most Likely to End Up a Middle-Aged Zombie. If he lived that long.

But then came spring semester of his sophomore year. Benjy was only about two pop quizzes away from flunking out when he took a survey course in modern art.

Magic happened.

Sitting in the dark lecture hall—stoned, of course—and looking at slides, in what was probably going to be his last semester at Yale, Benjy Woke Up.

A painting came up on screen. Benjy didn't look up until the instructor droned out the name of the painting. It was *The Great Masturbator* by Salvador Dalí. Benjy snickered at the title, looked up, and froze, his mouth hanging open. Dalí is supposed to be surrealism, I know. His paintings don't usually *mean* anything to most people. But to Benjy it was pure enlightenment. Something about that painting spoke to Benjy like nothing else ever had. He looked at the slide, and suddenly everything made sense. Benjy Woke Up.

He bought a reproduction of *The Great Masturbator* and stared at it for hours. It was even better after a few hits of dope. And that painting led him to other things that, weirdly enough, turned out to be just as compelling. Benjy was hooked on modern art.

It would be a sweet story if Benjy's new awareness turned his whole life around. It would also be a fairy tale. But he *did* cut down on booze and partying, and he brought his grades up. Enough so he could finish out Yale, go on to grad school, and take a master's in art. And when he was finished, he was a natural for a cushy job at the family museum.

Now in his thirties, Benjy had worked up to the noble position of curator. He was in charge of maintaining the collection, Acquisitions, and Special Events. Of course, his assistant did most of the work. Benjy was still a lazy-ass party boy with no ambition. And he still liked pot, especially White Rhino. He'd go up on the museum's roof a couple of times a day for a smoke.

That's how I found him, of course. On the roof, getting high. And that's how I took him out.

I knew what time he'd be up there. It was simple: as soon as the dope from his last trip up there wore off. And I knew something else, too. He turned off all the security on the roof before he went up— cameras, sensors, alarms, everything. Natural enough. He didn't want anybody to know what he was doing. That part didn't work too well. It was an open secret at the museum. Mr. Curator Benjamin Dryden was a doper, a true old-fashioned stoner, and he went on the roof to light up.

So I knew he'd be there. Even so, even with the security system off, he didn't make it easy. That's good. Like I said before, I don't like easy. So when I slipped up onto the roof and saw Benjy, I knew I would have to work a little harder. That made me feel a lot better about it.

He was sitting in the middle of the roof with his back to a stanchion. He had a fat spliff in one hand and a gold hip flask in the other, and he looked just mellow as shit.

So instead of cat-footing up behind him, I went racing over to him in my best synthetic dither. And Benjy, being totally whacked on Rhino and bourbon, just stared at me with his jaw hanging.

"Did you hear that scream?" I said, sounding as urgent as I could.

Benjy blinked. What else would he do? He was high as a kite.

"I think it came from over here," I said, and I quick-stepped over to the edge of the roof. I peered over. "Oh my God!" I said. "Oh, holy shit! Jesus, that's terrible!"

That did the trick. Benjy lumbered to his feet and hurried over, "What?" he said. "What is it?"

"Somebody must have fallen—there's a body in the street!" I said.

Benjy leaned over, blinked, searched for a long stoned moment. I looked at him in profile. There was a big clot of crusty wax in his ear hole. A big red pimple had bloomed on his neck. But his haircut hung just right, like it cost a couple hundred dollars, and it brushed against the collar of a shirt that cost even more. He looked just like what he was: rich, spoiled, useless. He'd done nothing his whole life except take with both hands, like he had a right to anything and everything. He was everything I hated.

I took a breath . . . and I felt the Darkness wrap around me.

"Do you see it?" I asked.

"No, I don't see anything," he said. "There's no body down there."

I put a hand on his back and pushed. Benjy went over the edge and all the way down.

I watched him fall. Then I watched him hit.

"How about now?" I said.

CHAPTER 23

You won't believe what happened today!" Katrina said breathlessly to Randall as she rushed in the front door of the house.

"Um, let's see. You went to a meeting? Oh—and they ran out of petit fours! My God, the inhumanity!"

"Randall, stop—this is serious!" she said, hanging her jacket on the rack in the front hall.

"Oh, I'm sorry. You should have said so." Randall came to attention and made a very serious face. "Seriously—what happened today?"

"My cousin Benjy," she said, hurrying on into the living room and sitting urgently on a settee. "He died! Benjy is *dead*!"

"He died at the meeting?" Randall said, sitting next to her. "Right there at the conference table?"

"What? No, of course not," Katrina said. "He was up on the roof!"

"The meeting was held on the *roof*?" Randall asked, rubbing a hand through his beard, half genuinely puzzled.

"Stop it, Randall, of course not," Katrina said. "The meeting was in the boardroom where it always is. Benjy was on the roof—he never made it to the meeting."

Randall was looking at her with real curiosity now. "Why was Benjy on the roof?" he asked. "Instead of at the meeting?"

"He goes up there to get high," she said. "Oh—I mean he *went* up. He's not going to— He's *dead*, Randall!"

Randall shook his head. "I'm sorry, this is— He died from getting high? Was it an overdose? Or poison dope?"

"Randall, the man is *dead*! My *cousin*!"

Randall put a comforting hand on her back and rubbed in small circles. "I'm sorry. Were you fond of him?"

"Not really," Katrina admitted. "He was kind of a borderline black sheep? But he was family, and I've known him my whole life."

"I'm sorry," Randall repeated. "How did he die?"

"What? Randall—he was on the *roof*!"

"Is it a very dangerous roof?" Randall asked.

"He fell!" she said. "Of course it's dangerous!"

"He fell—OFF the roof?" Randall asked.

"Yes, of course."

He nodded. "I guess that would do it," he said.

"He must have been so high, he just—I mean, he was probably looking at the lights, you know, after smoking pot? And he must've lost his balance, and . . ." Katrina stopped and took a ragged breath. "Anyway," she said.

After a pause, Randall, still rubbing her back, hesitantly said, "And, um, aside from that—how was the meeting?"

She stared at him, and then, in spite of herself, she giggled. "Shit," she said, holding a hand to her mouth. "I mean, I shouldn't—poor Benjy was just . . ." She got herself under control, sighed. "Anyway, with Benjy dead, the museum has a little problem. Because the Iranian crown jewels are coming, and—did I say that part of Benjy's job was Special Events?"

"You did not say that," Randall said.

"Well, so we need somebody very experienced in the art world—and we need them *now*! Because time is running out and there's so much to—I mean, Benjy liked to do everything at the last minute, so . . ."

"So the last minute is very soon?" Randall asked.

"Practically yesterday," Katrina said. "And it usually takes weeks and weeks to find the right person for a museum job."

"Well, I'm sure the right person will turn up," he said soothingly.

"And of course, technically," Katrina said, "it has to be somebody in the family. That's the tradition. Family. Either a blood relative or, you know, by marriage? So that makes it a lot—oh!" Katrina put a hand to her throat and literally bounced into the air. She turned in midair and launched herself at Randall. "Oh, Randall! Of course! I should have thought of it right away!" She hugged him with excitement.

"Thought of what?" he said.

Still holding his shoulders, she leaned back, beaming. "I know the perfect person!" she said. "Oh, Randall, of course! It's perfect!"

"Slow down, Katrina," he said. "What's perfect?"

"YOU are!" she said triumphantly.

"Thank you, I like to think so, but what . . ."

"For the JOB, Randall! You are perfect for the job!"

Randall could only stare at her.

No," Erik said. "Absolutely not."

"Just talk to him, Erik," Katrina said. "Give him a chance to—"

"I said no, and I mean it," Erik said. "I will not let some fortune-hunting guttersnipe take an important job at the museum!"

"'Guttersnipe,' for God's sake," Tim said. He'd come along to give Katrina moral support. "Listen to yourself, Erik—you sound like Grandfather!"

"I choose to take that as a compliment," Erik said. "Grandfather would never have let some penniless drifter get close to this priceless collection. And I will NOT be the one to grant access to this museum to some . . . *adventurer* . . . whose only qualification is that he's hypnotized Katrina into this ridiculous marriage!"

"This marriage has kept me out of prison, Erik," Katrina said, starting to get angry in spite of her vow not to.

Erik stared down his nose at her. "Well, perhaps it would be better if you—" he began.

Tim jumped to his feet and leaned over the desk to go nose-to-nose with his brother. "Erik, if you finish that sentence, I swear to God I will thrash you," he said with quiet anger.

Katrina could see a parade of different emotions march across Erik's face. For a moment she thought he would take his brother's threat as a challenge. But in the end, Erik's overwhelming love of dignity won out. He simply shook his head and said, "All right, Timothy. Sit down."

Tim lingered for a moment. But he finally let a breath hiss out between his teeth, and he sat.

While her two brothers faced off, Katrina had recovered her cool. And now, as evenly as she could manage, she said, "I'm just asking you to talk to Randall," she said. "See for yourself that he is completely qualified to, to, take on this job."

"He's nothing but a scam artist," Erik said stubbornly. "After your money."

"You don't know that," Katrina said.

"I think I do," Erik said. "What else could he want?"

"Don't be such an asshole, Erik!" Tim snapped.

"I'm not actually hideous," Katrina said. "And Randall hasn't taken a penny from me so far."

"All the better to take it all later," Erik said.

"Jesus Christ, Erik, you—" Tim began. Katrina put a hand on his arm and stopped his outburst.

"Erik, you're being completely unreasonable," she said.

"I don't think *you* are in any position to comment on anyone being unreasonable," Erik said.

Katrina mentally gritted her teeth and forced herself to go on calmly. "I met Randall because he is an expert on art. He stopped me from buying a fake Hans Hofmann. That's over a million dollars in savings, Erik."

"Well, but still," Erik said, but Katrina knew she'd scored a point with her penny-pinching brother.

"Remember what Dad used to say?" Tim said. "Don't let prejudice and ignorance make business decisions for you."

"Yes, that's true, but I don't think Father would have—"

"Randall knows what the job requires, and he can do it," Katrina said. "He's talked to Benjy's assistant, Angela, and even looked over Benjy's records—"

Erik interrupted, a shocked look on his face. "That was *not* an authorized—"

"Erik!" Tim said in an unexpectedly commanding voice. Erik looked at him with surprise. Tim locked eyes with him. "Ten days, Erik," Tim said firmly. "We have ten days until the jewels arrive. And you know bloody well it will take *twenty* to get ready." He spread his hands. "The man is good. I questioned him, and he knows his stuff. And he's right here." And then very softly, he added, "And like it or not—he is family now."

For a moment Katrina thought that was exactly the wrong thing to say; Erik turned red, and his face seemed to swell up. But at last he gave

a heavy sigh and flicked a glance to Katrina. He frowned. "Well . . . ,"
he said.

The face-to-face meeting between Erik and Randall went a great deal
more smoothly than Katrina had dared to hope. Erik had grudgingly
allowed her to sit in on it if she promised not to butt in. For fifteen minutes so far, she'd been sitting on the edge of her chair, trying as hard as
she could not to bite her fingernails and watching with increasing
amazement as Randall overcame Erik's objections. One at a time, with
smooth and careful logic, he knocked down every doubt Erik expressed.

But even though Katrina could see that Erik was impressed, he had
still not given his approval. She knew exactly what his last, unconquer-
able objection would be: money. Like so many people born into wealth,
Erik was an inveterate cheapskate. And beyond that, he had a completely paranoid conviction that absolutely everyone who approached
him, or anyone in the family, did so only to get at the family's money.
Katrina knew, therefore, that Erik was still more than half convinced
that Randall was a gold-digging scalawag. But since she was forbidden
to speak, she couldn't coach Randall on the subject.

And to her great relief, she didn't have to.

"Mr. Eberhardt," Randall said, "I'm aware that many people will
think I married your sister to get at her money. You may think so
yourself."

"Oh, well now, that's—" Erik said.

Randall held up a hand. "Please," he said. "You are head of the family and its financial watchdog. Protecting Katrina and her interests is
vitally important—and I would be dismayed if that thought didn't
cross your mind."

"Yes, of course," Erik said, mollified. And Katrina had to smile,
seeing Randall play her pompous brother so smoothly.

"So," Randall went on, "let me first state positively that I have not taken one red cent from Katrina—"

"So she says," Erik muttered.

"And I never will," Randall said with a moral force that even Erik had to find convincing. "I would find it demeaning and unmanly." He ran his hand over the top of his neatly shaved head, and his signet ring flashed in the light.

Erik blinked. "Your ring," he said, somewhat hesitatingly.

Randall frowned. "Sorry, what—oh, my class ring?" He held up the hand with the ring on it. "I guess it's kind of silly to wear it all the time," he said, shrugging.

"You went to Choate?" Erik said.

"Yes," Randall said.

Katrina could see that her brother was impressed, and for once she was grateful that he was such a snob.

"Well, well," Erik said thoughtfully. "I didn't realize you were—" And he waved a hand to finish the sentence—*because*, Katrina thought, *it doesn't sound good to come right out and say "upper class" or "one of us."*

"In any case," Randall resumed. "I think my experience and knowledge speak for themselves, and I realize this museum is a different thing, I understand that." Randall went on as if Erik hadn't said anything. "But the basics remain the same, and I am quite familiar with what's involved. Of course, as a matter of principle, I would never have tried to shove my way in the door here. That would be the kind of gauche, nouveau riche behavior I detest."

"Yes, that's right," Erik murmured.

"I didn't ask for this job. I'm not sure I really want it at all—but whatever anybody might think, I care deeply for Katrina," he said. "And this museum is important to her—because it's important to her *family*. YOUR family. And the museum—the family museum— Katrina's family—faces a crisis that I can help solve."

251

"That may be true, but—" Erik began.

"So for Katrina's sake—for the family's sake—I'm willing to look like something I find very distasteful," Randall said. He made a face like he'd bitten a sour lemon and rubbed his beard. "I can only hope that I do a decent job, prove my worth. And that in time I can overcome that negative opinion. To that end," he said, taking a deep breath, "give me six months with no salary. If you are pleased with my work after that, you can pay me. Until then, nothing. I won't even take the customary commission on buying new works."

"Who told you a commission is customary?" Erik said. "I can assure you, it is not."

Randall looked surprised. "Oh!" he said. "But according to the records Benjamin—" And then he shut his jaw with an audible click.

"What?" Erik said. "According to the records Benjamin did what?"

Randall shook his head. "Speak no ill of the dead," he said.

"If there is ill to speak about Benjamin filching money from the museum's budget, I bloody well want it spoken!" Erik said.

Randall looked embarrassed. "I, um—I had assumed that, that it was, you know . . . because on every single transaction, um . . ."

"Benjamin took a piece of every transaction?" Erik said, turning bright red with anger. "ALL of them?!"

Randall nodded.

"How much?" Erik growled through clenched teeth.

Randall looked down. "Five percent," he said.

Erik glared at Katrina as if it was her fault. "Why didn't we know this?" he demanded. Without waiting for her answer he turned back to Randall. "Bring me those records," he said. "I want to see for myself."

Randall looked up at Erik and raised an eyebrow. For a moment, Erik frowned back at him, apparently puzzled that he had not been obeyed instantly. And Katrina could no longer stay silent. "Erik, for the love of God," she blurted out, "you can't order him around if he doesn't have the job!"

Erik turned the frown on her and blinked. Then he got it. "Oh," he said. He turned back to Randall. "You're hired."

CHAPTER
24

Monique couldn't remember when it happened. It had probably been sometime in the last week, when all the prep was done and she'd started to work on the actual piece, but it really wasn't possible to say for certain. She had studied the photos Riley had given her, made a few notes, and then started collecting all the photos and information she could. She made some rough sketches, gathered materials, and began.

She started the actual crafting of the piece exactly as she always did, slowly, methodically, paying extraordinary care to each minute detail, even those that would not be visible when she finished. But as she worked in her usual way, she couldn't help thinking about what she was making, who she was making it for, and what all logic dictated had to be the result of trying something so completely insane. *They're going to kill him,* she kept thinking. *They're going to kill Riley.* She was certain of that: Riley would be killed. And it would be her fault because he'd said that his only chance would be if she made a perfect copy. That made it very hard to concentrate.

But Monique tried. She worked methodically, deliberately, carefully, and with a complete lack of inspiration. It all seemed mechanical, uninteresting—because no matter what she did, it couldn't possibly be good enough, and Riley would be killed.

She didn't want to think about why that mattered so much. She was not that interested in any of her other clients. She didn't necessarily want them to die, but if they did, she would regret only that she'd lost a client. She'd even said that to Riley. But with Riley, the thought felt different. If he died—if he was killed because her copy wasn't good enough—

She told herself he was just another customer. But she didn't believe herself. And when she asked why he was special, her mind would veer away from the question and tell her to get back to work. And she would try . . . But somehow, she knew that what she was doing was not good enough.

And then, for no real reason, it happened. As she worked and tried to kick her mind out of its self-digesting fugue, she stopped thinking and something else took over. Suddenly, Monique floated up out of her normal, careful working habits and elevated to a new, much higher plane. She didn't plan it, didn't do anything to make it happen. But she went from meticulous to obsessive. Time stopped having any meaning. Only this one small piece of work mattered—nothing else had any real existence.

Monique forgot to eat, sleep, bathe. She did nothing but work, rework, improve. When she was so exhausted she couldn't stand up, she would snatch a quick nap on her sofa, only to jerk awake in a sweat with some new detail suddenly flooding her brain, and she would leap up and get back to work. Whatever new space she now inhabited, wherever the obsessive thoughts came from, it didn't matter. She only knew this piece had to be the best thing she'd ever done. It had to be perfect. She no longer consciously thought that making it perfect might save Riley's life, but that belief began to grow in her, too, without any reflection at all about why that might matter to her. She simply worked on, approaching an exquisite artistry she had never touched before.

At some point she became vaguely aware that someone was standing behind her, watching her work. Annoying, but not enough to make her stop or look. She didn't know who it was, and she didn't care. She was pretty sure it was Riley, but that didn't matter. She was working.

"It's beautiful," the voice behind her said. Yes, that was Riley's voice.

"Go away," Monique said. "It isn't ready."

And it was, in fact, far from ready. The main jewel itself was set in the frame, with the crown filigree rising above it, but none of the detail was in place yet. So many smaller gems to set, so much elaborate fine work—and Monique was not really satisfied with the main setting, either. There was just so much . . . "Go away," she repeated, frowning with concentration.

Again, some small watching piece of her consciousness knew that he stood there for a long moment, studying her now and not the piece she worked on. But finally he left, and Monique worked on.

There were so many details, so many small but vital pieces that had to be just right—had to be *flawless*—and somehow she had to keep them all in her head, their relation to one another, their comparative size and color . . . So many things to think of all at once. But she did. Somehow she could easily keep it all whirling at the same time in a mental picture of complete clarity. She was raised up to a level where everything was clear and perfect and she was a part of it and could not possibly make a mistake.

And then one day, finally, it was done.

Monique stood up from her worktable and stared down at what she had wrought. For a moment she forgot that she was looking at something she had made and just let herself be dazzled by the thing itself. It was perfect, amazing, the most beautiful thing that had ever been. It was so remarkably flawless in every tiny detail that it just might work. It just might save Riley Wolfe.

Monique smiled.

And then a gigantic battering ram of total fatigue smashed into her and she barely managed to stumble across the floor to her sofa and fall onto it before a great wave of all-encompassing sleep wrapped around her and took her away to a timeless, thoughtless depth that washed away everything.

Monique had no idea how long she'd been asleep. There was no way to know; she'd fallen onto the couch completely oblivious to the hour, day, month, and slept so completely that she could not tell if she'd been out for an hour or a week.

A sleep that deep makes waking to reality seem a little bit unreal, out of focus, and Monique's waking was exactly that. It seemed to her, impossibly, that someone was leaning over and kissing her on the forehead. Nobody did that to her. Not even her father had ever done something like that.

So she blinked her eyes open with no guarantee that she would see anything that made sense. And for a moment, nothing did make sense. There was just a strange moving blur in front of her eyes, a blur that slowly receded, until it turned into a man's face standing over her and looking down with an awe-stricken expression. "Monique," the man said—Riley? "I have never, in all my life, seen such a perfect piece of work." Yes, it sounded like Riley's voice. "I can't even—it's—it's completely amazing. YOU . . . are completely amazing." And he bent over and kissed her on the forehead again.

She pushed him away and struggled to sit up. "What time—Jesus, what *day* is it?" Her voice was somewhere between a rasp and a croak, and she put a hand to her throat.

"It's Wednesday," Riley said, an answer that made her want to kick him, and so did the smile that came with it.

She jumped up abruptly, suddenly overcome with panic for no reason she could name. She ran to her worktable, the sweat already starting on her forehead—and there it was. Monique took a deep breath, and then another, and just looked down at it in wonder.

The Ocean of Light.

For a long moment she just stared. It was the most beautiful and perfect thing she had ever seen. She knew in her heart that she could not possibly have made anything so amazing—but there it was.

A firm but gentle hand came down on her shoulder. She didn't look to see who it was. She couldn't tear her eyes away from her Ocean of Light.

"Monique," a soft voice said—Riley's voice. "Go back to sleep." His voice was filled with a gentleness she never knew he was capable of, and she looked up at him and blinked.

Riley smiled, a smile that matched the softness of his voice. "You have done something wonderful," he said. "Something no one else in the world could ever do." He put his arm around her waist. "Now come on, go back to sleep. You have earned it."

Monique didn't resist as he led her back to the sofa. But she did turn back for one last long look at her creation. It caught a beam of light and seemed to glow from within with some kind of divine fire. "Yes," Riley said. "It is the most perfect thing I've ever seen. Really."

Monique looked a moment longer before she turned away. And as Riley eased her down onto the sofa, she was smiling.

She was still smiling, soft and gentle, as Riley covered her with a quilt. She closed her eyes and was already asleep when Riley bent over and kissed her. He stood above her for a long moment, staring down at her with a soft smile that matched her own. "Perfect," he whispered.

Then he wrapped the perfect copy of the Ocean of Light in velvet and left.

Frank Delgado stood in the sunshine and was grateful for its warmth. He still wore his light summer jacket, and it was just barely adequate on this cool late afternoon. There was a definite edge to the wind, a reminder that fall was here and winter was close behind. And here, on this exposed hilltop, he felt that chill.

He didn't care. He could have been lying nude in an ice bath for all he cared. Because he had been right, and he was here to prove it. It was real, and he'd found it. He was standing in the place where it all began.

He'd found the Big House on the Hill.

Delgado didn't really need to get out of the car and stand in the yard of the dilapidated old house. In fact, he didn't really need to come see it at all. He had all he needed. And he knew what his next move had to be. But he had started this trip to find out all he could about Riley Wolfe's past. He had wanted to dig out puzzle pieces and see how they fit in order to understand Riley Wolfe—in order, of course, to catch him.

Aside from that, though, there was a very real pleasure in simply looking at this place. And he'd spent enough time and effort finding it that he felt he'd earned a field trip to look at it. It was a kind of reward for a job well done, to see the place that had launched Riley Wolfe.

Not that the job was actually *done*. He hadn't even started on the real job, catching Riley Wolfe. But now he could. Now he had a picture of what was driving Riley Wolfe. Sitting there in his car, he flipped open his notebook one more time. Looking over the many notes he'd written, he allowed himself to feel satisfaction. He'd been right more often than wrong, and he was looking at the payoff for all his work.

There was one remaining question. He didn't know if it was important, and he knew he would not find the answer here, at the Big House on the Hill. Maybe he would never know the answer. Maybe it wasn't really important. He had to assume it wasn't because he had enough to go on. Still, it bothered him not to know.

Why "Riley Wolfe"?

Of every possible name in the world, why had J.R. Weimer picked *that* one?

It was a small thing, a detail that was probably unimportant—but it had been the question that started him on Wolfe's back trail, and it nagged at Delgado. He had the backstory now without it, but he also had a feeling it mattered, that it meant something. It was easy to make guesses, like, "'Wolfe' stands for 'lone wolf' or 'predator.'" But it could just as easily be something obscure—maybe J.R. had been a fan of detective fiction, named himself for Nero Wolfe. It was spelled the same. And why "Riley"? It was an Irish surname—did being Irish have some significance for the boy? As far as Delgado knew, there were no connotations to the name that would be meaningful for a thief, or a predator, or a lone wolf, or—what the hell. Whatever the reason, Riley Wolfe had picked that name. That was the *fact* of it. Any guesses Delgado could make didn't matter. It was all just cheap parlor psychology. J.R. probably just liked the sound of it.

What mattered was what Delgado *did* know now. It mattered that he had found and followed Riley's back trail, traced him to his roots, and learned more about him than anyone had known before. And more importantly—now he knew one truly significant new fact. And Delgado was sure it was the one that was going to bring Riley Wolfe down.

Riley Wolfe had a weakness.

And Frank Delgado had found it.

So he got out of his car smiling, and walked into the yard, and he looked at the Big House on the Hill.

It was no longer much to look at. Years of neglect had peeled the paint, nibbled away at the roof tiles, and weathered the trim to a sad grayish brown. Several of the windows were broken out, and a heap of rubbish had gathered on the porch, blown into the corners by winds that even now were tugging at the clumps of litter. But Delgado could see what this house had once been. It was not, by any means, a millionaire's estate. It was really no more than an upper-middle-class Victorian-style house. Still, it was light-years away from a collapsing double-wide trailer—even now, after it had been abandoned for many years. And in the imagination of a young boy who had lost it, it would seem like a palace.

He was very glad he'd come to see it, unnecessary as the side trip might seem. To Special Agent Frank Delgado, it was not unnecessary at all. This house was an essential piece of the profile, a tangible picture of a vital part of what had turned J.R. Weimer into Riley Wolfe. Delgado knew now that it had not been a fantasy, a promised future goal for a boy who wanted something better than a moldering double-wide. It was real. And it had been taken away from J.R. when he was young and very vulnerable. Getting back to a social and financial level where he could take it back—or even surpass it—that was a big part of what had pushed Riley Wolfe so hard, hard enough to make him a true master at crime.

Delgado knew most of the story now. Arriving in Nashville, he'd been so anxious that he'd put aside his qualms about using official channels and gone to the local field office of the FBI. And to his great relief, the SAC was Bill Kellerman, a man he had gone to the Academy with, and as close to a friend as Delgado had in the FBI. Delgado hadn't been in touch recently, didn't know Bill had been posted here. But when they spoke, it was like no time had passed. Bill had been happy to help, and had called his predecessor, now retired, and they'd gotten the whole story: How J.R.'s father, Ron Weimer, had run a string of scams, finally settling on a Ponzi scheme. How he'd made it work for two and a half years, pulling all the cash out to buy the Big House on the Hill and other big-ticket items for his family and himself. Until, finally, a record producer, a man from a very wealthy family, grew suspicious. He called in the Feds, and they began to ask questions.

The mounting pressure no doubt contributed to Ron Weimer's heart attack. Certainly his son would think so. And when everything J.R. owned was taken away, it would have been because the greedy, rich assholes took it—and so they became the group Riley Wolfe would forever blame. J.R. would vow to get back all that was rightfully his, and get it back illegally, like his much-loved father. But he would be smarter than Dad had been—he wouldn't let them catch him the same way. He would be bolder, stronger, smarter.

He would become the Wolf . . .

At the same time, he felt a need just as strong to protect the one person who had suffered through it with him—the only one who had stood by him and helped him reach a point where he could begin to take it all back: his mother. And because she was now helpless, the victim of a series of strokes that left her in a near-vegetative state, he would need to keep her close, to watch over her, to make sure she was there, near at hand, so he could tell her of each one of his triumphs.

All the pieces fit. For the very first time, Delgado began to understand Riley Wolfe, what made him tick, why he did things the way he did, and even what he might do next. Delgado had the picture, and he was ready to use it. He was going to catch Riley Wolfe.

And so, like a pilgrim to a shrine, Delgado came to understand that this was the starting point, the symbol—for both Riley and his mother—of the Good Life that would someday come again. The Big House on the Hill.

Delgado took a couple of photos with his phone. Then he walked forward through the brown shin-high grass, trying to picture the place as it had been, guessing which window had been young J.R.'s room— that one, just below the cupola? Maybe so. That's where he himself would have wanted a room when he'd been ten. He walked closer, moved by a strange desire to be near, actually touch the place, even breathe in the smell of it, just as J.R. had.

He reached the front porch and stopped, looking up at the house. *THE* house, he told himself again. The Big House on the Hill, with its cupola and wraparound porch—he could almost picture J.R.'s mother, Sheila Weimer, coming out onto that porch and calling her son in to dinner. Kellerman had helped him find Sheila, too. She was alive. Or she had been six months ago, when she'd been in an extended-care facility in Chicago. She'd recently been moved to some unknown new facility.

Delgado smiled again because he was sure he knew where. And also because it was the final piece, and it fit perfectly. Chicago had been the location of Riley's last heist, and it had been six months ago. He still kept her near, and that meant Delgado knew where Sheila was now. If Riley was in New York, Sheila would be, too, in one of the eleven facilities in the New York area equipped to give her the care she needed. And Delgado thought he could find her easily enough. He now knew Sheila's maiden name—Beaumont—and he had a list of all the medications she needed to take. That would narrow the search considerably, whatever name she might be using. He would find her. Finding her, he would find Riley Wolfe and close out a file that had been burning at him for years.

Delgado turned away from the porch and strolled aimlessly along the side of the house, just soaking it in. He put a hand out onto the wooden siding and caressed it—and got a splinter. It didn't matter. Seeing the house, touching it, even getting the splinter, reinforced his sense of its reality, and its importance to Riley Wolfe. And he smiled as he worked the little shard of wood out of his hand.

He walked backward, still looking up at the house, still smiling. When he got to his car, he paused for a moment and turned to look out at the view from the hilltop. Very nice. Rolling hills, the Nashville skyline in the near distance—maybe it wasn't quite the same as it had been twenty-some years ago. There were a lot more tall buildings, and closer to hand there were certainly more houses, and that large six-lane expressway was probably recent. But it was a good view, and Delgado lingered, looking at it, for several minutes. He had grown fond of Nashville. It was going to give him Riley Wolfe.

He turned back to look at the house one last time. Then he got in his car and began the long drive north.

CHAPTER
25

The week had been an endless buffet of manic activity. And even though her new boss was working as hard as she was, Angela Dunham had never been so busy before. The crew from Tiburon Security Systems had practically moved in, and they were, in Angela's opinion, a frightening lot. Of course, they were all ex-SEALs, which meant trained killers, and that was rather intimidating. There was just something about them, an air of potential menace, that made her feel rather odd; her knees got weak, and her pulse would flutter strangely. Worse, she would even shiver when one of them looked at her directly.

And one of them *did* look at her rather a bit more than absolutely necessary. Or it seemed so to her. He was one of the larger Tiburons, with a shaved head, a Fu Manchu mustache, and a face marked by several large scars. Every time Angela passed the men at their work, he would look up, and she could feel his eyes on her. It made the goose bumps run straight up her spine, and she had to hold herself in tightly to keep from shivering as he stared at her.

He never actually threatened her in any way, of course. None of the Tiburon men did. For the most part they were brisk, efficient, and polite, and except for that one large and frightening man, they ignored her and concentrated on their work.

Which was a very good thing since Angela had more than enough to worry about. And making things even more complicated, the Iranian advance team had also arrived. Most of them spoke very little English, but they were unfailingly polite—at least to Angela. Aside from that, they didn't seem to share Angela's feelings about the Tiburon team. In fact, there was a palpable feeling of hostile tension between the two groups. This situation was not improved by the habit the Tiburons had of muttering "raghead" whenever they were within hearing of one or more of the Iranians. Angela was quite certain there would be violence sooner or later—if not now, then almost certainly later in the week when the Revolutionary Guards arrived. From what she understood, they were rather like an Iranian equivalent to the SEALs: trained killers with itchy fingers. It was quite impossible to imagine the two groups coexisting peacefully. And to Angela's mind, it could only get worse when the armed team from Black Hat arrived.

But Angela had no time to worry about that except in passing. There were so many details to attend to, so many decisions to be made and so many different people trying to make them—and somehow it all ended up in her lap. It was so completely annoying that Angela was quite certain she would have gone stark bonkers if not for Mr. Miller, her new boss—Randall, as he insisted upon being called. She had resented him at first, of course. On top of the rumors about his sordid rise to "family" status, there was the fact that he'd been flung right into the job as curator, apparently without anyone considering Angela for the job—even after her years of experience at the museum in which she'd done virtually the entire job by herself while Benjy smoked pot on the roof.

She had expected Mr. Miller to be cut from the same cloth as his predecessor, and she'd been prepared to detest him. Instead, she discovered that he was very likeable, hardworking, and knowledgeable. He had an air of cheerful competence that Angela could not help thinking of as being rather British in nature—especially when she learned he had recently returned from a two-year stint in London.

And so, in very short order, Angela found that she could take many of these problems to Mr. Miller—*Randall*—with the expectation that he would actually solve them. In very short order, she realized that she not only liked Randall Miller; she respected him as well. She found herself leaning on his judgment and his quiet strength. Surprisingly, he was extremely well versed in the intricacies of the art world, and Angela learned to trust him. He was an island of calm and focused certainty in the midst of an ocean of chaos.

And as the week went on, to Angela's great relief, the hostility between the men installing the security system and the Iranians seemed to dissipate. The SEALs of Tiburon Security stopped saying "raghead" altogether, and instead nodded civilly to the Iranians and exchanged with them what Angela took to be polite greetings in their own language—Farsi, wasn't that it? The Iranians responded in kind, and Angela was pleased to think all sides were finally being diplomatically prudent. She was so happy with this apparent détente that she decided to participate. She listened carefully and learned a few of these Iranian greetings.

And so when Randall sent Angela to the supply room for a roll of blue bunting to decorate the lobby for the opening night gala, she was practicing one of her new Farsi phrases. As she walked into the restricted staff-only area at the back of the first floor, she was repeating *"Kir tu kenet,"* which she'd overheard and memorized this morning. She thought the phrase had a pleasant and musical ring to it. For no real reason, she decided it meant "good morning," and in the privacy of the restricted area she practiced saying it with a loud and cheerful voice, turning the last corner before the hall leading to the supply room.

"*Kir tu kenet! Kir tu*—oh!" she said as rounded the corner and ran into a solid wall of man. He was tall enough that Angela's face was in his chest, and for a moment she couldn't see anything except the badge around his neck, which was pressing into her nose. She could just make out, printed across the top of the badge, "TIBURON," at the point above the tip of her nose.

Powerful hands clamped onto her shoulders and moved her gently back. "The mouth on this girl," the man rumbled in a deep bass voice. "Where'd you learn to say that?" Angela blinked up at the man, and for a moment she could not breathe.

It was him.

The large, rough-looking man with the shaved head and Fu Manchu mustache. The one who had been staring at her.

He was staring now, with a half smile that frightened her more than an angry glare would have done.

"Somebody teach you to say that?" the man asked.

It took a moment for Angela to recall that she'd been speaking her Farsi phrase. And then it took another moment for her to overcome the sheer terror of being in his grip, and then remember to breathe. "It, it was—I heard some of your, ah—friends saying it?" she said hesitatingly. "This morning? You know, to the Iranians? And so, ah—it was just—I thought it must mean 'good morning'? Or something . . . ?"

The man snorted with amusement. "Or something," he said.

"Oh," Angela said, feeling oddly deflated—and still very frightened. In truth, her knees were wobbling just a bit. But she summoned her British spirit, took a step back, and soldiered on. "Then it—I had just thought it sounded so cheerful, and I do so want for everyone to get on nicely, so I thought that if I at least learned to say 'good morning'—and in any case I, I—" Angela jerked to a halt as she heard herself going on and on. *Stop babbling!* she told herself. "May I ask, what *does* it mean, Mr.— Ah . . . ?"

"'Chief,' not 'mister,' I work for a living," he said, with a great deal more force than Angela thought was strictly necessary. But he held out a massive hand. "Walter Bledsoe," he said.

Angela stared at the hand for a moment. It was covered with black hair, and the knuckles were enlarged and terribly scarred—and she realized he was holding it out in order to shake hands with her. "Oh! Yes, of course," she said as her manners came back online. "Angela. Angela Dunham. I, ah—I'm the assistant curator?"

"Nice to meet you, Angela," he said, with what was clearly meant to be a warm smile, but instead seemed to her like the sort of leer a jack-o'-lantern might wear.

"Likewise, I'm sure, Mr. Bledsoe," she said.

"Walter, not 'mister,' that's my old man," he said. "Or just call me Chief, like everybody else."

"Yes, of course—Chief," Angela said. She realized he was still holding her hand and pulled it back. "Tell me then, ah, Chief," she said, emboldened by his friendly attitude. "What does that phrase mean, if not 'good morning'?"

"*Kir tu kenet*," he said, with what seemed to Angela like a very authentic accent. His smile grew broader. "It means '*My dick in your ass.*'"

"Oh Lord," she said, and she felt herself blushing.

"It's really not something you oughta repeat. Not a pretty girl like you."

Angela floundered for some reply, her blush growing deeper. As far as she knew, she had never before been considered "pretty," even by boyfriends. She was, she knew, a prime example of British Plain: pale, with slightly pinched features, and a figure that tended toward the doughy. But this man said it with such sincerity, and it was tremendously flustering. "Well, that's—thank you, but—and then what *should* I say?" she finally managed. "I mean, to the Iranian gentlemen?"

"Well, if you have to say something," the chief said thoughtfully, "you could try '*madar ghahbe.*' That means 'motherfucker.' Or '*kirkhor,*' which is just plain old 'dick sucker.' Although my personal favorite is '*kire asbe abi too koonet.*'" He beamed. "That means 'hippo's cock in your ass.'"

In spite of herself, Angela laughed. She was not really fond of that sort of language, but the chief said it with such innocent joy that she couldn't help it. "I was really looking for something more in the line of 'good morning,'" Angela said.

"Waste of time with them," he said. "Only way they ever respect you is if you got your foot on their neck."

"Am I really to choose between a foot on the neck or a, ahem—a hippo's cock?"

"That's about the size of it," the chief said with a solemn nod.

"Perhaps I should remain mute," Angela said.

"Well," he said seriously, "if you're sure you don't like the hippo's cock?"

Angela opened her mouth, closed it again, and then, in spite of her shock—or perhaps because of it—she laughed. "I'm sure," she said. And then with a bit of a smile—since he *had* thought her pretty—she said, "Certainly not in that context, any road."

His smile broadened, which made Angela feel very uneasy—but also . . . What? She felt something else she couldn't name, which increased her uneasiness. And so she hurried a smile onto her face and said, "Well. Thank you for setting me straight, Chief."

"My pleasure," he said.

And then Angela could not make herself turn away, although she quite clearly had to, and they lapsed into a rather awkward pause—or at least awkward to Angela. It didn't seem to faze the chief at all. He just continued to regard with her with a fixed expression that reminded her of a large predator looking at its dinner. Angela felt her blush return and spread over her entire body, and she had no idea why. She really, truly wanted to leave, get on with her job, walk away from this man—and yet she did not, and she hadn't a clue why. "Yes, well," she said at last, determined to break away, "I'm afraid I have to get back to it. There's a bit of bunting I need to get and, uh—in the supply room?"

The chief nodded. "Just where I was headed," he said. "I'll give you a hand." And he did so quite literally, putting his large and powerful hand in the small of her back and shepherding her along the hallway to the supply room.

Angela opened the door, and he came in right behind her. He turned and closed the door, and then faced Angela. She stared at him, unable to speak, and the unknown feeling came back and washed over her and made her feel very wobbly and uncertain.

But the chief just nodded, walked over to Angela, and put both hands on her shoulders. Then he leaned slowly forward, and Angela did not move or try to pull away. Their lips met, and with a shock, Angela responded, putting her arms around him. His hands began to move over her, and she pressed against him harder.

And when it occurred to her what was about to happen, she broke away from him at last. He regarded her mildly, one scarred eyebrow raised.

"The door," Angela said in a husky voice she did not recognize as her own. "Lock the door."

CHAPTER
26

It was three nights before the gala opening, and Katrina surveyed the setting for the exhibition where it sat in the most secure interior room in the museum. The team from Tiburon was putting the final touches on the electronic security equipment, and every few minutes an alarm would squeal as they carefully tested each sensor.

Katrina barely noticed. In the first place, she was completely focused on making this event unfold flawlessly. But just as important, she was exhausted. Or, to be a little more accurate, she had been exhausted three days ago. Now she was so far beyond that she had trouble remembering where she was, let alone what she was supposed to be doing.

But she'd been doing it anyway. Because for the first two days that Randall had been curator at the Eberhardt, he hadn't come home at all. There was simply too much that had to be done before the opening and not nearly enough time to do it. And so naturally, Katrina had come to the museum to give what help she could. Since then, the days and nights had blurred together into an endless flurry of frantic activity, with no time for sleep except for short naps when it was absolutely essential. She and Randall—and Angela, the assistant curator—had been laboring around the clock.

Katrina took a deep breath and let it out audibly. She didn't dare close her eyes, even for a moment, or she would fall asleep where she stood. She took another look around the room. The collection itself would look absolutely fabulous in the setting they'd made for it. The individual pieces would sit in transparent cases that were locked in place, each one guarded by a half dozen devices that would detect any change in weight, any movement, any disturbance at all to the blast-proof glass of the case. Cameras were sited on each case—not merely for visual surveillance but for infrared, too. In addition to those measures, each case would have several human guards on a random patrol schedule that ensured there were always eyes on each item.

But the room itself was still littered with tools, scraps of wire and tape and packing materials. Stacked against one wall were a dozen poster-sized placards with information relating to each item, the general history of the collection, and something of Iran and the Persian Empire. They were not in place yet because, although each placard had its own easel to display it, the paint on the easels was still drying.

Katrina shook her head at the mess. They couldn't really clean up until the Tiburons finished their work. But at least they were finished in the museum's lobby. She could begin in there.

Katrina left the exhibition room and walked through the large marble archway into the lobby. She paused in the archway for a moment and surveyed the wreckage. The lobby was truly a disaster. It had been the staging area for all the individual work projects, and it looked like a combination of warehouse and dump. In just a few days, it would host the glitterati of the art world, all come in their finery to see an exhibition of wonders that had never before been displayed in the

United States. And when they arrived, if the lobby was not absolutely gleaming with quiet good taste, the multitudes would sneer as they sipped their champagne and end the evening by calling for Randall's head on a silver tray. They would be joined by the Iranian delegation, demanding an explanation for the dreadful insult and probably setting off an international incident, maybe even culminating in war.

Katrina knew there was only one way to avoid a long and bloody war that might eventually drag in most of the world and end in nuclear catastrophe. That was to set things right, make everything beautiful, turn the museum from a litter-strewn slum into a gleaming mecca of good taste. Only she and Randall could save the world, and time was running out.

And as Katrina had that thought, she saw her husband stagger around the corner from an alcove of the lobby. He was trying to balance a huge burden of trash, made up of four large boxes and two oversized trash bags. She watched him for a few seconds, smiling, and then, as the load began to slip from his grasp and onto the floor, she hurried forward.

"Randall, for God's sake," she said as she reached him, "didn't you ever hear the saying 'The lazy man breaks his back trying to do it all in one load'?"

Randall sighed. "That sounds very German. Is that another of your grandfather's pearls of wisdom?"

"Probably," she admitted. "But it's true anyway." She frowned. "Where's Angela? She could take some of this."

"She vanished a little while ago," Randall said. "She must have fallen asleep somewhere."

"Well, you can't carry it all by yourself," Katrina said. "Here—you take the boxes and I'll take the bags."

"Deal," he said, and in another moment they were walking together toward the back door, where the already-full dumpster awaited.

As they passed the exhibition hall, an alarm sounded, and Randall nearly dropped his armful of trash. "Jesus," he said.

"They're just testing all the alarms in there," Katrina said. "I think that means they're almost finished."

"I sure to God hope so," he grumbled. "There's this thing called *time*? And it's definitely running out."

"We'll get it done in time," Katrina said, trying to sound confident.

"Uh-huh," Randall said, making no attempt to match her tone.

"Well, but we sort of have to, don't we?" she said. They had arrived at the door marked "DO NOT ENTER: STAFF ONLY." It led to the loading dock and the dumpster.

"That's no guarantee that we will," he said. "I've known—hey!" He broke off as the door swung open, nearly hitting Randall, and Angela came hurrying through.

"Oh!" Angela said, clearly as startled as they were. And for some reason, she turned bright red. "I was just—I, uh—actually," she stammered. She looked around wildly, smoothing her skirt jerkily. "I'm just locating the catalogs," she said, pointing behind her. "Some twit has misplaced them, apparently." She squirmed, then said, "I'll have a look in the office, all right?" And before either of them could speak, she hurried off.

"What was all that about?" Katrina said.

Randall shrugged—and almost dropped his cargo again. "Oops, gotcha," he said, grabbing the trash and balancing it in his arms. "I have no idea," he said. "Maybe just British eccentricity?"

"She seemed embarrassed about something," Katrina said, pulling the door back open so they could get through.

"Like I said, probably fell asleep," Randall said. They walked down the hall toward the loading dock door. "I mean, if she did, and she thinks we caught her at it—"

"Maybe so," Katrina said. "I could use a nap myself right now."

They were only a step beyond the door of the supply room when it, too, swung suddenly open.

"Whoa," Randall said, dodging away from the door, and they both turned back to see who had opened the door.

A very large man stood in the doorway, adjusting his pants and fastening his belt, staring at them.

"Hello," Katrina said. She cocked her head to one side and said, "You're with the security people, aren't you? I've seen you with them. Aren't you the one they call Chief?"

The large man ignored Katrina and squinted at Randall. He gave his pants one last tug and tilted his head to one side. He raised one scarred eyebrow and pointed at Randall. "I've seen you before," he said. "I remember your face." And there was something in his tone that made the memory seem menacing.

"Uh, yes," Randall said. "I'm the curator of the museum."

The man shook his head. "That's not it," he said. "Somewhere before this. In the last six months."

"Uh, well, I've been in England until recently, and—"

But the chief was already shaking his head. "No," he said. "Somewhere else. Where you shouldn't have been." His forehead wrinkled in thought; the man moved around Randall, looking him over like he was sizing up an animal for the slaughter.

"Well, maybe you saw him on the news," Katrina said, trying to break the palpable tension.

The chief stopped between them and the loading dock and shook his head. "Someplace you shouldn't have been," he repeated slowly.

"You must be mistaken," Randall said. "Now, before my arms break from this trash—" And he tried to push past, but the chief put a huge hand on his chest and stopped him.

"I don't make mistakes. Not about this," the chief said. "I remember faces. It's kept me alive."

"Well, I'd love to play guessing games with you, but I have a lot to do, so excuse me?" And Randall finally managed to get past the chief. "Katrina—come on."

Katrina stood there a moment longer, looking with surprise at the chief. He was still staring after Randall. "I'm gonna remember," he said softly, his voice filled with menace.

"Katrina!" Randall called again.

Her husband's words jerked her into motion. "Coming," she said.

She caught up with him at the door to the loading dock. "What was that about?" she asked Randall.

"No idea," he said.

"He said, 'I'm gonna remember,'" Katrina said. "Like it was some kind of threat, or—"

"Shit," Randall said. "Give me a hand with this door?"

Between them they fumbled the outside door open. A rush of cool air came in, hitting Katrina in the face. But before she went out, she looked back one last time.

The chief hadn't moved. He was still standing in the hall, watching them. Katrina felt a chill go up her spine, and she hurried through the door and out onto the loading dock.

Chief Bledsoe watched the two wallflowers lug their trash out until the door closed on them. Then, still frowning, he turned away and headed back to rejoin the team. It bothered the shit out of him—he knew that fucknuts. Had seen that face. But where? When?

Never mind. It would come to him. It always did. And then he would decide what to do about it. Until then, why fuck with the good mood? Because he was feeling very pleased with himself. Not because he had just knocked off a piece of ass, either. It was a professional thing, too. His team had done a primo job installing the security equipment, even though some of it had never been deployed in the field before. That meant problems they couldn't anticipate, requiring solutions nobody had thought of yet. And they'd fucking well found them. So the men were happy that they were scoring with tech that nobody had seen before. And the chief had done his job, organizing the whole thing, dogging it all into place and keeping everybody clean and sober while they worked.

And yeah, best of all—once his duty was fulfilled, he had found a way to get laid on site, something he regarded as almost as important.

The piece of ass—Anabel? Abigail? something with an *A*—whatever her name was, she'd been surprisingly enthusiastic. He'd found that the plain ones usually were. He'd have to remember to ask somebody about her name. Wouldn't do to fuck that up. She might cut him off. Although, judging by her enthusiasm, he was pretty sure he could call her Fred and she'd keep fucking him.

The chief was thinking about that, and smirking, as he strolled down the hall—when a cold soft voice behind him said, "*Freeze.*"

Chief Bledsoe froze.

"Wipe that fucking simper off your face," the voice said. "And button your fucking fly, you cock-breath motherfucker."

A huge smile spread over Chief Bledsoe's face. "Sir," he said. "Permission to tell cocksucker officer to go fuck himself, sir?"

"Granted," the voice said, and Bledsoe spun around.

Standing there with a grin matching his own was Lieutenant Szabo, an officer he'd served under on the Teams.

"You dog-fucking bag of shit. Sir," Bledsoe said, grabbing the man in a bear hug.

"Jesus fuck, Chief, you're even uglier than I remembered. Like a warthog fucked a donkey."

"And you, sir. Without the beard you had in the sandbox, I thought I was looking at a monkey's ass."

"Guess you'd know, considering how many monkeys you fucked," Szabo said.

For a moment, the two just grinned at each other. "Shit, it's good to see you, sir," Bledsoe said.

"Likewise," Szabo said, and the two walked together toward the exhibit hall.

"So what the fuck are you doing here?" the chief asked. He nodded at Szabo's uniform. "And in that pretty shirt and all."

"I'm leading the team from Black Hat," Szabo said.

"Hoo-yah," Bledsoe said.

"And get this: We're supposed to 'coordinate and implement' with the Raghead Guards." He snorted.

"Lucky you," Bledsoe said.

"They get here same time as these jewels," Szabo said.

"When's that?"

"I can't tell you. You don't need to know," Szabo said. "It's the morning of the big opening shindig."

"Huh," the chief said. "We're scheduled to run final tests about then. And then we're outta here."

"Too bad, I could use you guys," Szabo said. He shook his head. "This place looks like a fortress, but it's got so many entry points we're going to need all the eyes we can get."

"Speaking only for myself," the chief said, "I may stay over a few extra days."

Szabo stared at the chief, whose face had taken on a look of massive innocence. "Well, fuck me dead," Szabo said. "Are you serious? How the fuck did you find pussy in a fucking museum?"

Bledsoe's smirk returned to his face. "Pussy everywhere. You just have to know how to find it."

"And in your case, you have to be willing to fuck some stuff that does not actually look human."

"As long as the important parts work," Bledsoe said.

"That's pure Navy all the way," Szabo said.

"Hoo-YAH, sir!"

Both men chuckled. "So you willing to share this girl?"

"Aw, she's way too ugly for an officer," Bledsoe said.

"Selfish bastard," Szabo said.

The two paused at the door to the exhibition hall. "Hey, you're gonna be here when we're gone—let me show you how all this stuff works," Bledsoe said.

"Absolutely," Szabo said.

Bledsoe took his old commander's arm and pulled him through the door, bellowing as he did, "Officer on deck!"

CHAPTER 27

It was just before dawn. The day of the gala opening had come. And with it, the Crown Jewels of Iran came, too.

The jewels had been waiting for this moment, in a remarkably secure vault at the Iranian Permanent Mission to the UN. It would take brass balls and a low IQ to try for them there. And now the jewels were on the streets of New York, headed for the Eberhardt Museum.

The Iranians were pretty sure nobody would try for the jewels while they were en route, either. I agreed with them. I wouldn't try it. Not without knowing the route, the timetable, the security—too many variables. And with a platoon of Revolutionary Guards riding with the jewels, you'd need a full company of veteran assault troops and a couple of tanks. Maybe air support, too.

No, nobody was going to hit the Iranian convoy. Not while it traveled through the streets of New York. But some overoptimistic idiot might be watching to make a stab at it when they were most vulnerable—when they arrived at the museum. It wouldn't be a whole lot easier, but you never know. The guards would be ready for it in any case.

So would I. I watched from the roof across the street. I hadn't seen anybody else watching, not on the roof or the street or from any neighboring building. I might have missed somebody, but I didn't think so. I didn't care. Nobody was going to get the jewels tonight. And after tonight, nobody *else* was going to get them. Just me.

So I was watching mostly from curiosity. I don't know why I chose to watch from a roof. There were plenty of places to stand and look once I found out when the jewels would arrive. But I picked the roof. Maybe because it made me feel powerful, invisible—shit, who knows? I'm not a shrink.

And who cares? I chose the roof. I liked it. I felt like Spider-Man up there, watching and waiting for Doc Ock to do something heinous. I'd been standing up there for twenty minutes, and so far nothing heinous had happened. But it was going to happen, and soon. That's me: Captain Heinous, Sticky-Fingered Superhero.

In the meantime, I watched the traffic. It was light at this hour, just before dawn. That's one reason it was happening now. And there was a definite chill in the air, so any people out on the streets walked a little faster to keep warm. I couldn't wait any faster, so I was getting cold. But I knew it would happen soon, and I thought warm thoughts and waited.

A black SUV turned the corner and drove toward the museum. It was followed by another black SUV, an armored car, and then two more black SUVs. The first two SUVs split up. One turned down the alley that led to the museum's loading dock; the other one parked at the mouth of the alley. Six bearded guys in dark suits jumped out. They were carrying automatic weapons, and they looked like they were going into combat— you know, eyes wide, hyperalert, looking for something to shoot. They fanned out fluidly, like they'd done this kind of thing before, and watched while the armored car turned down the alley.

No doubt about it. This was it.

The other two SUVs pulled onto the sidewalk and spat out their passengers, carbon copies of the bunch from the first SUV. All eighteen of them spread out, scanning the street, the alley, the nearby buildings.

And the rooftops, of course. I crouched down behind a chimney. I didn't want to show a profile. The guys in the street with the weapons were Revolutionary Guards. They would be well trained, and they'd be looking for any kind of silhouette that didn't belong on top of a building. I could still see around the chimney, and I watched for a little longer. Just curiosity. I'd seen all I needed to see. The jewels had arrived.

No more waiting. It was all going to happen now. Everything I had sweated my ass off to knock into place was about to click into action, like one of those Rube Goldberg machines. All the little pieces were about to move, nudge the others, and finally push the payoff out the last little door and into my hands.

I shivered. I don't think it was the cold. I think it was because this was really fucking *it*. I felt something that was in between excitement and raw terror. I knew it was going to work—and at the same time I knew just as surely that there were a million things that could go wrong, and almost all of them were bad news for me. And I couldn't tell which was more exciting: thinking of the payoff or knowing I was stepping into deep and dangerous shit. I just know I had this feeling, like a kind of rising tide of adrenaline and anticipation. I got it every time I made my play, and I loved it.

There was some shouting in the street—I couldn't make it out; it was in Farsi. I looked around the chimney. One of the suits was waving an arm, and the others were moving on him, double time, back down the alley with their weapons at the ready. In less than a minute they'd all disappeared. A minute after that, the SUVs and the armored truck pulled out in a column and headed downtown.

I waited another minute, just to be safe. Then I crab-walked back away from the edge of the roof and to the far side of the building. Then I put my earbuds in and cranked up my music: "Celebration," Kool and the Gang. I let the beat take over and drive me across the rooftops of the city.

Katrina took a last look around the exhibition hall. She had to admit, even if she had done some of the work herself, it looked absolutely spectacular. The glass cases, each with its own jeweled wonder, stood around the room, widely separated to allow for a crowd at each station. Dominating the area closest to the entrance, among a series of smaller cases containing bracelets and necklaces, was Empress Farah's crown, with its spectacular 150-carat emerald. Another case featured a bejeweled sword of a type known as a yataghan, then a pair of epaulets encrusted with hundreds of diamonds and emeralds and a case filled with lesser pins and brooches.

And at the dead center of the room, the greatest marvel of all. It stood alone, literally and figuratively. Nothing else in the collection—nothing else in the *world*—could compare. There it sat, isolated in its perfectly lit case.

The Daryayeh-E-Noor. The Ocean of Light.

Velvet ropes were up all around it to keep the crowds at a safe distance, and a pair of guards—one American, one Iranian—stood beside the case. More guards were stationed around the room, and another dozen patrolled on a random schedule, which might have been a little off-putting except that they were all dressed in full military splendor and ordered to smile and be polite.

Katrina frowned as she surveyed the room, looking for some flaw. She found none. Somehow they'd done it. The information placards were finally in place on their easels, the lights focused, the floor polished to a supernatural gleam—they were ready. She sighed, part contentment and part fatigue. It was done. And she even had time to get ready for the gala. She glanced at her watch. "Shit!" she said. She actually had only ten minutes to get across town to her cosmetologist. And then all the way home to get dressed, all the way back into town— it was going to be a horse race.

She hurried out of the room, looking for Randall. He had to get ready, too. He couldn't very well show up looking like the plumber's helper. Luckily, she found him in the lobby, in an intense conference with Angela, which Katrina had no qualms about interrupting. "Randall!" she called. He looked up. "I have to go get ready—and so do you!"

He hesitated, then shook his head. "I can't leave," he said. "They're doing a final test of the security system, the caterer is coming in an hour—and I just found out they don't handle the drinks—"

"Well, but you still have to get presentable, that's going to take some time," Katrina said. "You, too, Angela." Angela just bobbed her head and smiled.

"It takes time for you," Randall said with a small smile. "Men are different. Hell, I don't even have to shave." He ran a hand over his beard. "I'm a manly man," he said solemnly, and she smiled. "Just bring my tuxedo with you when you come back. I'll dress in the office."

Katrina shook her head. "Be *clean* when I get here," she said, leaning in to kiss him. "You smell like the Jets locker room at halftime."

He kissed her right back. "In that case," Randall said, "bring some of my cologne. The Agua Brava? That'll cover it up."

"Sometimes, my dear," Katrina said, "you get a little *too* manly."

That should do it, Chief," Mallory said. As the lead tech on this operation, he'd been working as hard as anybody, but he showed no signs of being tired. He tapped the control panel gently with the tip of his screwdriver. "We just need to tap in the pass code, and we're good to go."

"Let's get everybody together," Bledsoe said. "You can show the staff how all the pretty buttons and levers work."

"Ragheads, too, Chief?"

Bledsoe blew out a breath. "Fuck, I guess so. The lieutenant said we gotta liaise with 'em."

Fifteen minutes later everyone had gathered in the exhibition hall—museum staff, Iranian diplomats, American and Iranian guards, the Tiburon technicians, and even a representative from the State Department. The Iranians clustered together on one side, and the men from Black Hat opposite. The museum folks—Erik, Randall, and Angela—stood in the center between the two groups.

Bledsoe stepped up in front of the central case, the one that held the Ocean of Light. "Ladies and gentlemen . . . and others," he began in his you-are-a-useless-dim-pogue voice. "Welcome to a new day in security systems, brought to you by the most advanced team in the world today—Tiburon Security." He looked around at the crowd with what could only be called a self-satisfied glare. "You are in the presence of a genuine miracle of security systems innovation." He paused while one of the Iranians from the advance team translated into Farsi. "The major elements of this system have never been deployed before, anywhere in the world." Pause. "For starters, every possible entry point in the building has been fitted with motion detectors, infrared sensors, video cameras, and some slightly more standard alarm components." Pause. "Every single one of them is totally new technology that can. Not. Be. Hacked." Pause. "And every single display case in this room is equipped with similar safeguards—plus pressure sensors that detect the slightest change in weight." Pause.

"If any single alarm point is triggered, an alarm will sound. And the location of the intrusion is indicated on the main panel, which is always manned and always in communication with all active guards."

He pointed to the far side of the room, where Lieutenant Szabo stood beside the panel. Szabo waved.

"Also at every alarm point, you will find a multitasked camera," Bledsoe continued. "Additional cameras have been placed at strategic locations all around and through the museum, providing complete surveillance of every possible angle of attack, from cellar to rooftop. They send the image to the monitor on the control panel, as well as to a storage drive that keeps these images for up to two weeks.

"And, ladies and gentlemen—these cameras are not mere *cameras*. These devices capture and record every movement within their field of focus. Movement by anything within the programmed guidelines will cause an alarm to sound on the control panel, and the image will show on the monitor screen. And that's just the start.

"These cameras also scan in infrared, and when needed they can penetrate any solid object up to eight inches thick and capture an image of whatever may be inside. They contain sensors that record, analyze, and differentiate seismic shocks from a bunker-buster bomb right down to a sparrow's fart.

"The system as a whole is not even close to state of the art," Bledsoe continued. And he watched the crowd frown and mutter with a slight smirk growing on his face. "Because state of the art is not good enough for Tiburon. This system is twenty years *ahead* of state of the art." Pause. "It represents the most advanced, complete, futuristic technology ever deployed, and it is all brand-spanking-new."

Bledsoe looked around, nodded. "You are about to ask, 'If it's all new, how do we know it works?'" Bledsoe allowed himself a smile. It was not a pleasant sight. "Who wants to try me?"

His audience shuffled their feet, but no one stepped forward. Bledsoe waited, then nodded. "All right. We'll get a volunteer. Snyder!"

One of the Black Hat guards stepped forward. "Chief!" he said.

"Steal something," Bledsoe said.

Snyder handed Bledsoe his weapon, looked around at the display cases, and settled on the one holding Empress Farah's crown. He stepped to the case, hesitated, then reached a hand out to touch the glass—

The silence was shattered by the shriek of a loud siren, and bright red lights flared in a strobe-like rhythm. The stunned onlookers blinked and covered their ears from the painfully loud siren.

Bledsoe did not. He just smiled and waved to Szabo, who hit a button on the panel. Instantly, the siren and lights turned off and the room went back to normal. "That's just the beginning," he said. "Let's pretend that somehow, you bypass the exterior case." He raised a hand to Szabo. "Snyder, bypass the exterior case."

Snyder nodded. He carefully lifted the glass case off the crown and set it on the ground. He reached for the crown—and again, the ear-splitting siren and red flashing lights.

Szabo mercifully clicked the alarm off quickly. "But wait, there's more. If you get around *those* sensors—" Bledsoe said. He nodded to Szabo. "Snyder?"

Snyder reached forward again. This time he actually touched the crown. And once again, the siren and lights went off.

Szabo turned them off. "Redundancy," Bledsoe said, nodding to Snyder, who put the glass back on the exhibit and reclaimed his weapon. "Every single piece of the system is backed up at least three times. And if you are the greatest thing since Houdini and you somehow manage to bypass one or even two—three or four will get you." Pause. "And that doesn't even consider my colleagues from Black Hat, led by a decorated combat-wounded veteran, Lieutenant Szabo."

Szabo lifted his middle finger to Bledsoe—quickly changing it to a wave as the crowd turned to look at him.

"Oh," Bledsoe added with a shrug. "And of course, the Arabs," he said offhandedly, knowing very well that calling Iranians "Arabs" would be taken as an insult.

"Questions?" he said. He let his eyes rove across the faces of the onlookers. He paused when he came to Randall and frowned. But before he could say anything, a gray-suited man in the front row raised his hand—Mr. Wilkins, the representative from the State Department. Bledsoe pointed to him. "Sir?"

"I'm quite sure you have not neglected something rather basic," he said in a pure *Hah*-vahd drawl. "But what happens if the power is deliberately cut?"

Bledsoe nodded. "Absolutely right, sir!" he said. "We have *not* neglected that important point—Con Ed being what it is." He turned to Szabo and called, "Lieutenant! Cut the power!"

Szabo reached behind him to the control panel and flipped a switch. The room was instantly pitch black. A moment later the emergency lights flicked on, providing a dim glow. Bledsoe let people blink and get used to the faint light, then turned to Snyder and said, "Steal it again, Snyder."

Snyder reached for the crown once more. And once more, he had no more than barely touched it when the siren and red lights flared.

Szabo clicked it off, and Bledsoe called, "Lieutenant! Lights, please, sir!"

When Szabo restored power, Bledsoe gave his evil grin to the crowd. "Battery-powered backup," he said. "Will last up to twelve hours." He looked around once and raised a scarred eyebrow. "Any other questions?" There were none. "In that case . . ." He came to attention and looked to Erik Eberhardt. "Sir! I give you the Tiburon Security Mark IV Security System!"

Bledsoe watched the small crowd disperse, his eyes fixing on Randall. *Sonofabitch,* he thought. *I know I've seen that face before. Where? When?* His musings were interrupted when Szabo ambled over and shook his hand. "Nice pitch, Chief," he said. "You got a real future—selling aluminum siding."

"Fuck you very much, sir," Bledsoe said.

"You staying for the party?"

"I may have a date," Bledsoe said. "She says I should stay for it."

"Jesus," Szabo said, shaking his head. "She's got you leash-trained already?"

Bledsoe just smiled and shook his head. "How 'bout you, Lieutenant? You here for the big beer blast?"

"No choice," Szabo said. "I'm on duty."

"You better clean up, sir. That stubble on your face will bring discredit to the service."

Szabo rubbed his chin. "I was thinking I might grow the beard again," he said.

"You should, sir, absolutely," Bledsoe said straight-faced. "Totally changes your appearance—nobody can tell what you really look like, and that's a *good* thing. Sir." And before Szabo could reply, Bledsoe said, "Son-of-a-goddamn-bitch, that's it—the fucking beard . . ."

"What's wrong, Chief?"

"Nothing, just something about a beard," he said. "How it changes your face."

"Uh, yeah, it does. You just figure that out?"

"What I just figured out," the chief said, "is whose face it changed. And where I seen it before . . ."

"Is there some kind of problem?"

Bledsoe shook his head. "Nothing I can't handle," he said.

CHAPTER
28

Katrina looked around the lobby with a satisfaction that almost overcame her weariness—almost. As she had known it would be, it was a true horse race to get ready and get back in time. But she'd made it, with twenty minutes to spare, and now she rewarded herself with a glass of champagne—a Perrier-Jouët Grand Brut, thank God. The cheap stuff gave her a headache. She sipped and waved at a prominent gallery owner as she passed by. The whole top echelon of New York society was here. They packed the lobby, and the marble walls echoed with their excited talk, the clink of glasses, laughter. A string quartet played in an alcove; Katrina was fairly sure it was Brahms, and that made her smile. The quartet had started with Bartók. Randall had flinched, looked up, and gone over to have a quiet talk with them, after which they'd switched to Mozart and other, mellower selections.

Katrina covered a yawn, thinking with warm pride of the amazing job Randall had done, even to the details like the choice of the champagne and the quartet's musical selections. He really and truly had pulled off a miracle. Even Erik couldn't possibly find fault. She turned her head and saw Erik nodding gravely to a congressperson, who had no doubt shown up because it was an election year.

But where was Randall? He had vanished a few minutes ago—Katrina didn't know why or where he'd gone. There was no sign of him here in the lobby. She scanned the crowd for some sign of him, some gleam off his shaved head, but saw nothing. And then a scented hand flopped onto her shoulder. "Katrina, darling, what a marvelous thing you have done!" a voice cooed at her, and the search for Randall was forgotten as she turned to see a pompous aging woman who was a fixture of the art scene and a ubiquitous gossip. Her brother Tim called her the Dowager Empress.

"Galatea, so happy you could come!" Katrina said, accepting the woman's embrace and cheek-kiss. And then Katrina was ensnared by the Empress's monologue and could only hope that Randall would come back and save her soon.

Angela finished off a flute of champagne—her third. It was far too much if she wanted to keep a level head—she knew that—but in truth, she did not want a level head, which might make her think rationally about what she'd allowed herself to become enmeshed in. It couldn't really even be called an affair. It was no more than a series of quick encounters in almost every closet or dark nook in the museum. She was allowing herself to be used—and even worse, she was positively *loving* it.

Angela had never before experienced anything like this. It just wasn't possible for a rather plain British Midlands woman of her temperament. Such things simply didn't happen, either because someone like Angela would never consider it or, more likely, because no one would ever ask. And yet she'd gone along with Walter without even a cursory objection. If she was honest, she'd gone along with enthusi-asm, even while she knew it was stupid, wrong, whorish—

Angela took another flute of champagne from a passing waiter, sipped, and looked at her watch, feeling a flutter of excitement in her midsection. She'd agreed to meet him again, tonight, in five minutes—here at the gala, in the middle of an overflow crowd at a black-tie event. It was insane, stupid, absurd, and wildly exciting.

Sipping slowly, Angela worked her way toward the far side of the lobby. When she got to the large arched doorway, she finished the champagne, set down the glass, and slipped out of the lobby.

Katrina had finally managed to pry herself away from the Dowager Empress and was looking desperately for either Randall or a glass of champagne to help her recover. There was still no sign of her hus-band, but she had just snagged a new flute of champagne when all hell broke loose.

There was a sudden loud *BLAM!* down the hall, accompanied by a flash of hot blue light, and an earsplitting siren began to shriek, accom-panied by a painfully bright flashing red light. For a moment, no one in the lobby moved. Then the murmur of conversation started up, pitched much higher, as the confused people in the lobby tried to guess what had happened and what to do about it.

But then there was a second explosion, and all the lights went out. Somebody screamed, and the stunned guests lurched into action and began a crushing stampede for the exit.

Someone shoved Katrina against a marble pillar, smacking her el-bow hard and causing her to pour her entire glass of champagne down the front of her dress. She wanted badly to rush down the hall to see what had happened. It was a combination of her sense of duty and a biting worry that Randall might somehow have been there, been injured by whatever it was. But she was pinned to the marble pillar by the crowd. She struggled to break free but could not. And for a long moment the crowd kept her there, pressed against the pillar. Then a small break came in the mad rush, just enough to allow Katrina to slip through the horde and hurry for the hallway where the explosion had come from.

The hall was dark, but the emergency lights cast just enough dim light to allow Katrina to see at least a dozen guards, both American and Iranian, running toward the far end of the hall. She hesitated, wondering if she was charging headlong into danger. But she told herself that she was an Eberhardt, and this was her museum, and she hurried after the guards as fast as her spike heels would let her.

She arrived at the end of the hall to find all the guards standing in a half circle around the utility closet. The door was half open. Katrina could not see around the guards, but she could hear a muffled sound coming from the closet—a kind of hysterical mewling that was half sob and half wail. "Let me through, please," she said, pushing her way through the guards until she was in front of them with a clear view of the closet. And then she stopped dead, stunned.

Angela knelt in the closet with her fist shoved into her mouth, the keening Katrina had heard coming out around her hand. And slumped on the floor of the closet beside her was a large body.

". . . Angela?" Katrina said.

Angela dropped the fist from her mouth and let out a louder moan. "He's *dead*," she said. "Walter is dead . . . !" And then she resumed her wailing.

While the echoes of the first explosion were still ringing in the hallway, the guards in the exhibition hall reacted immediately. Moving their automatic weapons to the ready and switching off the safeties, they slid into combat postures all around the room. From his post opposite the doorway, Lieutenant Szabo called, "Reed! Snyder! Tremaine! Check it out!" waving three of his men toward the explosion. The three pounded off immediately, trailed by a handful of Revolutionary Guards.

The rest of the men stood ready—there were four, including Szabo, plus six men of the Revolutionary Guard—and it was a tribute to the high quality of their training that a moment later, when a man ran into the room, not a single shot was fired.

Szabo recognized him at once. It was Mr. Miller, the curator. "Hold your fire!" he yelled. "He's with the museum!"

The guards, both Iranian and American, returned to combat-ready positions, facing outward. Szabo waved Miller over. "What's up?" he asked. "What the hell happened?"

"The alarm system is all off!" Randall said excitedly.

"The backup is on," Szabo said. "What was the explosion?"

"I think it's a diversion," Randall said. "Somebody's trying for the jewels!"

"How many somebodies?" Szabo said.

"It would have to be a lot of them," Randall said.

Szabo nodded; he agreed. All the papers had run stories detailing the number of armed guards and the elaborate electronics. Anybody making a serious attempt at the jewels would have to bring a large, well-armed force. Szabo knew damn well there were plenty of people who would figure it was worth it. He looked quickly around the room. There were only two ways in—the main entrance and a fire door. "All right," Szabo said. "Let's—"

The second explosion cut him off. It was much closer than the first, and when the lights went out in the hall, Szabo went into action. "Cover the doors!" he yelled, waving an arm at his team. Out of the corner of his eye, he saw the museum guy, Miller, look around and then move over beside the case in the middle—the one with the huge fucking diamond in it. Szabo frowned. Miller was only a civilian, but he'd seen something Szabo had missed. With all the guards facing outward, that middle case was vulnerable. He pointed to one of his men and yelled, "Braun! Center!"

Instantly, Braun ran to the middle of the room and took position by the case holding the Ocean of Light. The Iranian commander yelled something, and two of the Iranians pounded over and joined him. The others had already split into two teams and were facing the two doors, fanning out in front of them, Black Hat and Iranians together.

The emergency lights flickered, then came on, and the guards held their positions, frozen in place as the tension grew.

For a full three minutes, nothing happened. Szabo glanced around, making sure he'd overlooked nothing. His men looked ready, as did the Iranians. Szabo noted that Miller was still standing in the center of the room, slightly behind the guards, right beside the case for that giant jewel, the Daria something. Miller looked just as alert as Szabo's team, like he would jump on anybody who tried to get past him, and Szabo almost smiled.

There was a clatter of footsteps, and one of the Black Hat men, Snyder, pounded into the room. "You better come see this," he said.

When Angela resumed her hysterical crying, Katrina had followed her instinctive impulse and stepped forward to hug the crying woman. They were not friends, barely acquaintances, but it seemed like the right thing to do. "All right," she said as she put her arms around Angela. "It's all right," she repeated, wondering why people always seemed to say that to someone who was hysterical. Especially since it really wasn't all right whenever the words were said. "Come on, now," Katrina said, pulling Angela out of the closet, away from the body. As they stepped clear, Katrina glanced back.

The utility closet was just big enough for two people to stand in, but only if they were on very good terms. On the back wall, the small metal door that covered the circuit breakers hung open. One of the breakers had been pulled out of the panel and hung by a wire. The wire was bare, a small sleeve of melted insulation around the end still connected to the breaker. The other end hung down, pointing like a slim blackened arrow to the body below.

The big man was stretched out with his back against the closet wall. In his right hand was a screwdriver. The tip was blackened like the hanging wire, smudged black as if it had been stuck into a fire—or a blast of electric current.

The man's face was contorted by death and what had to have been a tremendous electric shock. But Katrina recognized him. It was the man from the security team who had confronted Randall so strangely, with his weird threat to "remember." The one they called Chief. And he was most definitely dead.

A man pushed through the ring of onlookers. He was distinguished-looking, with perfectly coifed white hair and a tuxedo Katrina saw was a very nice Italian make, probably a Zegna. He frowned at the body, then looked up at Katrina, and she recognized him as the police commissioner. "I've called this in," he said. "I'll have officers here in five minutes."

"Thank you, Commissioner," Katrina said.

The police came in five minutes, as advertised. It seemed pretty clear that the chief had died by means of an unfortunate accident. Initially, the detectives were inclined to agree. But when they saw Katrina and realized who she was, they changed their opinion. "Coincidence" is a dirty word in police work, and all of a sudden the chief's death didn't seem so accidental. The cops didn't want to leave. At least not without taking Katrina along with them. The fact that she didn't know the dead man, had no reason at all to kill him, and had been in sight of a roomful of witnesses when the death occurred was not nearly as important to the detectives as the fact that someone they considered a known killer was in the building when a mysterious death occurred.

Luckily for her, her brother Erik arrived a moment later. He used his political and financial influence, which was considerable, and spoke a few words to the commissioner, who nodded, turned, and spoke to the detectives. They were reluctant to leave without Katrina, but in the face of the commissioner's raised eyebrow they had no choice. And then they were joined by the under secretary of state for Iranian affairs, who had naturally been in attendance. Katrina heard him use a few ponderous phrases like "unfortunate diplomatic implications" and "international incident," and finally, reluctantly, the detectives declared the chief's death an accident, and they were gone ten minutes later, leaving behind no more than a forensics team, with orders to be "inconspicuous."

It hadn't been easy. But it had to be done.

So I did it. I did it the only way I could.

No choice in the matter. None at all. The guy was a major problem. He was big, fast, mean, suspicious, well trained, experienced, strong—and he would be on his guard. He would expect me to try something.

So I wouldn't. But I would still get the bastard. Or, more accurately, I would let him get himself.

I found the right way to do it and the right place. In fact, I found four places that would work. Not hard in a big building where a lot of work was going on. Then I found out when he'd be near one of them. Easy—and it isn't snooping or eavesdropping if there's a really good reason for it.

And then I got there first.

It was a small closet, just big enough for two people to stand without touching. Its only purpose in life was to hold the master circuit breaker panel. That's what I wanted—with a couple of minor modifications. It only took about five minutes of very careful work. I was done when he opened the door.

He stood there for a good two seconds staring at me. "What the *fuck* are you doing, fucknuts?" he demanded, looking at the electric component in my left hand. It had a thick blue wire on one end that led back to an empty slot in the circuit breaker panel.

I didn't have to act real hard to look scared. "Oh!" I stammered. "I, I, uh—this was just—it goes right back in there," I said, waving the screwdriver in my right hand at the hole in the panel. "I just, uh—I'll put it back—"

"The fuck you will," he said. "Who the fuck knows what you'll try? Give it." He stepped in and grabbed it from me, just like he was following my script. And then—

The honest-to-God truth is, it isn't hard to get people to do exactly what you want them to do. People in general are pretty predictable. And to get at any little differences, you just have to watch them, read them, figure their pattern.

I knew this guy was ornery, hostile, nasty, and suspicious, even more than most people. On top of that, he was a gimme-that, screw-you alpha male. That meant that whatever he "caught" me doing, he wasn't just going to stop me from doing whatever it was—he would take it from me and do it himself. He'd have to. It's who he was.

So that's exactly what he did. I just stood there and let him. "Don't fucking *move*," he said. "I got business with you." He snarled and said,

"I remembered where I saw you, motherfucker. You got some explaining to do." And he pushed me flat against the wall.

I did my part. I acted flustered, scared, frantic. I had to do that for like four or five seconds while he figured where the component went. And then, following the script again, he jammed the piece into the slot on the circuit breaker, stabbed the screwdriver onto the retaining screw—

Flash.

Bang.

Thump.

Problem solved.

Lieutenant Szabo stood with the team from Tiburon Security, watching the cops pack up and leave. Szabo knew most of the Tiburons, of course. They'd served together in the SEAL Teams. Szabo had no reservations about speaking his mind in front of the others, even the ones he didn't actually know. They were still veterans of the Teams. It's a very small fraternity, and a very special bond.

"It's bullshit," he said as the last detective sauntered to the lobby and out of the museum. "It wasn't an accident."

Mallory, one of the Tiburons, nodded. "The chief didn't know which end of a screwdriver to hold," he said. "No fucking way he'd fuck with the fuse box. He would've called me to do it."

Szabo nodded. Mallory waited. When Szabo said nothing more, he said, "The cops are just gonna let it go . . ."

Szabo looked at him. "We are not," he said. "But before we do anything, we got to figure it out." He looked around at his men. "Who killed him?"

CHAPTER

29

Shit.

    Shit, shit.

    Shit, shit, shit.

And so on, world of shit without end.

I had been so fucking close, and just like that, just because of a little extra diligence by the guards, the whole fucking thing was off the track. It had been purring along like a well-tuned engine. But the purring stopped when the alarm shut down. It just hadn't rolled the way I'd thought it would. Taking care of the chief had gone like clockwork—and then, pffft. Like I said, when everything is going right, it just means you're being set up for the Big Dump. And everything after I short-circuited the big guy had been pure shit salad.

But I wasn't beat. Not even close. I've been doing this kind of thing long enough to know that nothing ever goes exactly the way it should. Riley's Sixth Law: Shit happens, so be ready with a roll of paper. I was ready.

In a way, I was kind of glad I'd hit a glitch. Like I said, when it's all going smooth and easy, I get nervous. So when everything was chugging along like a well-oiled bowling ball, I was already antsy. And then when it hit a snag—okay, two snags—when it went just slightly south, I actually relaxed a little bit. A fuckup! Great! Relax and enjoy!

And move on to plan B.

I always have a plan B waiting, sometimes more than one. Which one I choose depends on what shape the fuckup takes and when it comes. At this point, I was in the end game. If it hadn't been for a couple of small bumps, I would've been home free.

I still would be, just a little bit later. There was never any doubt about that. The only question was how I would do it. Or—to be more accurate—*who.*

So when things got quiet, I slipped away into the night. I put on my music and headed across town via rooftop express. It was a good night for it, cool and clear. I played some Buddy Holly: "Think It Over," followed by "Crying, Waiting, Hoping" and "What to Do." Then I stopped on a roof, right before I went down to the street, and switched it to Mose Allison. No reason for either choice. It just felt right.

By the time I got to my storage locker I was on the Pretenders and feeling pretty good. Sing it, Chrissie. I went into the locker and closed the door, pulled out a folder that held a bunch of alternate identities. I sat on a steamer trunk and flipped through them.

Who would work best this time? I had more than a dozen choices, each one right for a different situation. Full set of IDs, credit cards, and so on. That stuff is simple to get. You just need the right connection and a little bit of cash—or bitcoin, which is usually better. The so-called dark web has made everything easier and cheaper, but cryptocurrency works better than cash there. It's safer.

So a new identity is cheap and easy, and I always had a bunch of cool ones ready. The trunk I was sitting on had the rest of each identity—hair, clothes, etc. Like I said, Monique helps me design them, especially the details and accessories. She never knows which one I'm going to use when. That would be too much like telling her what I was doing, and that's a stupid risk—even with Monique. But it is kind of fun to have somebody to try them out on, and she makes them all better.

I studied each identity and thought about how I might work it from here on. Who was I this time? Aging Art Critic? Maybe—it fit the scene, but there was no real usable scenario. I flipped through a couple more. Big Fat Gawker. He would come in, have a heart attack, wait for a moment when everybody was running around panicked—and I had the fat suit already. It was hanging up right behind me.

But it bumped into the same problem that had blown up plan A. These guards wouldn't panic. They were too good. The second Big Fat hit the ground, they'd flip their safeties off and look for somebody to try something. And there were too many of them. I flipped past Gawker and looked at a few more. I needed to be somebody who gave me some way to create a distraction that could get the guards to react *my* way—and still leave me free to make the move when they did. Each one depended on the same kind of distraction, and each one ran smack into the same problem. Too many too-good guards.

What would work with these guys? They were so much better than the usual rent-a-cops, it was like a brand-new concept of security. What could get them to leave me an opening? I just needed five seconds. These bastards hadn't even given me two.

Near the end of the stack, I had a thought. The problem was not how good the guards were or how many of them there were. The real bitch was that it was too complicated for one guy, even me. What I really needed was two people. One to make the distraction and one to make the play.

That made sense. Except, of course, the part about the second person. Who? There was nobody else in the world I trusted that much. I mean, nobody at *all*. And why would I get somebody I *didn't* trust to help me?

Stupid idea. I shook it off and flipped through to the end of the file. Possibilities, but nothing really—

A moment, please.

Just one tiny fucking moment.

Every now and then, something comes at you from left field. If you're any good at all, you pick it up, look it over—and nine times out of ten, you throw it back into left field.

But that tenth time . . .

Riley's Tenth Law: There's always at least two ways of looking at everything.

I had figured that my problem was I needed a second person, and I didn't know anybody I could trust. I didn't have friends, and honest to God, how could I trust my enemies? And there were a lot of them.

Except—and here comes the thought—if I looked at it the other way around, I actually *could* trust my enemies. I could trust them to do the same thing every fucking time. They would always act in their own interest, and mostly against mine. That's what made them enemies. So if I knew they were trying to help themselves and screw me, all I had to do was set up a little booby trap that counted on them doing exactly that. So that whatever they *thought* they were doing, they were really doing something else. Something that helped me.

I was pretty sure I was onto the answer. I put down the folder and switched my music back on to think it over.

This idea came from left field, so I put on some real left field space music. Eno, "Music for Airports." I closed my eyes and let it space me out, take me to a place that was huge and open and vague. And I thought.

I thought about enemies. The list of my enemies was long, but it got shorter as I thought which ones would fit something like this and how;

which ones might jump at the bait; what bait that would be; and, mostly, which ones I really wanted to stick it to. And then I thought of one who had actually screwed me, and that still hurt. I looked him over, strengths and weaknesses, habits and hates. I really wanted it to be this guy, so I parsed him twice. Finally I had to admit it. Even though I wanted him to match, he actually did. Perfectly.

Great. Step two. How to set the trap, and who in my folder of New People could set it best.

I'm not sure how long I sat there on that steamer trunk thinking. I do know the Eno was over, and my ass was sore, so I guess it was a while. That didn't matter. What mattered was that I had a plan. I knew who I would be. Even better, I had just the right enemy.

I took a big breath and smiled. "There's always a way," I said, and I opened my ID folder. I pulled one from the middle of the pack. "And this is it," I said.

I looked at the picture. This would be fun.

He had plenty of people didn't like him," Mallory said. He looked around at the other ex-Team members gathered by the security control panel in the exhibit hall. "But he didn't have any *enemies*. I mean..."

"Nobody who'd want to actually kill him," Snyder said, nodding his head.

"Fuck," Szabo said. "I wanted to kill him plenty of times. But not seriously."

They were all quiet, thoughtful, for a long moment.

Tremaine broke the silence, sounding a little reluctant. "Um," he said. "Don't suppose one of the towelheads...?"

"No fucking way," Mallory said. "They're all being good little fanatics."

Szabo nodded agreement. "They want this whole thing to go smooth and easy," he said. "They're on best behavior."

"Um," Taylor said, frowning. "This girl he was banging . . . ?"

"She was all broke up about it, crying her ass off," Snyder said. "Why would she kill him?"

"No, I mean, not her. But, you know," Taylor said, shaking his head. "Maybe somebody, you know. Who was with her before? And they were, like . . . jealous?"

They thought about that for a minute. It was Szabo who spoke first. "Naw," he said. "I don't buy it."

"Well, fuck-a-shit-piss," Tremaine said, his Cajun accent making the words sound kindly somehow. "They's a reason it happened here and now. So if it ain't the chick, what the hell? Hey, Lieutenant?"

Szabo shrugged and stroked the stubble on his chin. "I dunno. Maybe it—" He broke off abruptly, tilted his head to one side.

"What?" Snyder asked.

"He said something, just before he bought it," Szabo said slowly. "How a beard changes your face—and whose face it changed."

"What the fuck," Taylor said.

"Shit," Tremaine said. "That girl's ugly, but she got no beard."

"But if Tremaine is right—" Szabo continued.

"'Course I am right," Tremaine said. "Right about what, Lieutenant? The girl's beard?"

"Here and now there's only one guy with a beard," Szabo said. "Not counting the ragheads."

"That metrosexual guy? He's just darling," Snyder said.

"Yeah, him. Miller," Szabo said.

"Lieutenant, a guy that pretty couldn't never get the drop on the chief," Taylor said.

"Somebody did," Szabo said. "Somebody with a beard." He looked around at the other men. "Can you think of anybody else who fits?"

They were silent for another minute.

"Okay," Taylor said at last. "So what do we do about this guy?"

Szabo nodded. "Here's what I'm thinking," he said, and the others leaned in closer to hear.

I have to admit," Randall said, "I have never been to a more exciting opening." He sat in an all-glass alcove in their kitchen, used as their breakfast nook, with Katrina seated across from him and empty breakfast dishes pushed to one side.

Katrina frowned. The morning sun was in her eyes, underlining the fact that she'd had too much champagne and not enough sleep. She reached for the rheostat that controlled the SmartGlass windows. The sun was climbing above the trees now, and it was much too bright. Katrina twisted the dial and darkened the tint of the windows a point, then another. "I could have used less excitement," she said, still frowning. She sipped her coffee and held up the morning paper. "The *Times* was not impressed."

Randall shrugged. "Not to worry," he said. "I'm sure the *Post* will *love* it."

"And that's a good thing?" Katrina said. She sighed, then smiled slightly. "Although it was almost worth it to see the look on Erik's face."

Randall snorted. "I didn't know he had any other emotions aside from disapproval," he said.

"Of course he does," Katrina said. "There's shock and anger."

"And now the face he pulled last night. What would you call it?"

"Hm," Katrina said. "Maybe nauseated disapprobation?"

Randall nodded and sipped. "Mm," he said. "I like it."

They were silent for a moment. "But my God, poor Angela," Katrina said. "She must be a wreck!"

"Her boyfriend even more so," Randall said. "He's dead."

"It's just hard to picture Angela with that, that . . ." She shook her head.

"You can't say it?" Randall said. "Speak no ill of the dead?"

"Something like that."

"Well," Randall said. "Everybody loves somebody sometime."

"I'm not sure it's love if it happens in a utility closet," Katrina said.

"That's right, we haven't tried it, so—"

"Randall, stop," Katrina said. "I mean, the man is dead."

"No argument there," he said. He glanced at his watch. "Oops. I'm late."

"Late for what?" Katrina said as he stood up.

"Oh—in all the excitement, I forgot to tell you," he said. "I'm going up to an auction house upstate—Busby's?"

"Never heard of them," Katrina said.

"Well, it's upstate," Randall said. "And when I say *auction*, I mean, you know. Boxes of farm tools and old encyclopedias. And the occasional moose head."

"Is that really a reason not to come in to the museum today?" she said, frowning again. "We don't actually *need* a moose head. And my God, Randall, there's just so much—" She broke off and shook her head.

"So much damage control," Randall said. "Smoothing ruffled feathers and so on. Your brother Tim is much better than I am at that sort of thing."

"I suppose I should go in, too," she said. "But even so . . ."

"It will be a huge feather in the museum's cap if this trip pays off," Randall said. "Old Mr. Busby thinks they've uncovered a Masaccio."

"Is that a painting or an automobile?"

"Normally a painting," he said. "There are very few surviving automobiles from the fifteenth century."

"And this Mr. Bisbo can tell the difference?"

"Busby," Randall corrected her. "And as unlikely as it may be that it's the real deal, I would be remiss in my duty if I didn't check it out. And," he said, standing and clearing away the plates, "Mr. Busby assures me that if I get there today, I am a step ahead of the competition. The Met is apparently still filling out the proper forms to get a tank of gas for the trip." He put the dirty dishes in the sink. "So if you think you can spare me for the day, I'm off to upstate." He bent and kissed her. "And even if the painting is a fake, I promise to bring you something wonderful—"

"Please," she interrupted, "not a moose head."

"Of course not, not for you," he said. "You deserve something far more elegant—maybe a 1964 set of *Encyclopaedia Britannica*, missing volume fourteen."

"That sounds fabulous," she said. "I never liked volume fourteen."

"So I may be back late," he said.

She reached up and pulled his face down for a longer kiss. "Mmm," she said. "Not *too* late . . . ?"

Hey, Lieutenant?" Tremaine stuck his head into the exhibit hall and Szabo looked up. "Some FBI guy here. Wants to talk to you."

Szabo blinked. Chief Bledsoe's death—his *murder*; Szabo was sure it was no accident, no matter what the dumb-ass local cops said—was something he took personally. He had been here at the museum, without sleep, for over twenty-four hours, and he was tired. His SEAL training included going without sleep, and he could easily stay on watch and alert for another twenty-four—or forty-eight, if he had to. Even so, he was tired, and his eyes were dry and filled with sandy gunk. "What does he want to talk about?" Szabo asked, rubbing at his left eye.

Tremaine shrugged. "He didn't say. Just, he wants to talk to whoever's in charge of security. That's all. I mean, he's a Fed," he added, like that explained everything.

And maybe it did. Whatever the guy wanted, you didn't say no to talking to an agent of the FBI. So Szabo took a deep breath, nodded at Taylor to stay with the security control panel, and followed Tremaine into the lobby.

The morning light was blasting in through the front doors of the museum, and Szabo paused in the doorway, blinking against the unaccustomed glare. "Over there," Tremaine said, nudging Szabo toward the alcove where the bar had been set up at last night's gala. Szabo looked and saw a gray-suited figure waiting, back turned toward him. He held a pair of glasses in one hand and, with the other, rubbed his forehead, as if massaging a headache.

The suit turned as Szabo approached, fumbling the glasses back into place on his face. For just a second, Szabo could see last night's bar through the lenses of the glasses as he put them on. The distortion was incredible—the lenses were so thick Szabo wondered how the guy could possibly see anything at all.

But this FBI agent apparently could see. He straightened up and faced Szabo. "Lieutenant . . . Zharbo?" the man said.

"Szabo," he corrected, looking the FBI man over. He was a man of average height and build, with receding reddish-brown hair, a large and bushy mustache, and glasses. And he was looking unblinkingly at Szabo, waiting for more. So Szabo shrugged and added, "They only call me Lieutenant because they're used to it. I'm a civilian now—I'm with Black Hat."

"So I understand," the Fed said. "I am Special Agent Shurgin, FBI." He held up his credentials. He didn't offer to shake hands, so Szabo simply glanced at the badge and waited.

Shurgin blinked, an enormous gesture seen through the thick

lenses of his glasses. "I understand you have updated the museum's security?"

"Not personally," Szabo said. At the last second, he stopped himself from saying "sir." Something about this guy bothered him. "But I'm running it now. It's unprecedented technology. First-rate."

Shurgin nodded. "Who has access to the system?"

"I do," Szabo said. "A couple of the guys from Tiburon—"

"Tiburon?" Shurgin demanded.

"They designed it. Installed it," Szabo said.

"And you trust them?" Shurgin asked. He sounded like he couldn't believe it was a good idea to trust anybody, and if you did, you were an idiot.

Szabo shrugged it off. "Completely," he said. "I know most of them. They're from the Teams."

"Which teams would that be, Lieutenant?"

Szabo took a breath. This guy was absolutely getting under his skin. Maybe it was a technique, a way to knock people off balance and get the truth out of them. Even so, it was pissing him off, and he couldn't let that happen. "The SEAL Teams," he said. "They all have a top security clearance."

"Mmm," Shurgin said. "Anybody else?"

"The director of the museum. Miller."

Shurgin nodded. He looked around the lobby. Szabo wondered if he could really see anything. "Can I assume that this wonderful, up dated, first-rate system includes video surveillance?"

Again, the guy was just being a douchebag. But Szabo reminded himself that he had lived through worse. "Of course," he said. "Archived for two weeks."

Still looking away, Shurgin said, "I'll need access to the archived footage."

"All right," Szabo said. "You going to tell me what this is all about?"

"We have reason to believe there will be an attempt on the jewels. By a man we take very seriously."

"And you think this guy can get past the electronics, AND my team, AND the rag— and the Iranians?"

Shurgin looked back at Szabo and blinked again. "*He* thinks he can," Shurgin said. "He might be right. It's kind of his specialty."

Szabo shook his head. He was pretty sure nobody could get past all the guards, electronic and human. "He must be Spider-Man or something."

"He is," Shurgin said, with no trace of humor. "He is an expert at parkour—you've heard of that, I assume?" Szabo nodded, but Shurgin went on without noticing. "That means he can come at his target from any direction. Even the unexpected ones. And he has used these skills to execute highly improbable—and *successful*—thefts around the world. He's smart, relentless, ruthless—and he doesn't mind committing murder if it will achieve his ends."

Szabo perked up at the word "murder." If this superthief had already made a stab at the treasure—and killed the chief in the attempt . . . "Did you get briefed on what happened here last night, Agent Shurgin? It might be connected—"

"That's why I'm here," Shurgin said irritably. He rubbed his forefinger across his mustache. "Last night's attempt—if it was, in fact, an attempt—will not be the last. He'll come again. And again. He'll keep trying until he succeeds. And if he has to, he won't hesitate to kill again—unless we apprehend him first."

He raised an eyebrow, which, for some reason, looked bizarre: a thick band of fur jiggling above the thick lenses. "This exhibition has powerful implications for our national security. A theft of any one of the items on display would have catastrophic diplomatic consequences." He gave Szabo another unnerving blink. "You understand, Lieutenant?"

"Of course," Szabo said. "Who is this guy?"

"A man named . . . Hervé Coulomb," Shurgin said, and he added, unnecessarily, "He's French."

Szabo installed Special Agent Shurgin in the conference room, with a video monitor and playback, and he began to go through the archived footage from the security cameras. Szabo left him there, hunched absurdly close to the screen, presumably so he could see through his thick glasses.

Szabo went back to his post at the security console, where a handful of his men were waiting. "Miller isn't coming in today," Taylor said as Szabo approached. "His wife just got here—alone. Said he's not coming."

"Why not?"

Taylor shrugged. "Dunno. Chief's girlfriend isn't here, either."

"She probably all busted up 'bout the chief," Tremaine said.

"Yeah," Snyder said. "Think Miller is, too?"

"He'd sure as shit stay away if he was guilty," Mallory said.

"Maybe," Szabo said. "And maybe it's a legit reason." He filled them in quickly on what Special Agent Shurgin had said.

"A Frog?" Snyder demanded. "You think it was some Frog killed the chief?" He snorted and shook his head.

"Why not? You can get badass Frenchmen," Tremaine said, looking and sounding injured. "Some of those ole boys in Marseille are badass as they come."

"Anybody can get the drop on anybody else, you know that," Szabo said. "The point is, we don't know. I mean, Miller doesn't come in today? Yeah, sure. That looks guilty. But we got to consider this other guy."

"Why?" Mallory asked. "Chief said that thing about the beard, and then the beard plays hooky?"

"FBI don't fuck around wasting time," Taylor said. "He says it's the Frog, he got a reason."

"Sure," Mallory said. "We all know how smart and efficient the government is, right?"

"Fuck is wrong with you?" Taylor demanded. "FBI is the best in the world at their shit, and—"

"I'm just saying I want some fucking proof!" Mallory said just as hotly. "You can't just—"

"Stow it," Szabo said. The two men went silent. "We can't do shit about Miller when he's not here. And we're gonna look like prize assholes if it is the Frog and we miss him." He looked around the small circle of faces. "We're not quitting on Miller," he said. "Not on anything or anybody. Not until we got the guy that scragged the chief. But Miller isn't going anywhere—he's fucking *married* to an Eberhardt. So right now we focus on this French guy. Okay?"

After a moment's thought, the others all nodded their heads. "Right," Szabo said. "Let's set our action stations."

CHAPTER
30

It had been the longest day Katrina could remember.

The morning had been bad enough. The phones had not stopped ringing for two minutes, and every call had been a network, or a bureau, or a newspaper—calls had come from all over the world, all wanting the details of what had happened last night at the disastrous gala. And even though Katrina's plan had been to hand all these calls over to her brother Tim, there had just been too many for him to handle alone, and she'd had to give statements to such unlikely places as Bahrain, Indonesia, and Guiana. She didn't know what to say, and she stumbled over every phrase, until, in the end, Tim had crafted a general statement, and they had both answered each call by reading it, thanking the caller for their interest, and hanging up.

And then, to have that FBI agent, with his ridiculously thick goggles, sitting in the conference room the entire time, staring at the video monitor and snapping irritably at anyone who interrupted him. His attitude of cranky authority, combined with his creepy appearance, were nearly as intimidating to Katrina as all the phone calls. She had never wanted so badly to have Randall there for moral support.

Katrina had tried to call Randall, to tell him what was happening and that she was staying here and why. But he hadn't answered his phone. She hoped that meant he was driving home, but she couldn't stop herself from worrying about him, on top of everything else. It was a long drive; some of the roads were very bad and filled with drunken rednecks—what if he'd had an accident? The way things seemed to be going right now, that made a kind of emotional sense to her, and she couldn't lose the mental image of a broken Randall lying in a cold upstate ditch. And all for some ridiculous painting that was almost certainly a fake of some kind.

Katrina sat in the office worrying and answering a few more telephone calls. When the museum closed for the day, she switched on the answering machine. With nothing to do now, she passed the hours fretting. She took turns worrying about Randall, then about the museum, then occasionally pausing to wonder if she was in any danger herself. Special Agent Shurgin had asked her to be there to represent the family, but he hadn't said why he thought that might be necessary, nor what she might be asked to do.

And then, at long last, the FBI man called them all to the conference room.

R ight there." Special Agent Shurgin pointed at the screen. Katrina leaned forward and watched as the video image of a shadowy figure flitted across the museum's roof and then vanished over the side. "That's him."

"*Khar too kharé,*" the Iranian commander, Iravani, muttered.

Szabo nodded. "Yup."

"Hervé Coulomb," Shurgin said with quiet intensity. "And he is not here to look at pictures. He is here to take the jewels."

Katrina took a ragged breath. So much had happened—*was* happening—and it was just a little too much to take in all at once. After last night . . . and now this, another attack . . . ? "Are you—I mean, how can you be sure?" she asked. "That it's—you know. This, this—criminal . . . ?" It sounded terribly feeble, even to her ears, but she didn't want it to be true, not on top of everything else.

Shurgin pushed back from the screen and looked at her. It was not a friendly or encouraging look. "How many men do you know who can move up walls like that?" he said. "And how many of them would be on the roof of your museum, knowing they could get shot for it?"

Katrina bit her lip and shook her head.

Shurgin nodded, once, and said, "That's him. Believe me, I know him when I see him."

Of course, Katrina thought. *That is, if you really can see anything.* The thick glasses made her nervous for some reason—more nervous than having an FBI special agent come into the museum and take over. But Erik had told her to do what the special agent told her to do. She probably would have anyway since she had a natural respect for authority. And in any case, the man was there to help them.

So she just folded her arms across her chest and watched as Shurgin turned his head back to the screen. "There can't be any doubt. That's Coulomb, and he was looking for a way in from the roof. If he doesn't find it there, he'll keep looking until he finds it somewhere else. But," he said, "I think he has found it."

Katrina looked around at the men gathered here in the conference room: Lieutenant Szabo, the leader of the Black Hat team; Iravani, the Iranian commander; Mr. Alinejad from the Iranian Special Interest section; and Wilkins, the man from the State Department. Tim had gone home, pleading a prior engagement, but Katrina was quite sure he just didn't like being there with all the law enforcement and security men around. And Erik had left at five o'clock without even making an excuse as feeble as Tim's. So Katrina was the only representative of the Eberhardt family, and the museum, currently present.

"I know this man," Shurgin said, still staring at the shadowy image on the screen. "He does. Not. Quit." He scowled at the screen, the lines on his brow deep furrows. "Last night was no more than a test run, to see what our defenses looked like from the inside." He frowned at the screen and ran the recording backward, running the same clip again.

"Are you sure this man was here last night?" Katrina asked. "*Inside* the museum? With all the people here? I mean, it was— The place was packed."

"That's exactly why I'm sure he was here," Shurgin said without looking away from the screen. "No one would notice him in the crowd."

"Wait a sec," Lieutenant Szabo said. He took a step forward closer to Shurgin. "So if he was here last night—he's the guy killed Chief Bledsoe?"

"That's highly likely," Shurgin said.

"Why?" Szabo demanded.

"Either because your chief was helping him, or because he wouldn't," Shurgin said.

Katrina actually heard a "click" as Szabo slammed his upper and lower teeth together. The lieutenant leaned a knuckle on the conference table and pushed his face close to Shurgin's. "If you're trying to hint that Chief Bledsoe sold us out to help this guy, you fucking well better rethink it," Szabo said, his voice filled with barely controlled anger.

Shurgin swiveled in his seat, bringing him practically nose-to-nose with Szabo. "Either he was helping Coulomb, or he would not," Shurgin repeated. "There is no other possible explanation."

"Chief Bledsoe would never. EVER. Flip on us," Szabo said softly.

Shurgin held his gaze for a long moment until Katrina wanted to scream. Then he said, very matter-of-factly, "I'm sure you're right," and turned back to the video screen.

Szabo took a very deep breath and then straightened up slowly.

"Perhaps we could get back to the point?" Mr. Wilkins said. "You said this French thief has already found a way in? So you believe he will be back?"

"I know he will," Shurgin said.

"Knowledge is wonderful," Commander Iravani said dryly. "Do you also know *when* he will return?"

"Yes," Shurgin said. "He will come back tonight. And he will keep coming—until he gets in."

"What do you suggest?" Szabo asked.

Shurgin faced Szabo and smiled, the first sign of humanity Katrina had seen from the FBI man. "I say—we let him in. Tonight."

The Iranian snorted and looked at Shurgin as if he was crazy. "You will forgive me if I do not share your infidel sense of humor?"

"I'm dead serious," Shurgin said, all traces of the smile gone. "If we give Coulomb one way in, he'll take it. And when he comes—*tonight*—we will be waiting for him."

"There's not a whole lot of time to set something up," Szabo said. "And how do we let this guy know the way in without him getting suspicious?"

"Coulomb has an informant on the inside who has been paid to clear the way for him," Shurgin said. Szabo growled, and Shurgin looked at him, shaking his head. "No," he said. "I meant it when I said you're right. The chief was not Coulomb's informant. But I know who is." He glanced around the circle of startled faces, and he smiled. "One of us, in this very room, has been selling information to Coulomb on the dark web."

"Who?" Katrina blurted. They all looked at her. "For God's sake, don't go all Miss Marple on us—who would do that?"

Shurgin's smile grew wider. "I did," he said.

The stunned silence lasted several seconds, and then everyone erupted angrily at the same time. Shurgin rode it out with smile in place and finally held up his hand for silence. He glanced at them one at a time, his gaze settling at last on Mr. Alinejad, the Iranian diplomat, who was smiling broadly. "Mr. Alinejad has understood," Shurgin said.

"I congratulate you—it is very nearly as devious as a Persian solution," Alinejad said, showing a double row of very white teeth. "You offer him a piece of meat—but it also has in it a hook, correct?"

Shurgin nodded. "I offered the information for sale on the dark web," he said. "And I sorted through the replies until I had Coulomb."

"Very clever," Alinejad said.

Shurgin acknowledged the compliment by inclining his head.

"What info did you give him?" Szabo asked. He still looked a little angry.

"I told him that cutting the power to the museum would take out the alarm system," Shurgin said. "And I said I would divert the guards and cut the backup system."

"Hold on a second," Szabo said. "Cut the backup?"

"Otherwise, the alarms will still go off and Mr. Coulomb will not come in to join us." He looked at Szabo, then at Iravani. "If he has one way in, and one time to use it, and we know it," he said carefully, "we will have him when he comes." He turned his unsettling gaze on Szabo. "If your team is as good as you seem to think, we will have him." He looked around again, as if daring anyone to object.

No one did, although Wilkins shook his head and murmured, "A bold plan. A bit risky."

"No risk at all," Shurgin said. "We know when and where he will come. We will be there waiting." He looked at Iravani. "I was going to suggest that your team move into position to make the capture, Commander Iravani." Wilkins nodded approvingly.

"Of course," Iravani said with heavy sarcasm. "So when this criminal attacks, it is my men and my country who are in danger, and if he succeeds, we are to blame."

"If you prefer, I will ask Lieutenant Szabo's men," Shurgin said. "I'm quite sure they can handle it if you can't."

"We'd love to snag the bastard," Szabo said. "Dead or alive."

"Alive," Shurgin snapped. "It must be alive!" He blinked angrily around the circle of faces, then appeared to calm down. "The FBI has a very long list of major crimes Mr. Coulomb has been connected with. We would very much like to get our hands on Mr. Coulomb, *alive*, and have a long conversation—"

"And so you will risk my country's greatest treasures?" Iravani said angrily. "To catch a simple bloody thief?"

Shurgin stared at Iravani. His eyes were huge through the lenses and somehow conveyed a weird menace. The Iranian backed up half a step, and Katrina thought, *Oh, good—I'm not the only one who finds this man a little alien.* "If we set the trap properly—if we do this in a *competent* way," Shurgin said flatly, "there is no risk. And," he added, raising a hand to forestall Iravani's objection, "whoever makes the capture will look like heroes. All the media around the world will grab at this, play it up big." He allowed a very small smile to play on his lips. "I can see headlines like 'Revolutionary Guard Captures Thief American Police Cannot.'" He let Iravani enjoy that for a moment, then nodded. "But if you don't think your people can handle this—"

"We will do this," Iravani snapped. "But only if we approve of the arrangements."

Shurgin looked at the Iranian for a few uncomfortable seconds, then nodded. "Very well," he said at last. "Then assuming you agree— here's what we'll do."

CHAPTER
31

don't trust that FBI guy, Lieutenant," Snyder said when Szabo rejoined the team. "Somethin' 's off about him."

"I don't trust him, either," Szabo said. "He gives me the fucking creeps, and there's definitely something off. That changes nothing. He's a federal agent."

"Yeah, but, Lieutenant," Tremaine said. He hesitated, then went on in his soft voice, "My brother-in-law, he's a cop? Louisiana State Police? And he was thinkin' 'bout trying for the FBI?"

"Is he a dumb cracker like you?" Taylor asked. "Cuz if he is—"

"Shut up, Taylor," Tremaine said without anger. "Point is, you got to have good eyesight—think he said, no worse than 20-40?"

"Which this motherfucker clearly don't have," Snyder said. "So what the fuck?"

They were all silent for a minute. "Maybe he had an accident in the line of duty," Szabo said.

The others looked at him dubiously.

"Well, shit, I don't know," Szabo said. "He's got a real badge, and he's got this French guy coming in tonight, and if there's a chance the Frog killed the chief, I want to know about it, all right?"

Slowly, one at a time, the others nodded. Szabo nodded back and said, "Let's get in position," and they began to move together out of the lobby and down the hall.

"Yeah, but," Snyder said, "even if he really is what he says—why the fuck did he make *us* the backup?" Snyder grumbled. "To a bunch of fucking towelheads, too—that ain't right . . ."

Taylor grunted agreement. "I fucking hate this," he said.

"Diplomatic reasons. Above your pay grade," Szabo said.

"And if we're backup, how we gonna get a chance at this guy, Lieutenant?" Tremaine added. "Like you said, we got to have a few words with him before the cops take him away."

"We'll get our chance, I'll make sure of that," Szabo said reassuringly, even though he wasn't entirely sure about that himself.

"Just saying," Snyder said. "Our country, and we let a hostile foreign power take point?" He shook his head. "That ain't right."

"And we cut the backup alarm system?" Tremaine said. "Don't much like that."

"We're the backup," Szabo said. "And we're better than any battery-powered high-tech gadget. Goddamn it, I want to get my hands on this guy just as bad as you do."

"Yeah, but, Lieutenant—" Taylor said.

"For Christ's sake, quit whining," Szabo cut him off. "Shurgin was right. We got to lure this guy in, or he'll get spooked and run. And that means cut the alarms—*all* the alarms. That just makes sense."

"Shit," Snyder grumbled. "I never did like *sense*."

"That's why you never made it past PO3," Taylor said.

"Fuck you," Snyder replied.

"All right," Szabo said. They'd arrived at the exhibition. "Take perimeter positions and stay awake. Okay, Taylor?"

"Fuck you very much, sir," Taylor responded, saluting smartly.

Szabo watched the men move off into position. *But goddamn it, they're right,* he thought. *There's something wrong about Shurgin.* But there wasn't a whole hell of a lot he could do about it for now. He shrugged it off and took his place near the exhibit hall's door.

A few minutes later, Szabo heard a clatter of feet and turned to see Special Agent Shurgin coming out of the door that led upstairs. He closed the door and approached Szabo.

"Lieutenant," Shurgin said as he neared. "Is your team in place?"

"They're deploying now," Szabo said.

"The Iranians are in position on the roof," Shurgin said. "And also at key points on the second floor."

Shurgin made no further comment and didn't move on; he just stood there looking thoughtful.

Szabo looked at him, and his doubts grew. His gut told him something was off about this guy. Tremaine thought so, too. Szabo was not a subtle man, and he needed to know if Shurgin was legit. So if he was going to find out, he would just come out with it, face-to-face.

Now or never, Szabo thought. "Special Agent Shurgin," Szabo said carefully.

"You don't trust me," Shurgin said abruptly. "Your men don't, either."

Szabo hesitated, taken aback. But then he nodded. "That's right," he said. "We don't."

Shurgin looked right, down the hall toward the back of the museum. "I tell you what, Lieutenant," he said. "Pretend you do trust me, just for a little longer. Until midnight."

"Why should I?"

"Because then you'll have proof," Shurgin said. He turned his hugely magnified eyes on Szabo. "If a thief comes at midnight," he said, "and he's French, I am legit and you were right to follow my lead. If a French thief *doesn't* come, I'm something else. And then . . . ?" The ghost of a smile flitted across Shurgin's face, then vanished. "I'm right here." He blinked. "Deal?"

Szabo thought about it. The man made sense. And it was only a little longer. If midnight came and went with no French thief, no deal, and Shurgin would have some very serious questions to answer. In the meantime, Szabo was right here with his eyes on the guy and his team around him. No risk.

Szabo nodded. "Deal," he said.

Shurgin rubbed his mustache with a thumb. Then he nodded, too, and looked up and down the hallway. "He could even come in the front door. So remind your men to watch all points, not just the tricky ones."

"They know," Szabo said.

"It's half-past eleven," Shurgin said, glancing at his wristwatch. "Coulomb will cut the power at midnight. But he's a devious bastard— be ready at all times."

"We're ready," Szabo said.

Shurgin looked at Szabo for a long moment, then nodded. "Good," he said. "Is the battery system off-line yet?"

"I'll do that right now," Szabo said. He went into the exhibition hall, and Shurgin followed him. They walked in silence to the far end of the hall, and Szabo disconnected the backup system, pulling the cables off the battery array. He straightened. Shurgin was watching him. Szabo raised an eyebrow at the FBI man.

"Shouldn't we have somebody at the control panel?" he said, nodding toward the command station at the far end of the room.

"No need, not with the whole system off-line," Shurgin said. "It's more important we have all eyes on the approaches—outside this hall." He nodded. "But just to be certain, I will wait here, with the jewels." Shurgin reached under his jacket and drew his pistol. "I'm the final backup," he said. "Just in case."

Szabo nodded. "He won't get that far," he said.

"You don't know him like I do," Shurgin said, showing a small and uncharacteristic smile.

"Maybe not," Szabo said.

"All right, Lieutenant," Shurgin said dismissively. "Take position and be ready."

Szabo nodded. "We will," he said. "Until midnight." He looked hard at Shurgin for a long moment, apparently without any effect at all. He shrugged and left the hall. From the doorway, he glanced back over his shoulder. Shurgin, pistol in his hand, was standing in the center of the exhibit, right beside the case for the big jewel, the one they called the Ocean of Light.

Szabo hesitated. Having the guy right there, right by the jewels—it didn't sit right. But what the hell, he was right outside the room, and his men were all around. There was no chance of anybody getting in or out, not without the Black Hat team seeing him. And it made sense for somebody to be right there. A central position, final backup, where he could see an approach from any direction. *If he can see at all*, Szabo thought, *with those fucking freak show glasses.* But if Coulomb made it this far, Shurgin had a clear field of fire in all directions. This was the right spot.

Satisfied that it was all as good as he could make it, Szabo left the hall. Until midnight. And then—all bets are off.

He glanced at his watch: twenty minutes 'til. He went down the hall to check on his men.

Katrina waited in the conference room, her heart pounding. Realistically, she knew she was safe here. All the action, and all the danger, was on the roof or in the vicinity of the crown jewels. And her rational mind was quite sure that one French thief, no matter how well he could scale walls, stood no chance against all those well-armed, well-trained men waiting for him in ambush.

But it's almost never our rational minds that get scared. It's the wild, untamable, irrational part, the part that believes in the monster under the bed—that's what sends the unnecessary adrenaline pumping through our veins. It did that now to Katrina. She felt clammy, her hands sweated, and her mouth was dry.

For the four hundredth time, she glanced at her watch. It was seventeen minutes before midnight—exactly three minutes later than the last time she'd looked. Shurgin had said it would happen at midnight. And he seemed so sure of it. So not long now. It would all be over soon. If she didn't burst from anxiety first.

She stood up abruptly. There was a coffee machine down at one end of the room, the kind that makes one cup at a time. She walked down and thrust a Styrofoam cup under the spout and pushed the button.

The machine seemed to take forever to get going, but finally it began to gurgle and hiss. Katrina waited, tapping her toe impatiently. When the coffee was ready, she took it back to her seat at the table. She called Randall for the four hundredth time. Straight to voicemail. So she sipped, put the cup down, glanced at her watch.

Twelve minutes until midnight.

It seemed to Lieutenant Szabo that he'd spent way too much of his life just standing around waiting for the shooting to start. On the plus side, the experience kept him from being really nervous right now—just a little revved up, like a racehorse waiting in the starting gate.

On the downside, this one was all out of his control. He couldn't do a goddamn thing except wait for a chance that might or might not come. And he was stuck down here, away from the action, as backup. That was frustrating as hell. He *had* to find a way to get to this Coulomb and find out if he'd killed Chief Bledsoe. Absolutely, positively no fucking way around it—he HAD to. The chief hadn't really been a close friend, and hadn't been one to most of the Black Hat team, either. That didn't matter. The chief had been one of them, and SEALs always balance the books. Nobody ever left behind, and nobody ever got whacked without an accounting. Whoever killed the chief would be paid in full, and Coulomb was the leading candidate. It was just that, so far, Szabo had no idea how he was going to get to the thief.

He glanced at his watch. Ten minutes to go if Shurgin was right. Szabo sighed and went to check each of his men.

Katrina lifted the Styrofoam cup to her lips for a sip of coffee. Nothing happened. She glanced into the cup—it was empty. She didn't remember drinking it all. But she had to admit her mind was not really tracking at the moment.

She dropped the cup to the tabletop and closed her eyes. She told herself to take deep, calming breaths. Slowly in, slowly out. It didn't work. She sounded like she was panting. And she hadn't calmed down at all, either. *When will this end?* she thought unhappily. And the answer came right back: at midnight, of course.

And when was that? Katrina opened her eyes to look at her watch—or she thought she did. But she couldn't see anything. Had she forgotten how to open her eyes? She blinked a few times; no, her eyes worked fine. But it was still as dark as if her eyes remained closed.

Her first thought, as rattled as she was, was that she had gone blind from the nervous strain. But then she heard a distant sound— *br-r-r-r-r-r-rap!*

Gunfire. Followed by voices shouting.

She wasn't blind—instead, she was an idiot. The electricity had been cut. And she didn't need to look at her watch, either. Because the sound of gunfire could only mean one thing.

It was midnight, and the thief had come.

Lieutenant Szabo was at the central point of his team's deployment, his men spread out on both sides and combat-ready. Szabo stood near the entrance to the exhibition gallery, eyes moving from side to side, weapon held waist high.

Szabo had just begun the move to look at his watch when the lights went out. A moment later, he heard the shots. They were not close, but he was positive they came from the roof—*Coulomb!* "*Fuck!*" he said aloud. If the Iranians had killed the thief before Szabo got a crack at him—

"Snyder!" he yelled, waving to his left. Snyder looked his way. "You got lead!" And without waiting for a reply, Szabo ran for the roof.

He sped through the door, up the stairs to the second floor, still in darkness. As he ran across the second floor to the roof door, he couldn't help but notice that there were no Iranians on guard anywhere—they had clearly all run to the roof when they heard the gunfire. Szabo felt a brief surge of pride; *his* men would never do anything of the kind. And then it occurred to him that it was exactly what he was doing right now, running from his post toward the first sound of gunfire.

Never mind; he reached the end of the hallway and ran through the access door, taking the stairs to the roof three at a time all the way up to the metal fire door. He slammed into it, shoved it open, and burst out into the cool night air of the roof.

After the darkness of the interior of the museum, the starlight was more than bright enough to light up the scene on the roof. The Revolutionary Guards stood in a loose circle, their AKM assault rifles pointed at a figure writhing on the ground at their feet.

Coulomb.

And he was alive—but obviously wounded.

Szabo hurried over and pushed through the circle of Iranians. The Iranians glared at him but let him through. He looked down at the figure on the roof. The Frenchman had been shot in the right thigh, and he was rolling around in pain, eyes shut. The wound was bleeding profusely, but it looked like Coulomb would live.

Shurgin had been right. The Fed was legit.

That meant the wounded man might be the chief's killer. And this could be his only chance to find out.

Szabo knelt by the Frenchman's side. "You're going to be all right," he said. "*Parlez-vous anglais?* Can you talk?"

Coulomb opened his eyes. "Talk!" he exclaimed. "Bloody fucking hell, mate, I'm fucking shot! They've buggered me leg!" he said in an accent that was pure Cockney.

Szabo blinked. "You're not French . . . ?"

"Oh, fucking Christ, no—and I'm not a bloody radish, neither, mate. So I am bleeding to death—how about a fucking tourniquet?"

Szabo felt his jaw drop. For a second that seemed a great deal longer, he just squatted there, his mind whirling. Not Coulomb—not even French. But Shurgin had been positive—the thief would be

French. What had he said? "If a French thief *doesn't* come, I'm some-thing else."

A French thief had not come. That meant Shurgin was something else. But what? Why was he here, waiting downstairs, when he had to know Szabo would find out and come down to confront him? All Szabo had to do was go down to where Shurgin stood waiting—

Waiting all alone—with the jewels.

Son-of-a-bitch—!

A strong feeling of panic combined with dread and anger flooded through Szabo, and he jumped to his feet. "Shurgin—!" he bellowed. The Iranians stared at him, but he pushed them roughly aside and ran from the roof and down the stairs, twice as fast as he'd run up only a minute ago. He clattered out into the hallway on the main floor and sprinted for the exhibit, passing several of his men, who gave him star-tled looks as he galloped past.

Szabo slid to a halt at the door to the exhibit. One quick glance told him he was too late.

Shurgin was gone.

Szabo spun and raced toward the lobby, skidding to a stop when he saw Snyder. "Shurgin!" he bellowed. "Where the fuck is he?"

Snyder shook his head. "He left, like, two minutes ago," he said. "Said he had to report, and he'd hook up again at the police station."

Szabo ran as fast he could through the lobby and out the front door onto the street. The traffic was light at this hour, mostly cabs. Shurgin would have had no trouble grabbing one and escaping. Szabo looked up and down the street anyway, but it was hopeless. Shurgin was gone.

Szabo walked back to the exhibition room, knowing he was just plain fucked, him and his whole team and by extension even Black Hat—and, much worse, his country. Because the Iranians would blame *him* and call it a plot by the crime-infested society of the Great Satan. And he would just have to take it because the Iranians were right. He had fucked up. His gut had told him there was something wrong about Shurgin, and he hadn't listened to it. And now he was thoroughly, totally fucked.

There was one remaining question before he made his report: What exactly had Shurgin taken? Szabo went into the hall, checking the cases one by one as he passed them. They were all apparently untouched, their contents still gleaming undisturbed in the glow of the emergency lighting. But that big jewel in the center, the one Shurgin had been "guarding"—that one was small enough to grab and conceal.

Szabo approached the central case with a sick feeling in the pit of his stomach, certain he would find that case empty. He reached it, looked down through the glass . . .

It was still there.

Bewildered, he looked around the room. And they were all still there, all the crown jewels, every fucking item.

The big, priceless, easily grabbed and concealed jewel was right there in its case. Shurgin hadn't taken anything, not one fucking thing. But he was gone—and wait a minute, what the fuck was going on here? Because the guy on the roof was not French but a *Brit*—which meant Shurgin was not legit and the whole thing had been some kind of setup—and the only reason for any setup was to take the fucking jewels—except they were all there, nothing was missing—and that meant . . .

What, exactly?

Szabo stood there for several minutes, just breathing hard and thinking. He couldn't think of anything that made sense of what had happened: A thief captured, but the wrong one. An FBI agent who wasn't, or maybe not, except then what the fuck was he? And he'd engineered what should have been a successful attempt on the jewels except nothing was taken. An absolutely perfect setup that worked like a Swiss watch—but a setup for what?

Because no matter how many times he looked into the case, the big fucking jewel was right there where it was supposed to be. They all were.

The main lights came back on, and the big jewel really came to life, glowing like it was filled with a living fire. Szabo stared at it. He hadn't really looked at it before, and it was worth a long look. Beautiful, completely filled with light. It was easy to understand why somebody would want to own this thing. It made the love of jewels reasonable, even inevitable. Its name, posted on the neatly lettered sign beside the case, was no exaggeration.

The Ocean of Light.

It really was just that, a deep pool of beauty that radiated a light so perfect you could almost swim in it.

And it was still right here. Untouched.

"What the fuck," Szabo said at last. It was about all he could manage.

CHAPTER
32

When Special Agent Frank Delgado heard on the news that there had been a death at the Eberhardt Museum at the grand opening gala for the Iranian crown jewels, he knew right away what it meant.

Riley Wolfe.

But the news also said that the collection was intact and open to the public. So Delgado waited. And the next night, when reports came of a thief captured on the roof of the Eberhardt Museum, he moved—but not to the Eberhardt, and not to the police station.

An agent who did not know Riley Wolfe as Delgado did would almost certainly have gone to one or the other immediately, with all possible speed. Delgado did not. He knew with absolute certainty that it had not been Riley Wolfe who had been captured on the roof of the museum. So there was no point in checking with the police, or going to the Eberhardt. Instead, he got into his car and drove through the Holland Tunnel, all the way over to Newark.

This might seem like a strange reaction to the news that Riley

Wolfe, the man he had devoted so much time and energy to finding, was on the job in Manhattan. It was not. Instead, it was the only possible reaction, and only Frank Delgado could know that. Only Frank Delgado knew what was there at this particular spot in Newark, and what it meant to Riley Wolfe. He had found this place after a week of careful and methodical search, and he had been watching it and waiting for this exact moment.

So Delgado drove through the Holland Tunnel and over to Newark and parked his car in the small and crowded parking lot of the Gentle Ease Long-Term Care and Rehabilitation Center. He had already been here, twice, but had not yet gone inside. This time, he did.

His destination was room 242, a private room on the second floor, one of the more expensive ones available, with guaranteed round-the-clock care from an RN and a doctor always on call.

The occupant of this room was one of seventeen in the New York area who was the right age and required all the appropriate prescription medications. But the woman in room 242 was the only one with a name that matched one of the names on the short list he had made of possible aliases.

Mrs. Sheila Beaumont.

Riley Wolfe's mother.

Mrs. Beaumont needed the full-time nursing care she got here. She was in what is commonly called a persistent vegetative state, and had been for many years. Only a great deal of expensive care kept her alive—if the unchanging comatose state could be called alive, which Delgado doubted. In his opinion, Sheila Beaumont had moved out a long time ago, leaving nothing behind but the furniture. But it wasn't Delgado's business; it wasn't *his* money keeping the body technically alive. Strictly speaking, it wasn't Riley Wolfe's money, either, since it was all stolen. In any case, since it was leading Delgado right to Riley, he wouldn't complain.

And it would lead to Riley Wolfe. Delgado had no doubt about it. During Riley's previous heist, six months ago in Chicago, his mother had been right there nearby, in an Oak Park full-care nursing home. And the day after Wolfe's robbery, he had taken his mother out of that home, and they had both disappeared.

Delgado knew that if Riley Wolfe had already hit the Eberhardt, there was no point in looking for him there. And he was completely sure that whoever had been captured on the roof, it was not Riley. Riley Wolfe would be coming here, to get his mother. Just like he had before.

And Delgado would be here, waiting.

He entered the nursing home as excited as he had been in years. He felt like a little boy on Christmas, seeing all the presents under the tree and knowing that the really big one had his name on it. *This was it.* After so many years of disappointment, false hope, dead ends—he was about to come face-to-face with his obsession. Cornered at last.

Feeling a confidence he hadn't felt yet in anything involving Riley Wolfe, Delgado left the elevator on the second floor and followed the signs to room 242. As he got close, he heard voices from inside the room—not voices, plural. Just one voice.

Delgado jerked to a stop outside the door and listened.

". . . so we'll be moving on today, Mom. I found a really nice place for you, and it's much warmer. There's a garden—they have roses, Mom. You're gonna really like it . . ." The voice changed, grew softer, filled with emotion. "It's a great place, Mom. Just like you always said—you'll be living the life of Riley, just like you always said."

There was an almost audible click in Delgado's brain. *The life of Riley.* That's where the name had come from. The life of Riley, a wolf's reward for successfully preying on the herd. Delgado nearly smiled. He had a full picture now, and—

The voice had stopped. *Now,* Delgado thought. He drew his gun, swirled around the doorframe and into the room—

The room was empty.

For a moment, Delgado just stood there and blinked. Then he stepped to the closet, opened it—empty. The same with the bathroom. And nobody under the bed. The room was truly and completely empty.

But the voice he'd heard . . . ?

Behind him, he heard music, a ruffle of drums, then an insistent bass line in a minor key. He whirled around. On the small table beside the bed stood an expensive, high-tech digital sound recorder and a small speaker. The music was coming from this—and as Delgado stared at it, still stupidly pointing his gun, the guitar and then the vocals came in.

He listened for a minute, until he recognized the song. It was an Elvis Costello tune, one Frank had listened to often enough when he was young: "Watching the Detectives." It had never seemed quite so ironically appropriate before. And as a bright, hot flush mounted up his neck and into his face, Delgado put his pistol back in its holster and sank into the bedside chair.

He just sat there and listened until the song ended. It had hit him with a nearly physical pain, no doubt exactly what Riley had intended.

Riley Wolfe, all along, had been watching the detective—Special Agent Frank Delgado.

Somehow, Riley knew he would come. Somehow, he had set up a mocking welcome, designed to let Delgado know he was completely outmatched and had been from the start.

When the song was over, he got up and went to the nurses' station. "The woman in room 242," he asked, holding up his badge. "When did she leave?"

The nurse glanced at her computer, clicked the keyboard a few times. "This morning," she said. "A private ambulance picked her up." She frowned at the keyboard. "But the room was paid for through tomorrow—we're not supposed to touch it until then." She shook her head. "That's weird . . ."

Delgado just nodded and walked away. It wasn't weird to him. The room had been left for him. And there was no point in asking any more questions. He already knew the rest. He would check, of course, but he knew what he'd find; the private ambulance would be registered to a company that didn't exist, going to a destination that was an empty lot, or a pet cemetery, and there would be no clues, no way to track it down, no way to find Riley Wolfe or his mother.

Until next time. And there would be a next time, for him as well as for Riley Wolfe. But in the meantime . . . ?

Delgado stepped into the elevator and rode down. He walked out to his car and got in, putting both hands on the steering wheel and staring straight ahead for several minutes. And then he slammed the wheel with both hands, hard. "God-*damn* it!" he said. Just once. Then he started the car and began the long trip home.

The sun was just coming up when Katrina got home. It had been a very long night, and the one before—with the ruined gala at the museum—had been nearly as long, and it occurred to her that she had not really slept more than a couple of hours for two days now. She parked her car in the huge garage, noting that Randall's car was back, neatly parked in the spot next to hers. She was filled with elated relief; she hadn't really believed he'd had an accident, but the possibility had elbowed its way into her mind and wouldn't go away. But his car was here, unmarked, and that meant Randall was, too.

Katrina turned the key and switched off the motor. She sat for a few moments, blinking at the tiredness in her eyes, in silence broken only by the ticking of the engine as it cooled. She was just so tired, and so much had happened, and she couldn't wait to tell Randall all of it. She smiled at that thought. It was just so damn *good* to have somebody to come home to, somebody who would listen and care . . .

She climbed out of the car, stepped from the garage into the cool bright morning, and walked up the path to the house. The rosebushes were bare, of course. Winter had stripped all the greenery from the yard, and the gray and brown of the trees and the stems of the roses were a stark contrast to the bright sunlight of the frosty morning. She stopped for a moment halfway up the path, yawning hugely. Two nights with almost no sleep—or was it three? She couldn't wrap her exhausted mind around the arithmetic. And it didn't really matter. But in any case, she could not remember when she'd been so tired.

That didn't matter, either. She would be in bed soon enough—and with Randall. She smiled as she thought that he was probably sleeping, and she could quietly slip in beside him, and softly, gently, put her ice-cold feet into the small of his back—

Still yawning, still smiling, Katrina went into the house. She hung her coat and scarf on the hat tree in the atrium and headed for the stairs. Up to bed, to Randall and sleep. *Mmmm,* she thought happily. *Perhaps not sleep—not right away.*

She was halfway past the double-sized doorway to the kitchen and breakfast nook when she noticed something out of the corner of her eye, something on the breakfast table that was not normally there. She walked backward, turned, and went over to the table.

The salt and pepper shakers had been dragged to the near edge of the table. Propped up against them was a buff envelope. Beside that, on the table's surface, was a single white rose. It wasn't fully opened, and drops of dew glistened on the flower.

It was so very much like Randall, so thoughtful, to bring her a rose. No special occasion, just a small token to say "I love you." Again she felt the glow of happiness and fulfillment that came from having somebody who cared. Katrina picked up the rose, sniffed—it had a full and wonderful aroma, not like the cheaper hothouse flowers you usually get in the city, especially during the winter. For a moment she closed her eyes and drank in the smell, thinking how lucky she was to have Randall. Then she remembered the envelope.

Puzzled, she opened her eyes and put the rose down on the table. She picked up the envelope, noting that it was beautiful stock, the kind that came with the very best stationery. Centered on the front in green ink was her name, *Katrina*.

Still wondering what Randall might be up to, she opened the envelope and pulled out a single sheet of stationery that matched the envelope. She unfolded it and began to read the neat letters, also in green ink.

Dear Katrina,

I'm sorry, but I have to say you have really terrible taste in men—

Katrina frowned. It was a strange beginning, clearly some sort of joke—but what kind of joke? What was Randall thinking? What did he mean? Shaking her head, she went back to reading.

—you have really terrible taste in men. Michael was bad enough. But at least he was only a simple pedophile. To go from him to somebody like me . . . Well, like I said, you have awful taste. I guess there really are some things money can't buy.

If it's any consolation, our marriage was totally invalid—I don't really exist! You can even pin Michael's murder on me. That should make Brilstein happy. And you don't really deserve to go to prison.

By the time you read this, I will be long gone. But after all we went through together, I couldn't leave without saying good-bye.

Good-bye, Katrina. Don't bother trying to find me. You won't.

It was a joke. Some kind of stupid joke, it had to be. Katrina felt horrid, sickening panic flood into her. She crumpled the letter and threw it to the floor. She ran from the room and yelled, "Randall!"

At least, she intended to yell. The sound that came out of her was nothing she recognized as her voice—it didn't even sound human. It was an animal screech, a yowl of agony ripped from her throat that echoed through a house that sounded so empty it killed her hope even as she looked for some small sign to feed it. "Randall!" she screamed again, and again there was no answer.

She went from room to room in the huge house, even the very faintest hope flickering dimmer and finally dying into bleak cold ashes as the last room proved to be empty.

Gone. He was really gone. Randall was gone.

Katrina felt all the air and light go out of the world, and for a while there was nothing there at all—no trace of sight or sound or touch or anything but a dark and excruciating blankness.

And then, without any idea how it had happened, she was sitting on the kitchen floor. She couldn't breathe, couldn't think, couldn't even see anything except the dark fog across the whole world around her, slowly oozing back and letting in a thin trickle of awareness. And that consciousness was much worse than the darkness had been.

Gone. Randall was gone . . .

She had no way of knowing how long she had been sitting there like that, completely wrapped in darkness, inside and out, clutching the crumpled letter in both hands. But at long last she was able to take a single, deep, painful, rasping breath. She looked around her, completely numb, and sunlight began to seep back in at the edges of her world. It shed light on the room, but none at all on Katrina.

What had happened? What did the letter mean? It had to be some kind of horrible joke—except Randall really was gone. She smoothed out the letter and looked at it. It seemed to be his handwriting—and down at the bottom, in place of a signature, he had put his initials with a flourish. R.M.

But no, wait—those were not his initials. She frowned at the letters, trying to make sense of them. The *R* was definitely an *R*. But the *M*—it seemed to be reversed, upside down. A *W*, not an *M*.

"R.W."? What the hell did that mean? She didn't know anybody with the initials R.W.

And apparently, she didn't know anybody named Randall Miller, either. The letter said he didn't exist. She had been sleeping with a figment of her imagination.

And it didn't matter if he was Randall or R.W. or totally imaginary. Whoever or whatever he was, he was gone.

And Katrina was more alone than she'd ever been.

CHAPTER
33

Frank Delgado stood beside the bed, looking down at the man lying there. His hands were behind his head and his leg was elevated and he was far too chipper for a man who had been shot only three days ago. He looked like he was lying in a hammock on a warm beach instead of the infirmary in a city jail.

He hadn't said much so far, but his fingerprints had come back from Interpol and they said enough. His name was Oliver Sneed, a British national who was skilled at parkour, and he had used those skills in a series of daring robberies—not all of them successful, since he had a record longer than his wounded leg.

Delgado had been halfway back to his home in Virginia when Special Agent in Charge Macklin had called and asked him to head back to New York, to question Sneed. Delgado didn't mind. And when he got a look at Sneed's history, he was glad he had returned.

Sneed had given smart-ass replies to the first few questions. That was okay with Delgado. The questions were pretty standard, just setting a tone and a rhythm for the interview. Delgado was using them to make Sneed relax, to set him up for one question in particular, one that Delgado really wanted to ask.

"I told you, mate," Sneed said breezily. "It was all a lark. Just a bit of fun on a lovely evening."

"Pretty cold evening," Delgado said.

"The parkour, mate," Sneed said. "Warms the blood like a tonic."

"And at midnight, too," Delgado said.

"Aw, I couldn't sleep, that's all," Sneed said. He shook his head slightly, as much as he could lying down, and his face took on an expression of innocence that would have done Shirley Temple proud. "How was I to know there was all those Ay-rab lads up there, automatic weapons and that?"

"You had no idea what was in the museum?" Delgado asked.

"Not a fucking clue," Sneed said with a shrug. "Never was much for museums."

Delgado nodded. "All right," he said reasonably. "Just a coincidence, then?"

"That's the word," Sneed said happily. "Co-fucking-incidence."

"Quite an amazing fluke, considering your record," Delgado said. He pulled a metal folding chair close to the bed and sat. "Seven counts of grand larceny, mostly jewels."

"Done my time, haven't I?" Sneed said with an air of injured innocence. "Changed man, I am."

"So you had no idea the crown jewels were at the Eberhardt?"

"Not a fucking clue."

"And you weren't there because you paid somebody on the dark web to turn off the alarm system?"

"The dark what?" Sneed asked.

"Somebody," Delgado went on, "who apparently double-crossed you, set you up to get shot?"

"Aw, now, who would do such an awful thing?" Sneed asked with great innocence.

Delgado smiled. This was what he'd been waiting for. "Riley Wolfe," he said.

Sneed's reaction was better than he could have hoped for. His mouth opened wide, but nothing came out, and then he closed his eyes and seemed to sink down into his pillow. "Bloody fucking hell," he whispered, and again, "Bloody fucking hell."

Delgado said nothing, and after a moment Sneed opened his eyes again. "Should have known," he said. "Riley fucking Wolfe." He sighed and shook his head slowly. "Bugger has it in for me."

"Why?" Delgado asked.

Sneed waved a hand dismissively. "Aw, I done him dirty a few years back. The old double-cross, jobbed him out of a right nice score." He closed his eyes again. "Should've known he wouldn't let that go. Not Riley. Not ever." He opened one eye and pointed it at Delgado. "What did he get away with?"

"Apparently nothing," Delgado said.

Sneed snorted. "Pull the other one," he said. "If he was there, I promise you he didn't leave empty-handed."

Delgado frowned. "The museum says there's nothing missing," he said. "It's all there."

Sneed shook his head vigorously. "Don't believe it," he said. "Not a fucking prayer. Riley leave empty-handed? Never in life."

Delgado didn't believe it, either. But the museum had been positive that nothing was missing. "If it was you," he asked, "if you'd gotten inside like you planned—what would you have taken?"

"The Daryayeh-E-Noor, nothing else," Sneed said, and there was a note of reverence in his voice. "It really is an ocean of light— beautiful, like you've never seen. One of a kind—and it's small enough to carry easy, and worth a fucking fortune." He opened both eyes now

345

and they shone as he looked at Delgado. "Fifteen *billion* dollars, mate. With a *b*."

"The museum says it's still there, in its case."

"Look again, mate," Sneed said. "Look again."

He stood right there," Lieutenant Szabo said, pointing to the space next to the Daryayeh-E-Noor's case. "He had his weapon out and ready, and he stood there while we chased after the other guy."

"What kind of weapon?" Delgado asked.

"Glock Model 23," Szabo said.

Delgado nodded. That was the weapon most agents carried. But that was well-known. It didn't mean much here. "Describe him for me again?"

Szabo shrugged. "I'd say five foot ten, average build, but a little bit of a paunch? So maybe a hundred seventy-five pounds. Reddish-brown hair and mustache." He frowned. "Like I said, the most notice-able thing was the glasses. Lenses were like an inch thick. Nobody could see through those unless, you know. If it was their prescription."

Delgado turned away and scanned the hall. With his years of expe-rience in the FBI, he could spot most of the electronic security devices. Szabo had already sketched out for him where the two teams of guards had been deployed. Nobody in their right minds would even try to get past all that—it was suicidal.

BUT . . . if somehow somebody *did* get past it, the real problem was getting the jewels and getting away. He looked at the rows of cases, each one with an apparently untouched item still on display. Szabo insisted that nothing had been taken. But to Delgado, all the signs pointed to Riley Wolfe. And he agreed with Sneed—Riley Wolfe would not leave empty-handed.

Delgado stepped closer to the case holding the Daryayeh-E-Noor and looked at it. Beautiful, amazing, and stunning. It was worth billions of dollars—but it could be easily concealed and carried away. It was a clear first choice for any thief. And yet there it sat. Unless—

Abruptly, he turned back to Szabo. "How long was he alone in here?" he said sharply.

Szabo looked away, embarrassed. "Ah—maybe five minutes?"

"Five minutes? With the alarm off?"

"Yeah. Uh-huh."

"Where were you?"

Szabo sighed heavily. "I ran up to the roof, like a fucking idiot," he said. "When I heard the shots." He shook his head and met Delgado's eyes. "I mean, my team was right here, but . . ."

"But nobody had eyes on . . . 'Special Agent Shurgin.'"

Szabo looked away again. "No," he said. "Nobody." He bit his lip, then looked back at Delgado. "But I told you—nothing is missing! I mean—it's all right there, see for yourself!"

Delgado nodded impassively. He looked once more at the case holding the massive jewel, and he was sure. "Call an appraiser," he said. "The best one you can find. Have him look at this one. The Ocean of Light."

Delgado looked at Szabo. "And keep it quiet. Nobody knows about this but you and the appraiser." He held out his business card, and Szabo took it. "Call me when that's done," he said.

"Uh, yeah, sure. Yes, sir," Szabo said.

Delgado turned and walked out of the exhibition hall, out of the museum. There was nothing more to say. He knew what the appraiser would find. And he knew how Riley Wolfe had done it. An FBI agent has inherent authority. Who would question him? Except the FBI had no Special Agent Shurgin. Delgado had been sure, but even so he had double-checked. The only thing he still wondered about was the glasses—glasses with lenses an inch thick. He knew Szabo was right about that—nobody could see through that unless it was his proper prescription. How the hell could Riley Wolfe?

Because somehow, he had. He'd used that impossible disguise to get five minutes alone with Iranian crown jewels.

And he had taken the Ocean of Light.

CHAPTER
34

The headache nearly killed me. For twelve hours I couldn't do a god-damn thing except lie there with my eyes closed and a cool towel on my forehead. I mean, I must've eaten half a bottle of Tylenol, and it did nothing to chill that fucking headache. The ophthalmologist had told me it would happen like that. It's a big reason why nobody but me would think of this trick. To everybody else, it's either impossible, or it's way too painful. You can't fuck with your eyes like that without paying the price.

I paid it. I didn't mind. Hell, I could afford it now.

The trick was pretty simple, when you think about it. Big, thick prescription lenses—nobody could see through them unless they need that prescription, that's obvious. So you know it's not a disguise—it's got to really be some half-blind guy. It can't possibly be Riley Wolfe, right?

Unless Riley Wolfe puts on contact lenses first—contact lenses with the exact *opposite* prescription of the lenses. Contacts with a pre-scription of minus 8.00, glasses with *plus* 8.00, get it? So the contacts and the glasses cancel out, and you see with your normal vision. But you look like a goggle-eyed freak—so you can't possibly be Riley Wolfe, and you can pull off some amazing shit.

And I had.

And then the absolutely killer headache. The opthamologist I'd paid to work this out for me had warned me. He was right. I was just about paralyzed with the pounding pain in my skull. But hey—who would ever say it wasn't worth it?

It totally was worth it. Even if the fucking headache lasted a month.

I was pretty sure somebody would figure it out soon enough. Probably the FBI guy. My only regret was that I wasn't there to see his face when he did—or when he "found" my mother. I should have left a camera, recorded that. I bet it was worth watching a few times. Shit, I would've put it on a continuous loop. Used it as wallpaper on my laptop.

Whatever. Anyway, it gave me plenty of time to split from New York, lose the headache, and get to my island.

Yeah, that's right. I have an island. It's not even on the maps, and it's all mine, nobody else lives there, mostly nobody even knows it's there. I want to keep it that way, too. So I'll just say it's probably either somewhere in the Caribbean or maybe the South Pacific. Someplace warm and very private. And I don't let anybody else visit, hear about it, know about it—not nobody, nohow, never . . . with one small exception. Just this once.

Every big win deserves a big prize, and this had been one hell of a win. It would need a world-class reward. And guess what? I had one all picked out.

Monique was having a very hard time believing it. She'd thought it was a very bad idea to begin with, and she was more than half convinced that it still was.

But here she was, wherever "here" was. Riley had been mysterious to the point of being psychotic about the exact location. All Monique knew was that the next-to-last leg of the trip had been twelve hours on a private jet, which had landed on a small and unidentifiable island. From there, Riley had hustled her off to a tiny marina on one end of the island, where they'd boarded a thirty-foot boat—a yacht, really. It had a cabin with a queen-sized bed and full kitchen. And it apparently had very large engines, because when Riley steered it out of the harbor and onto the open water and opened up the throttle, the acceleration had nearly pushed Monique through the back of her chair.

Eleven hours later, Riley slowed and steered them through a tight and unmarked channel, and finally to a well-hidden dock, where he tied up the boat, off-loaded their minor luggage, and led her onto his island.

There were a lot of security features, which she'd expected—everything from locked steel gates to electronic panels where Riley turned off unguessable devices, punching in long strings of numbers before proceeding. And finally, following a path up a gently sloping hill, they came to Riley's house, which was the biggest surprise of all. Not the fact that there was a house, of course. The surprise was the house itself.

Monique would have expected something small, sleek, and secure. Maybe more like a bunker with picture windows? What she found, perched on top of the hill in the center of the island, was a large, pseudo-Victorian house, with a cupola and a wraparound porch—really kind of a tacky, suburban house, Monique thought. It didn't fit here, in this tropical setting.

But Riley was clearly proud of the place. And from the inside of the house, it was clear that he had done a lot of work to make it more suitable to his personal tastes. There were floor-to-ceiling mahogany bookshelves, and they were loaded with well-worn books. And there was a large stereo system and several more shelves packed with CDs. The books were a bit of a shock to Monique. And the size and variety of the CD collection was just as impressive. It all hinted at someone she didn't know. Monique realized that by being here, she was getting a look at this unknown man—the *real* Riley Wolfe. She liked what she was seeing of this new person, so Monique kept her comments about the architecture to herself.

There was a faint whisper of air-conditioning, and it was cool and dry inside, in spite of the hot sun beating down outside. The windows had heavy steel roll-down shutters; the doors were thick and also reinforced with steel. "We are safe here," Riley said as she looked around the living room. "Completely, totally safe."

Safety would not have been the first of Monique's concerns in an isolated spot like this one, and she wondered why it seemed so important to Riley.

She wondered much more why she'd agreed to come with him to this completely secluded spot. She knew very well why he had asked her to come and what he would expect if she agreed, so why had she said yes? Why had she come along so readily, blurting out, "Okay, sure," the moment he asked, without really thinking about what she was agreeing to?

Part of it had been Riley's euphoric excitement. He was like a little boy who couldn't enjoy his new toy unless he shared it with his friend, and the bubbly glee was contagious.

But a deeper part was that Monique's feelings for Riley had changed. As she had worked feverishly to finish her replica of the great diamond, she had driven herself without mercy because Riley's life depended on her making something perfect. And as she repeated that, like a mantra, it gradually occurred to her that Riley's life was important to her. She cared. Monique's life without Riley Wolfe in it would be dimmer, less interesting. She wanted him alive, safe, and she wanted to be around him.

So she went along. Knowing what she was agreeing to when she did, Monique went with Riley to his supersecret, totally hidden, completely safe fortress of solitude. And for a while, she was glad she did. The odd shift in her feelings for Riley, the warming up to him that had come over her while she worked on this insane, lethal job, made it all a lot easier—even kind of natural. It even had her thinking, who knew what might happen between them? It no longer seemed annoying or unthinkable—even without losing the Bet.

That all changed the first night.

Riley made them both drinks, cooked a wonderful meal, decanted a wine that Monique knew was rare, even though she didn't know a lot about wines. And then, after dinner, he'd led her down to the beach. He built a beautiful bonfire, poured them each a large dose of brandy, and sat beside her.

And Monique, half enchanted by the evening, the starlight glittering off the water, and probably the large helping of alcohol, found herself leaning against Riley's shoulder, feeling secure and comfortable and happy, even when he put an arm around her. They sat silently in complete peace and harmony for half a glass of brandy.

And then she had to ask him.

The fire had burned down to a nice warm glow, and I was just about ready to get down to it when Monique said, "You promised you'd tell me everything." I tilted my head so I could see her. She was worth a look. I had my arm around her, and it felt better than almost anything else I could think of—although, to be honest, I was thinking very hard about a few things that would feel better. So hard I didn't really register what she was saying until she dug her elbow into my side. "Oh, right—what?" I said.

"Riley, you promised me," she said. "You said when it was over you'd tell me everything. About the job?"

I was pretty sure I hadn't actually *promised* anything, but I learned a long time ago that this is how women work it. You probably only said something like "We'll see," and they turn that into "You promised!" and they beat you up with it until you cave in and do whatever they want. And what the hell, Monique had earned it. And to be honest, she looked so good I would have told her just about anything right then.

"Okay, sure," I said. I frowned, thinking about how to start, which wasn't easy, between all the alcohol and Monique's warm body leaning on mine. "The big problem at the beginning was the security," I started. "I mean, I knew it would be too good and too new for me to just beat it. So I had to figure how to, to, what. To make it not matter. Irrelevant."

"Tall order," she murmured.

"Right, yeah, it was," I said. I realized I was rubbing her back, just gentle small circles, but she didn't stop me. "And you know. Only the family could do that. Only the rich-bitch Eberhardt family could ever get around all the cameras and sensors and shit."

"Mmm," she said. Which meant either she agreed, or she was getting into the back rub.

"So then the problem changes. It's not, how do I beat security, because I can't. The *real* problem is, how do I get into the *family*?"

I ran down the whole thing for her, how I found out about Katrina's asshole pedophile husband, which made her the weak link. How I had moved in on her, making her think it was all her idea, making her actually love me, then even *marry* me, and from there getting into the museum's in-crowd. And goddamn it, it was a great story! Maybe the greatest thing I ever did! And I told it well, too. Who wouldn't be inspired, sitting on a fantastic private beach with a beautiful woman?

But at some point, I felt Monique start to stiffen up under my hand. And then she reached back and pushed my hand away. "What's the matter?" I said.

She shook her head, but I could see she was truly upset about something. Her jaw muscles were clenched, and her face was knotted up in a frown. "Come on, Monique, what? What's wrong?"

"I think . . . ," she said slowly, "the fact that you don't know makes it even worse."

I thought really hard, trying to come up with something. I mean, I know when a mood has just dropped dead, and this had been a really good one, a mood I wanted to take further. But it was definitely deader than the dinosaurs. So what was up with Monique? What had I done that would turn her ice-cold in two heartbeats?

It wasn't stealing—I mean, duh. It's how we both lived. I was pretty sure she wouldn't mind me icing one asshole pedophile. So what had I done? What was "wrong" with the most brilliant rip-off in history?

I came up with nothing. And Monique was just getting colder. She hadn't even looked at me yet. So I decided to throw myself on the mercy of the court. Sometimes that works.

"I'm sorry, Monique," I said. "I wouldn't do anything to upset you, but . . . I mean, what did I do? So I can be sure not to, you know, do it again?"

Now she looked at me, and it was a lot worse than when she was looking away. The fire was back in her eyes—but it was totally the wrong fire. She looked like she wanted to shoot me. For a long and truly uncomfortable minute she glared at me. Then she hissed out her breath between her teeth and shook her head. "Riley," she said, and I could tell this was going to be a true zinger. But instead, Monique took a deep breath and looked away, down at her fingernails.

"Riley," she said again, a little softer this time, "you are probably one of the best—ever—at what you do."

"'Probably'?" I said. Bad move, I know, but I couldn't help it.

"I admire the hell out of the way you come up with these . . . schemes of yours. Schemes nobody else in the world would ever think of. And you make them work."

"Thank you," I said, maybe a little hopefully.

"BUT," Monique said. She turned back to me and all hope died. "There is one great big motherfucking important part missing inside you!" She poked my chest with each word, and it hurt. I mean, not the poking. What she said, and the way she said it.

"Monique," I said. But she wasn't done.

"You get all out there into these things, like, like—like some grand master in a big chess game. And you find a way to win when nobody else could."

"Why is that wrong?" I said.

Her eyes blazed up again, and she poked me a lot harder. This time, the poking hurt, too. "People! Are NOT! Chess pieces!" she said. And she glared at me harder than ever, and goddamn it, she looked great, even ticking me off like that, and some part of me wanted to just pull her close and get down to it, even when the rest of me was letting me know it wasn't going to happen. "Monique," I said. "I know that. And I know I—sometimes I do some stuff that, that—I mean . . . If I hurt somebody, they pretty much deserve it?"

"What did Katrina do?" she said. "How did she deserve that?"

I felt my mouth swing open, but nothing came out. I mean— Katrina? If it had been, oh, "Benjy didn't deserve to get thrown off the roof," or "Hey, that chief was a veteran," something like that—but *Katrina*?! "I didn't hurt her," I said. "I mean, not, uh . . ." I stopped talking because of what was happening on Monique's face.

"You *married* her," Monique said. "You made her *care* for you—"

"It wasn't *me*," I protested.

"You lived with her, you *slept* with her," she said.

"I had to!" I said. Was this just Monique being jealous? "Monique, that was the whole thing, the key to making it work! I swear, she didn't mean anything to me!"

"And that makes it even worse!" she yelled. "Goddamn it, Riley, what you did to Katrina was *worse* than killing her! You shattered her! That poor woman . . ."

"Poor?" I said. "For fuck's sake, Monique, she's a billionaire!"

"That doesn't give you the right to do what you did," she said.

I didn't say anything, mostly because I thought it did. People that rich, they're like leeches. Smug, fat-ass, do-nothing, self-loving leeches. I mean, Katrina's ass wasn't fat—but what did she ever do to earn all that money?

Monique finally looked away and got quiet. I let it stay quiet. It was a whole lot better than the talk had been. "I really like you, Riley," she said after a while. "And I respect you. A lot, maybe more than . . ." She shook her head. "But to *use* somebody like that. And then just walk away without—" She shook her head. "I'm sorry. I just can't . . . I could never . . ." She didn't finish, didn't say what she couldn't, but it wasn't hard to figure out what it was.

"Monique," I said at last.

But she just shook her head. And that's where it stayed.

At least Monique didn't ask me to take her home. She stayed on with me on my island. That gave me a little hope. I mean, as long as she was right there, hanging out with me every day, who knows? She could get over it, decide I was okay after all. It might be that a whim would take her over, or she'd have a couple of drinks and say what the hell. Or maybe even just change her mind, which women have been known to do?

So she stayed. I guess we even had some fun, just not the kind I'd been counting on. And when the money came in, I got hopeful again. The insurance company paid, and fast. Partly because I only asked for a fraction of what the Daryayeh-E-Noor was worth—but mostly because I knew the government would put the screws to them to get the thing back before the Iranians found out.

So they paid fast, and Monique and I watched the money come in. We watched it together, as it jumped via wire transfer from the Caymans, to Switzerland, to Hong Kong—maybe thirty-some transfers in all, impossible to trace. And I really thought that maybe seeing all that cash might loosen her up. I learned a long time ago the effect that money can have on a woman. It's even a law—Riley's Seventh Law: The only real aphrodisiac is money.

And it was a lot of money. Even with my low-ball demand, it was more money than Scrooge McDuck ever had. We watched the money, and I watched Monique, and she seemed just as jazzed about it as I was—but as far as I could tell, it didn't make her change her mind. I mean, when her cut was confirmed in her offshore account, and she saw how much she'd made, she loosened up enough to give me a hug—but it was a big-*sister* hug, with nothing on it except "Isn't that great?" Yahoo.

That was it. Her mind was made up. Riley was a great guy, but his greatness wasn't worth more than a few hugs. It wasn't what I wanted. Not even close. But what the hell—I liked being around her. And if it was a little frustrating sometimes—I mean, shit, a LOT frustrating! You should've seen her in her bikini!

But that was okay, too. You can get used to almost anything. The days passed, we had a good time, and I kept smiling. Someday, sometime, she would change her mind. I could wait. It was worth it. And if she didn't change her mind, well—maybe I could think of a way to change it for her. I didn't know just how I would do that. I just knew I could find some way.

Because there's always a way. And I always find it.

Just watch me.

ACKNOWLEDGMENTS

I am indebted to Ashley Koehler for her dedicated help in building Riley's psychological profile.

Dr. A. L. Freundlich gave me immeasurable help by sharing with me his vast knowledge of art and artists, among so many other things.

I also want to thank Bear, Pookie, and Tink for their patient support and blind faith that I would always find a way. Always.

Many male writers thank their wives and say their book could not have been written without their help. But in my case this is literally true. When I am lost in a sea of plot twists, when I have painted myself into a corner, it is always Hilary who applies her wonderful story-sense and finds me a way out.

Read the complete *Dexter* series now!

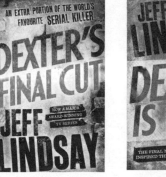